*Happy Dreams
at Mermaid Cove*

Happy Dreams at Mermaid Cove

Marie Laval

Published 2022 by Choc Lit Limited
Penrose House, Crawley Drive, Camberley, Surrey GU15 2AB, UK
www.choc-lit.com

A CIP catalogue record for this book is available
from the British Library

ISBN 978-1-78189-491-0

For Robert

Acknowledgements

My inspiration for writing *Happy Dreams at Mermaid Cove* was the photo of a yellow mobile library on a deserted Scottish road that author friend Melinda Hammond posted on Facebook at the beginning of last year. It captured my imagination so much that I had to start writing a story about it straight away. I knew a little about mobile libraries already because a long time ago I actually worked in one in the Wigan area for a few weeks, and what fun it was! During that time, I met the man who was to be my love, my companion and my happy dream for the following thirty-one years …

My thanks go to librarians who work so hard to provide an essential service for their communities – a service which often goes unappreciated and unrecognised. It is such a shame that so many libraries were closed these past few years. I would like to acknowledge too the brave and selfless men and women volunteers at the RNLI, who dedicate their time and risk their life everyday to rescue people at sea.

Thanks as usual to my fellow writers from Authors on the Edge for their friendship – Helena Fairfax, Kate Field, Melinda Hammond, Helen Pollard, Sophie Claire, Jacqueline Cooper, Mary Jayne Baker and Angela Wren. I would like to thank the Choc Lit team and my wonderful editor for her excellent suggestions which helped make the story stronger. My thanks also go to the designers who have come up with yet another beautiful cover. Of course, thanks as always to the Choc Lit Tasting Panel

(Amy Evans, Mel Appleyard, Deborah Warren, Gillian Hill, Bee Master, Liana Vera Saez, Julie Lilly, Nicola Whittaker, Jo Osborne, Alan Roberton, Lorna Baker, Jenny Mitchell, Honor Gilbert, Sharon Walsh, Fran Stevens and Gill Leivers). I am so happy that you enjoyed the story and gave me the chance to see it published today.

Merci beaucoup!

Chapter One

A gust of icy wind slapped Jenna's cheeks, yanked her hood off and whipped her hair around her face. She held on to the railing as the ferry climbed up to the crest of a wave, and slammed back down, hurling sea spray over her jeans and her brand new, supposedly waterproof coat which was turning out to be not waterproof at all.

Sailing through a storm wasn't how she had pictured her arrival in the small Arrandale peninsula of the Isle of Skye. It was hard to believe that it was the beginning of May, and that back in England trees displayed glorious blooms and shiny new green leaves. And yet there was nowhere else she'd rather be ...

'All right, love? A wee bit bracing, that wind, isn't it? You should come inside with me or get back in the van. You'll get *drookit* out here,' Brendon, the mobile library driver who had picked her up from Inverness train station, shouted above the roar of the storm.

Bracing? It was downright terrifying, and what on earth did *drookit* mean?

'Perhaps later,' she shouted back, fighting another wave of seasickness, as Brendon retreated into the passenger cabin.

She would feel ten times worse cooped up in there or in the mobile library parked on the deck, so bright and cheerful with its shiny new coat of yellow paint that she had baptised it Buttercup as soon as she'd seen it.

Ten minutes later, she was soaked from head to toe and the ferry rolled on the waves so much she feared being thrown overboard. Shivering, and combing a few soggy strands of hair back, she gave in and pushed the door to the cabin.

'Changed your mind, lass?' Brendon asked when she stumbled into the small waiting room and flopped on the bench next to him. 'I hope you're not worried about the storm. It's only a short crossing and Jim is a great skipper. He'll get us to Arrandale safely.'

She clasped her fingers in her lap. 'I'm not scared, but I do feel rather guilty for insisting we make the crossing when he didn't look so keen.'

He smiled. 'With the Skye Bridge closed, there was no other way to get to Arrandale today, and you seemed a wee bit anxious ...'

Anxious? She'd had an embarrassing panic attack and burst into tears when the *Riannog*'s skipper said he wanted to stop in Mallaig overnight.

'It's a shame you won't see Arrandale at its best today,' Brendon carried on. 'You won't find glens as beautiful, mountains as spectacular or beaches as fine anywhere else, especially not Manchester.' He chuckled. 'That's where you're from, isn't it?'

She nodded and rubbed the base of her fingers where her ring used to be. She may have taken it off months ago but she could still see the white band where it had been for two years, like the ghost of bad memories imprinted on her skin. She pushed her hands into her coat pockets.

'Living here isn't for everybody, especially a city girl,' Brendon remarked.

She looked at the window and the expanse of grey sky and the tall, white crested waves. 'I can see why, but I hope you'll be patient with *this* city girl. I have a lot to get used to, starting with driving the mobile library on single-track lanes.'

Brendon laughed. 'That can be a wee tricky, that's true, but you'll learn in no time. You'll have to watch the sheep and the *Heilan coos* too.'

She gave him a blank look, and he laughed. 'The Highland cows,' he repeated, toning down his Scottish accent.

'They're the ones with the shaggy ginger coat and the big horns, aren't they?'

'Aye, although they're not all ginger, you know. We've black or white ones in Arrandale too. You'll learn to be patient when they wander on the road to graze and to watch their horns if you don't want to get the van's new paintwork scratched.'

She had so much to get used to. So much to learn …

'It's very kind of you to come out of retirement to help me settle down.'

He winked. 'It's a pleasure, lass. To tell you the truth, retirement isn't all it's cracked up to be. It will be nice to be on the road again and have a good blether with folks.'

Brendon seemed like a cheerful, friendly kind of man. With his stocky build, red cheeks and bushy white beard he reminded her of Father Christmas, and she could imagine him dressing up as Santa to amuse the children.

She sighed. Why was she even thinking about Christmas? It was months away and many things could go wrong until then. They usually did. Better concentrate on the present, her new job and her new home.

'I read that Arrandale has been in the McGregor family for centuries, and that it is still one of the few privately owned estates on Skye.'

Brendon nodded. 'Aye, together with Glendale and Dunvegan to the North, and Carloch to the East. But it's the most beautiful, so beautiful we call it *Fearann nan Aislingean Sona*, which in Gaelic means the Land of Happy Dreams.'

She drew in a surprised breath. 'Really?'

How odd that she should mention happy dreams during her telephone interview with Daniel McGregor…even if it hadn't been much of an interview. She had expected questions about her experience, qualifications, and plans to improve the library service, but all McGregor wanted to know was how soon she could start and if she was prepared for difficult working conditions, a mediocre wage and the unlikelihood of any pay rise in the near future. She had to give it to him; he was abrupt, but at least he was honest! Little did he know that she was desperate ...

She had just launched into her carefully prepared speech about libraries providing essential services for people's well-being and employment prospects, being a portal into the world and a lifeline for remote communities, when loud cattle noises had erupted in the background. McGregor had rudely interrupted her to have a conversation with someone else – a vet, from what she'd gathered. Her well-rehearsed words had failed her, and her mind had gone blank ... In a panic, she had glanced at the newspaper on her coffee table, spotted an advert for the latest release in the popular Zonk McPurple children's fiction series, remembered that the main character caught happy dreams with his butterfly net, and without even knowing if Daniel McGregor was listening, she had improvised about books being like happy dreams she would share with the people of Arrandale.

'Sharing happy dreams? Isn't that a bit naïve?' McGregor had remarked abruptly. So he had been listening after all. Naïve or not, he must have liked her answers well enough because he offered her the job there and then, pending suitable references, copy of her criminal record check and proof that she was up to date with her Driver Certificate of Professional Competence.

That was just over two weeks before ... two weeks she'd spent in constant fear that something, or rather someone, would prevent her from leaving. She'd given notice to the landlord, moved the few possessions Adrian hadn't taken out of the flat, into storage, and tried to convince her mother that taking up the job in Arrandale and working for someone she'd never met in a place she'd never visited, wasn't the latest stupid thing in the long list of stupid things she'd done.

'What is Daniel McGregor like?' she now asked Brendon. She had googled him, of course, but there was surprisingly little to satisfy her curiosity. Her search had mainly turned out information about farming and articles from diving publications about a younger brother who had died in a freak diving accident five years before. There were also a handful of photos of two strikingly similar dark-haired, blue-eyed men in diving gear or formal Scottish regalia – green and red tartan kilt, white shirts and dark velvet jackets. In more recent photos, Daniel McGregor looked a rather windswept and rugged character, standing on the deck of a lifeboat, wrestling with a sheep at a sheep shearing competition, or again at a farmers' market standing next to one of those hairy Highland cows ...

Brendon took a moment to reply. 'What can I say? Some folk would climb Sgùrr Alasdair in the Black Cuillin with their bare hands and feet if he asked them to. And other folk would rather climb Sgùrr Alasdair with their bare hands and feet rather than having to deal with him. What's sure is that he's a hard worker and the man you can rely on in times of bother, even if he can be a bit *crabbit* at times ... but don't let that put you off.'

Crabbit? Another word to add to her glossary of Scottish words, although she could easily make out what that one meant, and it didn't do anything to improve the image she had of a grumpy despot barking orders to staff from his dusty dungeon ... or his busy farmyard.

Brendon shrugged. 'Whatever you think of Daniel, I hope you find your happy dream in Arrandale, lass.'

She crossed her fingers in her pocket. 'So do I, Brendon.'

Except that with the storm picking up and the ferry rolling from side to side, the happy dream she so wished for was fast turning into a nightmare. Her pub lunch of jacket potato and smoked salmon weighed like a stone inside her stomach. The cabin felt hot and stuffy and the smells of engine oil, brine and seaweed became overpowering. She needed fresh air, fast.

She jumped to her feet. 'I think I'm going to be sick.'

Making a quick exit onto the deck, she took a few long gulps of cold, salty air. The crossing was only supposed to last half an hour, and they'd already been at sea for over twenty minutes. Surely they should be able to see the Arrandale Peninsula by now ...

She glanced at the wheelhouse at the back of the ferry, and opened her eyes wide in shock. It was empty! Where were the skipper and his young crew member? She gave the cabin's window a frantic knock.

'What's the matter, love?' Brendon asked when he opened the door.

She pointed at the empty wheelhouse. 'Who is steering the ferry?'

His smile vanished as he glanced at the empty cabin. 'By heck! You're right. Stay put while I have a look.'

He strode to the wheelhouse and yanked the door open. Almost immediately, he gestured for her to come over, and she hurried to join him, taking care not to slip on the wet deck. The skipper lay unconscious on the floor. Next to him, a teenager sat holding a bloodied handkerchief to his forehead.

'He collapsed, just like that,' the youngster spluttered. 'I couldn't do anything. He fell on me, and I stumbled backwards and banged my head on that lever over there. Is he dead? Please tell me he isn't dead.'

Brendon gave the boy's shoulder a reassuring pat. 'Don't fret, lad. Jim will be fine. He must have fainted. Maybe something he ate at lunchtime didn't agree with him.' But the look in his eyes belied his reassuring words.

He glanced at Jenna. 'You don't happen to have first-aid skills, lass?'

She stood still, pulse racing, heart tight with panic and mind filled with swirling, disjointed thoughts. She'd never been any good in a crisis. What if she made the poor man worse?

Brendon cast her another imploring look. 'Lass?'

'Well, I … I did attend a first-aid course once, but it's a long time ago.' She knelt down next to the skipper, and gently tilted his chin up and opened his mouth. 'The airways are clear …' She lowered her cheek onto his chest and listened. 'He is breathing, and I can hear his heartbeat. That's a relief.'

She looked at Brendon. 'Help me put him in the recovery position while we call emergency services.' She bit her lip. She was being stupid. They were at sea, drifting in the middle of a storm. No ambulance could reach them here, and no rescue helicopters would fly out in this weather. It was her fault. If she hadn't insisted they sail despite the bad weather, the skipper would be all right, or at least he would be within reach of a doctor or a hospital.

'I'll call the coastguards,' Brendon said. 'There's nothing to worry about. Nothing at all …'

He mumbled the words several times as if to reassure himself, but his hand was shaking as he pulled his phone out of his pocket and made the call. 'This is the *Riannog*. We need help. Our skipper is unconscious and we're drifting at sea. Come in.'

A distant male voice crackled at the other end. Brendon explained what had happened in a few words, gave their approximate location, and ended the call. 'They'll be as quick as they can.'

As he spoke a huge wave washed above the deck of the ferry, which groaned as it swayed to one side, then the other. Jenna stifled a cry. It would do no good to show she was scared. She took hold of the skipper's hand. It was freezing cold.

'Is there a coat or a blanket I could use to cover the poor man?'

'Here, lass.' Brendon pulled down a padded anorak from a hook at the back of the door and covered him with it.

The young lad glared at her. 'It's your fault if he dies. He didn't want to sail but you made a fuss. What did it matter if the mobile library got to Arrandale today or not?'

'Hang on, lad,' Brendon interrupted. 'I know you're upset but it's not fair to blame Jenna – Miss Palmer. Jim wouldn't have left Mallaig if he was that worried about the weather … No, it's just plain bad luck that he should have fallen ill today.'

'I am sorry,' Jenna whispered as she clenched her fingers together. Brendon meant well, but the boy was right. It was her fault.

Anxious minutes ticked by. At last the skipper's eyelids flickered open and he drew in a long, wheezy breath.

'Try not to move,' she told him. 'How are you feeling?'

He winced. 'Weak. Dizzy. And my chest hurts. Is our Kieran here?'

The boy shuffled closer. 'I'm here, Jim.'

'How long was I like out cold, son?'

'Not long. No longer than ten minutes, I'd say.'

'Then we should be near Mermaid's Rocks … Can you see them?'

Brendon stood at the rain battered window and peered at the horizon. 'I can't see anything … except … the lifeboat!

It's coming. Hang on … it's the Black Wolf.' The relief was palpable in his voice.

'I'm going out to help,' Brendon said, opening the door to the cabin and letting in a freezing gust of wind.

'I'm going too!' The lad scrambled to his feet and rushed out behind him before Jenna could object that the wound on his head was still bleeding and he should stay put.

Soon there were voices shouting outside. Thudding noises reverberated through the ferry as the lifeboat bumped against the hull, followed by more shouting. Jenna stood up to look out of the window. Two men with white helmets, black waterproof trousers, yellow jackets and boots, climbed on deck. They carried an orange stretcher and a medical bag. Brendon talked to one of them – a tall, heavy built man – and gestured to the cabin.

She turned round again and crouched next to the skipper and lay her hand on his shoulder. 'They're here now. You're going to be all right.'

The door was yanked open behind her, and a deep voice she recognised instantly thundered, 'What the hell were you thinking of, sailing on a day like today? That was a stupid idea, Jim. That mobile library cost me a bloody fortune. It'll be no good at the bottom of the sea. Last time I checked, the fish couldn't read.'

Jenna gasped in shock. How could he be so rude to that poor skipper?

Jim however didn't seem to mind. He looked up and smiled faintly. 'Aye … but don't forget the mermaids, my lad,' he replied in a wheezy voice. 'They like a good love story, don't they, Daniel? You should know that, being a McGregor.'

Chapter Two

If Jim was cracking jokes, then it was a good sign ...

Daniel smiled. 'Mermaids? I've never met any ... never even seen the tail of one.' That wasn't completely true. Hadn't he once been foolish enough to believe himself in love with a beautiful siren? And what a mistake that had been ...

He focussed back on Jim, and the new librarian who stood stiff and pale in front of him. Daniel cursed under his breath. He shouldn't have shouted, but the gale still roared in his ears and he hadn't had time to adjust his voice level to the relative quiet of the wheelhouse.

Perhaps he shouldn't have said "what's the hell", "bloody" and "stupid" either. If she'd heard, Katrina would ask him to put three coins in the naughty words jar she kept in the kitchen at the farm ... and one extra coin for being grumpy, even if he had the right to be grumpy when he'd spent most of the day wrestling with the accounts at the farm, and worrying where to find the money for a new tractor and the vet's bill. He could have done without being called out to sea, especially to see the mobile library he'd just had refurbished pinned like a bug on the ferry deck with waves crashing over it.

'Mr McGregor?' the woman asked in a quiet voice. 'I am ...'

'Jenna Palmer, the new librarian, I know.'

She winced, probably at the shortness of his tone.

'Please don't shout at the skipper. It wasn't his fault we sailed today, but mine. I was the one who insisted ...'

He nodded. 'So I've been told.'

Jenna Palmer shoved her hands inside the pockets of her

flimsy coat, and tilted her face up to look at him. Her eyes were huge, her heart-shaped face pale and pinched, and her shoulder-length blonde hair soaked. She was probably cold and seasick as well as scared, which made him feel a lot worse for shouting ... but he didn't have time for niceties right now.

'Can I do anything to help?' she asked.

'You can stay out of the way.'

She gasped and moved to the side. 'Of course. Sorry.'

Daniel lifted his visor up, took his gloves off, before putting his bag down and crouching next to Jim who breathed in short, shallow breaths. He had closed his eyes again. His skin was pale and mottled, and his lips had taken on a grey tinge.

He put his hand on the man's shoulder. 'Jim ... I'm going to put the oxygen mask on, but before I do, can you tell me where you're hurting?'

The skipper opened his eyes. 'Aye, it's my chest, lad ...'

'Anywhere else?'

'My left arm.'

It sounded like the symptoms of a heart attack. 'OK. Don't worry. The lifeboat guys are going to take you back to Mallaig where an ambulance is waiting. You'll be in hospital in no time.'

'What about the *Riannog*?'

'I'll steer it back to Dana myself. Kieran, Brandon and ...' He looked up at the young woman who was still staring out of the window, back straight and shoulders tense, '... Ms Palmer are staying with me.'

'Thank you, my lad. I know I shouldn't have sailed today.'

'Forget I said anything. It was a poor joke. Just focus on getting better. I'm going to put the oxygen mask on now, and then we'll lift you onto the stretcher and down into the lifeboat. You'll be all right, Jim.'

11

He radioed for one of his crew mates to come in with the stretcher, opened his medical bag and took the necessary equipment out.

Ten minutes later, Jim was strapped to the stretcher and lowered onto the lifeboat, which immediately raced towards Mallaig, bouncing up and down on the waves. Daniel took his helmet off and stood at the controls in the wheelhouse, while Kieran kept watch for the treacherous Mermaid's Rocks. He'd patched up the lad's head, and thankfully the cut to his forehead looked worse than it was.

An experienced sailor, Daniel was used to navigating the stretches of open sea between Arrandale, the mainland and neighbouring islands, but it would still be a challenge to make the crossing in such poor weather conditions ... and with a bright yellow mobile library chained to the deck.

Her new boss was a scary bear of a man, with dark stubble, unruly black hair and a cold, mean blue glare.

Jenna squeezed her eyes shut and focussed on her breathing. Clenching her fists inside her pocket until her nails dug hard into her palms helped too. At least the pain distracted her from the rolling of the ferry and from her self-loathing. It was her fault Jim was on his way to hospital, young Kieran had got a head injury and Daniel McGregor now had to steer the *Riannog* back to Dana. Her fault she had made such a bad first impression to her new boss.

'Are you all right, lass?' Brendon's voice made her snap out of her dark, troubled thoughts.

She opened her eyes and nodded. 'I'm fine,' she lied.

'Are you sure?' Brendon frowned, looking concerned. 'I hope you don't believe a word young Kieran said about it being your fault Jim was taken ill,' he said as if he could read her mind. 'He was upset, that's all. He adores Jim – hero-worships him, actually. The lad's dad died at sea when he was a toddler and Jim more or less brought him up, you see.'

'But it *is* my fault, and that's what Mr McGregor thinks too.'

Brendon shrugged. 'Daniel? Bah ... he was probably in a bad mood because he got called out when he was busy at the farm.' He patted her arm. 'Don't mind him, lass. He's a good man, and you'll find that his bark is worse than his bite when you get to know him a bit better.'

Jenna almost replied that she had no intention of getting to know the man any better or have any interaction with him other than what was strictly necessary, but she bit her lip and said nothing.

Brendon craned his neck and glanced at the window before breaking into a wide smile. 'It looks like we're about to dock at Dana.'

The ferry was indeed approaching a small harbour nestling in a cove, and like by magic the gale died down and the sea became less choppy. Fishing boats danced on the waves, and a row of houses painted different colours – raspberry pink and baby blue, marmalade orange and lemony yellow – huddled together against a dramatic backdrop of black mountains shrouded in grey clouds.

Brendon rubbed his hands on his belly and let out a loud sigh. 'Strong emotions always make me peckish. What do you say about a restorative cup of tea and a bite to eat at The Buttered Scone? That's the best tea shop in Dana – the *only* tea shop in Dana, mind you. My treat, to help you recover from that bumpy crossing!'

Jenna glanced at her watch and frowned. 'I don't think there'll be time. I have so much to do and we're late already. I need to cross-check the new stock and make sure the mobile library looks good, ready for our grand opening. I was hoping that I could practise driving too.' She took a deep breath. 'To tell you the truth, I am a little nervous about tomorrow.'

It had been a while since she'd driven a mobile library, certainly one that size, and there was the prospect of meeting new people, and making sure she was up to the job. She was more than nervous. She was terrified.

Brendon pulled a face. 'Goodness, lass, you are keen. I have a much better idea. We have tea and cakes at The Buttered Scone before getting to work. Then I drive to my place, which is a converted barn on my sister's farm, and only ten minutes or so from Mermaid's Cottage where you'll be living. Ruth is desperate to meet you and said I was to invite you for tea before taking you to your new home and helping you get settled.'

'What about my driving practice?'

He grimaced. 'It can wait until the morning. If you don't mind me saying, you've had a heck of a long day and the weather is awful. I don't want to end up in a ditch. '

'Oh.' Jenna's throat tightened. What should she do? Brendon's suggestion was perfectly sensible. She was tired, having got up before dawn to catch the first train from Manchester Piccadilly to Edinburgh then changed for Inverness where Brendon had picked her up in the newly refurbished and kitted out mobile library. After the stormy and eventful crossing it would be stressful to drive Buttercup for the first time, especially in the pouring rain.

But what would Daniel McGregor say if she spent part of the afternoon in a tea shop on her very first day? He was her boss after all, and he was already annoyed with her. She could tell by the icy blue glare he cast in her direction when he tended to Jim and snapped at her to stay out of his way.

Brendon was waiting for her to answer, looking a little puzzled.

'Are you sure your sister won't mind me coming for tea?' she asked at last.

Brendon's smile faded and he suddenly looked quite cross. 'Of course she won't mind. She invited you, didn't she?'

'Oh ...' she said again as her heartbeat galloped hard and she couldn't seem to be able to breathe. She pressed her back against the wall; everything went white and blurry and the cabin spun around her.

'What's wrong, lass?' Brendon leant forward and put his hands on her shoulders. 'You're not having a funny turn like Jim, are you?'

Snap out of it, Jenna. Brendon was a nice man. He may have raised his voice but he wasn't going to hurt her. Nobody was! But it was no good. Fear and dizziness pinned her to her seat, and she shivered so hard her teeth clattered and she couldn't talk.

She was dimly aware of the door to the cabin opening, and of Daniel McGregor's tall silhouette filling the doorway. 'Come on, you two, we're at the pier now. You need to drive off ... Brendon, what's going on?'

'I think the poor lassie is having a bit of a turn.'

Jenna pushed a deep breath down. 'No ... I'm fine. Really.'

McGregor strode towards her anyway. 'It must be the crossing making her ill. I hope for her sake she doesn't get seasick every time she has to take the ferry.'

Jenna stiffened. What if McGregor decided that she wasn't up to the job and terminated her contract there and then?

'I'm all right now.' She tried to get up but her legs shook too much and she had to sit down again.

She may as well not bother. McGregor bent down, put his index finger under her chin and tilted her face upwards so that she stared straight into his eyes. 'Yes, she does look pale indeed. Are you hurting anywhere, Miss Palmer? Your chest ... your head?'

'No ... I'm fine. It's just ...'

McGregor straightened up and turned to Brendon. 'Get the mobile library started. I'll bring her over.'

Jenna tensed again. Bring her over – what, like a sack of potatoes? But before she could object he scooped her into his arms. Her fingers gripped his shoulders but his waterproof coat was wet and slippery, and she instinctively brought her hands higher. As she knotted them behind his neck, her nails grazed his skin. His arms tensed around her, his jaw tightened, and he glanced down at her. His piercing blue eyes looked even colder than before, but from close up she saw the thin yellow rays in the irises, dancing like minuscule flames.

'All right?' he growled.

A grumpy bear, yes, that's what he was. 'You can put me down. I'm better now.' Still dizzy, she kicked her legs and tried to slip out of his grip but he only lengthened his stride, and walked across the deck.

'Stop wriggling. We already had one suspected heart attack this afternoon and I'm not taking any chances. Brendon will take you to the doctor as soon as he drives off the ferry.'

'I don't need a doctor. I have lots of work to do if I want to get Buttercup ready for tomorrow.'

He frowned and this time a flash of humour warmed his eyes. 'Buttercup?'

Her cheeks heated. 'That's what I called the mobile library.'

'Why?'

'Because it's yellow, and buttercups are yellow.' Wasn't it obvious? She would have shrugged if she wasn't squeezed against his chest.

16

'Aye, they are yellow indeed … Buttercup is also the name of my prize heifer. I'll introduce you some day, although you might be disappointed. She's not yellow.'

He was making fun of her, and it annoyed her so much she instinctively tightened her grip on the back of his neck, and felt his arms tense around her once again. He put her down next to the mobile library, opened the passenger door and before she could slip away, lifted her onto the padded seat, pulled the seat belt and leaned over to fasten it for her as if she was incapable of doing it herself.

'Drive straight to the surgery,' he told Brendon who was already behind the wheel, 'and ask Doctor Kerry to give Ms Palmer a thorough check-up, then stop at The Buttered Scone and get her a hot drink and something to eat. I reckon she'll need it.'

Brendon started the engine. 'Will do … She does look very *peeley-walley* indeed.'

Jenna crossed her arms and shot both Brendon and Daniel McGregor a frustrated look. 'I may be a little out of sorts, but there's no need to talk over my head as if I don't understand.'

McGregor frowned. 'Good. If you understand then you'll do as I say.' He turned on his heels and strode back into the wheelhouse without giving her a second glance.

Chapter Three

'Here, pet, get that down you. You look as if you need it.' Brendon's sister handed Jenna a mug of tea.

'Thank you. It has been a long day indeed.' Jenna sighed with pleasure as she drank a sip of sweet, hot tea. It was exactly what she needed – invigorating and comforting, like the kitchen at Ruth MacDonald's farmhouse.

Everything there was big, bright and cheerful, from the green walls to the orange blinds at the mullioned windows, from the yellow Aga where a large pot of soup steamed away to the children's drawings pinned to the fridge. Ruth was a colourful woman too, with short ginger hair and sparkling blue eyes, dressed in a blue jumper, red corduroy skirt, and purple crocs. Next to her, Jenna felt dreadfully dull in her jeans – still slightly damp from being exposed to the elements during the crossing – dark blue jumper and black ankle boots.

Ruth's farmhouse stood solid and welcoming in the bleak, brown and grey landscape – peat bogs, hills and muddy fields as far as the eye could see. It was the kind of house Jenna had always yearned for, and judging from Ruth's happy smile and healthy pink round cheeks, it was fair to assume that she probably led the kind of life Jenna had always dreamt of, filled with laughter, and love ... Her throat tightened and tears filled her eyes. She looked down and drank a sip of tea, then another and willed for the wave of sadness to pass.

'Are you all right, my love?' Ruth asked. 'Are you still feeling poorly? Brendon said you had to see the doctor when you docked at Dana.'

Jenna put her mug down and forced a smile. 'I'm afraid

I wasted that poor doctor's time. There was nothing wrong with me. I tried to tell Mr McGregor but he insisted Brendon take me to the surgery.'

Ruth shrugged. 'Daniel can be a bit bossy at times, but that's because he's always busy dashing from one place to the next, dealing with the farm and sorting things out on the estate. You'll get used to his ways when you get to know him.'

Once again it was on the tip of Jenna's tongue to say that she had no intention of getting to know the man better. He may be her boss but she doubted he would ever set foot aboard Buttercup or in Dana's library office and it suited her fine.

Ruth pushed one hand into an oven glove, grabbed a wooden spoon with the other and lifted the lid off the slow cooker, before giving the soup an energetic stir. 'My Cock-a-leekie is ready. There's bread and cheese to go with it. I hope you're hungry,' she said as she put the lid back on.

Jenna gave Ruth an apologetic smile. 'I'm really sorry, but Brendon treated me to a cream tea at The Buttered Scone after my visit to the GP, and I would be quite unable to eat anything this evening.' Adrian's sneering voice echoed in her mind. *How can you eat so much? What a glutton you are. No wonder you're fat ...'*

And now Ruth would find her rude ...

Ruth smiled. 'It's all right, love. I know exactly what you mean. The scones are massive.'

The knot in Jenna's chest loosened a little. Ruth didn't seem to mind.

'The Buttered Scone is the best tea shop for miles around. We have lovely shops in Dana, you'll see.'

As Ruth listed names of shops, Jenna's mind wandered a thousand miles away, back to Manchester and the apartment she had shared with Adrian for over a year and where everything had been sleek and polished and perfect – everything, except her.

Ruth stopped talking. 'You're not listening, pet, but I don't blame you. I talk too much, that's what my husband says.'

Startled back to the present, Jenna jumped and almost knocked her mug of tea over. She managed to catch it before it tipped over and wrapped her hands around it to steady it.

'I'm sorry. I was listening but …' She may as well speak the truth, or at least part of the truth. 'I was thinking how lovely your house is and what a change it is from where I used to live.'

Ruth smiled. 'Thank you. It's a big, messy house but I wouldn't change anything.' She checked the kitchen clock and added, 'I'd better set the table. Brendon said he'd take you to Mermaid's Cottage after tea. I hope you won't be disappointed. It's a wee bit old-fashioned and out of the way.'

'I don't mind old-fashioned and out of the way.' The more out of the way, the better.

Ruth took a loaf of bread out of the oven and placed it on the table, before getting some plates and soup bowls out of a cupboard.

Jenna stood up. 'Would you like any help?'

'That would be lovely. You'll find placemats in there, and cutlery in that drawer. Just four sets, love. You'll be glad to hear that the bad weather is supposed to lift this evening, and it should be sunny for the mobile library's grand opening tomorrow.'

Ruth put four tall glasses and a pitcher of water on the table. 'I hope you're prepared to meet a lot of very nosy locals. Word about your dramatic arrival on the *Riannog* this afternoon must have already spread far and wide.'

'Ah.' Jenna's hand shook as she put the last spoon on

the table. What if locals blamed her for the skipper's heart attack, like young Kieran did? Or if they found her dull and stuck-up, or hated the books she'd ordered for the mobile library? Worries bumped against one another, making her chest tighter and tighter.

'Everybody is really excited about having a mobile library service again,' Ruth added in her cheerful voice. 'And folks on the Carloch estate are dead jealous. I wouldn't put it past Toby Drummond to try and poach you.'

Jenna forced a smile. 'Who is Toby Drummond?'

'He's the laird of the Carloch estate, otherwise known as "His Smoothness" – you'll find out why soon enough. His mobile library service was terminated at Christmas too, but unlike Daniel who set up the social enterprise venture and got a council grant to refurbish the mobile library, he hasn't done anything about it.'

Ruth gave Jenna a sheepish smile. 'Actually, since Brendon parked the mobile library in the courtyard, I was going to be cheeky and ask if I could take a peep at your new books.'

Jenna nodded. 'Of course. It will be a pleasure to show you around.' But she was worried again. What if Ruth didn't like the new look Buttercup?

'Brilliant! I'll ask Brendon for the keys. I won't be long.'

Jenna gazed at the drawings pinned to the fridge. Brendon had told her that Ruth had taken up childminding when her two sons left home, so the drawings must be from her young charges. One drawing stood out and Jenna walked over to take a closer look. Painted entirely in black and grey, it depicted a man standing at the centre of a stone circle. It was an unusual and striking piece of artwork which captured the sadness of the lonely figure perfectly.

Ruth soon came back with a set of keys dangling from her index finger. She glanced at Jenna, then at the drawing.

'I see you're looking at Katrina's masterpiece. It's good, isn't it, especially for a seven-year-old lass. The stone circle is the Weeping Stones, up at Dunfiadhaich. Katrina didn't say so, but I'm pretty sure the man in the painting is Daniel.'

She must have seen the question in Jenna's eyes, because she added, 'Daniel is Katrina's uncle. His younger brother Hugh was the lass's father. He died five years ago and Daniel has been looking after her ever since.'

Yes, Jenna remembered the tragic story from her internet search.

Ruth took her waterproof coat down from the coat rack near the door. 'He dotes on her, but he's a busy man so I take care of her most days after school and sometimes during the holidays too.'

What about the girl's mother, Jenna wanted to ask. Was she not involved in the little girl's upbringing? However the McGregors's childcare arrangements were none of her business, and she'd never been one to gossip, so she said nothing.

As she slipped on her yellow coat, still wet from the ferry crossing, she was aware of Ruth giving it the same dubious look as Daniel had earlier.

'You're going to need something better than this, my love,' she said. 'It may be good enough for showers in the city, but it will be useless around here.'

A few minutes later, the women climbed aboard the mobile library Brendon had parked in the courtyard. Jenna switched on the light, and Ruth gazed at the well-stocked shelves. 'Wow! Look at all these new books ... and you have audio books and DVDs too.'

Her enthusiasm made Jenna smile. She had made the most of the meagre budget McGregor had allocated to order new or nearly new books, audio books and DVDs at discount prices, and Brendon had collected some old stock from Inverness central library before picking her up from the station.

'I have rearranged the women's fiction area,' she explained, 'put all the children's books into plastic crates and bought cushions for them to sit on when they read or browse.' There was so much more she wanted to do, but it would depend on Daniel McGregor and the council, of course.

There was a timid knock on the door, and a child's voice called, 'Can I come in?'

'Katrina?' Ruth rushed to open the door and pulled a small, dark-haired girl inside. 'What are you doing out, and without your coat too?'

The girl stepped aside and stared at Jenna with serious, cornflower blue eyes bordered with thick black lashes, and Jenna was immediately reminded of Daniel McGregor. 'Are you the new librarian lady? Is it true that you're from England? Do you have stories about animals and mermaids?'

The little girl's delicate, elfin features and serious blue gaze were endearing, and Jenna couldn't help but smile. 'Yes, yes and lots are the answers to your questions.'

She walked over to the counter, opened a drawer and took out a pack of stickers with a bright yellow smiley face on. She peeled one off and handed it to the little girl. 'There you are. You are now officially Buttercup's very first customer. That's what I called the mobile library, but your uncle said he had a cow called Buttercup, so perhaps I should pick another name. What do you think?'

Katrina frowned. 'We do have a cow called Buttercup and she's massive, but it's a pretty name so I think you should keep it.' She walked to one of the floor cushions, and turned round. 'Can I sit down?'

'Of course. Actually I have a brand new book about

mermaids if that's what you're interested in,' Jenna said as she crouched down next to Katrina.

'My mummy is a mermaid, you know. She sends me beautiful shells by dolphin post because normal postmen can't go under the sea.'

Children came up with the strangest stories. 'Oh. Right. Does she write back by dolphin post too?'

Katrina shrugged. 'Oh no, she never writes. It's not her fault. She can't use pens and paper under the sea, but it does make me sad sometimes.'

Jenna had no idea what this story about dolphins and mermaids was about but the last thing she wanted was to make the little girl sad, so she flicked through the box and pulled out a book with a dark-haired mermaid on the cover. 'There it is …'

'She looks like my mummy.' Katrina gasped in wonder as she stared at the front cover.

'Oh crumbs,' Ruth said behind Jenna. 'I think you'd better put that book away, and quick. It will only upset the wee lass.'

Jenna turned round. 'I can assure you that it's a lovely story, perfectly suitable for children of Katrina's age.'

'I don't doubt it for a second, but … Please do as I say and take it from the lassie now,' Ruth insisted, eyes pleading.

Even though she didn't understand what was going on, Jenna did what Ruth suggested. She got up and held the book against her chest and out of Katrina's reach.

'Come on, Katrina,' Ruth said. 'It's time for tea. I made your favourite Cock-a-leekie soup, and you can have a piece of chocolate cake for pudding.'

'But I want to look at my mummy's picture,' Katrina said, scrambling to her feet and holding her hand out.

'It's not your mum on the cover, love,' Ruth protested as

the door of the mobile library opened and Daniel McGregor stood in the doorway.

He may not have been wearing his lifeboat crew outfit now, but he still looked broad and weather-beaten in a dark green waxed jacket and faded jeans tucked into muddy boots. He brought in the scents of the outdoors too – a mixture of rain, sea spray and farmyard smells.

He wiped his feet on the mat, glanced at the two women and the child and frowned. 'Katrina? Ruth? Miss Palmer ... Is there anything the matter?'

The little girl pointed an accusing finger at Jenna. 'Uncle Daniel, the new lady has a book about my mummy but she won't let me have it. Can you ask her to give it to me?'

Daniel glowered at Jenna, his eyes a frigid blue. 'What's going on here?'

His anger was so palpable Jenna recoiled, holding the book to her chest, with her heart beating at a hundred miles an hour, and stammered, 'Nothing. I ... It's a perfectly innocent storybook about mermaids and ...'

Ruth gave Jenna an encouraging smile then turned to Daniel. 'It's a misunderstanding, that's all,' she interrupted in a conciliatory voice. 'Let's go back in for tea.'

Daniel gave Jenna another hard stare then he lifted Katrina into his arms. 'Ruth is right. Come on, chick.'

Chapter Four

Shannon ... Would the woman follow him like a curse to the end of his days? Even now, when she was a continent away, it seemed she still had the power to wreak havoc in her daughter's life.

However frustrated he felt, he had to remain calm for Katrina's sake. Most of all he had to make sure she forgot all about that blasted storybook Jenna Palmer had produced, so as he carried the little girl across to the farmhouse, he told her about the two calves born at the farm that very afternoon.

'You can name them, if you like.'

'Can I? Great! I'll have to talk to them first so I can choose the right name.'

He walked into the MacDonalds' farmhouse and put Katrina down in the hallway. 'They're calves, love. They can't talk.'

She gave him a pitying look. 'They can. Miona says she talks to animals all the time.'

He sighed. Miona said all kinds of crazy things. However, she was also the closest Katrina had to a grandmother, so it didn't matter if she had strange notions about fairies, ghosts and talking animals. That said, she had given him one of her funny looks when he'd asked her to give Mermaid's Cottage a thorough clean for Jenna Palmer. 'The Cove has a new mermaid,' she had muttered. 'Perhaps she'll be the one who breaks the curse.'

The McGregor curse, otherwise known as the mermaid's curse ... He'd started to laugh but he didn't want to upset Miona, even if she talked nonsense, so he'd grabbed his toolbox and gone out to tinker with the tractor.

'The mobile library is called Buttercup because it's yellow,' Katrina declared.

'Aye, love, I remember.' He'd smiled when Jenna Palmer had told him. He remembered something else ... the feel of the young woman's body in his arms and the delicious but unwelcome sensations she had aroused when she'd linked her hands at the back of his neck as he carried her out of the passenger cabin.

Katrina pulled on his sleeve. 'Uncle, are you listening? I said it was my favourite colour.'

'I know, chick.' That was why he'd asked the garage in charge of the refurbishment to paint it a bright yellow instead of the old mustardy colour.

'Her eyes are very blue and very big.'

'Huh? What are you talking about?'

Katrina let out an impatient tut. 'The new librarian lady, of course! I think she's very pretty.'

'Is she?' He hadn't really looked at the woman, but she seemed rather plain and ... well, nothing special – then again, he'd had other things on his mind on the ferry that afternoon, like taking care of Jim and then sailing the *Riannog* back to Dana.

'She gave me a sticker and she made the mobile library look really good too,' Katrina added.

He'd hardly noticed that either. All he had seen was Katrina's pleading eyes as she asked for the mermaid storybook. What if she got upset again? Like when she was much younger and all Daniel could do was hold her tight, and make up fancy tales about mermaids he hoped she would forget as she grew up. But she clearly hadn't. More importantly, what would she say if she knew the truth?

They found Brendon slicing bread in the kitchen.

'It smells nice,' Daniel said as soon as he stepped in.

27

Brendon gestured towards a pot on the Aga. 'It's Ruth's soup. Have you heard about Jim yet?'

Daniel nodded. 'Julie called to say that he was still in intensive care but thankfully out of danger. The tests showed that he did indeed have a heart attack. It was lucky we got him to hospital so quickly.' Jim's wife had been full of praise for the lifeboat's rapid response, and he'd made a point of relaying both the news and thanks to the crew straight away. Not all call-outs ended that well.

'She wants to have a ceilidh at The Anchor when he's out of hospital.'

Katrina looked at him. 'Can I come? I love it when you play the fiddle.'

Daniel smiled. 'Sure. Why not?'

Katrina loved music, singing, and dancing … like Shannon. Hopefully these were the only traits she had inherited from her mother. Daniel took his coat off and hung it on the rack behind the door.

'I'll get some beers from the pantry. I won't be long,' Brendon said before nipping out, and a few seconds later Jenna Palmer walked in, her thin parka dripping water all over the floor tiles. She took her coat off, and looked around as if she wasn't sure what to do with it.

'Here … Let me hang it for you,' Daniel said, stepping closer to take the coat off her.

She stiffened and he was once again struck by the wariness in her eyes as she handed him the coat. 'Yes. Thank you.'

Surely she wasn't frightened of him? It was true that they hadn't met in the best of circumstances, and that he may have been a little abrupt on the *Riannog* and again in the mobile library just then, but he wasn't that scary … was he? He looked at his hands. They may be clean but they always looked rough, and his clothes carried a distinctive farmyard smell, even when they came out of the washing machine. Perhaps she just didn't want him to put mucky stains all over her fancy coat.

Whatever the reason, it was plain to see that she was ill at ease, and it was up to him to make an effort. The woman had had an awful journey, and the last thing he needed was for her to decide that Arrandale wasn't for her after all and that she wanted to go back to Manchester.

He forced a smile and gestured to the table. 'Why don't you sit down?'

She shifted from one foot to the other. 'I'm not sure I should.'

He frowned. What was wrong with the woman? 'I promise I don't bite. Well, not usually.' His attempt at humour fell flat and her face became bright red.

'No, of course not ...' She drew in breath. 'What I meant was, I'm not having anything to eat so I don't know if I should sit at the table.'

'It's a big table. There's enough room for you. You can sit here.' Katrina spoke with such a bossy voice Jenna Palmer had no choice but to do as she was told.

'Don't you like soup?' Katrina asked. 'I *love* soup! And cake and ice-cream too. What's your name, by the way? I can't call you Librarian Lady. It's not polite.'

'Katrina, what's not polite is to ask grown-ups for their name,' Daniel warned, but Katrina extended her hand over the table and spoke in a formal voice.

'Hello, my name is Katrina McGregor, but you can call me Katrina. I am very pleased to meet you.' She cast him a cheeky glance and added, 'You see, Uncle Daniel, I am being polite.'

This time, Jenna Palmer smiled and shook Katrina's hand. 'I am very pleased to meet you too, Katrina. I am Jenna Palmer, but you can call me Jenna.'

Katrina nodded. 'Jenna … that's pretty. It would be perfect for one of our new calves. You don't mind if I give your name to a baby cow, do you?'

Daniel held his breath. Not everybody appreciated Katrina's quirky ways, but Jenna Palmer smiled again.

'Not at all. I would be honoured if both the mobile library and I have cows' names.' Her cheeks coloured and she gave Daniel a timid smile.

He smiled back. 'By the way, Brendon said he planned to take you to Mermaid's Cottage after tea, but I'd rather show you around so I can explain how everything works. Is that all right with you, Miss Palmer?'

'Why don't you call her Jenna too?' Katrina interrupted, before turning to the librarian. 'Can my uncle call you Jenna? Don't be scared of him. He is big and sometimes grumpy, but he's really nice when you know him.'

'Katrina …' he growled again.

The young woman glanced at him. 'Well, yes, I don't mind … if he doesn't.'

He shrugged. 'Of course I don't mind. Why would I mind?' He sounded grouchy again, and Jenna Palmer's face immediately lost its appealing rosy colour and became as pale as the moon.

Great. He'd frightened her, again. Good job, McGregor. He had finally found a librarian who was qualified *and* didn't mind living in the Arrandale wilderness or getting paid a paltry wage, and it seemed he was doing his best to scare her off.

He rubbed his cheeks. He hadn't had time to shave that morning again and his hands made rasping sounds. Heavens, he was tired. Every muscle in his body ached too, and he was hungry. He would feel more amenable after he'd had some of that soup cooking on the Aga.

Katrina clapped, her eyes shining with delight. 'Great.

And you can call him Daniel too! There, we're all friends now, so you two should shake hands or better still, give each other a kiss on the cheek. I always kiss my friends at school.'

There was an awkward moment when Jenna Palmer gasped and looked as if she'd rather kiss a feral goat. Thankfully Ruth and Brendon walked in before she had to reply or before Katrina could cause any further embarrassment.

Ruth must have sensed the uncomfortable atmosphere in the kitchen because she arched her eyebrows and glanced at Jenna then at Daniel.

'Is everything all right?'

'Fine.' Both he and Jenna Palmer replied at the same time.

'Uncle Daniel and Jenna are friends now,' Katrina announced in a happy voice.

'Are they? That's excellent news. Come on everybody, let's eat. I don't know about you all, but I'm famished.' Ruth turned to Jenna. 'Are you sure you don't want anything, love?'

The woman replied that she wasn't hungry so Ruth served the soup, Brendon opened the cans of beer and handed one to Ruth, and Daniel poured some water out for Katrina and him, Jenna Palmer having said that she didn't want anything. Katrina mentioned the newborn calves, and the conversation veered onto the new arrivals at the farm, how hard Ruth's husband Colin worked and how desperately he needed help in his veterinary practice. Katrina said her best friend at school wanted to become a vet but she was going to be a ballerina, or a truck driver, or perhaps an artist.

Daniel smiled. At least she seemed to have forgotten about her mother and the mermaid storybook. For now.

'It's only a short ride to Mermaid's Cottage,' Daniel said

an hour later as the Land Rover splashed in puddles and bumped along on the track.

The road forked right and followed the cliff down to the cottage and Mermaid Cove. To the left was the way to Dunfiadhaich Farm and the old castle from which his ancestors had ruled Arrandale for centuries and fought their savage clan warfare, and which was now little more than a ruin. The McGregors, MacLeods and Donalds may now all be getting along fine, but relations with the Drummonds of Carloch were still proving tricky ...

Things had taken yet another nasty turn since Toby Drummond had inherited Carloch from his father. The man who had once claimed to be his brother's best friend was nothing but a sneaky weasel. Daniel's fingers clamped harder around the steering wheel, but he forced himself to relax. Better not think about Hugh or Drummond when he drove down the narrow cliff road to Mermaid's Cottage ...

'Here we are.' He parked in front of the small whitewashed cottage facing the cove. He got out, intending to open the passenger door for Jenna, but she had already jumped out and walked closer to the cliff edge.

The wind had blown most of the storm clouds away, revealing patches of pink and orange sky that reflected on the surface of the sea. The days were getting longer, and in a few weeks' time it would hardly get dark at all ... Gannets, gulls and kittiwakes glided over the cliffs, their shrill calls carried by the fresh breeze that smelled of salt and seaweed. This was one of Daniel's favourite spots to watch the sunset, and he often came down from the farm after work to sit on the beach. Sometimes he even brought his fiddle, although he'd not done that for a while. He guessed he would now have to share the view with Jenna Palmer, or – and it was more likely – find himself another beach.

'The cottage is very old but it has been modernised. It

was a holiday cottage for a few years.' He didn't mention that it wasn't a very successful holiday cottage as it was rather basic and isolated.

She didn't reply. In fact she hadn't spoken more than a couple of words since they'd left the McDonalds's farm. He hoped she wasn't changing her mind about taking the job. What if she hated the place? He had been surprised when out of the three cottages he had suggested she picked the smallest and the most remote.

'It's perfect,' she said at last. She looked at him as a ray of sunlight pierced through the clouds and touched her face and hair, painting them a glorious gold. Her blue eyes were as clear as the water at Fairy Pools, and her lips full, soft and pink. He held his breath and his heartbeat picked up pace as something – desire, longing, and a weird, forlorn feeling of loss and pain – churned inside him. How could he ever have thought her plain?

Her eyes widened, and she gasped. He'd better stop gawking at her or he'd scare her again. He took a step back, and said in a gruff voice, 'Good. I'm glad you like it. I'll get your things.'

He lifted her bag and small suitcase out of the boot. 'You'll have to let me know when the rest of your stuff is delivered so that I can help you move in properly.'

'This is all I have.'

He frowned. That didn't sound promising. 'I hope it's not because you're not planning on staying.'

'Oh no! I want to stay. This is the most beautiful place I've ever seen, and I can't thank you enough for giving me the chance to work here. I promise I'll do my very best for Arrandale ... and for you.'

Her slightly husky voice did funny things to him, and once again his pulse hammered hard and fast. What was wrong with him? He took the keys of the cottage out of his pocket, unlocked the front door and grabbed hold of the suitcases. 'Right ... Good.'

He cringed with embarrassment. She was a librarian, for Pete's sake – a woman with impressive degrees who was used to fancy words and clever people. She would think him an awkward, uneducated peasant, unable to string more than three full sentences together. It shouldn't matter what she thought. After all, he wasn't trying to impress her, was he? But he was annoyed to realise that it mattered.

Chapter Five

Daniel McGregor ducked down as he walked through the doorway. Jenna waited until her heartbeat returned to normal and the heat on her cheeks cooled. What had just happened?

It was as if the air had shifted and become charged with some strange energy and the light became soft and hazy and all she could see were Daniel McGregor's eyes, so bright and blue and filled with an intensity that took her breath away. It was almost as if he had touched her heart, her very soul.

And she was being fanciful and ridiculous. She hadn't come all the way to Arrandale to be dazzled by a pair of blue eyes. She would do well to remember they belonged to a bear of a man who was abrupt and unpleasant – a man who was her boss too.

McGregor turned round and frowned. 'Are you coming?'

An abrupt, unpleasant, grouchy bear … Definitely.

'Yes. Of course. Sorry,' she mumbled.

The cottage's hall smelled of detergent and furniture spray. Its whitewashed walls were bumpy and uneven and decorated with a small watercolour of Dana harbour and a rectangular mirror hanging above a hall table. A straw hat and an oversized umbrella hung from the old-fashioned coat stand next to it.

McGregor switched the light on. 'The cottage has been empty since last summer, but I came yesterday to check that everything was in working order, and put the heating and the hot water on for you.'

He pushed a door to his right. 'As you probably remember from the details I emailed, there's only one bedroom and bathroom upstairs, and through here is the open plan living area and kitchen. My housekeeper brought a few essential supplies when she came to do the cleaning this morning.'

The living room was rather rustic with its dark green two-seater sofa facing a stone fireplace where an old-fashioned gas fire had been fitted, a coffee table and a beige rug covering a patterned red and green carpet, but all she saw was the vase filled with a profusion of yellow roses on the dining table.

'How beautiful!' She stepped closer and bent down to breathe in the flowers' sweet and delicate scent. 'Thank you. But how did you know?'

He looked puzzled. 'Know what?'

'That yellow roses are my favourites.'

He shrugged. 'I didn't. Miona must have picked them in the garden at the back of the house.'

She bit her lip and her face burned so hard it hurt. Why had she said such a silly thing? Of course he didn't know she loved yellow roses. What's more the idea of the big, burly man picking flowers and arranging them in a vase was ridiculous.

He gestured to the suitcases. 'Where would you like them? I can take them up to the bedroom, if you like.'

She shook her head. 'No, thank you. Here is fine. I'll deal with them later.' The sooner he left, the better.

'Then I'll show you how to work the various appliances and where the fuse box and the stopcock are.'

The cottage was small and rather sparingly equipped, so that didn't take long. To finish, they crouched side by side in front of the gas fire.

'It gets chilly in the evenings even in summer, so you'll need it. See that button, there? You have to push it and turn this dial at the same time.' There was a hissing sound as the gas was released and flames popped up.

He glanced at her, probably to make sure that she

understood, and she was once again struck by the cobalt blue of his eyes, now warmed by the reflection of the flames in the fire.

He wasn't what most people would consider handsome, but there was something incredibly appealing about him, or rather there would be if he didn't frown so much, had a shave and a decent haircut, and if he smiled more – the kind of genuine, unguarded smiles he gave his adorable niece. Or if he looked at her the way he had on the clifftop earlier – that long, hot, dreamy look that had made her feel beautiful and enveloped in warmth and desire ... But that had only been her tired brain and overactive imagination playing tricks.

She rose to her feet and stepped back to put some distance between them. 'Thank you. I understand how it works.'

'The emergency phone numbers are in the visitors' book. I suppose I should warn you that the phone signal is patchy and the electricity supply can be hit and miss, especially in stormy weather, but there's an ample supply of candles and matches, and two electric torches under the sink with a box of spare batteries.'

Life at Mermaid's Cottage was certainly going to be very different ... different, and wonderful.

'I almost forgot,' McGregor said when they were both standing on the doorstep again. 'I arranged a meeting with Celia Kennedy for Thursday. She's the Council's finance officer who gave the mobile library project the go-ahead. She's been helpful so far, but I have the feeling that she intends to scrutinise how we spend every single penny of the council grant. I hope it's all right with you.'

'Thursday? Well ... yes, of course.' Jenna forced a smile but dread tightened her chest. What if the woman decided she wasn't up to the task of managing the library service? If the council withdrew their grant, the use of their premises in

Dana and access to the Highlands Library computer system, she would be out of a job, and out of this lovely cottage.

McGregor looked at her hands and frowned, and she realised that once again she was rubbing her finger where Adrian's ring had been. She pushed her hands into her coat pockets.

'About tomorrow,' she started. 'I planned a children's story time session in the afternoon. 'Do you think your niece will want to come?'

'I'm sure she will.' He gave her a warm, genuine smile which lit up his eyes and made her catch her breath. 'Katrina is insatiable when it comes to reading and has books about everything and anything.'

Only perhaps not about mermaids, Jenna thought, recalling the strange incident in the mobile library earlier.

He bade her good night, climbed into his old Land Rover, which was covered with so many rust and mud patches it was impossible to tell what colour it had once been, and drove away on the narrow, bumpy track.

And Jenna was alone.

The light was a dusky, transparent blue, with both the sea and the sky merging into one, with only the indigo line of the horizon to separate them. Suddenly the urge to go down to the beach and dip her toes into the water was irresistible, so she hurried down the cliff path and, avoiding the piles of green and black seaweeds strewn around on the wet sand, walked to the edge of the water where she took her boots and socks off and rolled up her jeans.

'Here goes.' She stepped into the sea, hissing a shocked breath at the bite of the freezing cold water against her ankles. She wriggled her toes and kept her eyes down as she paddled along the shore to the far end of the cove and back. The sea was so clear she could see every shell, every tiny pebble, almost every grain of coloured sand.

The waves whispered as they lapped the shore. A black and white bird flew overhead, the flapping of wings echoing in the quiet evening. The sky turned a more pronounced shade of mauve and the jagged rocks in the bay Jim had called Mermaid's Rocks looked dark and mysterious.

Bending down, Jenna picked up a piece of driftwood the sea had smoothed into a willowy shape that fitted perfectly in her hand. Her finger traced the grooves which looked like the outline of a woman's figure. Here was the oval of a face, there folds of a long dress draped over generous female curves, and the shape of one hand lifted in greeting or in prayer ... But she was imagining things. It was only a piece of wood.

As the moon rose, Jenna gripped the piece of driftwood like a talisman. Her new life in Arrandale may not have started under the best auspices, but her luck would change and she would make a success of her new job. As she walked back across the beach she couldn't resist picking up a smooth, round pebble and a delicate pearly shell. She placed her treasures in one of her boots and scrambled barefoot up the sandy cliff path, smiling to herself ...

And stopped short at the sight of a woman standing in front of the cottage.

'About time!' The woman scowled. 'I've been waiting for nearly twenty minutes. My stew will be cold by now.' She gestured to the basket at her feet and gave Jenna a disapproving glance.

She was short – even shorter than Jenna's five feet three, with piercing dark eyes and grey hair cut short, and wore a thick woolly cardigan, checked skirt and sturdy brogues.

She bent down to pick up the basket. 'Let's go in, lass. I haven't got all night.'

'Well ...' Jenna hesitated. Who was she?

The woman shook her head and let out a sigh. 'I take it

Daniel didn't tell you I'd be calling round with your supper.' She clicked her tongue. 'Typical! The man forgets everything that's not about his cows and sheep … and the wee lassie. I'm Miona McKinnon, Himself's housekeeper. I did the cleaning here earlier.'

Jenna smiled. 'Of course! I'm very happy to meet you, Mrs McKinnon.'

'You can call me Miona.' It sounded more like an order than a suggestion.

Jenna's smile faltered. 'All right … Miona. Thank you for making the cottage so welcoming, and especially for the yellow roses in the dining room. They are beautiful.'

The woman's expression softened a touch. 'They're from the garden, at the back.' Glancing down at Jenna's bare feet and the wet hem of her jeans, she added, 'If I may say so, it's not a good idea to go paddling when you don't know anything about tides and currents.'

Jenna's face grew warm. 'Oh … Well, I …'

Miona glanced back at the open door. 'And it's not a good idea either to leave the house with the gas fire on.'

Jenna gasped. The fire! She had completely forgotten about it. 'Oh no! I only wanted to go down to the beach. It was like …'

She looked back towards the cove. 'Like the sea was calling me, and once I was on the beach, I lost track of time. It's so beautiful, so peaceful … I am sorry, Mrs McKinnon … Miona. It won't happen again.'

Miona McKinnon stared at her in a strange way. 'Aye … You're the one all right. Come now.' And ignoring Jenna's puzzled look, she walked into the house.

Jenna left her boots in the hallway and followed barefoot into the living room where Miona put the basket on the dining table. She looked around and made a few tutting sounds.

'The cottage is all right for a holiday, but not to live in. I told Himself this very morning that you'd need things to make it more homely. I'll have a look at the farm to see what I can find for you.'

'The cottage is perfect as it is and I don't need anything ... but thank you.' She suddenly remembered about the garden. 'Actually, there *is* something I may need. Mr McGregor and yourself mentioned the garden. I was wondering if I could borrow some garden tools. I've always loved gardening.'

'Have you seen the state of the place?' Miona shot Jenna a sharp look. 'Don't take it the wrong way, lass, but you look way too scrawny to tackle the garden. It's a mess.'

Jenna repressed a smile. Scrawny? She wished! Nobody had ever called her scrawny before ...

'I must get back before it gets too dark,' Miona said as she walked back to the hall. 'There's fresh cream in the fridge, so you can have some with the apple pie. You'll have to warm up the stew.'

Jenna thanked her again and watched her disappear in the thickening shadows. She locked the front door and leaned against it for a moment, almost giddy with joy as she listened to the deep silence. There would be no noise of traffic, people shouting in the street or police sirens wailing in the night – only birds, the sea, and the mermaids singing on the wind.

She chuckled. Well, perhaps not mermaids ...

She retrieved the pebble, the shell and the piece of driftwood she collected on the beach, carried them to the living room and put them on the mantelpiece. These were her first treasures, and hopefully the first of many.

Chapter Six

'Watch that ditch on your left ... and the wall on your right ... Steady on. Now you can go into fifth gear.' Next to her, Brendon relaxed against the back of his seat and stretched his legs in front of him.

Jenna's fingers gripped the steering wheel so tightly pain shot up along her arms, all the way to her neck and shoulders. She had expected her first outing to be stressful. She had been right. Her heart beat at a hundred miles an hour, sweat dripped down her back, sticking her white blouse to her skin, and her legs shook every time she moved her feet from the pedals. Buttercup was older and more cumbersome than the mobile library she had driven in the past, and the roads in Arrandale were narrow, with many twists and turns, and she wasn't even mentioning the sheep waddling across the lanes without any regard for their safety – or hers. At least she hadn't come across any Highland cows so far.

Thank goodness Brendon would be with her for the next few weeks, until she was familiar with the route, the stops and the van. He had promised to introduce her to the locals too. She didn't know what made her more anxious – driving Buttercup safely or meeting new people. On top of everything, there was now that meeting on Thursday with the woman from the council to worry about.

She couldn't afford for anything to go wrong. She needed this job, this fresh start in Arrandale. Since being made redundant almost a year before she hadn't been able to find a permanent position and her savings had almost completely melted away. She could still hear the pity in Adrian's voice as he read out yet another rejection letter before ripping it to shreds and throwing it into the bin. "You don't have the profile they're after" or "They've already appointed for the post" or again "You're under qualified". She wasn't keen on him opening her correspondence at first, but after she twice lost the key to their letter box he had decided that he would collect their post, and that he might as well open it too. After all, they had no secrets from each other, and he was only sparing her hurt and disappointment ... He had done the same with her emails, and she had let him. How blind, stupid and pathetic she had been! Anger and shame battling inside her, she pressed her foot down on the accelerator and the van shot ahead.

Brendon let out a chuckle. 'Steady on, love. This isn't the Grand Prix!'

'Sorry.' She lifted her foot off the pedal and gave him an apologetic smile.

As the van turned round a bend in the road, the sun shone into her eyes and she pulled down the sun visor. It was hard to focus on the road when she was surrounded by such glorious landscape – the bright blue sea, the hills dotted with sheep and the meadows covered with wild flowers, and every so often, the ruins of a castle standing at the foot of a loch, the reminder of a proud and violent past. And suddenly, at a turn of the road there they were.

'The Highland cows. In that field over there ... They're huge, and beautiful, and so hairy!' she shrieked, as excited as a child.

Brendon laughed. 'That's why we call them the Hairy coos.'

Jenna slowed down as she drove past the field and stared at the animals. 'But how can they see where they're going with that massive fringe?'

Brendon laughed again. 'It protects their eyes from flies. You'll have to ask Daniel about the coos.'

She grinned. 'Perhaps I will. He said he had one called Buttercup, like the mobile library. Wouldn't it be great to have a photo of Buttercup the cow in here?'

'That's a smashing idea, love. So, how was your first night at Mermaid's Cottage?'

'It was fine.' She bit her lip. 'No, actually, it was wonderful.'

For the first time in months, she hadn't had one of these horrid and all too real nightmares about Adrian when she sobbed, pleaded and cried out in her sleep, and it was the calls of seabirds and sunlight flooding the bedroom that woke her in the morning.

She slowed down as she approached a crossroads.

'We're coming into Dana now,' Brendon said. 'Take the first right, then left to the seafront and the library office.'

She indicated and turned right. Thankfully there wasn't much traffic. 'How clever of Mr McGregor to ask the council to let us use their former facilities in Dana and their computer systems for loaning books. It would have been difficult to run the mobile library service without it.'

'Daniel's a clever lad.' He winked. 'The lady from the council was very impressed by his business proposal, and even more impressed by his sparkling blue eyes.'

Yes, Jenna could very well believe that. Daniel McGregor's blue eyes had a strange effect on her too … enough to make her forget his grouchy personality.

'Take the next left and we're there.' Brendon grinned and rubbed his hands. He must be as relieved as she was to have made it to Dana in one piece.

She turned into the main street and gasped in shock.

A small crowd had gathered outside the library office. A "Welcome to Dana" banner hung above the door, and a long trestle table on the pavement was covered with food, cups and saucers and a couple of big old-fashioned tea urns. People stood around chatting while children played at sword fighting with blue and white flags.

'Why are all these people here?'

Brendon arched his bushy eyebrows. 'They're waiting for you, lass.'

He pointed at two elderly gentlemen sitting on camping chairs. 'I bet Donald and Murdo have snuck a dram of whisky in their tea, unbeknownst to their misses! You'll have to watch these two. They're terrible flirts.'

Jenna giggled. 'Flirts?' The men looked ancient.

'Donald is the one with the sideburns, and his old pal Murdo has the tweed cap,' Brendon explained. 'Over there under the banner is Enid.' He gestured towards a stout lady serving food and drinks. 'Her sister owns The Buttered Scone which is handy because she always brings us buns and pastries. However she runs the book club and can be a wee bit bossy.'

Jenna cast Brendon a suspicious glance as she drove down the street in second gear. 'Did you know about this welcome committee?'

He gave her a sheepish smile. 'I may have had an inkling.' He looked away and pointed at a tall and gangly man. 'I see Donaldson from the *Gazette* is here too.'

'The newspaper? I'm not dressed smart enough. I haven't even got any lipstick on.' Appalled, Jenna glanced down at her boring white shirt and navy trousers and pulled a face.

'You look bonnie exactly as you are. Stop fretting and park that van. Your arrival is the highlight of the week – no, make that the month.'

That did absolutely nothing to calm Jenna's nerves.

'You can park in that space, over there.'

'I'll never fit. It's too small.'

'You'll be fine.'

She cast him a dubious look, but what choice did she have, short of showing the whole of Port Dana and the local press that she was incapable of handling their mobile library? Her heart was in her throat as she manoeuvred the van. She checked the mirror and reversed into her allocated spot, holding her breath all the way through.

'Almost there … Watch out, there's some traffic coming this way. Stop!' Brendon warned suddenly.

She slammed her foot down on the brakes as a cacophony erupted outside – the furious beeping of a horn, the screech of tyres on the tarmac, and the shouting from the small crowd waiting for her.

'What happened? Did I hit someone – something?' She unclipped her seat belt and got out from behind the wheel while Brendon opened the door and stuck his head outside.

'It's Drummond,' he said in a harsh voice as he climbed down the steps. 'Trust him to cause trouble today.'

Jenna followed him out and looked at the convertible sports car, stopped inches from the mobile library. Behind the wheel, a slim blond man gesticulated. Had she caused him to be injured, or damaged his car? It looked like an expensive one. What if she'd dented Buttercup when it had just been repainted? This couldn't be happening. Not on her first day. She lifted her hand to her throat. She was going to be sick.

People had assembled around the sports car, and they all fell silent and stared as she walked over.

The driver glared at her. 'You are a menace on the road – a dangerous lunatic! You almost backed into my car with that … yellow monstrosity.'

Jenna opened her mouth to apologise but Brendon was faster. 'With all due respect, Mr Drummond, you were driving so fast we couldn't have possibly seen you. In fact, I'd say you were well over the speed limit.'

There was a rumble of agreement from the crowd. 'Aye, he sure was.'

'That was never thirty miles an hour.'

'Definitely over the speed limit.'

'Where's the constabulary when you need them?'

Drummond raked his fingers into his floppy blond hair. 'Well, I may have been driving a little fast, but only because I was late to pick up mother from the station and I wanted to surprise her with a box of pastries from The Buttered Scone. It was a total waste of time anyway. They were sold out. At ten o'clock in the morning! What kind of cake shop is that?'

The woman who had been looking after the cake stall and who Brandon had called Enid pushed her way to the front. 'That's because we took them all to our wee welcome party. It's Miss Jenna's first day, you see … She's our new mobile librarian.'

Drummond turned to Jenna again, but this time his gaze was pensive. 'Of course … Now I remember that the council took pity on McGregor and sold him their old van for peanuts. I didn't realise he'd hired a new librarian though. I thought you'—he gestured to Brendon—'and the old crone would carry on as before.'

Brendon's face turned crimson. 'The old crone? How can you be so disrespectful to Gwen McCreed?'

Drummond shuddered and got out of his car. 'She was one scary lady. And she had a moustache.' Suddenly oozing boyish charm, he gave Jenna a broad smile and she remembered Ruth had called him "His Smoothness" the day before. 'I realise that I didn't introduce myself. My name is Drummond – Toby Drummond. Lord Drummond, actually. My family own Carloch estate, a stone's throw from here.'

He extended his hand and Jenna had no other option but to take it.

'Dear Jenna. You don't mind if I call you Jenna, do you? Good,' he carried on, still holding her hand. 'I have a proposition for you. Dine with me tonight and we'll talk no more about your driving mishap.'

'*My* driving mishap?' Jenna pulled her hand out of his

47

grip. Now was the time to put into practice her resolution to be more assertive. She tilted her chin up and squared her shoulders. 'I did nothing wrong, Mr Drummond. You were the one driving too fast. And your car doesn't appear to have suffered any damage.'

'The lass is right. There isn't a scratch on that fancy car of yours, so you can quit your shenanigans!' the elderly gentleman with the bushy sideburns Brendon had called Donald remarked.

This was followed by more murmurs of approval from the crowd.

'We know what you're trying to do,' a woman said then. 'You're trying to steal our new librarian for Carloch.'

Drummond's lips stretched into a thin smile. 'Now, that's an idea … But the truth is I only want to show Jenna our Michelin-starred restaurant, and I think a three-course meal at the Three Fishes is a fair trade-off for an insurance claim, especially'—he massaged the back of his neck and pulled a face—'since I think I may have a touch of whiplash.'

Bending down, he opened the glove compartment and flicked through a few papers. 'Now, where did I put my insurance details? I'll ask my lawyers to get in touch with McGregor so that we can sort out my claim as soon as possible. Of course, there will need to be a full inspection of the Jag then I must arrange a visit to the doctor's and the physio … I believe whiplash claims can mount up quite quickly.'

Jenna's throat tightened. She may have done nothing wrong, but dealing with a claim would be a major inconvenience for Daniel McGregor, not to mention an increase in insurance premiums.

'All right! I'll have dinner with you,' she blurted out, only too aware of the surprised looks and mutterings from the people around her.

'You don't have to do that, lass,' Brendon said. 'It's blackmail, pure and simple. Let me call McGregor now. He'll send *him* packing!' He gestured towards Toby Drummond, who paled and immediately brought his hand to his nose as if to check it was still there.

Jenna put a calming hand on Brendon's forearm. 'It's fine, don't worry. The last thing I want is to cause Mr McGregor any trouble. Besides, being invited to a nice restaurant isn't exactly an ordeal, is it?'

Drummond nodded. 'Very wise words, dear Jenna. Now, where are you staying?'

'Mermaid's Cottage.'

'That old croft on the cliff road? I'm surprised it's still standing.' He grimaced and sighed. 'Very well, I shall brave the potholes and McGregor's scraggy sheep and hairy cows, and pick you up at seven tonight.'

He got back behind the wheel, and gestured to the villagers standing around the car. 'Now move along, my good people. I don't want to drive on anybody's feet or risk any of you scratching my new paintwork.'

He revved the engine a few times and beeped his horn, which had the immediate effect of dispersing the crowd, and drove off.

'That Drummond, he's a right *chancer*,' Donald said.

'He thinks he's better than us because he lives in a fancy castle and drives a fancy car,' a woman agreed.

'That green paint is very fancy indeed,' Donald's friend Murdo remarked, lifting his tweed cap to scratch his head.

As the Jag turned round the corner a seagull dived, hovered over it for a few seconds and let out a big dropping onto the car's shiny new paintwork.

'But Arrandale gulls don't care about fancy,' he finished with a broad grin, pulling his cap back down.

Chapter Seven

'And Zonk, the big purple monster, who was so grumpy he scared everybody away, found his happy dream at last and lived *zonkfully* ever after ...' Jenna smiled as she closed the book, and the mobile library echoed with the deafening sound of children clapping.

'*Zonkfully* isn't a real word,' Katrina whispered in his ear.

He arched his eyebrows. 'Are you sure?'

Shaking her head, she threw him a despairing look. 'Of course. Even *I* know that.'

Daniel checked his watch. 'Story time is over. It's time to go home.' And thank goodness for that. He was thoroughly *zonked* out, and had pins and needles from the knees down. He was far too big and old for floor cushions.

He was also the only man amongst the dozen mothers and children who had squeezed into the mobile library to listen to Jenna Palmer reading the improbable tale of Zonk McPurple, the clumsy monster chasing clouds and happy dreams with a butterfly net and getting into all kinds of trouble as he did so.

Happy dreams ... It reminded him of Jenna's telephone interview. It had been a rather embarrassing conversation, with him being in the cowshed at the time while one of his cows was giving birth. He hadn't really paid much attention to what she was saying, until she mentioned books being like happy dreams that had to be shared. The image had struck him, and not only because of Arrandale's Gaelic name.

He may have told Jenna she was naïve about books making people happy, but hearing the children's giggles today and looking at their beaming smiles as they hung on her every word, he had to admit that she was right.

He tried to shift his position, and his elbow bumped into a little boy's ribs next to him. The place was full, and it was getting hot and stuffy. Perhaps he should have stayed outside with Brendon to enjoy the spring sunshine and a mug of tea from the welcome stall. He glanced down at his shirt and frowned. He could have done with changing it before Katrina dragged him away from the farm. There were a few suspicious stains where he carried the sick calf into the cowshed after lunch.

Jenna put the book down. 'I will tell you more stories about Zonk when I visit your school next week. Thank you all for coming. Don't forget your books and help yourself to a complimentary bookmark.'

There was a cheer from the children as they all scrambled to their feet, clutching their library book against their chest and grabbing a free bookmark before exiting the van with their mothers. Who would have guessed kids could be so enthusiastic about free bookmarks?

Katrina pulled on his sleeve. 'Can we ask Jenna to come for tea?'

He frowned. 'I don't know, love. I don't have time for guests. There's too much going on at the farm.'

Katrina folded her arms and stuck her lower lip out. 'You never have time for anything fun. You're like Zonk – big and grumpy and you have no friends!'

Ouch, that hurt, but then again the truth often did. Katrina was right. He did feel like that Zonk monster most of the time. He may not be purple or wear a kilt every day but he was often short-tempered and he didn't have many happy dreams either. His thoughts usually revolved around the estate and the ever pressing issues of paying bills and looking after the farm. As for friends and family, well, he had Miona and Iain, and the lifeboat lads and lasses. More importantly he had Katrina, and she was the only one who mattered. The more he thought about it, the more he realised that the only thing he had in abundance in Arrandale was clouds – literally and figuratively.

'Someone's got to look after the farm, love. We can always invite Jenna another day.'

'But she doesn't know anybody. It would be kind to invite her. You always say we have to think of other people.'

Abandoning the sulking child posturing, she arched her eyebrows and gave him a serious and very grown-up look which almost made him laugh. How was it possible that the girl was only seven years old? Then again, Miona claimed that she was an old soul …

'All right, you win.' He winced when his knees creaked as he got up. His thighs hurt and he couldn't even feel his feet. He strode around the estate all day, climbed fences and carried tools, wooden posts or bags of cattle feed on his shoulders, but one hour sitting on a cushion in a cramped mobile library and he felt like a hundred-year-old granddad!

Katrina held on to his hand and they shuffled in the queue towards the front door of the van.

'Thank you so much for coming everybody. I hope you had a good time. See you soon,' Jenna was saying as people left. She pointed at a book that a little girl clutched to her chest. 'Good choice! That's one of my favourite Zonk McPurple books.'

At last it was their turn, and Katrina didn't waste a second before embarrassing him. 'My uncle said you must be lonely and would like to invite you for tea,' she said without drawing breath. 'I'll show you the new calves. They're really cute and fluffy, but one of them is poorly. I called her Maisie. I called the other calf Jenna because my uncle says she's pretty and you're pretty too.'

Jenna looked at him, and heat crept up his face and neck. Katrina made it sound as if it was his idea to invite the woman over for tea. Worse still, Jenna now believed that he said she was pretty. He couldn't deny either of these things without being rude and tactless, so he forced a smile.

'Yes, well, hmm … if you have time after you finish here, we would both be happy if you came over to the farm for tea.'

Jenna shook her head. 'That's very kind of you, and I would love to accept but unfortunately I already have plans for tonight.'

'Oh. Are you going for tea somewhere else?' Katrina asked in a small, disappointed voice.

'That's right, but I would love to come and look at your calves another day.'

'Where are you going?' Katrina insisted.

Daniel pulled the girl closer to him. 'Katrina, it's none of your business where Miss Palmer is going.'

'You said you would call her Jenna,' the little girl interrupted.

'Yes … right. Like I said, it's none of your – our – business where Jenna is going tonight.' But he too was curious, even though he had absolutely no right to be. Perhaps Ruth had invited her again, or Brendon was taking her to the pub.

Jenna seemed hesitant, and rubbed her thumb over the ring finger of her right hand, like she'd done the day before.

'I was going to tell you earlier but it's been so busy I didn't get the chance. There was a rather unpleasant incident this morning when I arrived in Dana.'

He frowned. 'What kind of incident?'

Her cheeks coloured and she drew in a deep breath. 'As I was reversing the mobile library, a sports car came out of nowhere. I didn't hit it, but the driver had to brake hard and said he may have whiplash …' She let out a shaky sigh, and rubbed her finger again.

He frowned harder. 'Carry on.'

'He threatened to put in a claim with his insurance company and it would be very costly for you unless …'

'Unless?'

'Unless I had dinner with him tonight,' she finished quickly. 'The last thing I want is for you to be inconvenienced, so I agreed.'

Only one man would pull such a stunt. 'Was he driving a racing green, convertible Jaguar by any chance?'

Jenna nodded. 'How do you know?'

So he'd been right. It was Drummond. 'Why did nobody tell me about this? Brendon or you should have phoned me straight away.'

He dug his mobile phone out of his jeans pocket. 'You certainly don't have to go out with him if you don't want to. I'll give him a ring now and tell him he's out of order. He can't go round threatening my staff.'

'Please don't! It doesn't matter, and I don't want to create any bad feelings between you and Lord Drummond.'

'Lord Drummond, eh?' So the man had used his title, to scare Jenna off, no doubt. He shook his head. 'Don't worry about creating bad feelings between Drummond and me.' It was far too late for that.

'Where is he taking you?'

'The Three Fishes.'

Of course. He should have guessed Drummond would take Jenna to the best restaurant on the island. The kind of restaurant he couldn't afford. In fact, the last time he'd been there was for Hugh and Shannon's engagement party. The memory left him with a bitter taste. It was the night Shannon had announced she was pregnant … and the night she started blackmailing him.

Katrina pulled on his sleeve again. 'Please, Uncle, don't be cross with Jenna. She said it wasn't her fault but you're frowning.'

She looked at Jenna and added, 'I told Uncle Daniel that he was like Zonk McPurple, with no friends and no wife and no happy dream.'

'That's enough, Katrina,' Daniel interrupted, more sharply than he'd intended. The little girl glanced up, her chin wobbled and her eyes filled with tears.

He sighed. Katrina was right. He was a stroppy, miserable brute, and an idiot for letting Drummond affect his mood so much. He bent down and scooped the little girl into his arms. 'Sorry, love, I didn't mean to shout at you.'

He looked at Jenna. 'I am sorry too if I gave you the impression that I was cross with you. I wasn't – at all.'

He sighed. Now wasn't the time or the place to air his grievances against Drummond. 'I'm sure you will have a very pleasant evening. The Three Fishes is an excellent restaurant.' Drummond may be sly but he could be charming too. Didn't people call him "His Smoothness"? He had no idea what people called *him*, but if Katrina had her say, she would probably suggest "His Grumpiness" or even "His Zonkiness".

'I don't like Mr Drummond.' Katrina linked her hands behind his neck and hooked her legs around his waist like a monkey. 'He talks posh and every time I see him he looks at me funny.'

Daniel forced himself not to react but he tensed with anger. He'd have a word with the man if he ever upset Katrina – more than a word.

'If it's any consolation,' Jenna told Katrina, 'I'd much rather look at your baby cows. I came across a herd of Highland cows this morning ...

'It's called a fold,' he corrected without thinking.

She arched her eyebrows. 'Sorry?'

'We don't say "herd" but "fold" for Highland cows,' he said.

Jenna Palmer blushed and bit her lip, and he felt bad once again. What did it matter what a group of cows was called?

'I know!' Katrina said then. 'You can come for lunch tomorrow. It's Sunday, and Miona always makes loads to eat on Sundays. Can Jenna come, Uncle? Then we can show her all the cows.'

'Sure.' He nodded. Not that he had much choice. Katrina would make a fuss if he said he was run off his feet and wouldn't have time for a long, leisurely lunch, and even less for a grand tour of the farm afterwards.

'Then I would love to.' Jenna's aquamarine eyes sparkled as she directed a beaming smile at Katrina. She toned down her smile to look at him. 'Thank you for inviting me.'

'Then it's agreed. I'll come for you at noon,' Daniel said. 'Now it's time we left you and Brendon to tidy up. I think everybody enjoyed the day. The children certainly loved your stories.'

'I love Zonk.' Katrina gave him a big sloppy kiss. 'And I love you, Uncle Daniel.'

Chapter Eight

Jenna put on her grandmother's moonstone earrings and looked at her reflection in the mirror. She hadn't worn them in ages and yet they were so pretty. Her chest tightened as she recalled how the few times she'd worn them, Adrian had made a show of sniffing the air and complaining she reeked of old lady and naphthalene. And she'd said nothing.

Well, she would wear them every day from now on. It would be the symbol of her new self – of her new life.

The earrings were the only item of jewellery she had taken with her. Everything else she left at her mother's, including her engagement ring. Especially her engagement ring. What she should have done was to send it to Adrian, or give it away. The clunky gold and garnet ring had been one of Adrian's grand gestures when they first went out together. At the time when he showered her with flowers – yellow roses, her favourites – and took her to expensive restaurants and romantic weekends in country hotels.

He took her shopping to Selfridges and Harvey Nichols too. He claimed she needed a complete wardrobe overhaul and desperate to please him she bought a few designer outfits and accessories, which had been a complete waste of money. Not only were they ridiculously expensive, but she felt uncomfortable wearing them and they were hardly sensible for driving a mobile library, running a toddler sing-along session, or clearing shelves in the library stockroom.

So she kept them in her side of the flat's walk-in wardrobe and hardly ever reached for them. The thought of the small, claustrophobic room made her shudder and catch her breath. How she hated that walk-in wardrobe. She'd even refused to keep her clothes in there, but if Adrian first found her phobia endearing, he had quickly become annoyed to the point of playing a cruel prank on her. One evening he'd asked her to fetch his tie and locked her in before switching off the light. When she banged on the door and cried for him to let her out, he claimed he wanted to cure her from her childish phobia, and she would thank him for it. He unlocked the door three hours later, took her into his arms and comforted her as she sobbed, claiming he was sorry and was only trying to help. And she had been stupid enough to believe him.

Memories of her life with Adrian flashed in front of her. Her pitiful desire to please; her constant anguish at not being good enough, pretty enough, slim enough, clever enough; tiptoeing around his moods; and the abject, sticky fear that she was losing her mind.

It was bad enough that she regularly misplaced her keys, her phone or her watch, but after a few months she started sleepwalking too, and would find her shoes on the balcony, her phone charger in the fridge, or her handbag in the shower. She forgot random things too, like which brands of granola Adrian didn't like or which type of hummus he was allergic to, and constantly got dates of meetings and family parties wrong, even when she wrote them down.

Adrian's parents had made it clear that she wasn't good enough for their son. The last time she'd seen them, she mixed up dates again and when they'd turned up for lunch, she'd had nothing ready and had to run out to the local Sainsbury's to buy party food. Jenna had been aware of the wary glances they cast in her direction throughout lunch, and when they left, Adrian's mother hugged him and said he had the patience of a saint.

A saint? Jenna clenched her fist and stared at her reflection in the dressing-table mirror. A saint indeed … How blind everybody had been where Adrian was concerned, but she'd been the biggest, blindest fool of all.

How she had cried when he left at Christmas to start his new life in London with a woman who he said was everything she wasn't: ambitious, beautiful, successful ... She could recall every one of his parting words, hear the sniggering tone in his voice, and suddenly it was as if he was right there whispering in her ear. Her heart beat faster. Black butterflies fluttered around her, filling the room with darkness. She didn't want to remember him when she was awake. The nightmares were bad enough.

Something puzzled her however. Adrian had been texting her these past two months, at first sending cute emojis, and short messages such as *"How are you?" "I miss you"* and *"I've been thinking about you"*. She'd been so shocked that she hadn't replied at first, but as the texts kept coming she made the mistake of replying that she was coping just fine and was thinking of moving away to Scotland.

There had been a period of silence then Adrian's texts had come in thick and fast. *"Scotland? Doing what?" "You can't possibly be serious." "You're being silly. You'll never cope"* or *"What about your mother?"* Her mother only ever cared about herself, but that was another matter. Annoyed, Jenna replied that she'd already found a job in Arrandale and was moving out of the flat. This time as well as texts about the supposed breakdown she must be having, he left voicemail messages promising to come to Manchester to talk her out of her "crazy idea".

She didn't want to hear from him, even less see him, so she'd bought a new phone and asked her mother not to give her number to Adrian should he ask. She had however spent the past week expecting Adrian to turn up at the flat to stop her from leaving, as if what she was doing with her life was any of his business. It was only when she'd stepped down from the train in Inverness that she'd breathed a sigh of relief. She was in Scotland at last. Nothing would go wrong now … But it had. The storm had closed the Skye Bridge and the *Riannog's* skipper wouldn't sail.

But why was she even thinking about Adrian tonight? Jenna pushed herself up, walked to the window and watched the sunset colour the sky orange and pink, and the birds dipping in and out of the waves. There was only the sea, the cliffs, the beach. She was safe. Adrian would never come all this way for her. Gradually her breathing returned to normal, and her heart rate slowed down.

Her thoughts turned to her busy first day in Buttercup. She had enjoyed every minute of it, especially story time. And if she was being honest, she enjoyed very much seeing Daniel McGregor looking big and uncomfortable, and very endearing as he sat on the floor with little Katrina by his side, the only man amongst the mums and grandmas.

He had been even more appealing when he'd blushed as Katrina invited her to the farm, and when he'd held the little girl in his arms and looked at his niece with love painted all over his face. Jenna sighed and slipped a cardigan over her white dress. Unlike Katrina's claim, and even with his grouchy disposition, Daniel McGregor was a million times more attractive than Zonk McPurple, and she would have much rather spent the evening on the farm than in a fancy restaurant.

The roaring of a powerful car engine followed by loud beeping echoed in the quiet evening. Toby Drummond obviously didn't believe in making a discreet arrival. He mustn't believe in driving inconspicuous cars either, she thought when she ran downstairs, opened the door and saw the shiny black SUV parked at the front. He got out and gave her a dazzling smile; as dazzling as the cream linen suit and light blue shirt that made his tan stand out.

She smiled back. 'Good evening, Mr Drummond.' Or should she say Lord Drummond?

'Please call me Toby. There's no need for formality between friends.' He looked at his watch. 'Are you ready? I booked a table for eight o'clock.'

'I hope you don't mind riding in this ugly tank,' he said a moment later as he opened the passenger door for her.

An ugly tank? The four-wheel drive oozed luxury with its sleek, shiny dashboard and soft grey and cream leather seats that smelled brand new. It certainly was a world away from Daniel McGregor's rusty, creaky and mud-spattered Land Rover.

Toby grimaced as he started on the cliff road. 'I can't understand why McGregor doesn't care more about his estate. The place is falling to pieces while he plays at being a sailor on his lifeboat.'

It was so unfair Jenna couldn't help herself. 'Actually he came to our rescue yesterday with the lifeboat crew when the skipper of the ferry had a heart attack during the crossing. Without them the poor man could have died and the rest of us would have been in serious trouble.'

He glanced at her, and arched an eyebrow. 'Is that so?'

She nodded. 'And Mr McGregor does care about Arrandale, enough to give me a job and a house, and to have the old mobile library refurbished.'

She stopped talking, and bit her lip, stunned by her outburst. What had just happened? She hadn't been so outspoken for a long time!

Drummond's jaw clenched and his profile hardened. 'It seems McGregor has made quite an impression on you.'

Her face grew hot. 'No, not at all, but I thought you were being a little unfair.'

'Very well, my dear. I do apologise. There is quite a bit of history between myself and McGregor, as you'll probably get to know when you've been here a while and that may have coloured my judgement.'

He shrugged. 'Let's talk about you. I want to know everything – where you're from, what you did before coming here ... and most of all, why you agreed to work in this godforsaken place?' As he spoke the last words a seagull flew in front of the car with a squawk and let out a huge dropping that splattered onto the windscreen.

'Not again! I swear these gulls lay in ambush for me to drive by. I think McGregor is so jealous of my cars that he puts them up to it, don't you?' He smiled, and Jenna couldn't help smiling back as she remembered that it was exactly what had happened that morning in town.

'Anyway, where were we? Ah yes, you were going to tell me why you chose to work here ... in the land of potholes, evil gulls and grumpy McGregors.'

She was prepared for such questions, and she gave him the same brief and well-rehearsed answers she had given Ruth, Brendon and the people who asked about herself during Buttercup's opening day, before diverting his attention to the landscape. What was that loch called? What was the story behind the ruined castle in the distance? Was that a stone circle she could see on the hill?

Drummond was both knowledgeable and entertaining, and despite his complaints about the roads, the drive was smooth and fast. A large, ornate black and gold sign announced they were entering Carloch. He slowed down and turned off the main road, and the tyres crunched on the gravel of a driveway lined with blooming purple rhododendrons. At the end was a pink-stoned mansion, flanked with pointed, slate-roofed turrets and a large orangery.

'Here we are. I come here quite a lot. I think you'll like it.'

'It's beautiful.' Beautiful and very grand, as befitted a Michelin star restaurant. It reminded her of the places Adrian used to take her when they started dating – luxury hotels in the Cotswolds or the Lake District. She would have preferred a quiet B&B or a cottage where they would be alone and she wouldn't embarrass him because she wasn't elegant enough, was too friendly with the staff, or couldn't eat langoustines without squirting the juice all over her dress.

The restaurant was full but the atmosphere cosy, and mouth-watering aromas floated in the air. Crystal chandeliers hanging from high ceilings reflected on the silver cutlery laid out on crisp white tablecloths.

Their table overlooked the garden, where green, red and yellow lanterns flickered from tree branches even though it was still daylight. After a brief look at the menu, Jenna ordered the scallop starter, followed by lamb and a salad, while Toby Drummond chose oysters, venison and vegetables. A sommelier brought over a bottle of French champagne which Toby tasted and declared excellent before launching into a conversation about his recent holiday in Sardinia.

'One of the best holidays I've ever had. Have you been there?'

When she said she hadn't, he proceeded to describe the stunning coastline, quirky villages and secluded beaches he'd visited.

'Where have you travelled to?' he asked when he ran out of stories about Sardinia. 'The South of France? Paris?'

She nodded. 'I have been to Paris, a long time ago.' Or rather it felt like a long time. It had been a spur of the moment trip she'd booked as a surprise for Adrian who claimed to love French food, French cinema, and pretty much anything French. It had been a disaster from the start. He'd hated that she spoke some French when he couldn't, that she knew about French history or literature. "Blah de blah de blah. Boring Little Miss Librarian in all her glory," he had sneered with so much venom words had stuck in her throat. He had spent most of the weekend on his phone and she had been too upset to enjoy any of it. The funny thing was that he later told people how much he loved their Parisian mini-break, and how proud he was of her for speaking French and knowing so much about the country, so much so that she doubted her own memory and wondered if she hadn't imagined his bad mood and nasty comments.

'Ah, Paris, what a wonderful city.' Toby Drummond smiled. 'If, of course, there are no yellow-vest protesters throwing chairs around or setting fire to your car. I remember ...' And he launched into yet another account of a holiday – in Paris and Normandy this time. The man seemed to spend an awful lot of time on holidays.

After a delicious pudding of chocolate and raspberry charlotte, they ordered coffee, and for the first time since he'd picked her up at Mermaid's Cottage, he fell silent and stared out at the garden where the lanterns created oases of colour in the dusky evening.

His blond hair flopped on his forehead. He flicked it back with his fingers and sighed before turning to her. 'Jenna, I must come clean and confess that I had an ulterior motive when I invited you tonight. There was no whiplash – not even the hint of one – and no scratch on my Jag either, only a disgusting gull dropping.'

He gave her a sheepish smile. 'The thing is, when I met you this morning, I knew you were the only person who could help me.'

Jenna arched her eyebrows. 'Help you? In what way?'

'Help me find out what McGregor is plotting. The man

has been scheming against my family for years. He is the most pig-headed and unreasonable man I've ever known.' His fist clenched on the white damask tablecloth and his gold Omega watch glittered in the light of the chandelier.

That she could very well believe, but the idea of McGregor as a devious schemer didn't fit in with the impression she had formed of him. Then again, she knew nothing about the man – except that he was bad-tempered, had gorgeous blue eyes and a soft spot for his little niece.

'I would like you to be my friend on the inside, so to speak … keep your ears and eyes open, and report to me anything you find out about McGregor's plans, however menial they sound to you.'

She recoiled with a sharp gasp. 'You want me to spy for you?'

He tutted. 'Spy? What an ugly word … but yes, I guess I do. The brute wishes my family harm and my poor mother is in a permanent state of anxiety, so much so that her health is suffering.'

'I am sorry for your mother, but what you are asking of me is completely out of the question. It would be wrong, and disloyal.'

His eyes narrowed to slits. 'You think McGregor deserves your loyalty? The man is a villain of the worst ilk – a brute who caused his brother's death after having an affair with his fiancée. And worse still, he prevents the girl's heartbroken mother from having any contact with her. And that's only the start. I could say much more …'

Shock rendered Jenna speechless. How could Toby Drummond's conversation have switched from quirky holiday memories to these most appalling allegations?

She bent down to gather her handbag and rose to her feet. 'I don't want to hear any more. Thank you for a very nice meal … well, it was very nice until a few minutes ago.

Don't worry about driving me back. I'll ask the receptionist to call a taxi.'

He stood up immediately too, a contrite expression on his face. 'You will do no such thing. I am sorry. I should never have said anything.'

He ran his fingers through his fringe and flicked it back again. 'Hugh was one of my closest friends, you see … Please, Jenna, don't be angry with me. Let's be friends again.' He extended his hand.

Friends? They weren't friends. She hardly knew the man, and the only reason he invited her was to use her, but what was she supposed to do? People at nearby tables stared at them, and she didn't want to embarrass him so she took his hand. 'Yes, of course.'

He broke into a smile. 'Thank you. Now let me take you home. Please?'

She didn't want to look churlish, so she nodded and they were soon on their way back, but his terrible accusations swirled in her mind during the journey back to Arrandale. Did Daniel McGregor have an affair with his brother's fiancée? Was he stopping Katrina's mother from seeing the little girl? Was that what the mermaid story was all about?

This was nothing to do with her. She didn't know the family or their history. One thing was certain: there was a lot of bad feeling between Daniel McGregor and Toby Drummond.

It still wasn't completely dark but a shiny full moon reflected on the sea and the lochs they came across, and outlined the rugged contours of hills and distant mountains. Drummond only spoke to ask if she wasn't too hot, or too cold, and it was a relief when he finally turned into the track leading to Mermaid's Cottage. As the SUV's headlights swept over the bumpy lane, she kept her head turned towards the sea, glittering in the moonlight.

Mermaid Cove. She had only been there one day, so why did it feel like she was coming home? 'Please, stop the car,' she said as an impulse. 'I'll walk back from here.'

'But there's still a mile or so …'

'It's a lovely evening. I'll be fine.'

He stopped the car and gave a doubtful look. 'Are you sure?'

She nodded, unbuckled her safety belt and opened the door. 'Thank you for the meal. Good night.' She jumped down, and started on the path back to the cottage.

Chapter Nine

'Good night, love.' Daniel pulled the duvet up to Katrina's chin and kissed the tip of her nose, like he did every night after reading her a bedtime story. Tonight, of course, he had to read that silly story of Zonk McPurple chasing happy dreams with his butterfly net. Katrina liked it so much he'd had to read it twice. He'd never heard of that Zonk character before Jenna Palmer arrived, but he had a presentiment that the books would become standard bedtime reading material ... unfortunately.

'Good night, Uncle Daniel,' Katrina replied. 'I can't wait until tomorrow. Do you think Jenna will like her twin?' She laughed.

'Her *what*?'

'The calf we called Jenna, you silly!' Katrina burst out laughing.

'Ah ... I'm sure she will. Now sleep tight, love. It's late.'

'What can I dream of?' she asked in an already sleepy voice.

That was the question she asked every night. 'Dream that you're on a beautiful ship that's taking you to Antarctica and you can see penguins.'

'And mermaids?'

His heart missed a beat. 'Well ... I'm not sure there are any over there. The sea is too cold.'

'Oh ... I like penguins. Good night, Uncle Daniel.'

'Good night, love.'

He went to his room, undressed and took a long shower. The hot water soothed his sore muscles but did nothing to help him relax. Heavens knew he had put in a long enough day and should be exhausted, and yet he felt restless.

'What's ailing you?' Miona asked as he came down to the kitchen and opened a cupboard to take a glass out. 'You're wandering like a lost soul.'

'I have no idea what you're talking about.'

'You've been *crabbit* all evening – well, more *crabbit* than usual.'

He poured a glass of water. 'I'm preoccupied, that's all. There's that poorly calf and its mother, and Iain's tractor I need to replace, and a thousand other things to fix …'

But Miona had practically brought him up and knew him better than anybody else. She wasn't so easy to fool. 'I say there's something else. It's *her*, isn't it?'

'Who?' But he knew exactly who she was talking about. Jenna Palmer. There was something special about her. It was silly how he couldn't stop thinking about her – her kind and sunny smile, her soft voice as she read out stories to the children … and that strange, irresistible attraction he felt as they stood on the clifftop and again in the mobile library that afternoon. It was almost as if his heart, his soul recognised her. He'd better watch out or he'd soon believe Miona was right about the McGregor curse. There was a curse, all right – his own stupidity.

Perhaps he should be honest with himself and admit that he was attracted to the woman. After all, it was only natural. He was a man, and she was a pretty woman. She was also his employee, which meant she was probably out of bounds … More importantly there was no place in his life for a relationship, and that's assuming an educated woman like Jenna Palmer would be remotely interested in a peasant like him. No, the only feminine presence in his life for many years to come would be Katrina and she was more than enough to keep him busy.

He put the glass down a little too forcefully on the granite counter and it made a sharp sound.

'Watch out, my lad, or you'll break that glass and make a mess in my kitchen. I'll make you clean up, mind, like when you and your brother were lads and ran into the house covered with sheep muck, or dripping water everywhere after swimming in the Cove.' Miona's eyes misted up as she evoked the happy old days Daniel and his brother spent roaming the hills, diving and looking for the Spanish gold.

They had so much fun then, even if they tempted fate far too often and had a few near misses with the tides and the currents. They always tricked the sea in those days, but in the end, the sea had won, in the cruellest possible way …

The memory hit him like a punch in the stomach, and he squeezed his eyes shut. Five years since Hugh had died, and it still hurt like mad.

Feeling a hand on his forearm, he opened his eyes and met Miona's kind gaze. 'I know it hurts. I miss him too, every single day. You were my boys and as good as my own flesh and blood.' Her voice shook, and she wiped her eyes with a corner of her apron. It wasn't the first time she'd said that …

'But it won't do you any good to deny yourself any joy and happiness,' she added, now with a fierce scowl on her face. It wasn't the first time she was saying that, either.

'You're a good man, Daniel McGregor, but you work too much, and you worry too much. Why don't you go out for a wee while? Go to the pub. You need to see folks your own age, have a drink and a natter, take your fiddle and play a tune or two with the lads.'

It was tempting. When was the last time he'd had a drink at The Anchor? It was even longer since he'd played any music. He didn't feel like talking or drinking tonight, but he could take his fiddle to the beach like when he was younger and believed he could serenade mermaids – a feat his ancestor Angus McGregor was rumoured to have achieved, and with dire consequences if you believed the folk tales. Daniel had never enticed any mermaids out of the sea, but when he was younger his music had helped him charm a few pretty tourists holidaying in the area.

Jenna Palmer was out with Drummond tonight, so the cottage would be empty and nobody would hear him play, apart from the birds, the seals ... and the mermaids, of course.

He smiled at Miona. 'I'll take my fiddle and go down to the beach. I need to clear my head. Thanks, Miona.'

'It's all right, my love.' She lifted her hand to his face and gave his cheek a pat.

Miona and Iain MacKinnon had lived at the farmhouse for as long as he could remember. Miona had been the McGregors's nanny and housekeeper while Iain worked as farm hand, gardener and handyman. They were above all friends, family almost, especially since his parents had passed away when he was in his first year at university and he'd had to come back to manage the estate.

Cutting short his studies hadn't bothered him that much. In fact, if he was honest, it had been a relief to leave university where he'd felt like a fish out of water. He'd struggled at school and sixth form, and unlike Hugh had never been academic, preferring hands-on work on the farm.

He loved the land, the people and the glorious and ever-changing landscapes ... but he could feel his old insecurities resurface when he was in Jenna Palmer's company. She was bright and well read, and had degrees in English Literature. He hoped she wouldn't try to discuss any bookish matters with him and expose the glaring gaps in his education.

He retrieved his fiddle from the library and walked out of the farm. His dogs Eddie and Sam barked as he walked across the yard, and he spent a minute patting their heads and throwing their rubber ball around before strolling down to the cove.

The cottage was dark and it was safe to assume that Jenna was still out, so he went straight down to the beach. It wasn't night yet, but it wouldn't have mattered if it had been pitch black. He knew every rock, every tuft of grass, every crevice and wouldn't even need the moonlight to guide him. Once on the beach, he walked to the edge of the water, took the fiddle and the bow out and set the instrument on his shoulder. Touching the bow to the strings, he teased the first few melancholic notes out.

He hadn't played for so long his fingers felt awkward and clumsy at first and he had to start again a few times, but soon the tunes flowed and the notes flew towards the horizon and the stars. When he played in the pub sometimes friends accompanied him on the guitar, the harp or the accordion, but tonight all he needed were the sounds of waves sliding softly over the sand as the night darkened and the moon rose in the sky.

He had no idea how long he played when suddenly the skin of his back prickled and he knew he wasn't alone any longer. He lowered the fiddle, turned slowly and held his breath. What if his old dream came true and he had charmed a mermaid?

It wasn't a mermaid, but she was just as breathtaking, basking from head-to-toe in white silvery moonlight she appeared to sparkle and glow. There were even tiny stars at her earlobes.

'Jenna?'

She took a few steps towards him. 'Your music … it's wonderful.'

'Thanks.' His voice came out all funny and hoarse and he coughed to clear his throat. Playing his music always made him a bit emotional, but seeing her on the beach as he was thinking of love and mermaids and magic was like a weird dream.

'Have you been here a while?'

She nodded. 'A while, yes.'

He looked around. He hadn't heard a car engine, but then again he'd been immersed in his music. 'Is Drummond here too?'

He seriously hoped not. He didn't feel up to dealing with Drummond and the snide remarks he would no doubt make about him playing the fiddle on the beach at night.

Jenna shook her head. 'No, he left me at the crossroads. I wanted to walk. I thought I was dreaming when I first heard the music, and I'm sorry I disturbed you.'

'You didn't.' How embarrassing to feel so awkward and tongue-tied again. Why couldn't he think of anything clever or witty to say?

'Do you often come here to play in the evenings?'

He shrugged. 'I haven't for a while, but I used to. Locals used to say I was trying to serenade the mermaids.' Why had he said that? Now she would find him even more stupid.

'Serenade the mermaids ... what a wonderful thought.' She smiled. 'You must be disappointed it's only me. Would you play one more song, please? But don't feel you have to, I don't want to impose.'

Her eyes were as shiny and enchanting as the stars. He took a deep breath. Get a grip, McGregor, and stop staring at the woman ...

'You're not. It's all right.' He put the fiddle back on his shoulder, lifted the bow and struck the first notes of another lament, every fibre of his being aware of her standing close by, watching him. She may not think so, but with her white dress she did look like a mermaid tonight – a moonlight mermaid.

'It was beautiful. Thank you,' she said when the last notes died down.

A fresh gust of wind blew from the sea, tousling her hair, moulding the thin fabric of her dress to her body, outlining her every curve so that she may as well be naked, triggering a primeval response. His body hardened, heat coiled inside him and his fingers itched to touch. Instead they gripped the fiddle more tightly. He turned round, picked up his case and secured his violin inside.

'Time to leave. It's late, and the wind is freshening.'

She gave the cove one last look. 'There is something special about this place, isn't there? I can't explain it. I've never been here before, yet when you emailed me the photo of Mermaid's Cottage, I had the strangest feeling … as if, somehow, I knew it.'

She cast him a sidelong glance and smiled. 'And now you probably think I'm weird.'

'Not at all. Mermaid Cove is a very special place.'

They reached the bottom of the cliff, and he gestured towards the path. 'Would you like me to lead the way?'

'I think I'll be fine. The moonlight is bright enough.' She looked up. 'And the stars … there are so many of them. I don't think I've ever seen such an incredible sky.'

He looked up too. 'My brother and I used to sneak out of the farmhouse at night in summer to come down here and swim in the cove.' He had no idea why he mentioned it. He rarely spoke about Hugh – and certainly not to strangers.

Her foot must have caught in a root or on a rock because she let out a weak cry and stumbled in front of him.

'Careful …' He managed to catch her with his free arm to stop her from falling. He only held her for a few seconds but it was enough to breathe in the flowery scents in her hair – iris, rose, and jasmine. It smelled like summer in the cottage's abandoned garden.

He released her. 'Are you all right?'

'I'm fine. I wasn't looking where I was going.'

She only spoke again when they reached the top of the cliff. 'I'd better say goodnight now. Like you said, it's late.'

She sounded colder suddenly, and didn't even look at him.

'Of course. It's been a busy day. Are we still on for lunch tomorrow? Katrina can't wait to show you the calves.'

'I'm looking forward to seeing her again. She is a lovely little girl.'

'A very chatty little girl, who will probably talk you to death tomorrow.' He couldn't help his voice softening.

She rummaged in her handbag for the keys and unlocked her door. 'Well, until tomorrow then. Goodnight.'

He waited until she closed the door and he saw the light through the curtains in the living room window before making his way back to the farm. All the peace and serenity from his music had vanished, leaving him as restless as before ...

Chapter Ten

The wooden gate squealed as Jenna pushed it open, revealing a riot of blues, pinks, whites and yellows and exuberant vegetation spilling over the gravel path. Sheltered from the wind by high stone walls, the cottage garden was alive with colour and movement – buzzing bees, fluttering butterflies and damselflies darting around like shimmering arrows of light. Foxgloves and lupins shot up towards the sky, and rambling yellow roses covered one of the walls with sunshine. The air was heavy with earthy smells from the damp soil, scents from roses, rosemary and thyme bushes and the carpet of wild garlic hiding under rhododendron bushes.

It would take a determined gardener to get things back under control, but it would be worthwhile. Jenna had spent many weekends helping her father in their small garden. It had been their time together, when they would chat about school, homework, and her friends – or rather, her lack of them …

Her father used to tell her not to worry. She was shy, but she was also clever and had a kind heart and a lovely smile, and in time would become self-confident and meet like-minded people. He was right. If she had been lonely at secondary school and college, she had made a few good friends at university – friends she had unfortunately lost touch with … by her own fault.

She caressed a rose's velvety petals with the tips of her fingers. Her father would have known straight away what variety it was, like he would have known how best to tackle the garden. She missed him so much. What she wouldn't give to be able to snuggle in his arms and breathe in the smells of earth and plants that clung to the old woolly jumper he used to wear for gardening.

The cottage garden was bigger than she'd first thought. At the far end, irises created a patch of vibrant blue amongst a mess of weeds, grasses and thorns that snagged on her clothes as she pushed her way through. Half hidden in the undergrowth was a stone slab covered with ivy. Jenna kneeled down to rip some off and brushed off the dirt with her fingers. The stone looked ancient, with some marks on the surface that looked like writing that had long since been erased by the passage of time.

'Hello? Jenna? Miss Palmer? Are you out there?' Daniel called from the garden gate, startling her.

She glanced at her wrist, and remembered she'd taken her watch off to do the washing-up after breakfast. Was it midday already?

'Over here!' She waved.

'I couldn't see you back there,' Daniel McGregor said when he reached her. He looked at her muddy pumps and dirty jeans and gave her a puzzled look. 'Are you all right?'

She wiped her hands on her jeans then smoothed her dishevelled hair. 'Yes, I'm fine, but I lost track of time. I'm sorry.'

He frowned. 'It's all right … What do you think of this place? It's a bit wild, isn't it?'

'Yes, but it's wonderful too.' She gestured to the slab of stone. 'I hope this isn't a grave.'

He smiled. 'No, don't worry. It's only the entrance to a sea cave which was sealed off a long time ago.'

'What are the inscriptions?'

'That's an old story.' He crouched down next to the stone and his fingers followed the patterns on its surface. He had strong, tanned hands, criss-crossed with cuts and scratches – the hands of a man who worked outside in all weathers.

But they were also the hands of a man who played the violin on a moonlit beach to serenade mermaids, and who ruffled a little girl's hair to comfort her …

He looked up, and she was drawn once again by his bright blue gaze.

'An old story which has to do with the McGregor curse,' he finished with a tight smile.

'The McGregor curse? What is it?'

Daniel stood up and smiled – a real smile this time, like the ones he gave Katrina, and her heart did a little flip. 'Only another fanciful tale about the cruel and bloodthirsty McGregors.' He exaggerated his Scottish burr for effect as he spoke the last words.

'There are many of those, I'm afraid, but I doubt you want to know what brutes my ancestors were. It might scare you off and you'd never want to come for lunch at the farm, never mind work for me.'

He checked his watch. 'In any case, I've never been known for my storytelling skills, and Miona gave me strict instructions to be back for half-past twelve.'

'Of course. I only need a minute to wash my hands and change my jeans.' Perhaps she would ask him for the story later.

It took less than ten minutes to change into some pale blue cropped chinos and a lemony yellow shirt, slip on a pair of canvas pumps, and run a brush through her hair.

Daniel was waiting outside, arms folded and facing the cove. He turned round when she came out of the cottage. 'Ready? I don't want to make Miona angry or she won't give me any pudding, and she made rhubarb crumble – my favourite.'

She smiled at the idea of him getting told off by his diminutive housekeeper and they started on the steep path that followed the clifftop.

'What a change from Friday,' she said as she paused to catch her breath.

The view of Mermaid Cove was breathtaking, with the sapphire blue sea dotted with a rainbow of sailing boats and feathery clouds floating in the sky.

'With the beach so white and the sea and sky so blue,' she said, 'we could almost be in the Caribbean.'

He looked at her. 'Almost ... Please don't feel that you have to answer if I'm being nosy, but what made you decide to come here?'

She couldn't tell him about the miserable existence she'd led for months, about the shame and the guilt of having let a man destroy her self-respect, about her desperate need for a fresh start far away, somewhere new where nobody knew her and she didn't risk bumping into Adrian or his family or friends, but she could tell him about the glorious memories of her childhood holiday to Scotland.

'When I was about ten, my father took my mother and me camping in Scotland. I don't remember exactly where, except that it was the seaside and I loved every single day. The wind sweeping across the vast, empty beach, the white sand and the turquoise sea ... I had so much fun. It was wonderful.' Her mother on the other hand had hated every minute of the holiday, complaining about midges and the rudimentary shower block, the stodgy food which she said gave her heartburn, the husband who couldn't do anything right and the daughter who was a constant source of disappointment.

Poor Dad, Jenna thought. For as long as she could remember everything he did or said was an embarrassment to her mother – his second-hand Ford Fiesta. His job as a caretaker in the local primary school – the only job he could find after his accident on the building site where he was a construction manager. Jenna's mum hated his gardening too, saying that it turned him into a boring old man. She even resented him for the horrible cancer that caused his death, and which she said forced her to stay at home and nurse him.

If she had ever loved him, there had been only recriminations and dissatisfied silences by the time Jenna was old enough to understand that her parents' marriage was not a happy one … As usual when she thought of her mother, her stomach and throat burned as if she'd drunk acid.

'Will your parents be visiting you?' Daniel asked.

She shook her head. 'My father died of lung cancer three years ago.' Her voice wobbled, and she turned away from him.

'I am sorry. It's a terrible disease.' He sounded genuinely sorry.

She nodded. 'A cruel, horrible disease. It stole my dad from us – from me. He would have loved it here, and he would have loved doing up the garden. Will you let me look after it?'

He frowned. 'It's an awful lot of work – back-breaking work.'

'I can cope.'

She didn't think much of the doubtful look he gave her but he didn't say anything. At least he hadn't called her scrawny, like Miona had.

They started on the path again, and after another ten minutes of strenuous walk uphill reached a ruined castle. Perched on a rocky outcrop, it looked part of the cliff itself.

'What is this place?'

'Welcome to Dunfiadhaich Castle – the once proud home of the McGregor clan chiefs,' Daniel announced in a mocking voice.

'You mean it's your family's castle?'

He nodded. 'What's left of it.'

'It must have been formidable in its heyday.' Formidable and sinister, and her skin prickled with goosebumps at the sight of one of the towers rising like a threat against the pure blue sky. 'Why is it ruined?'

Daniel's gaze hardened as he stared at the ruin. 'Clan warfare. Neglect. The McGregors were a particularly nasty, belligerent and stupid lot.'

She glanced at him. 'That's a bit harsh.'

'Not at all, although to be fair I should add that they also suffered from a massive amount of bad luck as well as of a total lack of diplomatic skills. When they wanted something, they went for it even if it meant losing useful allies and making powerful enemies. Fortunately, a few of the more astute, or less bloodthirsty, family members decided to put their claymores and war paint away, build the farmhouse and become gentlemen farmers.'

The path snaked around the tower and the remains of the castle, carried on through a small copse of gnarled and twisted trees and led to a large and rather handsome stone two-storey farmhouse. It was more a small manor house than a farm, with large windows, three gables and four lots of chimneys rising from a steep slate roof. There were outbuildings dotted about, and more sheds and barns in the distance. A tractor, a quad bike and Daniel McGregor's old Land Rover were parked in the courtyard. The strong smell of cow dung pervading the atmosphere made her nose twitch.

She must have pulled a face, because he frowned. 'The cows are in the lower field today – hence the smell.' Was it her imagination or had he looked embarrassed for a second?

He turned away to open the gate and two sheepdogs came running towards them, tongues out, ears pulled back and yelping excitedly.

'Don't be scared, they won't bite you.' He stroked the

bigger dog's white and black coat. 'This one is called Eddie. And young Sam here is his son.'

Jenna crouched down and ruffled the older dog's ears. 'Hello, Eddie. You are beautiful, and such a good dog.' The younger dog nuzzled her arm for attention and she couldn't help but laugh and stroke him too. 'And hello Sam! Don't be jealous. You are gorgeous too.'

'You like dogs.' Daniel sounded surprised.

'My dad and I always wanted a dog but my mother wasn't keen on the idea of muddy paws on the carpet, hair on the couch, and vet fees. After I left home, I shared a house with a flatmate, Suzie, who had a cat.' They had remained friends for years, but Adrian said that Suzie was jealous and snooty, and Suzie called Adrian cold and controlling. In the end their meetings became so strained they stopped calling or texting each other … It turned out that Suzie had been right all along.

'After university,' she carried on, 'I went back to live with my parents as my dad became ill and my mum needed help to nurse him, and then …'

She sighed. Then her father had died and she met Adrian. After a few months they'd moved in together, and a dog would have been out of the question in a fashionable city-centre flat and with a man as fastidious as he was.

'Well, feel free to come up here any time you want to give Sam and Eddie a wee cuddle,' Daniel said, before leading the way across the courtyard.

He pushed open the front door and called, 'We're back!' before standing aside to let her go in first.

The hallway was dark after the sunshine outside, and Jenna blinked a few times. Her eyes had hardly adjusted to the dim light when Katrina came bouncing over and sneaked her little hand in hers.

'Here you are at last. You took *ages*!'

Chapter Eleven

Katrina chirped away about Miona's rhubarb crumble and the yellow dress she was wearing in Jenna's honour even if it was too short because she'd had a growth "splurt", but Daniel had promised to buy her a new one for the ceilidh in a few weeks' time. Hardly pausing for breath, she then asked Jenna if she liked rhubarb crumble, and what her favourite colour was.

As usual the little girl hopped from one topic to the next, but Jenna seemed to cope very well and managed to answer at least some of the questions fired at her. He couldn't help but smile at Katrina's delight when Jenna said that yellow was her favourite colour too and she laughed as Katrina mentioned that growth splurt. It was a long time since a woman's laughter other than Miona's had echoed at Dunfiadhaich.

'It's this way to the dining room.' Katrina now pushed the heavy door open. 'I call it the gloomy room but it's prettier today because Miona gave me vases for my flowers, and Uncle Daniel spent ages cleaning the posh cutlery to make it shine. He was grumpy at first, as Miona told him to wear one of her aprons so that he wouldn't stain his nice new shirt he'd changed into especially for you. He even said a bad word and had to put a pound in the naughty words jar.' She pulled a face. 'But I can't repeat what it was or I'll have to put in a pound too.'

'It wasn't really a bad word,' he protested, embarrassed that Katrina should once again give so much away.

Jenna glanced at him over her shoulder. 'I'm sorry you went to so much trouble. You didn't need to. I'm only ...'

'You are a guest, and Katrina talks far too much.'

'You looked very silly with Miona's apron on,' Katrina added. 'It's very girly with frills and flowers all over, and it's far too small for you.'

'Remind me to buy one my size next time we go to town.'

As Katrina chuckled and Jenna smiled, he quickly reviewed what else he had done that morning that could constitute another potentially awkward revelation, and his breath caught in his throat. There was something, but with any luck, it would skip Katrina's mind.

'And after he cleaned all the knives and forks, Uncle Daniel pretended to be a princess and danced like a girl!' Katrina blurted out suddenly.

He winced with embarrassment and was about to explain that he only wanted to make Katrina laugh when Iain arrived.

Big and burly, Miona's husband had a wild mop of ginger hair and a bushy beard that showed no sign of greying despite his seventy years of age. He showed no sign of slowing down either, and worked at the farm with the younger farmhands from dawn to dusk most days, having rejected Daniel's offer of retirement or even of part-time work.

Iain stopped in front of Jenna and gave Daniel a mock surprised glance. 'By heck, my lad, you didn't tell me our guest was such a bonnie lass! You don't look at all like Gwen McCreedy!'

Jenna blushed, but Katrina shook her head. 'Of course, she doesn't. Not all librarians are old with grey hair and glasses, you know.'

'Aye, I can see that, pet, but with such a bonnie librarian, I bet your uncle will find time for books now, and who knows, even I may start reading something other than the *Farmers Weekly*.'

'Uncle Daniel never reads books for grown-ups,' Katrina interrupted. 'He says books are for kids and for people who have nothing better to do than sit around all day.'

Jenna turned to look at him, a shocked expression in her blue eyes, and heat spread on the back of his neck. Damn. Now she would really think he was an uneducated peasant … and she would be right, but after spending sleepless nights pouring over accounts and worrying about making bank repayments to keep the farm going, the last thing he wanted was to sit down. He'd much rather go out for a walk.

'I didn't say that,' he muttered. 'Well, not exactly …'

Iain laughed. 'Never mind, lad. I'm sure Jenna doesn't care about your lack of enthusiasm for literature, or perhaps she'll try to convert you.' He winked, put his hands on Jenna's shoulders, and pulled her to him. 'Come here, lass, and let this auld man give you a wee peck on the cheek.'

He gave her a loud kiss and released her. 'You smell as nice as you look!' Turning to Daniel, he added, 'Can you go and see if Miona needs a hand in the kitchen while I look after our guest, lad? I'll tell her a few stories about the McGregors while we're waiting for our dinner, so she can put names to this depressing rogues' gallery over there.' He pointed at the portraits hanging on the walls.

Daniel smiled, relieved to be off the hook. 'Good idea.'

It was true that the paintings didn't improve the general gloom and doom of the dining room. They usually ate in the kitchen but Miona had decreed that today only the dining room would do for Jenna …

She had also asked him to take out the dinner service from the dresser, and polish the silver cutlery that hadn't seen the light of day for years – as if he wasn't busy enough as it was! He'd done what she said, of course. He always did. She was right anyway. It was a long time since they'd had anyone stopping over for lunch and he wanted Jenna to enjoy her visit.

His pace slowed and he froze halfway down the stoned-flagged corridor leading to the kitchen. Why did it matter so much that Jenna enjoyed her day at the farm? For a start it would make Katrina happy ... and he wanted to see Jenna smile and look at him with eyes shimmering like stars, the way she had the night before on the beach.

He took a deep breath.

There was something about the woman, something that affected him in the weirdest way whether he wanted it to or not. Sleep had been a long time coming after their meeting on the moonlit beach. He had tried to convince himself that it was because playing the fiddle on Mermaid's Beach had brought back too many memories and because the mug of strong coffee he'd had when he'd come back to the farm had made him jumpy, but he was kidding himself. Images of Jenna in the white dress that the breeze moulded to her body were etched into his mind and had done nothing to help him fall asleep ...

That morning the same feelings had slammed straight back into him when he'd seen her looking right at home in the cottage's garden, and they'd only become stronger as she smiled, stroked his over-enthusiastic collies without a care for their muddy paws, and held Katrina's hand as she answered her nonsensical questions with patience and good humour.

Could he be falling for her? Was this what the tightness in his chest, the raised awareness of all his senses and the erratic dancing of his pulse was, not to mention the shyness that overcame him when he was near her, and turned him into a human version of that dim Zonk McPurple monster?

Bad idea, McGregor. Very bad idea, indeed. Eight years before, he had promised himself never to feel vulnerable again. He'd better nip whatever it was he was feeling in the bud, and quick.

Miona greeted him with a frown. 'Here you are at last. You took your time. Now my tatties will be mushy and my roast will be as tough as an old boot … Here, take that to the dining room before it gets cold.'

He muttered an apology, grabbed hold of the serving dish with the leg of lamb and spring vegetables and the sauceboat filled with gravy while Miona followed him with a bowl piled high with roast potatoes.

They found Jenna and Katrina laughing as Iain was finishing a story, 'And this is how Robbie McGregor exchanged his wife for a cow at Oban market.'

'Not that old tale again!' Miona put the dish of potatoes on the table, curled her fists on her hips and glared at her husband. 'I wish I had changed you for a cow a long time ago – my life would have been a lot more peaceful.'

'Aye, perhaps that's true, my sweet Miona,' Iain retorted with a wink, 'but a husband gives better cuddles than a cow, especially a husband as braw as me.'

The couple exchanged a smile as Daniel put the sauceboat and dish of lamb and vegetables on the table. Iain and Miona MacKinnon had been married for over forty years, and despite their often stormy arguments they had the kind of union anyone could envy.

As usual Miona handed Daniel the carving knife since she considered that it was his duty as master of the house to carve the roast and dish out the food.

He was about to slice the first piece of lamb when he froze and looked at Jenna. 'You're not a vegetarian, are you?'

She shook her head. 'No.'

He let out a sigh of relief. 'I never thought to ask.'

Iain grabbed the bottle Miona had insisted he bring up

from the cellar. 'Here, lass, have some red wine.' He poured everybody a glass, except for Katrina, of course.

'I don't want pretend wine.' The little girl pulled a face as she pointed to her tumbler of blackcurrant juice.

'Tough. Blackcurrant is all you'll get,' Daniel said. 'Or you can have water instead.'

Katrina folded her arms. 'But it's not fair!'

Jenna raised her glass of wine and turned to Katrina. 'You can still toast like grown-ups with blackcurrant juice, you know.' Her soft voice diffused the tension at once. 'Say "Cheers", or like they say in France, "*Santé!*"'

Katrina laughed before clinking her tumbler of cordial against Jenna's glass of wine. 'Let's all do it,' she exclaimed.

'Shall we speak posh French or will *Slàinte Mhath* do?' Iain asked in a mock grumpy voice, raising his glass too. He and Miona had always looked on Katrina as their adoptive grandchild and the girl could wrap them both around her little finger – and often did.

'French, of course!' Katrina replied.

After they toasted, Daniel served the meat, potatoes and fresh green beans from the garden, and sat down to eat.

'This is delicious,' Jenna said after a few mouthfuls. 'In fact, it is as tasty as the food I ate last night at The Three Fishes.'

'You're too kind, lass,' Miona said but the faint blush on her cheeks indicated that she was pleased. That was a first. Miona didn't usually care much what other people thought, especially people she didn't know.

Iain looked at his wife and nodded. 'Miona's food is something else … So you enjoyed The Three Fishes? Who did you go with?'

The young woman's fingers tightened on her knife and fork. 'Toby Drummond invited me.'

Daniel arched his eyebrows. 'Invited or blackmailed?'

She bit her lip. 'Well … a bit of both, I suppose.'

'How's that?' Iain looked confused so Daniel put his cutlery down and explained.

'He almost caused a crash with the mobile library Jenna was driving but had the cheek to threaten to put in an insurance claim unless Jenna had dinner with him.'

Iain shook his head and muttered, 'That lad was always in need of a good *skelping*.' Remembering the day Daniel did just that, he gave him a knowing glance then turned to Jenna again. 'What did you make of him?'

'He is very … entertaining,' she answered after a moment of hesitation. 'He spent all evening telling me very interesting holiday stories.'

Why did Daniel have the feeling there was more to it? It wasn't hard to guess that Drummond must have made derogatory comments about him.

'He does seem to spend much of his time abroad,' he remarked.

Daniel's chest tightened when Jenna didn't make eye contact. Surely Drummond wouldn't have gone as far as to repeat what he'd said at Hugh's funeral five years before?

'He's always abroad because he wants to avoid his mother,' Miona said. 'The old dragon puts the fear of God in everybody, including her son.'

'He said she wasn't well,' Jenna remarked.

Miona blew a breath. 'Not well? The woman will bury us all.'

'I want to go on holidays too,' Katrina announced then. 'All my friends go to Spain.'

He sighed, relieved that Katrina should steer the conversation away from Drummond, even though it sounded like they were heading for yet another tantrum.

'I'm sure that's not the case, love. Many people don't have holidays. What's more, we're at the seaside already, and who would mind the farm and the animals if we all went away?'

'But I want to go to Spain … and to Disneyland!' Katrina folded her arms. She was getting more petulant by the day. He dreaded to think what she would be like as a teenager.

Miona folded her napkin on the table and got up. 'And so you will one day. For now, stop mithering your uncle and help me fetch the pudding. Didn't you say you wanted some ice-cream with your crumble?'

'What are you young people going to do with the rest of the day?' Iain asked after Miona and Katrina had left.

'Katrina wants to show Jenna the farm,' Daniel said.

'I would like to take a photo of Buttercup the cow to put in Buttercup the van,' Jenna said.

'Buttercup is a heifer,' Daniel corrected.

'What's the difference?'

'A heifer is a cow that has never born a calf.'

'Ah … sorry. Then I am looking forward to meeting Buttercup the heifer and the little calf who is my namesake.'

'Jenna? She's a strong one,' Iain commented. 'In fact, she's pretty much perfect – with a thick coat, broad feet, big ears and a lovely pink nose.' He winked at Jenna. 'You've a lovely pink nose too.'

Jenna laughed, and lifted her blonde hair to show her ears. 'What about my ears?'

'Aye … Although they're only tiny, and I bet your feet are too.'

The woman was indeed of small stature, but he would have had to be blind or cold-blooded not to notice that her trousers outlined a very shapely bottom and her pale yellow shirt clung to some very generous forms. His thoughts having taken a direction definitely not suitable for a family Sunday table, Daniel deliberately focussed his attention onto one of the ugliest McGregor portraits and poured himself a glass of water.

Sipping his water, he concentrated on counting the warts on Murdo McGregor's bulbous nose. One, two, three … Heavens, the man was ugly, with his bushy grey whiskers and bloodshot eyes. He was also a mean bastard who had imprisoned his child bride in the dungeon and left her to die of thirst and hunger to avenge his honour and punish her for being unfaithful, thereby reigniting the clan war between the McGregors and the Drummonds. Poor Lady Jane. She'd barely been seventeen when she died …

Staring at Murdo's ugly face did the trick, and soon Daniel's blood was cool enough for him to rejoin the conversation and look at Jenna without fantasising about peeling her clothes off.

'Jenna – the calf, that is – is already running around the field, chasing after her mother,' Iain was saying. 'Not like poor Maisie.'

Jenna frowned. 'What's wrong with Maisie?'

'She has an infection due to complications when she was born,' Daniel answered. 'Her mother is poorly too. I think I should prepare Katrina for some bad news, but she'll take it hard.'

'You mean you don't think the calf and her mother are going to make it?' Jenna asked.

He gave her a sharp nod. 'It doesn't look like it.'

'The lassie will take it badly, that's true,' Iain said, his blue eyes full of sympathy. 'She's very soft-hearted, that lass.'

Daniel sighed, tired suddenly of the responsibility of carrying all the worries of his small family, the farm and the estate on his shoulders. Every animal was precious, and every loss of life was mourned.

'If the worst happens,' Jenna said, 'perhaps you don't have to tell her the truth.'

'You mean that I could pretend they have gone to sunny pastures on the other side of the rainbow bridge?' He let out a harsh laugh. 'I don't think so. The sooner Katrina understands the realities of farming, the better.'

He wasn't about to make up any more improbable fairy tales about mermaids returning to their watery kingdom and heroic sea captains getting lost on the oceans while looking for treasure. That had been a mistake. He should have told Katrina that Hugh was dead and that Shannon lived in Florida and was too busy diving and partying to be a mother. When he finally got round to telling Katrina the truth about her parents, she would probably hate him for inventing the stupid stories in the first place.

It was far simpler, and in the long run, far kinder, to be honest and help her accept the facts of life – and death.

Chapter Twelve

'But it would be heartless to tell her the truth. She's only a little girl.'

'I am well aware of that, thank you.'

He glared at her and all the happiness from the day shrivelled and died inside her. Her cheeks burned under the rebuke, and her heart hammered hard. She looked away and interlinked her fingers. What had possessed her to speak out? She was a guest, an employee – a complete stranger to the McGregor family. Even if she disagreed with Daniel, it wasn't her place to comment on his decisions regarding Katrina's upbringing. No wonder he was annoyed. And now she had ruined the friendly atmosphere around the dining table.

Suddenly she was thrown back to her childhood, when her mother constantly reprimanded her, or again to a not so distant past when Adrian found fault with the way she looked or grimaced at something she'd said, and the sunshine in her heart dimmed and was replaced by black butterflies that choked her and stopped her from breathing …

'Do you have itchy fingers, lass?' Iain asked, next to her, a puzzled expression on his face. 'An allergy, perhaps? I used to have terrible eczema a few years back. Turned out I was allergic to some weedkiller we used at the farm.'

She froze, looked down at the red raw finger she hadn't even realised she was rubbing once again, as if trying to erase the memory of Adrian's ring off her skin.

'It's nothing, a touch of eczema, like you said,' she stammered, forcing a smile and hiding her hands in her lap.

The fast tapping of small feet running in the corridor heralded Katrina's return. 'Look at how much ice-cream I've got!' The little girl burst into the dining room, brandishing a plastic bowl filled with crumble, topped with two large scoops of vanilla ice-cream.

She set it on the table, climbed on her chair, and stuck her spoon in.

Daniel frowned. 'Mind your manners, Katrina. It's polite to wait until everybody is served before eating.'

'But my ice-cream will melt!'

'Not for a couple of minutes, it won't.'

Katrina put her spoon down with an exaggerated sigh. 'Very well. I'll wait.'

He gave her a strained smile. 'Good girl.'

'After pudding we'll go and see Jenna and Maisie, won't we? I do hope Maisie is better today. Her mummy's been poorly too. Poor Maisie. What if her mummy dies?'

The girl's voice quivered and Jenna's throat tightened again. What was Daniel going to say now, since he seemed to favour the honest, no nonsense approach?

He surprised her by rising to his feet. 'Don't worry, love, I'm sure they're all right. Scot and Jamie are looking after them today and they would have called me if anything was amiss. To put your mind at rest, I'll go to the cowshed to check on them now.'

Miona pointed to the bowl of crumble in front of him. 'What about your pudding?'

'I won't be long. It'll keep.' He walked out without looking at Jenna.

Perhaps he wasn't that heartless after all …

As if reading her mind, Iain leant over and said in a very low voice, 'He's a good lad, is Daniel. Despite what he says, he'd never do anything that makes the wee one unhappy.'

Katrina clanged her spoon against her bowl. 'Do I have

to wait for Uncle Daniel to return before I can eat my pudding?'

'No, lass, you can eat it now.' Miona looked at Jenna. 'Did you have a chance to look at the cottage garden? You said you liked the yellow roses I picked for you.'

Jenna nodded. 'I went in there this morning. It's a wonderful garden – or at least it must have been at one time.'

'It's been overgrown for as long as I can remember,' Iain said.

'I can't wait to look after it. I'm not afraid of hard work, and it will keep me busy in the evenings and at weekends.'

Miona smiled at her enthusiastic response, and for some odd reason Jenna felt that she had passed some kind of test. 'Iain will give you some tools to get you started.'

'Thank you. By the way, I found a large slab of stone with some strange inscriptions at the bottom of the garden. It was most peculiar. Daniel says it masks the entrance to a sea cave. Do you know about it?'

Miona and Iain exchanged a glance, and Miona leant over to Katrina, who had made fast work of her dessert and was busy scraping every last bit of melted ice-cream from the bottom of her bowl. 'Why don't you go to your room and bring down some of the books you'd like to show Jenna?'

The little girl grinned and dropped her spoon on the table, before clambering down to her feet. 'I'll get them now!' And she ran out of the room.

'So you're curious about the stone,' Iain started.

Jenna nodded. 'Especially since Daniel mentioned some old story about a curse. He didn't go into any details, though.'

Iain pointed at the painting of a dark-haired man, dressed in a white shirt and a red and green tartan kilt. He was brandishing a claymore and had a fierce expression on his hawkish face.

'That's the man who started it – Angus McGregor, one of the clan chiefs. He ruled Arrandale from the old castle …' He looked at Jenna. 'You've seen the castle, haven't you – or rather, what's left of it?'

Recalling the ruined building and the half-derelict tower on the cliff, Jenna nodded.

'The McGregors were always at war with the other clans – the Donalds, the MacLeods, and the Drummonds. Those were the worst by far. They caused us all kinds of bother.'

'They still do,' Miona said.

Iain stroked his beard. A cloud passed over his eyes. 'Aye, that's true.' He shook his head, and carried on. 'Anyhoo, the story goes like this. After a few too many ales, Angus McGregor boasted that no woman alive could ever resist him.' He winked at Jenna. 'He did have quite a reputation with the ladies, you see. His old enemy Donald Drummond then challenged him to catch and bed a mermaid, who he claimed were women too.'

Iain scratched his beard. 'Although quite how that was supposed to work, I have no idea, what with the fishtail and—'

Miona slapped his forearm with her napkin. 'Get on with it.'

'So the McGregor went on his boat day after day and night after night with his giant fishing net and tried to capture one of the mermaids who came out to sit on the big rocks in the cove.'

'Mermaid's Rocks?' Jenna asked. So there was the origin of the name.

'Aye … but they were clever, those mermaids, and they always stayed out of his reach. Time passed, and he still hadn't caught his mermaid. Scared of losing his wager, he went to an old crone who dabbed in magic. The woman gave him a magic whistle, put a spell on it and taught him a special tune he had to play on the next full moon.'

He arched his eyebrows and a cheeky glint shone in his eyes. 'I've always wondered if that flute, or whistle, wasn't a polite way of talking about his ... you know ... his ...'

Jenna giggled, and Miona slapped his arm with her napkin again. 'What's gone into you, Iain MacKinnon? You're a very naughty boy this afternoon.'

He gave her a fond smile and carried on. 'Come the full moon, McGregor went down to the cove, played his whistle, and a beautiful mermaid swam close enough for him to capture her. He brought her back to the castle and they spent the next few days ... ahem ... getting to know each other better. Now the story goes like this ... They fell madly in love. She grew legs and shed her fishtail and he hid it so that she could never leave, but after a few months the poor mermaid was pining for the sea. She spent days and nights at her window in the tower and constantly begged for her tail back. McGregor flew into a dark rage, bricked up the windows so that she couldn't see or hear the sea, and burned her fish skin so that she could never return to her former life. He also put heavy stone slabs on the entrances to all the sea caves on the clifftop so that the mermaid couldn't escape that way. It is said that the old crone used her nails to scratch a spell of eternal doom on the flagstones to anyone who dared remove them. The poor mermaid wasted away, but still the McGregor wouldn't release her.'

'He was a cruel, cruel man ...' Miona shook her head, as if they were talking of a real story as opposed to an ancient folk tale.

'He was a man in love, who didn't want to lose his woman,' Iain countered in his deep voice. 'In the end the poor thing died, and on her death bed she cursed the whole

McGregor bloodline. They would all be unhappy in love and all die by drowning.'

It was as if a shadow had passed in front of the window, making the dining room colder and darker. Jenna shivered. Fairy tale or not, it was a sad story indeed.

'That's not all,' Miona said. 'The old crone said that the curse would only be broken by a very special mermaid who relinquished the sea for the land of happy dreams.'

Jenna pulled a face. 'How very odd.'

Miona nodded gravely. 'Perhaps but they were her exact words.'

There was no point in remarking that the old crone probably never existed, let alone talked about curses, mermaids or happy dreams.

'Arrandale is *Fearann nan Aislingean Sona* – the land of happy dreams,' Miona added. 'You believe in happy dreams too, don't you lass?'

'Well, yes, but don't we all?' Why was the woman looking at her like that?

'And you love the garden and the flowers too.'

'That's true, especially yellow roses. They smell divine.'

'And yet you love the sea too. You said it was calling you the other night.'

Jenna smiled. 'It was a figure of speech. I don't quite see what …' She gasped. 'Surely, you don't think that I could have anything to do with ending the McGregor curse, do you?' Jenna let out an incredulous laugh.

The couple looked at her. They weren't laughing.

'There is a major flaw in your thinking,' she added quickly. 'I am no mermaid. I have never had, and will never have, scales or a fishtail.'

Miona arched her eyebrows. 'Time will tell.'

Iain chuckled. 'Aye, time will tell indeed.'

Jenna shook her head. Time was irrelevant. She would

never grow a fishtail! The elderly couple were mad or had drunk too much wine, but she didn't want to offend them, especially not after upsetting Daniel earlier.

'I'm not even that good at swimming,' she added in a weak voice.

'It doesn't matter. According to the tale, the mermaid who ends the curse will give up her sea-life to tend her garden,' Miona said. 'It's you, lassie … You are the cove's new mermaid.'

So that was why Miona was so interested in her plans to look after the garden at Mermaid's Cottage. This was crazy – completely crazy. She had to distract her before she could spout any more nonsense, so she pointed at the portrait of Angus McGregor, the mermaid murderer. 'How did he die?'

'He went mad and he drowned,' Daniel said quietly from the doorway.

Jenna's heartbeat picked up and heat spread inside of her. She hadn't noticed he was there, leaning against the door jamb, arms crossed. Had he been there a long time? How embarrassing if he heard what Miona and Iain had said about her being the one who would end the McGregor curse.

Daniel strode in and sat down at the table. 'People said he could hear his dead lover call to him from Mermaid's Rocks.'

Miona nodded. 'That's right. 'Twas the curse.'

Daniel clenched his jaw. 'Curse, stupidity or pure bad luck, take your pick. I know which one I'd choose.'

'And I know which one *I'd* choose,' Miona retorted with fire in her eyes. 'Don't forget all the other McGregors who drowned near the rocks.'

Iain put his hand on her arm. 'Hold your *whisht*, woman. You've said enough.'

She paled and nodded. 'Aye. Sorry, Daniel. I … I didn't think.'

Daniel's face became stony as he sat at his place, in front of his untouched bowl of crumble. He had rolled up his sleeves. A few sprigs of straw stuck to his shoulder, probably where he had been holding the calf.

'What news, lad?' Iain asked.

'Not great. I called Colin MacDonald. He'll be here in half an hour.' He looked at Jenna. 'I'm sorry but the vet is coming over so we have to reschedule your tour of the farm. Where's Katrina?'

'Gone to fetch some books,' Miona replied, getting up. 'I'll make some coffee while you eat your pudding. Come and help me, Iain.'

Her husband pulled a face. 'Why?'

'Because I'm asking.'

He frowned. 'Do I have to?'

She gave him a stern look. 'Aye, you do if you know what's good for you.'

After Iain trailed behind his wife out of the dining room, Jenna shifted on her chair, unsure of what to say or where to look. Hopefully Katrina would come back soon, and fill the awkward silence. Daniel wasn't eating, but leaning against the back of his chair and staring straight ahead.

The moment had come to be brave and apologise for her earlier faux pas. 'I am sorry for speaking out of turn, for calling you heartless,' she started in a shaky voice. 'It was very rude of me. It's none of my business what you tell Kat—'

'No. I'm the one who should apologise,' he interrupted, turning the full force of his bright blue gaze onto her. 'You were right, and I overreacted. It's not always easy to know what to do for the best with a child. To be honest, most of the time I'm making it up as I go along.'

He looked so contrite, so defeated that she itched to touch him, take his hand, and reassure him that he was doing great.

'Katrina will be upset when the vet arrives,' he added, 'and even more upset if the animals have to be put down.'

An idea formed in Jenna's mind. 'Why don't you leave her with me this afternoon? I could take her to Mermaid Cove to collect shells and pebbles.'

Daniel raked his fingers in his hair. 'Actually, that's a great idea if you're sure you don't mind. Spending time with a chatty seven-year-old may not be your idea of a relaxing Sunday afternoon.'

'I'd love to. Katrina provides me with the perfect excuse to play on the beach instead of doing something grown-up like cleaning or ironing.'

'Then, I would be very grateful. Thank you.' The smile he gave her was like sunshine pouring into her heart.

Miona and Iain came back with the coffee. Katrina brought an armful of books, but dropped them all on the wooden floor as soon as Daniel announced that there had been a change of plan and Jenna was taking her to the beach while he was busy with the vet. She ran to her room again to get changed into jeans, tee shirt and trainers and to pick up a sweatshirt, before shooting back in like a cannonball to decree that she needed a bucket, a spade and her fishing net from the shed. Daniel dutifully abandoned his cup of coffee to fetch them for her.

Twenty minutes later, Jenna said goodbye and thanks to Miona and Iain, and holding Katrina's hand firmly in hers, stood in the courtyard in front of the farmhouse. The little girl slung her pink backpack onto her shoulders and Daniel crouched in front of her. 'You're sure you have everything? Did you pack an extra jumper and some socks?'

The girl sighed. 'Yes, Uncle Daniel. You asked already.'

'Right then, you have a good time, and I'll come and get you later.' He rose to his feet.

'Will Colin cure Maisie?' she asked before they set off.

He gave her a smile that didn't reach his eyes. 'I'm sure he will but he may have to take her to a special hospital for baby cows.'

Katrina nodded. 'That's all right, then. Come on, Jenna, let's go,' she said as she pulled on Jenna's hand and dragged her out of the courtyard.

As they walked past the tower of the ruined McGregor castle, Jenna spared a thought for the poor mermaid who had once been imprisoned there, who couldn't even look at the sea because her window had been shut down by her heartless jailer and who had cast a terrible curse on all the McGregors.

Chapter Thirteen

The late afternoon sunlight cast oblique shadows on the fields, and turned the sea a bright, almost purple blue as Daniel walked down to Mermaid Cove with Sam and Eddie. He could have asked Iain to bring Jenna the garden tools she'd asked for but he needed the walk to clear his head ... and if he was totally honest, he wanted to see what Jenna and Katrina had got up to.

Colin MacDonald, Ruth's husband, had spent over an hour at the farm, and had ended up taking Maisie away to have her operated on at the veterinary hospital in Portree. It was its only chance, he had said. He had also administered another dose of strong antibiotics to the calf's mother, but reserved his prognosis. 'If there's no improvement by tomorrow evening, then ...' There was no need for the vet to finish his sentence.

Daniel took his time walking down the path. Hopefully Katrina would be tired out after her afternoon at the beach and forget to ask about Maisie. But there was as much chance of that as of the old Dunfiadhaich Castle being rebuilt overnight or of seeing actual mermaids in the Cove.

He heard Jenna's and Katrina's voices as soon as he reached the cottage. Before he could even see them their laughter and enthusiastic off-key singing put a smile on his face and lifted all his worries from the farm. By the – terrible – sound of it, Katrina was trying to teach Jenna the "Boat to Skye" song that she had learnt at school and Jenna was putting random words in the lyrics.

Daniel propped the tools against the garden gate and made his way to the cliff path.

'No, silly, it's not "baby goat" it's "bonnie boat", and it's not "our cows stand by the shore" but "our foes stand by the shore!"' Katrina protested in-between fits of giggles.

'I like my song better,' Jenna said, 'yours is far too gloomy.'

'I like it better too,' Daniel said as he jumped down onto the sand and strode towards them with the dogs running in circles around him.

Jenna was still laughing as she turned to greet him. Her cheeks were pink, her hair tousled and pale blonde in the afternoon light, and her eyes as clear as the purest summer dawn. She had rolled up her trousers and taken her shoes off and her feet were just as small as he'd imagined, with the toenails the colour of the most delicate shells. He tightened his lips. What was wrong with him? Since when did he notice women's toenails?

Next to her was a pile of shells and pebbles, as well as a few pieces of polished glass and driftwood of various shapes and sizes.

'I see you've been busy,' he told Jenna.

'We found lots of pretty rocks and shells, Uncle Daniel,' Katrina said before falling to her knees on the sand and making a fuss of the dogs. 'Sam! Eddie! Give me a wee cuddle.'

Daniel pulled a pretend hurt face. 'I see. You'd rather give the dogs a kiss than your old uncle.'

'You're not old.' Katrina pulled a face. 'Well, not *very* old.' She laughed again as Eddie licked her face. 'Yuk, you smell … And you too, Sam. Come with me to have a wash.'

Perhaps he should be relieved that she hadn't kissed him after all. She would have decreed that he too smelled after spending hours in the cowshed!

Katrina jumped to her feet and clapped her hands as she ran towards the edge of the water, the dogs by her side. Daniel smiled as he watched her skip and hop in the waves and bending down to flick water at the two collies. 'Don't get too wet!' he shouted, but she paid no attention and splashed happily in the waves.

'We can always go to the cottage,' Jenna said next to him. 'I'll put the fire on and make Katrina a cup of hot chocolate. I brought some biscuits back from the welcome party yesterday.'

She gave him a tentative smile. 'We could have a hot chocolate too, or some tea or coffee?'

'I could do with a coffee. Thank you for looking after Katrina this afternoon. It looks like she had a good time.'

'We both did.' Looking down, she pointed her foot in the manner of a dancer and traced a few shapes in the sand with her toes, before tilting her face towards him. 'May I ask what happened with the vet?'

'Colin took Maisie away to the surgery and is going to operate on her today. As for her mother ...' He made a defeated gesture. 'Who knows? Perhaps there will be a miracle and she'll pull through.'

'I see. I'm sorry.'

He nodded. Losing both the calf and the cow would be a serious setback he could ill afford, but he didn't want to bore Jenna with his troubles. The air was freshening and shadows moved across the beach. He cleared his throat. 'Perhaps we should head back up.'

She put her hands on her hips and looked at the pile of shells, stones and pieces of wood. 'I'll start gathering everything.'

But Katrina had other ideas and it took almost half an hour of running around on the beach, playing with the dogs and skimming stones before she agreed to leave. They traipsed back up the path, Daniel carrying a now wet, cold and tired child, as well as the rucksack laden with stones, shells and driftwood.

'The dogs can come in, I don't mind,' Jenna suggested, but Daniel said they should wait outside, so she led the way into the living room and pointed to the sofa.

'Why don't you sit down?' she asked Katrina. 'I'll get a blanket for you to snuggle into.'

Jenna ran up the stairs while Daniel switched the fire on. Ten minutes later the room was warm and cosy, the kettle was boiling and the tin of biscuits was open on the coffee table; Katrina munched on shortbread fingers, while wrapped up in a fluffy blanket up to her chin.

Jenna put a mug of hot chocolate down. 'Take care not to burn yourself.' She looked at Daniel. 'I only have instant coffee. I hope it's all right. I need to go shopping tomorrow after work.'

'Instant is great. How will you get around without a car?'

'Brendon kindly offered to take me to the supermarket tomorrow, and he said he would ferry me to and from work.'

'That's good of him. I hope you're not feeling too isolated here.'

'Not at all. This cottage is my haven, and all I could ever have wished for.'

A haven? From what? He frowned. What an odd thing to say.

'Wait until we have a proper storm and the gale cuts the electricity off and it gets so wild you can't even get out of the front door,' he said.

She stopped spooning instant coffee into one of the mugs. 'A proper storm? You mean what we had on Friday wasn't a proper storm?'

He laughed. 'On the scale from one to ten, I'd say that one was a four.'

Her eyes grew wide. 'In that case, I shall make sure I stock up on food and get myself some good waterproof clothing.' She poured some hot water into the mugs and added a splash of milk. 'Do you take any sugar?'

He shook his head, and she handed him a mug, took the other one and followed him back to the living area where they both sat on opposite ends of the couch, with Katrina between them. The blanket she had wrapped around her shoulders now had biscuit crumbs all over the front.

'It was great on the beach, thanks Jenna,' Katrina said before slurping her hot chocolate. 'We'll have to do it again, but this time you'll sing the proper words to my song.'

Jenna laughed. 'All right, Little Miss Bossy Boots.'

'I like singing, and I like music. My Uncle Daniel plays the fiddle. He's very good, you know.'

'Hmm … I'm sure he is.' Jenna glanced at him, half a smile on her lips. He smiled too and a faint blush coloured her cheeks as they shared the memory of their late night meeting on the beach. His body tingled and grew warm as they locked eyes. He wasn't paying attention to what Katrina was saying any longer.

'Be careful!' Katrina pulled on his shirt sleeve. 'You're going to spill your coffee all over me.'

He blinked, and put his mug down. 'Sorry, love. You were saying?'

'You didn't tell me how Maisie and her mummy were doing.'

So much for Katrina forgetting about the vet's visit. 'Colin took Maisie away to the animal hospital, and gave her mum an injection.'

'So they'll be all right?' There was so much hope in her blue eyes that all he could do was nod.

'Sure, love. They'll be fine.' He would have to think of something if the worst happened.

Katrina yawned. 'That's good … I'm a bit tired now.'

She climbed onto his knees, curled up against his chest

and closed her eyes. As he drank his coffee and the only sounds disturbing the quiet were Katrina's breathing and the hissing of the gas fire, he was reminded of the time Katrina was little and could only fall asleep in his arms.

Tonight however there was something more than the contentment of holding a sleeping child. His senses were on high alert, there was a spark in his heart, and it was thanks to the young woman who sat quietly a few feet away, sipping her coffee and gazing at the flames in the gas fire.

A cynical voice sneered right back and his arms stiffened around Katrina. It was no wonder he was all in a twist about Jenna. She was pretty, intriguing, and seemingly available, and of course he lived like a monk at Arrandale, working all hours without a break. He knew nothing about her apart from what was written on her CV.

After all, he was hardly a good judge of character, and it wasn't the first time he was taken in by a pretty face and a pair of beguiling eyes. Hadn't he believed that Shannon was the perfect woman once? The thought was like a freezing cold shower chilling him to the bones.

A ringtone chimed somewhere in the living room, and Jenna jumped up from the sofa. 'Sorry. It's my phone.' She picked up a mobile from the dining table, and her face grew pale and her eyes wide as she looked at the screen and read a message.

'Is everything all right?' he asked. 'I hope it's not bad news.'

She let out a nervous laugh but her hand shook as she put the phone down. 'It's nothing.'

She looked upset, but it was nothing to do with him, so he rose to his feet with Katrina still fast asleep in his arms. 'I'd better take this wee lassie back. She has school tomorrow.'

'Yes, of course. Let me get her things.' She picked up the

rucksack from the floor, as well as the net, and the bucket and spade. 'Will you be able to carry everything?'

'I'll take the rucksack but I may leave the rest here for now, if you don't mind.' The cynical voice inside him sniggered again. He wasn't kidding anybody. He was only looking for an excuse to come back.

Slinging the bag over his shoulder, he walked out of the cottage, with Katrina clinging to him.

'Thanks again for looking after her,' he said in a low voice. 'I shall see you on Thursday for our meeting in Mallaig. I'll pick you up from the library office at around nine thirty. In the meantime, if there's anything you need, please call.'

He walked away, with Katrina's head resting in the crook of his neck, and Eddie and Sam bouncing on the path ahead of him, but he couldn't resist turning round when he was about halfway up the path.

Jenna was back on the beach. He could just about make out her silhouette on the white sand. She was standing still, feet in the water, facing the horizon, her pale yellow shirt and blonde hair in perfect harmony with the evening's muted pastel blues and lilacs. Miona's words echoed in his mind.

It looked like the cove had found a new mermaid …

He shook his head and resumed walking. He would end up believing Miona's fancy stories if he wasn't careful.

Her breathing followed the rhythm of the waves as they climbed on the sand then withdrew, and the tangle of confused and angry thoughts caused by her mother's text unravelled.

How she had managed not to have a full-blown panic attack and to say goodbye to Daniel McGregor, she'd never know.

She pulled the phone out of her pocket and read her mother's text again.

Adrian came round today. I gave him your new phone number. I know you said not to but he was terribly upset that you cut him out after everything he's done for you. Poor Adrian. He came back from London especially to give you another chance, and now you've gone away on that hare-brained scheme of yours. We tried to call you but keep getting your voicemail. Call me so we can talk properly. Mum.

Her fingers tightened around the phone, and she let out a strangled, rather hysterical laugh. How dare Adrian visit her mother, play the concerned boyfriend, and claim he was prepared to give her a second chance? She didn't want a second chance. She wanted a new start in Arrandale, as far away from him and from the past as possible.

She could just see him as he paid her mother a visit – smartly dressed, holding a bunch of flowers from a posh florist in town, the sad look in his eyes as he pretended to be hurt that Jenna had left without giving him her new number. He would have been very convincing, as usual. Hadn't he told her mother that the break-up was due to Jenna's erratic and unreasonable behaviour and she'd believed him?

Jenna read the text again. What exactly had Adrian done for her except destroy her self-confidence and push her to believe that she was mad?

It had taken her only a few weeks to realise that there had never been anything wrong with her, except her readiness to accept Adrian's mind games and put-downs for which she would never, ever, forgive herself. She had managed not to lose her purse or her keys, misplace her phone or flood the bathroom. She hadn't forgotten to pay the bills, burned any of her food or got food poisoning from eating out-of-date ready meals ... all things that had happened before Adrian left and she had always blamed herself for.

Adrian had done that to her ... and now he had the cheek to claim he loved her and wanted her back? Jenna kicked a pile of sand. What a sick joke! Whatever he said, and whatever lies he poured into her mother's ear, she would never, ever, let him back into her life.

Chapter Fourteen

Daniel drove up the ramp and onto the *Riannog*'s deck, muttering under his breath as the Land Rover jerked forward and a cloud of black smoke puffed out of the exhaust. Blasted car. It was on its last legs.

He stopped the engine and turned to Jenna who looked very formal in her white blouse and navy trouser suit – very formal and very nervous, with her hands clasped in her lap, and doing that nervous tick again with her fingers. Memories of her last ferry crossing must be making her anxious, even if today the sun was shining and only the slightest breeze ruffled the crest of the waves.

'It's going to be a very smooth sailing,' he said to reassure her.

She nodded. Perhaps she was tired after her first few days at work, which according to Brendon had been very busy. There had also been a bit of trouble during the mobile library's visit to Katrina's school the day before. Katrina had said that Jenna had to send a few boys back to class. 'They were throwing books around. They even said that Buttercup was a rubbish name!' Katrina said, indignant, before shaking her head in disgust. 'Boys are horrible.'

Daniel opened his door, pocketing the car key. 'Should we get out?'

Hopefully she would feel less nervous in the fresh air. There was another car on deck today and several foot passengers too, and at the far end Kieran was busy making sure the ramp was up and secure. The lad smiled and waved at him, but his smile faded when he saw Jenna and he gave her a black stare.

'He still blames me for his friend's heart attack,' she remarked in a quiet voice.

'Of course not,' he protested, although he feared she was right. Perhaps he'd better clear the air up once and for all.

'Give me a minute,' he said before walking over to the teenager at the far end of the deck. 'Hi Kieran, I believe Jim is on the mend. Have you seen him recently?'

'Yeah … He's still in hospital but he's getting better. The thing is, he'll probably have to retire now, and he's really gutted about it.' Kieran narrowed his eyes and pointed his chin towards Jenna who stood a short distance away. 'That's all *her* fault.'

Daniel frowned. 'What are you talking about, lad? Jim could have had that heart attack anytime, anywhere – when he was driving or fishing or watching TV alone – and then what would have happened? It was actually lucky for him that you were there, and that the lifeboat could get to him quickly.'

He put his hand on the lad's shoulder. 'I know it's hard on you and on Jim too, but at least he's going to be all right.'

'Suppose so.' Kieran looked down and kicked a small pebble on the deck with the tip of his boot.

He left the boy to mull things over while he worked and returned to Jenna as the ferry left the harbour and Dana's colourful houses became smaller and smaller. The ferry sailed across the bay past Mermaid's Rocks' and Daniel's mood grew dark. This was where Hugh had died, trapped in the *Santa Catalina* wreck a hundred feet under.

Daniel closed his eyes and let the sounds of waves sloshing against the hull of the ferry, the calls of the seabirds gliding on the breeze and the warmth of the sun soothe him … the bitter taste of guilt however remained. It would never go away.

He opened his eyes to see Jenna's puzzled gaze next to him. 'Is there anything wrong? Are you not well?'

He gave a sharp nod. 'I'm fine.'

She didn't insist but pulled her phone out of her bag and took some snapshots of the coastline, of birds flying low and diving into the sea, of the distant, hazy blue mountains of Rùm that floated above the line of the horizon like a mirage.

When Mallaig harbour drew nearer, they climbed into the car again, ready for the *Riannog* to dock, and Daniel drove off to the library on the other side of the harbour. There was a café in the building and as they walked in the tempting smell of coffee tickled his nose and reminded him that he'd been up since before dawn.

He checked his watch. They had twenty minutes to spare before their meeting. 'If I don't get an injection of caffeine I may fall asleep during the meeting. To tell the truth, I find these meetings extremely tedious, and usually daydream about what needs doing at the farm ... Please don't tell Celia.'

Jenna smiled. 'I won't say a word.'

They ordered two coffees and sat down.

'How is the gardening going?' he asked.

Her eyes immediately lit up. 'It's going well even if I don't have much to show for my efforts yet.'

'Give me a shout if you need any help with digging up roots or doing any heavy lifting. I'll survey the garden at the weekend to make sure it's safe. I don't want you to fall in a hole or get injured on some old piece of rusty equipment that has been left behind.'

Her smile broadened. 'Don't worry about me. The garden is wonderful even as it is now. When the sun is shining like today, it's like a dream come true.'

*

Jenna stirred a spoonful of brown sugar into her coffee. There was something she wanted to discuss with Daniel. She had planned to do it during the crossing but he seemed so remote she hadn't dared. She drank a sip of coffee to give herself courage.

'I would like to ask your opinion about an idea to promote children's literacy which I hope you'll find interesting,' she said without taking a single breath.

He arched his eyebrows, and gave her an amused smile. 'Go on …'

'I was thinking of a short story competition. The theme could be Happy Dreams, which would be both a celebration of Arrandale's Gaelic name as well as a nod to the Zonk McPurple books children like so much. Of course, we could change the theme if you don't like it,' she carried on, just as quickly.

'Happy dreams? I like it. And a writing competition is a great idea.'

'So you agree?' She let out a sigh of relief and reclined against the back of her chair. She had passed the first hurdle and it had been a lot easier than she'd feared. Now for the second one.

'I know you're very busy but I thought that perhaps as Laird of Arrandale, you could judge the entries and give out the prizes.'

His eyes widened in surprise. 'Me? But I know nothing about books or children's literature.'

'It's only a bit of fun, not a proper literary competition,' she insisted. 'I think it would be great for the kids if you were there.'

He drank some coffee and reclined in his chair. 'It looks as if I have no choice. All right, I'll do it, but only if you help me.'

'That's a deal. Thank you.' Since everything was going

well, she felt bold enough to jump over the third hurdle. 'And perhaps you could wear a purple tee shirt and a kilt on prize-giving day? I'll sort out the purple tee shirt if you supply the kilt.'

He coughed and put his cup down. 'Why do I have the feeling that I'm being ambushed here?' He cocked his head to one side. 'So you want me to dress up like that Zonk McPurple monster? Do I have to saunter around, hold a butterfly net and try to catch clouds too?'

She laughed and put her hand on her heart. 'No sauntering around or butterfly net required, I promise.'

'Well, then, why not? I'm used to making a fool of myself, especially where Katrina is concerned. We could have the prize-giving event at the Summer Fete. Would that leave you enough time to get organised?'

She nodded. 'It would work if I made the posters this afternoon, got them photocopied and handed them out tomorrow. Of course, we have to decide on the prizes first.'

He drank the last of his coffee. 'Hmm … Let me think. What about a hamper of goodies from The Buttered Scone or a free pass for the sailing club? Perhaps even a family ticket for the Jacobite steam train …'

'Those would be great prizes. The children are going to love it!'

'What children? What event?' A woman spoke behind her.

Daniel rose to his feet. 'Celia. Good morning.'

Jenna turned round. An attractive ginger-haired woman, dressed in a smart pencil skirt and fitted white shirt stood behind her.

'Why didn't you let me know you had arrived? We could have had coffee together,' she said, her manicured fingers toying with her gold necklace that immediately reminded

Jenna of the bold and clunky jewellery Adrian used to like her to wear and she had given away.

The woman glanced at Jenna who got up too. 'You must be Jenna Palmer. It's nice to meet you.'

Five minutes later they walked into a light and spacious office with windows overlooking the bay. A file was open on the table, with a newspaper folded next to it. Celia had giggled a lot as Daniel told her about the short story competition and his dressing up as Zonk McPurple. She had however hardly spoken two words to Jenna, which suited her fine. Her nerves were back with a vengeance, and her new-found confidence had deserted her by the time she sat down.

Celia flicked through the folder, and there was no trace of a smile as she pulled out a piece of paper. Jenna recognised the printout of the curriculum vitae she had emailed Daniel when she applied for the job.

'I would like to go over your employment history, if you don't mind, Miss Palmer,' she started in a formal voice. 'There are a few details I would like to clarify.'

Opposite her, Daniel frowned. 'Is that really necessary? I was satisfied with Jenna's qualifications, professional experience and references when I offered her the job.' He looked at her and smiled.

Celia Kennedy pouted. 'Perhaps, but Miss Palmer is using premises and resources belonging to the council, she has access to our computer network and manages the grant the council allocated to your project. I need to make sure everything is above board.'

Jenna's heartbeat picked up pace. She knew exactly what Celia Kennedy was about to say next. The woman cleared her throat and pointed her manicured index finger on the printout, making a splash of blood red on the white paper. 'There seems to be gaps in your employment history. You were made redundant about twelve months ago ...'

Jenna nodded. 'The council made budget cuts and the mobile library services were axed.'

'You didn't work much after that, did you?'

'Well ... it was difficult. There weren't many jobs around. I did apply, but ...' She couldn't explain that she lost her confidence, thought she was losing her mind too, and that Adrian was refusing offers of work on her behalf while all the time claiming that her applications were unsuccessful. Both Celia and Daniel would find her completely pathetic. And they would be right.

Celia shuffled a few papers on her desk then looked up again. 'I have your attendance record. You seem to have had an unusually high number of sickness days before you were made redundant. Do you have recurring health issues we should know about?'

Jenna's stomach contracted. She had taken time off work when the effort of getting dressed, putting make-up on and pretending she was all right was too much. When she had felt so tired she couldn't even get up in the morning, the night terrors kept her awake and the black butterflies threatened to choke her ...

'No.' Her voice was barely audible. 'I don't have any health issues that I know of.' She felt fine now, except for the nightmares. She still had those sometimes.

She gripped her hands together in her lap and forced a few deep breaths down. She wasn't going to be sick – not here, not now. It would only confirm Celia Kennedy's suspicions that there was something not quite right about her, and that she wasn't up to the job.

Daniel glanced from one woman to the other. 'Celia. I told you before ... I am more than satisfied with Jenna's qualifications and the glowing reference I received.'

Celia shrugged. 'Fine. Regarding last Saturday, things didn't exactly get off to a great start, did they?'

She opened the newspaper and Jenna's heart sank as she saw the headline. *"New Librarian's Smashing Dana Debut" by our reporter Ron Donaldson.* There were photos of Toby Drummond's Jag, of the "Welcome to Dana" banner, and of Brendon and her standing in front of the mobile library.

'It seems that Toby Drummond wasn't very impressed to have the mobile library crash into his sports car.' Celia pushed the paper towards Daniel.

Daniel didn't even glance at the paper. 'What happened was that as usual Drummond was driving too fast, as many witnesses would be able to tell you. The mobile library didn't make any contact with his car and there wasn't even a scratch to report.'

Celia nodded. 'Still, this type of headline doesn't reflect well on us, as partners in your venture, especially with the local elections looming and fierce scrutiny of the council's accounts.'

She paused, and reclined against the back of her chair. 'I am afraid there is something else.'

Daniel drummed his fingers on the table and gave an impatient sigh. 'What is it now?'

Celia looked at Jenna. 'There was a complaint about the way a child was treated yesterday. Apparently you sent several school boys out of the mobile library. One boy in particular was very distraught about the incident, according to his mother.'

Jenna cleared her throat. 'The boys were throwing books around. I had no other option than to send them out.'

Celia pouted again. 'The thing is, Miss Palmer, the grandfather of one of the boys is a councillor and he isn't very happy about the way you handled the incident.'

'Are we talking about Councillor McLean, by any chance?' Daniel asked.

Celia looked surprised. 'Well, yes.'

'Jenna is perfectly within her rights to discipline a child whoever his grandfather happens to be and I completely stand by her. I will deal with any further complaint regarding the incident, if Councillor McLean cares to pursue the matter.' A ray of sunlight caught the harsh glint in Daniel's blue eyes.

'Now, can we move on to what really matters, what we came here for – the plans for the use of the council's grant over the next few months? Jenna had some good ideas about buying a laptop and creating a space for people to use the internet in Butterc—I mean in the mobile library, and providing a regular meeting place for young mums.'

He gave her an encouraging smile, but Celia tutted. 'That's not what a mobile library is about.'

Jenna cleared her throat. 'Perhaps not in the past, but I am convinced that it's what mums and young children need now ...' She carried on explaining her ideas, warming to the subject as she talked, leaving out the hot drinks machine for now. She didn't want to make too many changes all at once.

One hour later, after a thorough review of the mobile library's business plans, and promises to consider Jenna's suggestions, Jenna and Daniel were out in the sunshine again.

Daniel checked his watch. 'We'll take the one o'clock ferry back. I'm sorry for this morning, Jenna. I had no idea Celia was planning to go over your employment history with a fine toothcomb.'

He looked as if he was waiting for her to respond. She should be brave and tell him the truth, get it out of the way. She clasped her hands together, opened her mouth to speak ... but she couldn't say the words.

He frowned but didn't insist, and they made their way back to the ferry.

'By the way, I know why McLean is complaining so much about what happened to his grandson. He is annoyed that I gave you the job instead of his niece. He insisted that I interview her even though she wasn't qualified. The girl had no idea about running a mobile library service, didn't have the right driving licence, and from what I gathered, no interest in books – or at least she was in no way as eloquent as you about books and happy dreams.'

He smiled. 'Even if there had been no incident with his grandson yesterday, McLean would have found something else to moan about.'

The *Riannog* had just left Mallaig harbour when Jenna's phone buzzed in her handbag. She ignored it at first, but it buzzed again, and again. Frowning, she unzipped her bag and took the phone out.

She clicked on the first text and the blood drained from her face.

It was an emoji – a yellow rose. There was no name but she didn't need one. Her fingers started shaking. She hadn't heard from Adrian since her mother's text on Sunday and had foolishly hoped that he'd changed his mind about contacting her.

The second text had a full line of red hearts and crosses and *I miss you.*

She opened the third text. *How are you, my darling? Your mother and I are very concerned about you. Please come back to Manchester. We have so much catching up to do. And by the way, don't worry. I'm not angry with you. We all make mistakes …* This was followed by more emojis and kisses.

Jenna let out a slow breath as she leant her elbows on the railing and gripped the phone between her fingers. He was back to his mind games, and twisting reality again to suit him. She had done nothing wrong – nothing at all!

'It's none of my business,' Daniel McGregor said next to her, 'but I wouldn't hold my phone over the railings if I were you. Not unless you want to drop it in the sea, of course.'

His deep voice startled her so much she almost did just that.

'Pardon?' She looked down at her phone. 'Ah ... yes.'

There was only one thing to do – one thing she should have done on Sunday evening. Block Adrian's number.

Chapter Fifteen

'Let's sit in the garden,' Ruth suggested as they walked into the tea shop. 'Come on, it's through here.'

They chose a table near a trellis covered with climbing roses. 'This is wonderful.' Jenna put her shopping bags down and smiled at Ruth, who today again dazzled in a patchwork of bright colours. The blue tee shirt, bright green skirt and purple Crocs shouldn't have worked together, especially with the woman's bright ginger hair, but strangely, they did, and once again Jenna felt rather lacklustre in her jeans, canvas pumps and pastel pink shirt.

Ruth had called at Mermaid's Cottage late morning and invited her to go shopping in Dana. 'I'll take you somewhere you can buy a proper coat.' After nipping in and out of a few boutiques, they had walked along the seafront, and Ruth had bought two ice-cream cones they had eaten sitting on the sea wall, watching fishing boats sail back to the harbour, seagulls dive into the bright blue waves with strident cries, and children build sandcastles or play football on the beach.

'Now you've been here a week,' Ruth said as she studied the menu, 'what do you think of Arrandale?'

The words shot out without Jenna having to think. 'I think it's the most stunning, the most beautiful place I've ever seen.'

Every day brought new surprises as Buttercup stopped in quaint hamlets nestling in peaceful glens or sheltered coves, drove past rugged peaks poking through the early morning mist, or ruined castles keeping watch over lonely lochs or meadows carpeted with wildflowers. Of course, it helped that the weather had been warm and sunny, and that everywhere Buttercup stopped people were friendly and welcoming.

'So you think you'll stay?'

This time she took more time to answer. 'I would like to. Yes. Hopefully.'

Ruth frowned. 'You don't sound so sure. Brendon said that he enjoyed working with you and that everybody spoke very highly of you.'

'Everybody except that little boy and his grandfather ... and Celia Kennedy,' Jenna objected.

'Don't mind them. The boy is a spoiled brat, and his grandfather an obnoxious bully. I know the family. They're always complaining about one thing or the other. As for Celia, it's well known that she's fancied Daniel for years. She probably sees you as a threat.'

'A threat? Me?' Jenna let out an incredulous laugh.

'Don't look so surprised. You're pretty, smart, kind ... and different. It's only natural if Daniel shows an interest in you.' Ruth looked down at the menu again, which was lucky because Jenna's cheeks were on fire.

Was Daniel interested in her? And why did the thought make her giddy? She tried not to picture his blue eyes and his rare but breathtaking smile, recall the soulful melodies he played on his fiddle on a moonlit Mermaid's Beach, or again the way he leapt to her defence during that awful meeting with Celia Kennedy... Her giddiness evaporated. Of course he had supported her. He was her boss after all. The man who'd hired her. Her boss is all he would ever be.

'Thank you for taking me shopping today,' she said when her face had cooled down. 'It's been fun, and I love my new yellow coat.' She pointed at the thick coat folded in a shopping bag at her feet.

Ruth smiled. 'You're welcome, love. But what is it with you and yellow?'

'It's the colour of sunshine, and it matches Buttercup, of course.'

'Is that why you asked Joe at the ceramics shop to make a necklace from that quirky piece of majolica you found on the beach – because there's a big yellow sun painted on it?'

Jenna nodded and toyed with her new pendant. The glaze was cracked but the colours were still fresh and vibrant, which was surprising since the piece was quite old. At least that's what the owner of the ceramics shop had said as he fitted a blue leather thong into a tiny hole he had drilled.

'It's lovely, isn't it? I couldn't believe it when I saw it, lying on a pile of seaweed this morning. It was as if it was waiting for me.'

A waitress came to take their order, and while Ruth was having a chat with her, Jenna's phone buzzed once, then twice again in rapid succession. She resolutely looked away from her handbag, but the phone buzzed again.

'Gosh, you're popular!' Ruth laughed once the waitress had left. 'Are you not getting that?'

'It's probably nothing.' How could she explain that she was a coward and as long as she ignored the phone she could still enjoy the afternoon and pretend that everything was all right? That Adrian hadn't found a way to get in touch?

'Really, love, you should check your phone,' Ruth insisted, a slight frown on her face as she looked at her. 'What if it's important?'

Jenna sighed. 'All right …' Her chest tight, she extracted the phone from her bag, but her fingers shook so much she typed the wrong code twice before finally unlocking the device.

The first text was a yellow rose. So her fears were founded. Adrian had somehow found a way to get around her blocking his number.

The second, a short sentence. *I miss you so much, darling.*

Then another. *I am worried about you.*

And another. *I'm keeping your engagement ring safe for you.*

And finally. *I don't understand why you are being so stubborn. Don't force me to come and get you.*

She threw the phone on the table and shuddered, as if a slug was crawling up her back, leaving a cold, slimy trail.

Ruth glanced at the phone, then at her. 'Whatever's the matter, love? Is there a problem?'

Jenna didn't reply but rubbed her finger frantically over the place where she'd worn her engagement ring. Her chest was getting tighter as dark thoughts swirled in her mind, like bats at dusk. Adrian was coming. He would spoil everything. Make everybody see how pathetic she was.

'Jenna! Are you all right?' Ruth's voice was sharper.

Jenna made a conscious effort to snap out of her dark thoughts and stop scratching her finger. Adrian wouldn't come to Arrandale. He only wanted to make her scared and confused … and he had succeeded.

She took a deep, calming breath. 'It's nothing – nothing at all. I am sorry.'

Ruth didn't seem convinced but the waitress was heading their way with a tray laden with a pot of tea, delicate china cups and cream tea for two. The buttery scent of two freshly baked scones filled the air. Ruth wasted no time in cutting one in half and spreading bilberry jam all over it before adding a generous spoonful of cream.

'Yum … It's still warm from the oven.' She bit into her scone and rolled her eyes. 'Delicious. Pour us some tea, love, will you?'

Jenna did as she was told, but her hand was still shaking and she was glad not to spill tea all over the table.

'By the way, how did your evening with His Smoothness go?'

Jenna dipped her spoon into the pot of bilberry jam and spread some jam on her scone. Adrian's texts had wiped out her appetite but she didn't want Ruth to ask her what the matter was. 'The restaurant and the food were stunning.'

Ruth gave her a cheeky grin. 'And the man?'

'He was quite nice too, but there seems to be a lot of animosity between him and Daniel McGregor.' She didn't want to mention Toby Drummond's shocking allegations against Daniel or the fact he'd asked her to spy for him.

'You can say that again. He and Toby don't get on, especially since … well, it's a long story, but five years ago Daniel and Toby had a fight and Daniel broke his nose.'

Jenna dropped the spoon, which clattered on the table, leaving blobs of bilberry jam all over the tablecloth. 'He did *what*?'

Ruth shrugged. 'Drummond had it coming.'

Jenna grabbed hold of her napkin, and proceeded to wipe the jam off the tablecloth. 'I didn't think Daniel was a violent man.'

'He isn't. He is a good man – the best, with my Colin, and Brendon, of course.' She gave her a puzzled look. 'Are you not eating, pet?'

'Yes, of course. Sorry.' But she could only nibble on her scone as her friend chatted away about her plans for the summer holidays and hardly heard what Ruth was saying. Her mind was on Adrian's texts and what to do next …

She phoned her mother as soon as she returned to Mermaid's Cottage. She didn't really want to, but she had put it off for long enough, and she had to make it clear that Adrian was history and there was no point insisting she come back to Manchester.

'At last!' her mother snapped when she answered the

phone. 'Why haven't you called any sooner or returned any of my messages?'

'It's only been a week, Mum, and I've been busy. I have a new job, a new house, and I have to learn to drive the mobile library, which can be a bit tricky around here.'

'That's exactly what Adrian and I have been saying. You are in no fit state to cope with such upheaval. You need to quit this silly job and come back before you have an accident or another breakdown.'

She launched into one of her monologues. Jenna was selfish and headstrong, and she didn't care about anyone but herself. Poor Adrian was so upset she hadn't been in touch.

'He was even more upset when I told him you'd given to charity most of the lovely clothes and jewellery he bought you and left his engagement ring here with me.'

Jenna glanced at her bare finger and for once found the strength to challenge her mother. 'Upset? What does he have to be upset about? He's the one who broke up.' As for the designer clothes, she wanted to add, Adrian may have chosen them but it was Jenna who had paid for them.

As usual her mother wasn't listening. Why was Jenna so vindictive? Why couldn't she forgive and forget? As if she was completely blameless herself – Adrian had told her a thing or two about what had been going on before they broke up.

Jenna's blood ran cold. 'Really? What did he say?'

'He said you didn't want him anywhere near you and even made him sleep in a different room. What did you expect? Of course he was going to find somebody else – someone more … amenable.'

Jenna's fingers tightened around the phone. Once again Adrian had twisted the truth. He had a sofa bed in the study because he often had to work late on a project, and he said he didn't want to disturb her – which was pointless because he played his music so loud at night she couldn't get to sleep anyway. As for the more physical aspect of their relationship, it had fizzled out quickly after they'd moved in together, and Adrian's critical words about her body and lack of sex appeal still rang in her ears.

Her mother wasn't finished. 'He said you used to leave your things lying around everywhere, you bought foods you knew he didn't like or was allergic to, got muddled with important dates and acted weird and confused most of the time – which I had noticed myself, by the way, when you came to visit.'

Jenna had nothing to say to that. It was all true. Her mother would never believe that her so-called forgetfulness was the product of Adrian's scheming, all the more because she had no proof.

'In the end,' her mother carried on, 'the poor boy felt that walking out was the best thing he could do for you. That way you would have to take charge of your own life. He did it for you, Jenna. The boy really loves you very, very much.'

Disbelief rendered her speechless for a few seconds. 'Are you saying that he had an affair and left because he loved me?'

'That's right. His escapade with that girl in London was never going to last. You should have waited for him to come back instead of rushing to Scotland on a whim. Now you two need to talk and sort it out. I told Adrian that you can both move in here with me until you find somewhere suitable.'

She couldn't believe what she was hearing. It was like being in two parallel realities, with Adrian up to his usual tricks to make Jenna doubt her own recollection of events. She had to put a stop to this nonsense.

Her mother was still talking, but this time she interrupted.

'I'm not interested in what Adrian had to say, Mum. I don't love him. I don't want to see or hear from him any more, and I won't come back.' As for moving in with her mother, the very thought made her stomach convulse.

There was a stunned silence at the other end, but then again she had rarely spoken to her mother so bluntly. 'I've just started this new job, and I love it here,' she added in a more conciliatory tone. 'It may sound odd, but for the first time, I feel that I could belong here, and make friends.'

Her mother tutted. 'You never had any friends. You were always such an awkward child. You didn't like sport, cubs or brownies, had no interest in normal things, like going shopping or watching telly. All you did was bury your nose in books, push me away as you plotted with your dad, and look down at me for not being as clever as you ... and for what?' Her laugh rang, short and harsh. 'What did you achieve in the end? You're driving some old mobile library in the back of beyond.'

Where was all that coming from? All that bitterness, anger and resentment – all that dislike?

'You need to sort things out with Adrian,' her mother carried on. 'You'll never get another man like him, who accepts you despite all your flaws and doesn't get annoyed by your quirky ways.'

But Adrian did get annoyed ... A lump formed in Jenna's throat and her heartbeat raced as memories she had buried deep inside crept back to the surface. Adrian's face when she displeased him. His grey eyes darkening, his lips stretching into a thin line; his face turning to marble; a tic pulling the side of his mouth, announcing the coming of the storm.

She flinched and tried to shut down images and sensations but the black butterflies were back, fluttering all around, crowding her, and stopping her from breathing.

'Jenna, are you listening?'

'I have to go now.' She ended the call and closed her eyes, drained and frustrated as she leant against the wall, pushing the memories back into oblivion.

Chapter Sixteen

Jenna drew open the curtains and blinked at the bright sunshine. It was another beautiful day but for the first time since she'd arrived in Arrandale she didn't smile as she looked at the shimmering sea or the sailing boats bobbing up and down as they criss-crossed Mermaid Cove. Her old nightmares had returned to torment her, together with the usual anger and self-loathing.

Yawning, she showered, tied her hair into a ponytail and dressed in jeans and an old long-sleeved khaki tee shirt, not bothering with any make-up since she planned to spend most of the day in the garden. Hopefully physical work would tire her out and help her fall asleep tonight.

As she sipped her hot tea and spread a thick layer of marmalade on her piece of toast, her mother's bitter words echoed in her mind. They had never been close, but was Jenna partly to blame? Perhaps she could have done things differently. She'd always known her mother was disappointed that she wasn't more "normal" as she called her friends' daughters who played netball or went to Brownies or dance club every week, and enjoyed shopping outings. Jenna had however never considered that her mother could have felt excluded by Jenna's studies or her closeness to her father.

She put the knife down. Perhaps she had a point. It was always her father she confided in or turned to for help and advice. Always her father she spent time with in the garden, whether to help out or to keep him company as she sat on a bench with a book. Her mother rebuffed her so often that Jenna stopped talking to her about anything meaningful.

On the other hand, Adrian complimented her mother

on her dress, her hair or her cooking, and listened to her ranting against neighbours or family members, always making the right noise at the right time, behaving in every way as the perfect son.

They may not be close but it hurt that her mother always took Adrian's side. Once, Jenna had told her about him pushing her into the walk-in wardrobe when he was annoyed, but her mother snapped that she should be ashamed for telling such horrible lies. It turned out that Adrian had already told her that Jenna had tripped and locked herself in there several times by accident but was too embarrassed to admit it.

There was the noise of a powerful car engine outside, and a shiny black SUV stopped in front of the cottage. Toby Drummond ... She hadn't seen him since Saturday night. Now Ruth had told her about Daniel breaking his nose, she could understand why he didn't like him.

She opened the front door as he stepped down from his car, holding a box of chocolates and an extravagant looking bouquet of white lilies, cream orchids, red roses and gerberas, all wrapped in pink tissue paper and a shiny ribbon.

He handed her the flowers and the chocolates with a contrite smile.

'These are for you, dear Jenna, to say sorry for our little disagreement last Saturday. I hope you can find it in your heart to forgive me for spoiling the end of our meal with my ... err ... indelicacy.'

She smiled back. 'It's very kind of you, but it wasn't necessary.'

'I also wanted to invite you to lunch. There's a nice country pub which I think you would like.'

There was an uneasy silence as she frantically searched her brain for a kind way to turn him down. She had planned to spend the day in the garden and really didn't fancy having to get dressed up for an impromptu lunch.

Daniel's collies charging towards her at full speed saved her from having to reply. Toby cursed and jumped aside as the dogs leapt onto Jenna's thighs, pushing her backwards.

'Hey, careful, boys!' She laughed, struggling to regain her balance.

'Sam! Eddie! Down,' Daniel's voice called.

The dogs immediately lay down, panting and heads resting on paws. Jenna put the flowers and the chocolates on the hall table and crouched down to stroke them. 'Hello, you two. What good boys you are.'

'Good boys? These beasts are thugs, like their master,' Toby muttered. He was a bit pale. Perhaps he was afraid of dogs ... unless it was Daniel he was scared of.

'Are you all right, Jenna?' Daniel said as he came closer. 'The dogs didn't scare you, I hope.' He frowned at Toby, who took another step back and lifted a hand to scratch his nose.

'Drummond.'

'McGregor ... Fancy seeing you here,' Toby replied. 'You need to keep these dogs under control. They almost toppled Jenna over.'

'They're just being friendly,' Jenna protested. Making a fuss of the dogs gave her a few seconds to compose herself. It wasn't the dogs' boisterous greeting that had caused her heart to gallop and her breath to catch in her throat. It was seeing Daniel and remembering what Ruth had said about him liking her. It was nonsense, of course, and she was stupid for believing a word of it.

'I can't believe you're letting Jenna live in this dump, McGregor.' Toby gestured to the cottage. 'If she worked for me, she would have an apartment at Carloch Castle.'

'I have no doubt about it.' Daniel arched his eyebrows as

he looked down at him. The contrast between the two men couldn't be greater – Toby the picture of casual chic in his chinos, linen blazer and pale blue shirt, and Daniel rugged and unshaven in jeans and grey tee shirt.

Turning to Jenna again, Daniel handed her a couple of plastic bags. 'These are for you.'

She glanced into the first bag which contained a box of a dozen eggs. 'How wonderful … Are these from the farm?'

He nodded. 'Collected this morning by Katrina.' The second bag was filled by what looked like two dozen twigs.

'They're raspberry canes, aren't they?' Jenna smiled.

Daniel smiled. 'I thought you might want to grow your own raspberries in the garden. They probably won't give any fruit this summer, but you may get some in the autumn, you never know.'

Toby shook his head. 'What's the point of growing your own when you can buy perfectly good raspberries from the shops?'

'It's a lot more satisfying.' She looked in the bag. 'There is something else.'

She took out a photo of two adorable baby cows in a cardboard frame painted yellow and decorated with drawings of daisies and buttercups, and another photograph of a massive Highland cow – or rather heifer. 'That's Buttercup, isn't it?'

Daniel smiled. 'Indeed. And the other photo is of Maisie, who is almost fully recovered now as is her mother, and Jenna, the calf Katrina named after you.'

Toby Drummond guffawed as he crossed his arms. 'Tell me I'm dreaming. You actually named a cow after Jenna?'

Jenna and Daniel looked at each other and smiled. 'What's wrong with that?' Daniel asked.

'I was actually very flattered,' Jenna added.

Toby let out a loud sigh. 'You have no idea how to treat women, McGregor. It's no wonder Shannon ditched you for Hugh. At least he knew how to give girls a good time.'

The smile vanished from Daniel's face. He clenched his jaw, and his eyes took on a hard glint. In a split second the atmosphere changed, the banter was gone and the air became charged with darkness and danger. Toby no doubt felt it too because he retreated towards his car.

'Right, I'd better dash,' he said. As he climbed behind the wheel, a seagull flew overhead and a massive white dropping splashed over the bonnet's shiny black paint. He cursed, and started the car so quickly that the tyres screeched and spit gravel behind them.

'Shame that gull didn't fly over his head two seconds earlier,' Daniel muttered, glaring at the back of Toby's SUV until it disappeared in a cloud of dust at the bend of the lane, a positively murderous glint in his eyes. If Jenna had ever doubted the ill-feeling between the men, she couldn't any longer.

'Would you like a drink? Coffee or tea, or a glass of lemonade?' Jenna asked, probably to diffuse the tension, but right now he needed to be on his own.

'No thanks.' His voice came out as a growl.

He made himself unclench his fingers. 'I'll plant those raspberry canes now, and while I'm here I'll give the garden a quick survey.'

She gave him a timid smile. 'Thank you. I'll come round to help you in a minute. I must put Toby's flowers in a vase and the photos on the mantelpiece.'

He grabbed hold of the raspberry canes, whistled for the dogs to follow and made his way to the garden. Jenna must be wondering what the hell was wrong with him, but it was always the same. Drummond brought out the worst in him.

At least he had managed not to smash his fist into his smug face – not that he hadn't felt like it, mind.

He pushed the garden gate and paused in surprise. What a transformation in a few days ... He grabbed hold of a shovel and walked towards the garden wall, choosing an east facing spot. He crouched down, touched the ground. The soil was moist, but not waterlogged. This was a good sheltered place which would get plenty of sunshine. He dug holes for the canes. The physical activity helped him get rid of some of his frustration and gave him something to focus on instead of Drummond ... and Shannon. The midday sun was hot already and he was sweating by the time he finished.

'I'm sorry it took me so long. I couldn't find a vase big enough for Toby's flowers. I had to split it into four bunches, which completely ruined the effect.'

When he didn't reply, she pointed at the canes now all sticking out of the ground. 'You've almost finished already.'

'There weren't that many.' He turned round, and gestured to the garden. 'You've done an amazing job.'

'Thank you. I'm really pleased with the way it's going. I've been lucky that the weather has been nice all week and I was able to work in the garden every day.'

She was toying with some kind of pendant secured around her slender neck by a leather thong. Tendrils of blonde hair caressed her skin as they tumbled down from her loose ponytail. Suddenly all he wanted was to twirl a strand of hair around his finger, and kiss the curve of her neck, trail back up to her lips and ...

He cleared his throat and pushed a deep breath down. What was it about the woman that made him so worked up? She was still playing with her pendant. He narrowed his eyes, looked at it more closely and held his breath ... It wasn't ... It couldn't be, surely?

He pointed at it. 'Your necklace – it's rather striking.'

She held it out for him to take a look. 'Do you like it? I found it on the beach yesterday morning. It's pretty, isn't it? The manager of Dana's ceramics shop turned it into a necklace for me. He said it was a very old piece of pottery – he called it majolica. I haven't had a chance to look it up.'

His throat became dry and excitement raised his pulse. Jenna's piece of pottery was almost identical to one of the majolica pieces he'd seen at a museum in Edinburgh, which had been recovered from the wreck of a Spanish Armada ship at Kinlochbervie over twenty years before.

'Majolica is a type of tin-glaze earthenware pottery originally from Spain in the Renaissance period,' he explained. 'Some pieces were extremely valuable.'

He carried on examining her pendant. This was an old, sixteenth century piece, he was sure of it. If he didn't say anything, everything would remain as it should – forgotten, buried or hidden in whatever place the captain of the *Santa Catalina* and his men had chosen, and no more lives would be lost.

'Are you annoyed with me?' She looked at him, and he realised he was frowning. 'Should I have left it on the beach or perhaps given it to you? Ruth thinks it may be valuable. I am sorry… There … take it.'

She started untying the leather thong at the back of her neck.

'No. Keep it. It's nothing.' He sounded harsher than he intended. 'Of course you're allowed to keep things you pick up on the beach,' he added in a softer voice. 'Unless it's gold or anything valuable, in which case it all goes to the Crown – that's Scottish law.'

'You mean that if you ever found a treasure, you wouldn't be able to keep any of it?'

His neck and shoulders tensed, and strain radiated all the

way down his spine. 'That's right. All you can hope for is a reward, and the same goes for the landowner. But as I have no intention of looking for any treasure, it doesn't matter.'

He turned round. 'I'll give the garden a quick check now.'

He would try to forget that Jenna may have found a vital clue about the *Santa Catalina*'s treasure – the treasure Hugh and him, and so many more had spent years looking for, and which had cost Hugh his life.

Chapter Seventeen

Jenna pulled the handbrake up and winced as her arm ached. 'I think I may have been overdoing the gardening.'

Brendon undid his safety belt. 'You're really keen on Mermaid's garden, aren't you?'

She nodded. 'I love it. It's a little piece of paradise.' *Her* little piece of paradise, like Mermaid Cove was her very own private beach ... or at least that's what it felt like when she walked on the beach every morning before work, or paddled in the sea as soon as she was home after work. From the very first day she had felt she belonged there.

'I told you, didn't I, that Arrandale was the best place on Skye – no, make that the whole of Scotland.'

'Yes. The land of Happy Dreams.' She smiled. 'Whether it's the sea air, the busy days in Buttercup or working in the garden, I'm so tired in the evenings that I fall asleep as soon as my head touches the pillow.' And she'd only had nightmares once, and that was after her telephone conversation with her mother ...

Brendon glanced at the dozen people queuing patiently outside. 'It's time to open. There's quite a queue already.'

A smartly dressed middle-aged woman climbed onboard first.

'Good morning, Mrs Robertson, how are you today?'

'I am very well, thank you, my dear. Nice day, today, isn't it?' The woman took a handful of hardbacks out of her shopping bag and put them down on the counter. She pointed at one of them. 'I didn't like that one at all. I thought it was cosy crime.'

Jenna gave her an apologetic smile, although the title *Autopsy* written in blood red and the photo of a morgue on the cover should have been a giveaway that there would be nothing cosy about the story. 'I am sorry you didn't enjoy it. To tell the truth, it's not my cup of tea either.'

She shuddered. She would never enjoy reading about abuse and violence. 'By the way, I have received the novel you reserved last week.'

The woman's face lit up. 'Well, thank you, my dear. Enid put it on the book club reading list for next Tuesday. She said you would sort it all out for us.'

Jenna's smile didn't falter although she winced inwardly. Why didn't Enid warn her? Now she had to get hold of multiple copies of the novel in time for the club's next meeting. She logged onto the internal council library website on her laptop. By chance, Mallaig library happened to have three copies, which was a start. She reserved them all. She would pick them up later in the week.

Donald and Murdo were last in the queue, and they were bickering again, today over a pint of beer Murdo claimed Donald owed him for winning a bet about who had the longest whiskers.

'Good morning, gentlemen,' Jenna said as they put their books down on the counter.

Murdo took his tweed cap off with a flourish. 'And a good morning to you, fair maiden. You look as bonnie as ever. I wanted to buy you flowers but couldn't find my wallet when I got to the shop.'

Donald winked at Jenna. 'Aye, and who took that wallet? The wee fairies? Ye're a tight-fisted old devil, that's all.'

Murdo made an indignant face. 'I am not! I won't have you cast doubt on my good character. Take that back this instant.'

They both carried on arguing as they shuffled to the back of the van where they sat on the folding camping stools Brendon had brought from home, to read the *Gazette* and bicker over the latest football results, or whatever was in the news that day.

They were still there half an hour later when Daniel climbed onboard. Tall, tanned, broad-shouldered and looking attractively rugged in his faded jeans and a navy blue tee shirt, he immediately seemed to fill all the space. She hadn't seen him since Sunday, when he had left with barely a goodbye after planting the raspberry canes and surveying the garden.

'Morning, boss,' Brendon said from the back of the van where he was putting newly returned books back on the shelves. 'We don't usually see you in here.'

'Good morning.' Daniel gave her a tight, almost shy smile and stood in front of her, fiddling with his mobile phone and looking ill at ease.

'Good morning. How can I help?' She winced at her annoyingly squeaky voice.

Daniel nodded, and looked around. 'I'd like to borrow a book or two.'

Jenna smiled. 'Then you're in the right place. What are you after? Fiction, non-fiction? These are the recommended reads for this month.' She pointed at the display that she'd put together. 'You will find that they are all very good, in their own way.'

'It's not for me,' he said quickly, putting his mobile phone into his pocket. 'I was in town when Katrina texted that she wanted a couple of Zonk books. We read the ones she borrowed last week every single night and she's had enough. And so have I. In fact, I'd be happy never to read another of those silly books ever again, but Katrina wouldn't forgive me if I came home without them, so here am I ...'

He gave her a disarming smile, and she sat there, mesmerised by the intense blue of his eyes and her mind completely blank. His smile faded slowly as they held each other's gaze and it felt as if they were alone in some kind of dream.

'They're very popular, these Zonk books,' Brendon shouted from the back of the van, startling her out of her daydream. 'All the kiddies love the character because he's big and scary, but also very silly with his kilt and purple tee shirt … not to mention his butterfly net.'

Daniel groaned but there were sparks of humour in his eyes. 'Aye. Don't remind me that that's what I'm going to wear for the prize-giving in a few weeks' time, minus the butterfly net, and all because Jenna said it would draw the crowds.' Did she imagine it or was there something soft and gentle in his eyes as he looked at her, something that made her head spin and her heart thud.

She had to stop behaving like a silly girl with a crush. She made herself look away and took a few deep breaths. Hopefully he hadn't noticed the effect he had on her.

'I'll show you where the books are.' Trying to sound professional, she rose to her feet, walked the few steps to the children's section and pulled out the crates of books.

'Here are the Zonk McPurple titles. You'll also find lots of other books Katrina may want to try.' They crouched down together in front of the box, so close their thighs, arms and shoulders touched.

'Sure.' He pulled a few books out, smiled at some of the titles and selected a couple. 'I'll take this one, that one … and that one too.' He then took another, and this time his face closed and he dropped it straight back into the box as if he'd been burned.

He rose to his feet. 'These will do.'

Curious, Jenna leaned forward and caught a glimpse of the cover. It was the mermaid book she had shown Katrina on her very first day. What was it with mermaids around here? She got up too fast and stumbled backwards. Daniel reached out to steady her. His arms circled around her waist, and for a few seconds her body was pressed against his, her breasts were squashed against his broad, solid chest, and this time it was she who reacted as if she'd been burned.

She pulled away and stepped back. 'Sorry ...'

'There isn't much room in here.' He glanced at Donald and Murdo who were still engrossed in the *Gazette* at the back. 'Especially with those two behaving as if they're in their living room. I bet they wouldn't mind a cup of tea and a biscuit too,' he said in a jokey voice loud enough for them to hear.

'Och, McGregor! That's a splendid idea,' Donald shouted back. 'Young Jenna did mention installing a hot drinks machine in here the other day to give punters refreshments.'

Daniel arched his eyebrows and turned to her. 'Did she now?'

Her face heated up under his gaze. This was her chance to pitch her idea. 'Actually it was something I wanted to discuss with you when you had a minute, along with a few other suggestions.'

He nodded and glanced at his watch. 'It's almost lunchtime. Why don't we have a coffee and a bite to eat, and you can tell me about your plans?'

Brendon offered to look after Buttercup over the lunch hour, and ten minutes later, Daniel and Jenna were out in the sunshine, walking along the seafront.

'Shall we try The Buttered Scone? We could sit in the garden,' Daniel suggested. She agreed and they strolled towards the tea shop. Daniel smiled and waved at a few people on the way, stopped a couple of times for a chat. Suddenly he muttered an oath and his fingers clenched around the Zonk books he was holding.

Toby Drummond was coming towards them, smirking.

'Good morning, Jenna … McGregor. I see you got yourself some books. Are they not a teeny bit ambitious for you?'

'Shut up, Drummond.'

'Brief, but eloquent, as usual.' Toby sighed and added, 'Enjoy your reading, although you may need a dictionary to understand some of the words.'

Next to her, Daniel hissed a breath. 'Why don't you bugger off?'

Toby winced and tutted. 'Manners, McGregor. Mind you, you learned yours from your hairy coos … and you'll look like one if you don't go to the barber soon.' He flicked his floppy blond fringe back before hurrying away, glancing uneasily around him. Was he worried about another seagull dropping, perhaps?

Next to her Daniel sighed and opened the door to the tea shop. 'I'm sorry I was rude, Jenna. Drummond and I don't get on.'

'I had gathered that.' The bad relations between Daniel and Toby were none of her business, so she didn't say anything more as Daniel let her go through into the shop.

He could kick himself. He should know by now that Drummond always goaded him into behaving like a thug and yet he always fell for it.

As Drummond walked away in his fashionable beige linen suit, Daniel glanced down at his rough hands, his forearms criss-crossed with nicks and grazes, his faded jeans with a rip on one knee and scuffed work boots, then at Jenna, pretty and fresh like a burnet rose in her pale yellow blouse, white cardigan and skirt, and cringed inwardly. What was he thinking of, taking her out for lunch when he looked so scruffy?

They were lucky to find a table in the garden, sat down

and ordered a pitcher of water, two coffees and a cheese sandwich for him and a crab salad for Jenna.

'So, tell me your plans for Buttercup,' he said after the waitress left with their orders.

Jenna took a deep breath. 'Well, as Donald and Murdo said earlier, I would like to have a drinks machine in Buttercup ...' She hesitated, but soon gained confidence. Her face lit up as she laid out her ambitious plans for turning the mobile library into some kind of community hub. Some of them she had already mentioned at the meeting with Celia Kennedy. She had clearly done her research, but he couldn't afford any more expenses at this time. He hated to have to burst her bubble and disappoint her.

The waitress came back with their food. He poured out some water into their tall glasses filled with ice cubes, and took a bite of his sandwich.

'If you put everything in writing, then I'll be able to pass it onto my accountant. He may be able to find us some government grant. As for the drinks machine, we could cost a few and see how it goes.'

Jenna gave him a happy smile, picked up her fork and stabbed a cherry tomato. 'So you think it's a good idea? I know there will be risk assessments and extra insurance costs but I am sure—'

She stopped suddenly, dropped her fork to her plate and stared at something behind him. Curious, Daniel glanced over his shoulder and frowned. Was Jenna looking at the couple sitting near the rose trellis, and who judging from the man's thundery expression and the woman's downcast eyes were having an argument, or the family of four giggling with delight as they dipped their spoons into enormous ice-creams tipped with clouds of whipped cream?

He looked back at Jenna. Her face was pinched and colourless, her eyes an icy blue, and she was rubbing her ring finger in the frantic way he'd seen her do before. 'Jenna? What's the matter?' he asked in a quiet voice. 'Is there something upsetting you?'

She nodded.

'Who? Is it the man behind me?'

She nodded again. 'He's a bully. A nasty bully.'

He angled his body so that the couple was in his line of vision. The man was leaning across the table and talking in a growling voice to the woman who was dabbing a ketchup stain on the front of her dress with a napkin. 'You're so clumsy,' he was saying. 'Now we're going to walk around the shops with you looking a mess, and make me look stupid, as usual. Not to mention that your dress is ruined. How much did it cost, I wonder – that's my money you've been spending. My money, because you're too fat and stupid to get yourself a real job.'

The woman dabbed her eyes with her paper napkin. 'I'm sorry, John. Please, stop … please. People are listening.'

'I'll stop when I'm ready.'

Damn. Jenna was right. The man was a bully, and if there was something he hated it was a mean bastard taking out his nasty temper on people too weak or too scared to put up a fight.

Daniel put his sandwich down, got up and walked straight to the man. 'You should watch your language, apologise to the lady, and find yourself some other place to eat,' he said calmly.

'Really? Or what?' the man snarled, but as he looked up, his face lost some of its belligerence. Like every bully, he was a coward. Daniel was younger, fitter, and bigger. He would have no chance against him.

'You have two minutes to get up and leave.' Daniel gestured to the waitress, and asked her to prepare the couple's bill. The girl nodded and hurried inside.

147

'Fine. Keep your hair on, man. We're leaving,' the man said. 'The food was crap anyway. Come on, Nicola, get your stuff.'

The woman sat, rigid, in her chair. She didn't even look at Daniel.

'She'll be out in a few minutes, when you've settled the bill inside.' There was no way Daniel was going to let her leave without making sure she was all right.

'Fine. Suit yourself.' The man snorted and strode across the garden before disappearing inside the tea shop.

Daniel bent down closer to the woman but not too close as to unsettle her, and asked in a soft voice, the voice he used to reassure people he rescued at sea. 'Are you all right, ma'am? Nicola, isn't it? Is there anything I can help you with?'

The woman let out a sigh, shook her head, and put her napkin on her untouched plate of jacket potato and tuna salad. 'I have to go.'

'You don't have to do anything or go anywhere you don't want to. Are you scared this man will hurt you? Physically hurt you?'

She looked at him and gave him the saddest, most resigned smile he'd ever seen. 'He is right, you know. I am clumsy ... but thank you for your kindness.'

She got up, took her handbag and gave him a pat on the forearm before walking away slowly, her shoulders hunched as if she carried a huge, but invisible, burden.

Daniel glanced at Jenna. 'I won't be long.' He followed the woman. He really wasn't happy with letting her go away, but there were families queuing at the ice-cream counter inside, blocking his way, and by the time he made it out of the tea shop, he looked around and spotted the couple in the distance. Perhaps he should run after them to check if the woman was really all right.

'I hope she gets away before he destroys her,' Jenna said in a quiet voice next to him as if she knew what he was thinking.

He looked down, surprised that she had followed him out, and even more surprised to see the tears shining in her eyes. Just then the lifeboat station sirens howled and his pager went off.

'Sorry,' he said. 'I have to run. I don't like to leave you like this. Will you be all right?'

She nodded. 'Of course. Don't worry.'

But as he sprinted towards the lifeboat station, he wasn't sure she was telling the truth ...

Chapter Eighteen

They had been busy all morning and they were about to close for lunch when a stout man with florid cheeks and sparse brown hair combed over his shiny bald head climbed in. Panting as he reached the top of the stairs, he took a handkerchief from his pocket and mopped the sweat from his forehead. He was followed by the reporter from the *Gazette* who had attended Buttercup's opening day.

'What are these two doing here?' Brendon muttered in his beard before standing up. 'Councillor McLean. Ron ... To what do we owe the pleasure of your visit?'

Jenna's heartbeat quickened. Councillor McLean? This must be Archie's grandfather – the councillor who had complained about the way she treated his grandson the week before. She rose to her feet too and forced a smile. 'Good morning, and welcome to our mobile library.'

McLean didn't return her greeting. 'I'm here to make sure that taxpayers' money is being put to good use,' he started in a loud, querulous voice.

Brendon nodded. 'In that case, you need to speak to Jenna. She's the one in charge.'

McLean turned to her. 'Ms Palmer. Yes, I heard about you, and not all in good terms, I'm afraid.'

The journalist took a couple of photos of her close up with his mobile phone, the flash startling her and making her blink.

'Hey! Do you mind? Aren't you supposed to ask people's permission before taking photos?'

He shrugged, and took another few more shots. What was wrong with the man? It was as if he was deliberately trying to irk her.

'I see you have a bit of a temper,' the councillor remarked. 'Perhaps working with members of the public – children especially – isn't the most suitable occupation for you. There was a very unpleasant incident regarding my grandson the other day, an incident for which I would like you to apologise.'

Jenna's pulse picked up. The thought of a confrontation made her palms clammy and turned her stomach. She probably should apologise and get it over with. At least that's what the old Jenna would have done, even if she believed that she had done nothing wrong ... She remembered the woman in The Buttered Scone garden, and something hardened inside her. She wasn't that woman any more so she kept her lips firmly clamped.

'I am waiting for that apology, Ms Palmer.' As the odious man leant towards her, she caught a whiff of perspiration and stale cigarette from his clothes.

'I have nothing to apologise for, councillor,' she said, trying very hard to keep her voice from shaking. 'I was only making sure the class experience wasn't being spoiled by your grandson's and his friends' boisterous behaviour, as Brendon here and Archie's teacher will tell you.'

'Boisterous? Children are boisterous ... not a crime being boisterous.' McLean harrumphed and puffed and muttered under his breath, but he didn't insist. Instead he pointed his finger at the poster advertising the short story competition. 'What's this? A writing contest, with extravagant prizes? Family trips on the Jacobite steam train, Glenfield zoo and Dana's sailing club ... and free books for all competitors? Is that your idea, Ms Palmer?'

She nodded. 'It's a wonderful way of encouraging children to write, don't you think?'

'I call it an outrageous waste of the council's grant and taxpayers' money!' He turned to Donaldson. 'Make sure you record my words, Ron, when you write your article. This is exactly what I feared would happen when McGregor launched his hare-brained mobile library scheme and hired somebody totally unsuitable for the post, somebody who had spent more time off sick or out of work than actually working.'

Silence fell in the mobile library and Donald, Murdo and the remaining customers looked at her. The blood drained from Jenna's face, a wave of nausea rose inside her. How dare Celia Kennedy disclose her personal details to the councillor?

Brendon wasn't smiling any longer. 'Jenna is extremely well qualified, councillor, and—'

Jenna put her hand on his forearm. 'Thank you, Brendon, but I can take it from here.'

Brendon frowned and cast a worried glance towards her. 'Are you sure, lass?'

She nodded and drew in a deep breath. 'Councillor, if you wish to issue a formal complaint about my work, I would kindly ask you to write to my employer, Daniel McGregor. Otherwise, please refrain from making allegations in public against me, as I am sure that you are aware they could constitute slander.'

The knot of anger was growing bigger and harder in her stomach with every word but she forced her voice to remain calm. 'Moreover, this is not the time or the place to discuss my employment record – record that you should not have been given access to according to data protection regulations. I will certainly investigate this breach of my right to privacy.'

'Go, lass!' Murdo cheered her on from the back of the van where he and Donald sat on their usual camping stools, reading the paper.

'You tell him!' Donald called, looking over his copy of the *Gazette*.

She gave them a nod and a smile. She had friends here, people who took her side, and it made her feel instantly stronger.

'On the matter of the short story competition, all the prizes are being paid for by Mr McGregor himself, and this includes the books we will give to the children. You can therefore rest assured that no taxpayers' money has been wasted. Now would you like me to give you a tour of Buttercup and show you what we have done to modernise the service so far? If not, I will ask you to leave as we must shortly close for lunch.'

'Don't take that tone with me, young lady,' McLean spluttered at last, his cheeks regaining their florid colour. 'And who the devil is Buttercup?'

'It's the mobile library, councillor,' Murdo replied. 'As a taxpayer, I must say that I am delighted to have some kind of library service back, but that's no thanks to you. I'm sure I speak for everybody around here. It was a shame the council decided to axe it.' Looking at the journalist, he added, 'And you can put that in your report for the *Gazette* too, Ron.'

There was a chorus of 'Ayes, he's right' from the few people in the van.

'Arrandale always comes last with you lot,' someone shouted from the far end of the mobile library.

'How come the council is wasting money on a new logo when the kids' playground is still a mess?' a woman asked then.

'And the bin collection is a disgrace,' another complained. 'We'll soon see rats running wild in the streets.'

McLean took out his handkerchief and patted his forehead once again. His cheeks had turned beetroot red and his mouth twisted in a thin line. 'Well, regarding the cuts … we had to make tough decisions … and the logo …'

The rest of his sentence was garbled. He nudged the journalist. 'Time to go, Ron. I have seen enough.'

Everybody started talking at once as soon as the two men had left.

'Don't you fret about McLean, lass,' Donald said as he folded his newspaper and put it back into the rack. 'He likes to throw his weight around.'

'You did great,' Murdo agreed before turning to his friend. 'Come on, old man, I'll buy you a pint.'

Donald winked at Jenna. 'Found your wallet, have you? And who are you calling an old man?'

The two men rose to their feet, tidied the camping stools against one of the shelves and made their way out. 'See you next week.'

'Do you mind taking Buttercup back to the garage on your own?' Jenna asked Brendon when everybody had left. 'I want to catch the lunchtime ferry to Mallaig. I reserved some books for Enid's book club at the library, and I'd like to do a spot of shopping afterwards.'

'No problem, love. You go and enjoy yourself. You did well with McLean back there. I'm proud of you.'

'Thanks.' She felt rather proud of herself too, so it was with a spring in her step that she made her way outside. The weather was warm and sunny again and she almost felt like she was on holiday as she took her blazer off, and bought a crab sandwich and a bottle of water from The Buttered Scone, before rushing along the seafront towards the pier.

The ferry was already there, and so was the lifeboat, with a familiar tall and athletic figure standing on deck, his dark hair ruffled by the sea breeze. Her heart started racing, but she told herself that it was from walking fast and absolutely not from seeing Daniel looking tanned and rugged, the muscles of his arms and shoulders working hard as he rolled up a thick coil of rope.

She gave him a timid wave as she walked past. 'Hi.'

He straightened up. 'Jenna.' He had a way of saying her name that made her pulse dance. A way of looking at her that made her forget everything, even to breathe. 'How are you?'

She nodded. 'I am well. Thank you.' She pointed at the ferry. 'I'm going to Mallaig to collect some books from the library.'

He smiled, and the sunlight made his eyes as bright and blue as the sea and the sky. 'Good ... And how are things on ... err ... Buttercup?'

'It's busy, but wonderful ... most of the time.' She told him about McLean's visit, and by the time she had finished, Daniel wasn't smiling any longer.

'Ron Donaldson was there too,' she added, 'so I'm afraid there might be an unfavourable article in the *Gazette* soon.'

His face closed and his eyes narrowed as he stared at the open sea beyond the harbour walls. 'The man is completely out of order, and so is Celia Kennedy for disclosing your personal details, but don't worry, I'll sort it,' he said at last.

Was it pride or her new-found self-confidence, but she shook her head. 'I'd like to deal with this myself, if you don't mind. But thank you ... How did your rescue go the other day?'

He ran his fingers through his dark hair and sighed. 'It was a close call – couple of teenagers gone bodyboarding got swept away by rip current near Sìthiche Point. They should never have been there. The place is notoriously dangerous. It was lucky we got to them in time.'

Arrandale's geography was still a mystery to her and she had no idea where Sìthiche Point was, but she nodded. 'I'm glad it went well.'

The deafening sound of a horn made her jump, and she gestured to the *Riannog*. 'I'd better go or I'll miss the ferry.'

She said goodbye and walked to the end of the pier, aware of him watching her, making the skin of her back and neck tingle.

It wasn't Kieran helping out today, but a woman. As she bought her return ticket, Jenna was relieved that she wouldn't have to put up with the teenager's sour mood and the guilt she still felt, rightly or wrongly, for his friend Jim's heart attack.

The sailing was pleasant even if the sea was a little choppy, and once in Mallaig, she found a bench to eat her sandwich on and watch the fishing boats as they came back to the harbour. A dozen cars lined up to board a massive ferry bound for the Small Isles. Next to it, the *Riannog* looked tiny and a little worse for wear.

'Jenna?' A woman called next to her. 'It's Jenna Palmer, isn't it?'

She turned round, and narrowed her eyes against the bright sunlight. The young woman calling her looked vaguely familiar, but huge sunglasses hid half her face and a white cap covered her hair.

'Don't you recognise me? Becky. Becky Crolla. We worked together at Butterfield Library. I was with the homebound service.'

Jenna gasped. 'Of course! Becky … I am sorry. I should have known you straight away. How are you?'

'I'm great, thanks. What are you doing here? Are you on holiday?'

'No. I work here. Well, I work in Arrandale, on Skye. What about you?' Becky had been made redundant at the same time as her and she had lost touch with her. In fact, she'd lost touch with all her former colleagues, except Safiyya, the Butterfield library manager who had given her references when she'd applied for jobs.

'I'm a full-time mum now. Actually we're about to board

the ferry to Rùm for a camping holiday. I'm not looking forward to the mud and the midges but Tom and the kids love camping, so …'

She cocked her head to one side. 'So you work here. It must be a change from Manchester. What about your boyfriend? Does he live here too?'

Jenna drew in breath. 'Adrian? No … We're … not together any more. We split up a few months ago, before Christmas.'

Becky's smile widened. 'I'm glad to hear that. You're so well shot of him. The man was a creep, everybody thought so.'

'Did they?' Jenna found it hard to breathe suddenly.

'Oh yes, and we were all sorry for you. We couldn't believe that someone as nice and clever as you could put up with him and the way he treated you. I remember that time he was waiting for you in the library and he had a go at you in front of everybody for being five minutes late.'

Jenna's throat tightened. Yes, she remembered that day. Adrian accused her of making him wait on purpose when she hadn't even known he was coming to pick her up. He said she must have forgotten, and once again accused her of losing her mind … and she had apologised.

Becky carried on. 'And the night we all went out to that Indian restaurant in Rusholme and he kept texting you to come home, and in the end you left without even eating your curry. You never wanted to go out with us after that.'

No, she hadn't, and they had stopped asking her.

'Funny how he seemed the perfect man at first – handsome, loaded, charming, taking you out to all those posh places, showering you with gifts. That gorgeous ring he gave you …' Becky sighed and glanced at Jenna's bare fingers. 'I bet he made you give it back, didn't he?'

Jenna drew in breath and forced a smile, but her face felt

tight and brittle. 'No, it's at my mother's. I didn't want it any more.' The ring had meant nothing – or rather, it had meant too much.

There was some beeping from a white Kia lining up for the ferry. 'I have to dash,' Becky said and showed Jenna the plastic bag she was holding. 'I only jumped out of the car to get some sweets for the kids. Listen, Jenna, take care of yourself. I'm so glad I saw you. You look so much better, so much happier.'

And with a smile and a wave, Becky hurried towards the Kia, and her family.

Jenna wasn't hungry any more, so she wrapped what was left of her sandwich and disposed of it in a nearby bin. Her throat was too tight even to drink, but she forced some water down. She could feel the beginning of a headache pulsing behind her eyes. How naive of her to think that she could fool people and hide how miserable she was.

She made her way along the harbour to the library building, walking slowly to try to calm down and clear her mind, but her happy mood was gone.

She collected the books and went straight back to the harbour to catch the return ferry. She didn't feel like shopping any longer. All she wanted was to go down to Mermaid's Beach, and think.

She had been a coward for too long. It was time to be brave and revisit the past, including memories of Adrian's outbursts, broken promises and random acts of nastiness – all the jumbled snapshots and dark echoes of what their life together had been like that sometimes seeped out of her subconscious and into her nightmares …

Chapter Nineteen

Buttercup bumped along the one-track road, its tyres splashing into puddles, en route to the nursing home which was their last stop before the weekend.

'I'm surprised a bonnie lass like you isn't married, or at least doesn't have a steady fellow,' Brendon remarked all of a sudden.

Jenna focussed on the road and pretended not to hear, which would be perfectly plausible given the loud drumming of rain on the roof of the van and the mad swish of the wipers. The weather had changed from summery to positively autumnal. There would be no gardening for a few days.

'Look out for that pothole on your right.' Brendon gestured to the road ahead. 'We don't want to damage Buttercup and have Celia Kennedy complaining on the phone – or worse, in person, do we – even though it was Daniel who bought the van with his own money?'

Jenna sighed. 'I certainly don't. In fact I wouldn't be sorry never to hear from her again.' Since McLean's visit the week before, Celia Kennedy had been in touch almost every day with enquiries about Jenna's spending plans and modifications to the routes for the summer holidays.

On the positive side, there had been no article about Buttercup in the *Gazette*, and Jenna had warned the woman against divulging her personal details in the future, which had resulted in Celia coming down from her high horse and apologising profusely.

'We're here.' Brendon indicated a one storey building in the distance.

She slowed down and parked at the side of the road,

unable to repress a satisfied smile when the vehicle didn't jerk or stall. She was definitely getting better at this.

'Look at you, parking like a pro.' Brendon smiled. 'But you didn't answer. Is there no young fellow pining for you in Manchester?'

She might as well give him it straight. 'No and I like it that way.'

She grabbed hold of the flask of tea he had made and the tin of shortbread Enid had brought that very morning to thank her on behalf of the book club.

'Let's have a cup of tea and a biscuit,' she said.

Brendon glanced at her and frowned. 'I'm sorry if I upset you, love. I'm a nosy old bugger, that's all. You've been through a lot these past few weeks. Coming here, starting a new job, putting up with the weather … Ruth and I think you're very brave.'

Jenna sneered. 'Brave? I'm not brave at all.' Brave would be to confront Adrian instead of blocking him, or ask her mother why she chose to believe Adrian over her own daughter. And brave would be to tell Daniel, Brendon and Ruth what she had hidden for so long, even to herself.

She poured two mugs of tea and handed him one. Perhaps she could be brave right now, and tell Brendon about the past. She drank a sip of tea and faced the windscreen although it was raining so hard she couldn't see anything.

'I was in a relationship with a man who not only managed to convince me that I was worthless, but that I was losing my mind too. And do you know what the worst thing about it is?' She shook her head. 'I was stupid enough not to understand what he was doing, and I let him treat me like dirt.'

Brendon glanced at her hand, as if he too could see the white band where Adrian's ring had been. 'This man, was he your husband?'

'No, we weren't married, thank heavens, only engaged.'

She put her mug down on the dashboard. 'From the outside, I had a lovely life. I lived in a beautiful flat with a boyfriend who was good-looking and attentive and had a successful job, who drove a fancy car – the latest Audi sports model with his own personal number plate that he paid a fortune for. But inside it was cold and scary. I was eaten by self-doubt and thought I was becoming mad … And I probably was.'

'He left me just before Christmas for another woman and a job in London, and it's only afterwards that I fully understood what he had done to me.' She hissed a harsh breath, drank a sip of tea and carried on. 'He didn't give me any signs of life for months except to ask for his stuff to be shipped to him, until a few weeks ago.'

Brendon frowned. 'What did he want?'

'Apparently, things didn't work out in London, he's worried about me, says I made a mistake coming here, and he wants me back. So now you know why I don't want to talk about my love life – although in my case, there was no love and not much of a life either,' she finished, forcing a smile.

Brendon's eyes were full of sympathy. 'I understand, lass.'

After a few seconds, he hardened his stare. 'What's the name of the bastard?'

She couldn't help but smile at his fierce expression. 'Adrian – Adrian Jones.' She looked down at her cup, and her hands shook a little.

'The truth is, I'm a bit scared.' There. She'd admitted it. 'I don't want to see him. I don't want to talk to him. Ever. I want this chapter of my life to be over.' She sighed. 'I hope you're not too disappointed in me.'

Brendon gave her shoulder a quick pat. 'Why would I be?

You had the courage to move on and start a new life here. Did you not talk to anyone about him?'

She shrugged. 'I pushed away the few friends I had. Adrian didn't like them. And I was too confused and ashamed to talk to the people at work, even though I now know they'd guessed all was not well and would have helped if I'd asked.'

'What about your mum?'

'I tried, but she didn't believe me. In fact, you're the first person I've told. Please promise you won't say anything …'

Brendon gave her hand a quick pat. 'Don't worry, lass, I'll look after you. We all will.'

'Thank you.' Jenna smiled, feeling much lighter suddenly.

She glanced at the clock on the dashboard, and finished her tea. 'I've been talking for ages and now we're late.'

'It won't take long to get the books ready.'

Brendon pulled out a couple of plastic boxes which he filled with a selection of large print books he pulled from the top shelves. One of the books fell at her feet. 'I hope it didn't hit you.'

'No, I'm all right.' She bent down to pick the book up. *Lady Jane and the Spanish Captain*. Lady Jane … why did the name sound familiar? 'The cover looks intriguing. It's a painting of Mermaid Cove, isn't it? And that castle on the cliff, it looks like the old Dunfiadhaich castle.'

'It is indeed. Rob Ferguson, the author, is a resident at the nursing home, and this book is his pride and joy. He likes to see it from time to time.'

She turned the book over to read the blurb.

"September 1588. The Santa Catalina, a Spanish Armada galleon, is shipwrecked on Mermaid Rocks, off the coast of Arrandale. Among the survivors is Spanish grandee Don Pedro Flores de Valdes who finds

*shelter with his crew at Dunfiadhaich Castle, with tragic
consequences ... One of Arrandale's enduring mysteries
is the fate of the treasure the Santa Catalina was
rumoured to carry, and this is the enigma this book tries
to piece together."*

Jenna looked at Brendon. 'A treasure? Really?'

'Why don't you talk to Rob Ferguson about it?'

'I may just do that. I'll borrow the book too.'

Half an hour later, Brendon pointed to a gentleman
sitting on his own in the nursing home lounge. 'That's Prof
Ferguson over there.'

Armed with the book, Jenna approached the table. 'Good
afternoon. I've only just come across your book and was
wondering if you could tell me a little about the *Santa
Catalina* and the treasure.'

'I would be delighted, my dear.' He gestured for her to
pull out a chair. 'What would you like to know?'

'What kind of treasure did the *Santa Catalina* carry?'

'Around fifteen million ducats in gold coins,' the elderly
professor answered, 'which represented half the Armada
paymaster's chest, as well as religious artefacts and some
very expensive majolica.'

Majolica? Instinctively, Jenna's hand flew to her throat,
but she wasn't wearing the ceramics pendant today. 'And
nobody ever found anything?'

'Not even a coin, and that's not for want of trying.'

'What happened to the Spanish crew?'

Professor Ferguson pulled a face. 'All massacred by
McGregor and his men when they wouldn't say where the
treasure was hidden. But the worst was what happened to
poor Lady Jane – McGregor's child bride. The man was
a jealous brute so when he heard rumours of an affair
between her and Don Pedro he threw her into the dungeon

where he left her to die. She is buried at the McGregor's old burial grounds at the Weeping Stones.'

The stone circle ... Jenna remembered Katrina's drawing, with the man's silhouette in the centre that Ruth MacDonald claimed was Daniel. Perhaps she would go up there one day and visit poor Lady Jane's grave.

'What about Don Pedro? Was he thrown into the dungeon too?'

'Nae – McGregor chopped his head off with his claymore.'

'Oh.' Daniel was right to say that his ancestors were brutes. Jenna shuddered and rose to her feet when the professor yawned. She'd better not keep him any longer. 'Thank you so much for your time. I can't wait to read your book now. Would you mind if we talked about it again some time?'

He looked at her. 'It will be my pleasure, my dear.'

When it was time to leave, Jenna packed away books the residents were returning. Brendon grabbed one box while Jenna slipped her yellow coat on and took the other box. It was still pouring down so Jenna pulled her hood down before crossing the road, smiling as a bedraggled sheep followed her. Suddenly a green sports car appeared, racing towards her. There was the deafening screech of tyres biting the wet tarmac, and she froze as the car veered to one side and hit the sheep.

The engine coughed and spluttered as Daniel drove along the windy road. Droplets of cold rain slid from his hair onto his neck and behind him Sam and Eddie gave out a distinctive pong of wet, mucky dogs. They had all got thoroughly drenched on the hills that afternoon, and all he wanted now was a change of clothes, a cup of tea and a plateful of Miona's stew.

The mobile library appeared after a twist of the road, bright yellow in the murky grey light. Colin MacDonald's Range Rover was there too, and Brendon and the vet were kneeling down in the middle of the road next to a sheep which had blood smeared all over its wet ragged wool. It was one of his. He could just about make out the blue cross on its back.

'Stay here, boys,' he told Sam and Eddie as he parked, pulled his collar up against the driving rain, and got out.

'Colin? Brendon? What's up?' he called.

The vet looked up and shook his head. 'I'm afraid there was nothing I could do for the old chap except putting it to sleep. The injuries from the impact were too severe.'

'What impact?'

Brendon stood up. His white beard glistened with rain drops, and his hair was soaked through. 'Drummond was driving his Jag like a lunatic again. He saw the sheep too late, couldn't avoid it and almost ran Jenna over in the process.'

Daniel glanced around. 'Is she all right? Where is she?'

'She's fine, but she was badly shaken so Drummond said he would drive her back to Carloch and look after her there.'

He glared at Brendon. 'You let her get into his car?'

'I didn't know what else to do. She was upset, and I didn't want her to see the poor animal suffer and be put down, so when Drummond suggested he take her back, I thought it was a good idea … He did promise to drive slowly.'

Daniel drew in a deep breath. 'Right. I'll go to Carloch now. Can you drive the mobile library back to Dana?'

Brendon nodded, and Daniel turned to Colin. 'Thanks for coming out.'

'No worries. I'll ring the NFSCo and ask them to come and collect the sheep.' The vet tidied up his medical bag before standing up. Together they lifted the dead animal and carried it onto the grass verge. Colin then passed a bottle of hand sanitiser around and Daniel hurried back to the Land Rover.

His jaw clenched and his throat tight with frustration and anger, he started his engine. Drummond again! How dare he race around Arrandale and cause mayhem on his land? Why couldn't he stick to his own estate ... even better, why couldn't he disappear from his life altogether?

The rain showed no sign of easing as he drove through Carloch Castle's imposing gates half an hour later. He left the dogs in the car again, and walked to the grand portico sheltering the entrance. Given the state of his clothing, he should probably walk straight to the service entrance and wait in the utility area ... but he didn't.

He rang the bell outside the main entrance and a member of the household staff opened the door, and wrinkled his nose as he looked him up and down. He couldn't however leave him outside. Daniel may look and smell like he'd just rolled in a muddy field, but he was the laird McGregor, so the man showed him in and asked him to wait. It wasn't long before he came back and asked him to follow him to the drawing room.

The place hadn't changed much since Daniel's last visit. He wasn't a violent man but memories of the day he smashed his fist into Drummond's smirking face, breaking his nose and a couple of ugly antique vases in the process, still gave him a great deal of satisfaction.

Drummond was reading – or pretending to – when Daniel walked into the drawing room. He put his book down, uncrossed his legs and looked at Daniel with mock dismay.

'Good grief, man, what happened to you? Did you fall into a dung pit?' He rose to his feet, but didn't offer his hand. Instead, he slipped it into the pocket of his tweed blazer.

'I've been working on the farm while you were driving around like a maniac and running over my livestock,' Daniel retorted.

Drummond sighed. 'Yes, that was unfortunate. I never meant for that to happen, all the more because that blasted sheep made a dent in the bonnet of the Jag and it's going to cost me a few bob to have it put right.'

'That blasted sheep, as you say, had to be put down,' Daniel said through gritted teeth.

Drummond shrugged. 'That's too bad. I'll pay you back, of course. I know that for farmers like you every sheep is valuable.'

'Farmers like me?'

'Farmers who are struggling to make ends meet. Anyone can see that Arrandale is in trouble. You only have to look at the state of your roads.'

'The roads you insist on driving on.'

'Well, you know me. I do like a challenge. Give my accountant a ring and let him know how much I owe you for the sheep.'

Daniel nodded but he clenched his fists hard inside the pockets of his coat. 'I will, don't worry.' He looked around the elegant drawing room. 'I came for Jenna.'

'She's in the library. I gave her a tour earlier and she wanted to stay behind and explore our collection. Literature is a passion we both share – one you couldn't possibly understand since you only read kids' books, farming magazines or the back of cereal packets.'

Daniel didn't reply. Drummond had a point. He didn't read. Not enough time, and no idea where to start …

'Do you really want to drive Jenna home in your old banger?' Drummond asked, lifting an eyebrow.

This time Daniel tensed. 'Never mind what I'm driving. At least I don't go round causing accidents because I drive too fast.'

'And no wonder. I bet your rusty can of beans can't go over forty miles an hour. Why don't we let the lovely lady decide? A good meal in the luxury of Carloch Castle and a drive back in the comfort of my new, top-of-the-range Range Rover, or a wet, miserable drive in your old banger with wet, miserable you at the wheel. Knowing you, you probably have your smelly dogs in the back.'

The door to the drawing room opened, Jenna came in and looked at him, her eyes wide with surprise. 'Daniel ...'

Was it his imagination or she sounded relieved?

'Brendon told me what happened,' he said. 'He said you were upset after the accident. How are you feeling now?'

She tilted her face up, and he gazed into the pure clear blue of her eyes. 'I'm a lot better, thanks.'

'I took good care of you, didn't I?' Drummond interrupted. 'And I promise to drive you home at a sedate pace after we have dinner tonight ... once our unexpected visitor has left'—he glared at Daniel—'which will be very soon now he's reassured about you.'

Daniel ignored him. 'Do you want to stay here or would you rather come back home with me?' he asked Jenna.

'I'd like to go home, please.' Turning to Drummond, she added, 'It was very kind of you to invite me to dinner, but I'm tired and I'd rather go back to the cottage straight away. I am sorry.'

Drummond pulled a face. 'My mother was looking forward to meeting you. She will be dreadfully disappointed.'

Daniel looked at him. 'She'll get over it. Where is your coat, Jenna?'

A few minutes later, he was opening the passenger door

to the Land Rover and helping her climb inside. She turned round to the dogs straight away.

'Hello Eddie. Hi Sam!' The dogs yapped and wagged their tail as she greeted them with a pat on the head and a quick caress behind the ears, seemingly not bothered that they were wet and muddy and smelled of sheep dung.

'Thank you so much for coming,' Jenna said after strapping her seat belt on. 'I suggested calling a taxi but Toby insisted on driving me back later. I didn't know how to refuse without being rude, especially when he invited me for dinner with his mother.'

He glanced at her and smiled. 'So because of me you have now missed the chance to meet the formidable Lady Drummond.'

She returned his smile. 'Is she that terrible?'

'Worse. She has reduced more than one grown man to tears over the years, me included.'

She gave out an incredulous laugh. 'What happened?'

He grimaced. 'She stabbed my foot with her stiletto heel at a function a few years ago. I limped for days.' He didn't say that it was payback for breaking her precious son's nose.

He was about to start the car when his phone rang. It was Iain calling from the farm. 'What's up?' he asked. Iain said that a group of walkers had reported a ewe and her lamb trapped on a narrow ledge on Beinn Dhubh. They alerted the police who had in turn rung the farm since they animals both had blue crosses on their back and were on Arrandale land.

'I'm on my way. Hopefully I can get them to safety,' he told Iain before ending the call and turning to Jenna. 'There's been a change of plan, I'm afraid. I need to rescue a couple of sheep who got into mischief. It shouldn't take too long but it's a bit of a wild drive, and it means I can't take you back to Mermaid's Cottage straight away. Do you want to go back inside'—he gestured to Carloch Castle with his chin—'or should I call a taxi for you?'

'Can I not come with you?' she asked. 'I don't mind the detour.' She gave him a quick smile. 'And I'd rather avoid the formidable Lady Drummond, especially after what you just told me.'

He nodded. 'If you're sure …'

It was still raining and the mist had now descended from the hills so he put his headlights on. The Land Rover rattled over a cattle grid, and up they went on the bumpy hill track towards the mountain pass.

The fog thickened as they reached the end of the road and Beinn Dhubh rose in front of them. As if on cue, Eddie and Sam growled a warning from the back of the Land Rover. 'Here we are,' he said. 'Beinn Dhubh. The Black Mountain.'

'It certainly deserves its name,' Jenna whispered as the fog ripped apart, revealing the dark rock and scree covering the hillside. 'How will you find the sheep?'

'I have an indication where they are, and I'll take the dogs.' He stopped the car, zipped his coat up and turned to her. 'Stay here. There's no need for you to get wet.'

She nodded. 'Daniel?'

His heart missed a beat. It was the first time she called him by his name. His hand already on the door handle, he turned round. 'Yes?'

'This place looks dangerous. Please be careful.'

She looked at him with such concern that all he wanted to do was to lean over and kiss her, and it took all his willpower to open the door. 'I will.'

Chapter Twenty

Jenna watched Daniel walk away, shoulders hunched against the rain, with the two collies by his sides. He went up a steep path and was almost immediately swallowed by the mist. Would he find the two stranded sheep? What if he fell, or got lost?

To stop herself from worrying, she took Professor Ferguson's book out of her bag and read about the circumstances in which the *Santa Catalina* happened to be shipwrecked on Mermaid's Rocks in late September 1588, one of the sixty-eight ships that never made it back to Spain out of the one hundred and thirty that had formed the Spanish fleet.

Ferguson dedicated his first chapter to Arrandale and the clan McGregor, relating episodes of savage warfare and brutal murders between rival clans on Skye and the mainland. The union of Jane Drummond and Murdo McGregor had been an attempt to bring peace between the two clans, but Jane was young and pretty, and Murdo was old, ugly and mean. As she gazed at the photo in the book, Jenna recognised his portrait from the dining room at Dunfiadhaich Farm.

There was no portrait of Jane herself, so Jenna used her imagination and pictured a vivacious girl with long red hair and rosy cheeks, a girl dreaming of a kind and dashing lover and lumbered with a brutish old husband ...

The second chapter explained how villagers from Dana lit great bonfires on the beaches to lure the passing Spanish ships and loot them, like so many had done in Ireland and the West coast of Scotland. They must have thought they had struck gold when the *Santa Catalina* crashed against

Mermaid's Rocks that night, and yet they never laid a hand on the treasure it carried. According to contemporary reports, Don Pedro and his men managed to salvage and hide most of their hoard before the ship sank – where, was the burning question.

By the time Jenna finished the second chapter, the light was noticeably dimmer and the air had become chilly in the Land Rover. It was almost an hour since Daniel had left, and she was getting cold and stiff. She lifted her eyes from the book and worry fluttered in her chest once again as she glanced at the bleak and damp landscape partly shrouded in fog.

She got out of the car, closed the door and pulled her hood down before taking a few steps on the path Daniel had taken earlier to go up the hill. Digging her hands into the pockets of her coat, she looked at the mountainside for any sign of Daniel or the collies. The mist moved, gathered and thickened in gullies and then tore away on sharp rocks. The air smelled of minerals and rain, damp soil and vegetation, with a sharp salty tang from the sea Daniel said was close by but which remained hidden by the fog.

The mist shifted again and this time she spotted Sam and Eddie, black and white dots against the scree, and then she saw Daniel. He was on a ledge halfway up the mountain, and Jenna could just about make out two sheep next to him. Daniel knelt down, grabbed hold of the smallest sheep and lifted it up before dangling him off the ledge. Incredibly, the animal landed on its feet. Daniel now turned to the larger sheep. Surely that one was far too big for him to pick up …

He didn't have to. When it saw the lamb run away, the ewe tottered towards the edge and Daniel only had to nudge it for it to jump off. She was soon reunited with the lamb and they both scarpered off. Daniel stood up and jumped too, but he lost his balance, rolled down the slope, and came to a brutal halt as he hit a craggy rock.

Jenna's heart lurched. Was he dead? Injured? But he clambered to his feet and went down the slope with the two dogs, and she ran up the path to meet him. The dogs came down first, and jumped at her legs, leaving wet and filthy paw prints all over her trousers.

'Good boys, you were fantastic up there.' They were wet and muddy, but it didn't matter.

'You're drenched. You should have stayed in the car,' Daniel said as he came nearer.

She looked up. His dark hair was soaked, he had deep scratches on his cheek and his coat and trousers were ripped in places from his tumble down the hillside, but she only saw his eyes, bright and blue in the dim and murky light. So many conflicting feelings raged inside her she wasn't even sure she could breathe, let alone speak.

'I was worried … You were gone such a long time,' she said at last. 'I thought you were going to break your neck up there.'

He nodded. 'It was a wee bit hairy, but it ended up well for everybody. Well, almost.' He glanced down, and now she saw that his right hand was bleeding.

'You're hurt!'

'It's only a scratch.' But he winced and his shoulders were stiff as he walked. 'Let's get back to the car. I have a first aid box in the boot.'

He asked her to get the box and to open it, all the time holding his hand in his lap partly covered by his coat, jaw clenched, as if he was angry at the weather, the mountain, and above all, at himself.

Jenna did a quick inventory of the depleted contents of the box. 'There's one antiseptic wipe, some gauze and a roll of bandage that looks pretty old, that's all.'

'It will have to do. I keep forgetting to replace the stuff I use.' He gave her a quick smile. 'You'd better turn round if you're squeamish. I'm afraid my hand is rather a mess.'

'I'll help. You can't do much with one hand.' She unrolled the bandage and took the backing off the sticky plaster that would hold it in place then tore open the wipe wrapper and unfolded it. 'Please turn your hand over.'

It wasn't a scratch, and she repressed a gasp when she saw the torn skin, and the deep, bleeding gash slicing the palm of his hand. 'I think you may need stitches.'

He only grunted. 'How clumsy of me to get injured like that ... Katrina would no doubt compare me to that Zonk McPurple monster again,' he said, probably to lighten the mood as she cleaned some of the blood away. 'Except that I wasn't chasing clouds or happy dreams but sheep, as usual.'

'I didn't think you would manage it.'

'Can I be honest with you?' He looked up and gave her one of his heart-stopping blue gazes. 'Neither did I.'

She swallowed hard, and looked down again. 'Ah ... There, I can't really do any more. I'll wrap your hand now, but ...' She bit her lip. 'I don't think you'll be able to drive.'

He frowned. 'No. You're right. You'd better do it.'

'Me?'

He must have seen the panic on her face because he smiled. 'If you can drive Buttercup, then you can drive this old thing. Come on, let's switch places.'

He was right. There was no one else to help. Once she was behind the wheel he gave her some advice about starting the car. 'Go easy when you release the clutch.'

After two failed attempts when the Land Rover jerked and stalled, they were finally on the road. 'We'll have to go down the cliff road. It's quite steep. Keep your foot on the brake.'

Quite steep? She hardly breathed as the road plunged

into an abyss of sea fog. The headlights hardly made a dent in the fog, and she couldn't see more than two feet ahead. If Daniel was getting impatient with her crawling down that scary, vertiginous mountain road he was hiding it well.

'You're doing great,' he said. 'Not too far now. Keep the car in the middle of the road ...' As if she had any idea where that was!

Suddenly the engine made an ominous rattling sound and died. The car stopped. Jenna pulled the handbrake up, and looked at Daniel.

'What happened? Did I do anything wrong?'

'Damn. Damn. Damn,' he muttered. 'Of all the places, of all the times it could happen, it had to be here and now.'

He looked at her. 'The engine has been playing up. I'll get my toolbox and take a look at it, but it won't be easy with one hand out of action.'

Half an hour later, he admitted defeat and got back into the car. His dressing was now wet from the rain and stained with engine oil.

'There's a cottage at the bottom of the road which I rent out to university students for their research and ecological surveys. Let's see if they're home and can give us a lift back.'

Jenna took her handbag, zipped her coat up, and they set off on the road. Her feet were cold and wet and slid in her muddy pumps, and she was shivering by the time the little white cottage appeared like a ghost out of the mist.

There were lights at the window, but no car outside.

Daniel knocked, and a gangly young man with a shaggy beard, ginger hair twisted in a man bun and a puzzled expression on his freckled face opened the door. 'Holy Basil!' he gasped. 'You two almost gave me a heart attack.'

Daniel explained about the car breaking down, and the young man opened the door wide. 'Come in. You look as if you could do with a hot drink and a rest.'

'Thanks. That would be great.' Daniel gestured to Sam and Eddie. 'What about the dogs? Can we let them in too? They'll stay in the porch.'

The young man nodded. 'Sure. There's an old blanket they can lie on.'

Jenna and Daniel followed him into a very untidy living room. Clothes, books, and papers were strewn around, and a very distinctive smell of wet socks hung in the air.

'I'm sorry for the mess. I wasn't expecting any visitors.' The young man picked up a handful of tee shirts, socks and jeans from the sofa, gathered them in his arms and stood there, eyes darting around the room as if looking for the best place to hide them, before throwing them in an untidy pile on one of the armchairs.

'I'll make you a cup of tea – if I can find any clean cups, that is.'

Daniel smiled, and laughter danced in his eyes as the student dashed out of the room. 'If the kitchen is in the same state, we may be here a while. I suggest we sit down.'

He gestured to the small and rather battered sofa. Jenna glanced at some of the books and reports littering the carpet. They all seemed to have something to do with research and marine biology ... except one. It was Professor Ferguson's book about Lady Jane and the *Santa Catalina*. She bent down to pick it up and showed Daniel.

'What a coincidence! I found that very same book in Buttercup this afternoon and talked to the author at the nursing home. The story of the lost *Santa Catalina*'s treasure is fascinating.'

'Fascinating, and deadly,' Daniel whispered as if he was talking to himself.

The student came back, holding two mugs filled to the brim with steaming hot tea that he put on the carpet in front of Daniel and Jenna. 'There you are. I'm vegan so I put soya milk in your tea. I hope you don't mind.'

He sat on the floor near the fire. 'I'm Hamish, by the way, Hamish Forbes. I'm doing a PhD in marine biology at Glasgow Uni, as you can probably guess from the books.'

'I'm Daniel McGregor, and this is Jenna Palmer,' Daniel said.

The boy gasped and opened his eyes wide in shock. 'Daniel McGregor? *The* Daniel McGregor? Then you are ...'

'Your landlord, that's right,' he said quickly before the young man could say anything else.

'Holy Basil ... If I had known you were coming, I would have tidied up, but Ben – that's Ben Kershaw, the student I'm sharing the cottage with, went back to Glasgow for a meeting this morning and I've been busy reading and doing stuff for my next assignment.'

'Don't worry. I'm not checking up on your housework skills. We need a lift back to Dana and I was hoping you could help us out.'

Hamish pulled a face. 'I'm sorry, man. I don't have a car and Ben won't be back until tomorrow afternoon. You can't even call a taxi or anyone since as you know there's no landline and no mobile signal here.'

He looked at Daniel's bandaged hand and the blood that had seeped through the layers of wet, dirty gauze. 'You're hurt. How bad is it?'

Daniel shrugged. 'Not too bad.'

Typical man, Jenna thought. He'd rather suffer in silence than admit he was in pain. 'I think he needs stitches,' she said.

Hamish's face lit up. 'Then I can help. I trained as a first-aider. One could even say I'm as good a nurse as you'll ever get ... I'll sort you out in no time, man. Let me get my things. I'm in charge of first aid here, and with all the diving and the climbing we do, our kit is well stocked.'

'That's brilliant,' Jenna said as Hamish rose to his feet and disappeared into another room. She looked at Daniel. 'Isn't it just?'

'If you say so …' His face had turned a sickly shade of grey.

Was he scared? Was that big, strong man who thought nothing about climbing up and down almost vertical mountain slopes for a couple of sheep and who captained a lifeboat in stormy seas, scared of having his hand stitched up? Her heart softened and turned to mush at the thought.

'It will be all right, don't worry,' she whispered.

'Easy for you to say,' he whispered back. 'I only have his word that he knows what he's doing. Perhaps I should ask him to produce his first aid certificate. He could be making it all up and for all I know the closest he's ever been to a needle is to sew a button or darn his socks.'

She couldn't help but laugh. 'He looks like a very nice young man, but not the kind who'd be bothered mending his socks. However, I hope he finds a clean spot to stitch you up in. The place is a biological hazard.'

This time his lips quirked into a smile and a bit of colour came back to his cheeks. 'Thanks for that reassuring comment.'

They sipped their tea in silence and Hamish came back with a green box, a large bottle of disinfectant and a tea towel he unfolded and spread out on the dining table. 'I'm ready,' he called a few moments later.

'That makes one of us,' Daniel muttered. He sighed and gave her a meaningful glance before finishing his tea and getting up. 'Wish me luck.'

Chapter Twenty-One

'We're done. How are you feeling, man?' Hamish smiled as he pushed a bottle of whisky and two tumblers across the table. 'I reckon we both deserve a dram or two to recover. I'm sorry the needle slipped earlier. It's been a while since I had to do this and I was a wee bit nervous.'

'You don't say …' Daniel muttered between gritted teeth. It felt like the student had well and truly butchered his hand. Heavens, the stinging and the burning had even brought tears to his eyes … He hoped neither Hamish nor Jenna had noticed.

He poured whisky out for the both of them and drank the contents of his tumbler up in one big gulp.

Having tidied up his first aid box, the student now leaned back on his chair to sip his whisky. 'I think you two had better stop over tonight. There's no way you can walk to Glendale Farm in this weather. It's the nearest place where you could find a phone or someone who could take you home. Jenna looks shattered, and you need to keep your hand dry.'

Daniel had been thinking along the same lines. He didn't fancy walking the six miles or so to the next farm to phone Iain and ask him to pick him and Jenna up, especially since Hamish's bungled stitching job had left him a little shaky.

Iain and Miona wouldn't be unduly worried if he didn't come home. He sometimes stayed out and slept in a bothy or camped out in the wild when he was out in the hills, but Katrina would miss her bedtime story. She was obsessed with those silly Zonk McPurple tales and he'd had to read one or two every single evening that week.

'It's really nice of you to offer,' Jenna said to Hamish. 'Are you sure we won't be in your way?'

The young man laughed. 'I'll be glad of the company, and honoured to spend an evening with one of my teenage heroes. Ben will be dead jealous when he comes back and finds out you stayed over ... and that I stitched your hand too!'

He smiled as he looked at Daniel, and Jenna glanced at each of the men in turn, frowning. No doubt she was wondering what Hamish was talking about, but he didn't want to get into it now – not ever.

'You must be hungry,' Hamish said. 'Shall I make us something to eat? It won't be fancy – frozen chips and baked beans.'

'It's fine with me,' Daniel said, perking up at the prospect of a hot meal.

Hamish lent them both some dry clothes to change into, and soon the three of them sat in the kitchen with their plates piled high with chunky chips and baked beans, and glasses of red wine in front of them. Jenna's cheeks were pink, her eyes sparkly and she kept smiling.

Daniel hadn't seen her so relaxed before. Her blonde hair curled as it dried in the heat of the kitchen and framed her face like a halo. Hamish had given her a khaki sweatshirt and some sweatpants far too big for her but she looked sexy as hell, and Daniel had to force himself to stop gazing at the tantalising glimpses of her pale skin and delicate collar bones every time the sweatshirt slipped off her shoulder.

He too had changed into an old jumper and a pair of the biggest shorts Hamish could find at the bottom of his wardrobe, because if they were roughly the same height, the young man was as thin as a rake. Thankfully the shorts had an elasticated waist which meant he could enjoy the food and the wine now that the pain in his hand had reduced to dull throbbing thanks to a couple of painkillers.

They had toasted to the mountains, to Skye and Arrandale, and Hamish opened another bottle of wine. His freckled face was bright red as he raised his glass and smiled at Daniel. 'This time, I propose a toast to the great Daniel McGregor himself. Man, I can tell you that you and your brother have been my inspiration for years. I read all about your diving exploits. You were the ones who inspired me to get into diving … I was gutted when you announced that you were giving it all up.'

Daniel's fingers tightened around his glass but he forced a deep breath down. 'Well … thanks,' he said in a hoarse voice.

'Of course I completely understood why you didn't want to dive again after what happened to your brother,' Hamish added.

Jenna looked at him from across the table. She wasn't smiling any longer. Her eyes were soft and filled with kindness, sympathy, and questions too … He never talked about Hugh's accident. Would he be able to tell her what happened? Or rather, give her the official version of events leading to Hugh's death? The truth was another matter.

He nodded. 'Thanks, Hamish, but we weren't heroes at all, especially not me. I only ever dived for fun.'

'Don't you miss it – being down there?' Hamish asked after a few moments of silence.

'Sometimes … but I have responsibilities.' He had the estate to look after, and more importantly, he had Katrina. 'The thing is, I was never as driven as Hugh about shipwreck diving. He was determined to find the *Santa Catalina* treasure.'

Jenna gasped. 'You were looking for the Spanish treasure?'

He looked at her, and answered dismissively, 'Us and everybody else around here. When we were kids we spent every holiday scuba diving, and as we got older we undertook diving proficiency qualifications and ventured further afield.'

'You were legends, man – proper legends, and Shannon O'Keeffe as well.' Hamish carried on, oblivious to Daniel's darkening mood. 'She was a babe too ... if you don't mind me saying.'

Daniel let out a non-committal grunt and looked away. Born and brought up in Florida, Shannon was gorgeous, funny and clever, and followed her maritime archaeologist father around the globe. The man had nicknamed her "the Siren" because she swam like a fish – a beautiful, deadly one, like those lion fish that hypnotise you by waving their colourful fins before stabbing you with a venomous spike, straight into the heart.

'Her dad came over with a team from Florida University to do some research on Skye, didn't he? That's how you met.'

Daniel let out another grunt. Michael O'Keeffe and his team had stayed a few weeks in Arrandale, with Shannon tagging along, but when they left at the end of their mission, Shannon had stayed. Hugh was in London at the time, and only met her when he came back a few weeks later ... and the rest was history.

Hamish finished his wine, and poured himself another glass. 'Wasn't she a singer, too?'

Once again he felt Jenna's eyes on him, and he forced a smile. 'Yes, Shannon had a great voice.' And a talent for making you believe she was singing for you and only you ...

'Where is she now?' Hamish asked. 'Has she gone back to Florida?'

'Hmm ...' Daniel drank a sip of wine, but didn't

elaborate. Perhaps Hamish would take the hint and drop the subject.

He didn't. 'She left her kid with you, didn't she? Is it because she's busy diving with her dad?'

Daniel drank another sip of wine, aware of Jenna looking at him and frowning. 'Aye.' He cleared his throat. 'I don't like to talk about the past, Hamish. Can we drop the subject?'

Hamish shook his head and sighed. 'Sorry, man. I only wanted you to know how much I admire you, and not only for the diving. You go out with the lifeboat and that takes guts.'

Daniel's throat tightened. 'I wasn't able to save Hugh, though.'

Nobody talked for a while as they sipped their wine. Outside the rain still lashed against the windows. Jenna got up and gathered the dirty plates which she put in the sink. 'I'll do the washing up. It's only fair since you cooked for us and are kind enough to put us up tonight.'

Hamish nodded enthusiastically and pointed to the dirty plates and bowls piled up on the worktops. 'Thanks ... As you can see, doing the dishes isn't my forte.'

He turned to Daniel. 'I'll take the dogs out for a walk so that you don't have to get your dressing wet. If you don't mind me saying, you look shattered. You should go to bed. I changed the sheets on both twin beds and you'll be nice and cosy if you push the beds together. I'll kip on the sofa.'

'No, *I'll* sleep on the sofa,' Jenna said quickly, her face red. 'It makes more sense to me to leave you two men together.'

Hamish looked at Daniel and Jenna in surprise. 'But I thought you two were an item.'

Jenna's face turned a deeper shade of red. 'Daniel is my boss, that's all.'

Why did her heartfelt dismissal feel like a slap in the face? Of course he was her boss. What else could she have said?

Hamish frowned as he looked between Daniel and Jenna. 'No worries. Sorry I got the wrong idea. I'll take the dogs out now.'

Daniel stood up. 'I'll come to the front door with you. They may need a bit of encouragement to go out again, especially in this weather.'

Jenna was doing the washing-up when he returned to the kitchen.

'Sorry I can't help,' he said, 'but I don't want to risk messing up my bandage and give Hamish an excuse to come anywhere near me with his first aid kit again. He did enough damage the first time round.'

She turned round and smiled. 'Was it that bad?'

He pulled a face. 'Aye … I apologise for ruining your evening, by the way. You would have been far better off staying with Drummond at Carloch and letting him drive you home tonight.'

He looked down at her feet. Hamish had lent her a pair of thick woolly socks far too big for her while her shoes were drying near the gas fire.

'You wouldn't have had to walk in the rain and ruin your shoes. You'd have eaten a much better meal than beans and frozen chips, and you would be sleeping at Mermaid's Cottage tonight, not on a scruffy student's sofa, wearing a scruffy student's clothes.'

Jenna smiled. 'You don't have to apologise. It was my decision to stay with you. I don't mind the sofa or the clothes. The chips and beans were delicious. And I like Hamish. He is a lovely young man.'

Curly strands of hair fell across her face. She pushed them back with a hand covered in washing-up liquid suds, leaving a blob of foam on her cheek.

He stepped closer, until he was within touching distance. 'You've got bubbles on your face. There …'

She tilted her face up as he lifted his hand and brushed the foam with his index finger. Her skin was soft, her pulse beat in the small hollow at the base of her throat … And desire shot through him, electrifying.

He withdrew his hand, shocked by the brutal, primal ache in his body – the overwhelming need to kiss and take her in his arms. Her cheeks were pink, her eyes soft and slightly unfocussed, her lips parted slightly, as if she was expecting a kiss. He couldn't. He mustn't. His life was messed up enough as it was, and there was Katrina to consider …

'I'm going out. I want to see how Hamish is managing with the dogs. They can be a bit of a handful.'

Anything, even getting soaked or having Hamish stitch him up again would be better than the torture of staying close to Jenna and being unable to touch her, take her in his arms and kiss her until he forgot everything.

Chapter Twenty-Two

As soon as the front door banged shut, Jenna gripped the edges of the worktop and let out a trembling breath. Could one actually crumble into a pile of dust from mortification? If so, now would be a good time.

Had she imagined it all – the way his jaw hardened, his eyes darkened and his finger lingered on her cheek? Of course, she had, and it wasn't the first time either. She was the only one feeling that tingling, simmering, irresistible attraction, and she was completely deluded if she believed that Daniel would take her in his arms and kiss her. She could only hope that he hadn't seen how badly she wanted him to.

She finished the dishes, stacked them up in the plastic drainer at the side of the sink, and wiped her hands on a tea towel as Hamish walked into the kitchen, his coat dripping wet and his boots muddy. He was alone.

'Holy Basil, what a night!' His face was red and raw from the wind and the rain.

He opened the utility door onto a small room packed with boxes of diving equipment and several wetsuits hanging from pegs like human shells, kicked his boots off and hung his coat up to dry, and padded back into the kitchen in his socks. 'Daniel stayed outside with the dogs. He said he wanted to walk down the hill to try and get a signal for his phone.'

His shoulders sagged a little. 'I think he wanted some time alone. I upset him, going on about his brother the way I did.'

He extracted a rubber band from his jeans pocket and tied his wet hair into a ponytail. 'The thing is, I got a bit overexcited when you two turned up at the door and I realised who he was. Daniel and his brother were considered legends amongst divers in Scotland, and beyond.'

'Was Shannon a legend too?' she asked, aware of the tightening of her voice and the unwelcome nip of jealousy to her heart. Why should she even care about Shannon ... or about the way Daniel's eyes clouded and his voice deepened when he mentioned her name?

Hamish nodded. 'Like I said, Shannon was a babe – at least according to the photos and the videos Hugh posted online. She was a great diver too – so good she was called "the Siren". It's no wonder since she'd grown up travelling around the world with her dad.'

Siren ... what an appropriate nickname for a beautiful woman, who not only dived like a pro but sang beautifully too. It also explained why Katrina said that her mum was a mermaid.

'Hugh's death must have been traumatic for her,' Hamish carried on. 'Their kid was only young when it happened.'

Jenna didn't comment. She could understand why Shannon wouldn't want to live in Arrandale, but not that she had seemingly abandoned Katrina. Hugh's death should have made her cling even more tightly to their precious daughter. Then again, grief affected people in different ways, and who was she to judge? On the other hand, there was that allegation Toby Drummond had made about Daniel stopping the woman from seeing her daughter ...

'Ben and I have been looking into the mystery of the *Santa Catalina*'s treasure,' Hamish carried on. 'Of course, many have tried and failed before us, but we're going to search for it in our spare time.'

'Was the *Santa Catalina* the reason why Shannon and her father came here originally?' Jenna couldn't help being curious.

Hamish nodded. 'Her father was doing research on lost Armada ships. He and his team searched the wreck and the area around Mermaid's Rocks for several weeks but they found nothing apart from the usual lead bullets and ingots, and a few housekeeping items such as pewter plates and goblets, candelabras and pieces of muskets ... and the odd broken piece of majolica pottery.'

She frowned. 'Majolica ...' Professor Ferguson did write about majolica in his book.

'The ship was carrying some very expensive pieces – a dinner service fit for a king, apparently,' Hamish said.

'I see ...' A strange idea formed in her mind. Could the piece of majolica she found on the beach come from the *Santa Catalina*? She dismissed the thought straight way. It was a silly idea.

'Why did Hugh go back to the wreck if Michael O'Keeffe's search turned out nothing of interest?'

Hamish shook his head. 'I have no idea. He went there alone and without telling anyone – a mistake no experienced diver should ever make.'

'Who found him?' But the moment she said the words, she realised she already knew the answer. 'It was Daniel, wasn't it?'

Hamish sighed. 'He pulled his brother's body back up to the surface and onto his dinghy, and brought him back to Dana.'

No wonder Daniel hadn't dived since. It also explained why he looked distressed as the ferry sailed past Mermaid's Rocks on the way to Mallaig the other day.

'Anyway, about the treasure. We've been piecing old stories and testimonies together, but haven't come up with any new lead yet. Both Ben and I think Lady Jane knew where Don Pedro had hidden it.'

The front door opened and slammed shut, the dogs

yapped, and Daniel walked in. He was wet through, raindrops slid down his hair onto his face, and ran down his coat so that a puddle soon grew at his feet.

He shrugged the coat off, unlaced his boots and took them off without giving her even a glance. 'Would you have an old towel I could use to dry the dogs? They need a good rub down,' he asked Hamish.

Hamish laughed and pointed at Daniel's drenched hair. 'They're not the only ones.' He disappeared into the utility, and came back with a bath towel and a smaller one he gave Daniel. 'That one's for you.'

'Thanks.' Daniel wiped his face, his neck and gave his hair a quick rub dry, leaving it all spiked up.

'You're welcome. Any luck in getting a signal?'

Daniel shook his head. 'No. I'm afraid you're stuck with us tonight.'

'I told you. It's no bother.'

While Daniel was seeing to the dogs, Hamish fetched his first aid box and laid out the bottle of disinfectant, some cotton wool and a pack of dressings on the table. When Daniel walked back in, he gave the medical supplies a wary glance. 'What's all this for?'

'I need to redo your dressing. It's wet and you don't want the wound to get infected. Come on, man, take a seat and I'll sort you out.'

Daniel pulled a resigned face and sat down, and Jenna couldn't help but smile.

'I could do with a coffee,' she said in a light-hearted voice as she flicked the kettle on. 'Would you guys like one too?'

'Yes, please, Jen. You could even sneak in a dram or two of whisky.' Hamish gestured to the bottle of Talisker on the worktop.

Daniel looked at her for the first time since coming back

from his walk. 'Thank you. It's exactly what I need to cope with Hamish's ministrations.'

She smiled. 'What? The coffee or the whisky?'

'Both, although I may need more whisky than coffee in that mug.' Daniel smiled back.

While she spooned instant granules into three mugs, poured hot water and added generous glugs of whisky to the men's drinks, Hamish sorted out Daniel's dressing. He didn't take long, and they soon took their mugs into the living room. Hamish sat on the only free armchair with his long legs stretched in front of him and the floppy tip of his woolly socks dangling from his toes. The other chair was still covered with a messy pile of clothing, so Daniel and Jenna had to squeeze together on the tiny sofa again. It sagged in the middle, so they kept sliding down within touching distance of each other.

'Sorry.' They spoke at the same time, tried to shuffle away from each other, but it was like fighting a losing battle.

The men talked about Hamish's studies and the ecosystem of the area, and what should be done to preserve it, and Jenna relaxed against the back of the sofa and sipped her drink. Safe and warm next to Daniel, her body softened and mellowed as she listened to their deep, quiet voices. She finished her drink, rested her empty mug on her lap and closed her eyes, and didn't even notice when she drifted to sleep.

Jenna's head pressed lightly against his shoulder. The feel of her body next to his was intoxicating, and scents from her hair and skin filled his senses, making his head spin as if he was drunk.

'It looks like Jenna has fallen asleep,' Hamish remarked with a smile.

'She had a hard day.' His chest tightened at the thought

of the incident with Drummond, and of what he had put the young woman through that afternoon – the detour via Beinn Dhubh, the drive in the fog and his car breaking down, followed by the long trek in the pouring rain. And now she had to wear Hamish's clothes and stay in an old and uncomfortable cottage.

All that because he was too proud to leave her at Carloch Castle with Drummond! She would have been far better there. Tonight was definitely not the kind of evening that would impress a woman – not that he wanted to impress her, of course. And because of Hamish she now knew about Hugh … and Shannon.

'I'd better take her to the bedroom. I know she said she wanted to sleep on the sofa, but it's hardly comfortable enough, and she deserves a good night's sleep after today's events.'

He rose to his feet and scooped Jenna up in his arms, careful not to wake her up. 'Which one is Ben's bed?' he asked Hamish who followed him as he carried her to the bedroom. 'I'll take the sofa, so you can sleep in your own bed tonight.'

Hamish pushed the bedroom door open and switched the light on.

'No way, man. You'll both stay here, I'll crash on the couch, and I don't even want to hear a word of protest.' He pointed at the beds that he'd pushed together so that they looked like a double bed. 'Shall I … you know … pull them apart since you're not … ahem … together?'

'I'll do it later.' The painkillers had long since worn off and pain stabbed and twisted in his hand. Right now Daniel needed to put Jenna down.

He lowered her gently to the bed. She'd lost one of her socks so he pulled the other one off too before covering her with the brightly coloured superhero duvet, making a mental note to order new bedclothes for the cottage. These were more suited to kids than grown-up students.

Jenna didn't open her eyes, didn't make a sound. She must be exhausted. Suddenly he was bone-tired too, and couldn't think of anything else but going to bed .

'Right, I'll leave you two alone, then,' Hamish said. 'Good night.'

'Thanks, Hamish. You've been great'—he glanced at his bandaged hand and made a pretend grimace—'even though you'd make a rubbish nurse.'

Hamish laughed softly and closed the door, and Daniel switched off the light and pulled his bed away from Jenna's, but with only one hand he hardly managed a few centimetres. It would have to do. The young woman was fast asleep, and he would make sure he got up before her the following morning. He was always up at dawn anyway.

It almost made him smile that for the first time in years he shared a bedroom with a woman, she should be completely oblivious. So much for his power of seduction ...

Hamish banged about a bit in the kitchen, then in the bathroom. Then the lights went off, the night grew dark and the house became quiet, except for the rain lashing at the windows.

Daniel must have drifted to sleep because he was suddenly awakened by sounds of crying. His eyes flew open, and he lifted himself on his elbow and looked at Jenna, but she was facing the other way and as there was no moonlight he could hardly see the outline of her body under the duvet.

'Jenna? What's up?' he called softly.

She didn't answer but carried on sobbing. What should he do? Was she even awake? He called again, and when there was no reply he reached out, and touched her shoulder. 'Jenna, are you having a nightmare?' It was a silly question, of course. If she was, she would hardly reply.

She was talking now, between gasps. 'No … not in there. I don't like it in there. It's too dark. You know I'm scared in the dark … Please, Adrian. It's not my fault. Not my fault …' This was followed by a long, anguished cry that made Daniel clench his jaw and his heart grow cold.

'It's dark … and it hurts,' she carried on in a small voice. 'You're hurting me …'

He had no idea what this was about – if it was a memory or a random dream, but it was clear that she was in pain and he'd be damned if he let her suffer. He shuffled closer to her, slipped his arm under her and pulled her against him, so that her head rested on his chest. With one hand he patted her back, the way he patted Katrina's when she was upset. With the other hand he stroked her hair while making shushing sounds to calm her down.

It seemed to work. After a few minutes the sobs became less frequent and her whimpering died down, replaced once again by regular breathing. It felt strange holding her – strange, but completely right. Her hair was silky and smelled of flowers and rain as it tickled his throat … Her body felt shapely and so deliciously feminine that primitive feelings swelled and surged inside him. Desire, of course, so strong it made his whole body hard. But also the need to protect the woman who lay so small and soft in his arms, find out who that guy she was crying about was and sort him out for causing her pain.

He hissed a breath. She was quiet now … It was time he disentangled himself.

He was about to move away when her fingers gripped his shirt, and she moulded herself more closely to him. Of course, she didn't realise what she was doing, she didn't even know she was in his arms, but the last thing he wanted to do now she'd calmed down was to wake her, so he remained still, and hardly dared breathe.

He'd wait until he was sure she was fast asleep again then carefully extricate himself. After all, a few more minutes wouldn't do any harm …

Chapter Twenty-Three

She was safe and warm, wrapped in a powerful male embrace and lying on top of a broad, hard chest. A strong, regular heartbeat radiated inside her. Her nose rubbed against soft fabric smelling ever so faintly of salt, rain and sandalwood. She stretched her legs, her foot rubbed against a hairy calf and she burrowed in the man's arms with a hum of pleasure …

Awareness suddenly pierced though the fog of sleep. Whose arms were these? Whose leg were her bare toes stroking, and whose heart beat next to her cheek? This was far too real to be a dream.

Her eyes flicked open and her gaze trailed upwards to a square jaw covered with dark stubble. Her heart missed a beat as she stared at the man who was holding her so tightly in the morning sunlight filtering through the curtains. Daniel … What was she doing sprawled all over him?

Holding her breath, she lifted his hand off her waist very slowly and put it down on the bedcovers, but his other arm was still wrapped around her shoulders, effectively pinning her to him. Perhaps if she wriggled out of his grasp, moved over his body and slumped down to the other side of the bed, she could sneak out of the room without waking him.

So she edged over him, one careful inch at a time, hardly daring to breathe, and was about to finally slide off him when he muttered something in his sleep, grabbed hold of her and put her back in her exact previous position she'd been in at the start, except that this time, after encircling her in his arms once again, he slid one hand down her back and firmly cupped her bottom.

Her skin tingled all over; heat exploded inside her and

her blood fizzed in a confusing array of sensations. 'No … no …' she whispered. This was not good. Not good at all. This time there was nothing to do but to wake him up before things got out of hand.

'Daniel, I'm sorry. Please let go. I want to get up,' she started in a soft voice, but he only hummed as his arms tightened around her and his hand moved and stroked her bottom in the most delicious, arousing way.

Flushed and hot, she panicked and shouted, 'Wake up!'

This time he opened his eyes and for a second or two it wasn't only his arms that pinned her to him, but his intense, searing glare too.

'Jenna? What …? Damn!' Immediately he snatched his hands off her, looking as embarrassed as she was.

Her face burning and her pulse racing she gave him a faint smile.

'It's all right. I'll get up now. If I could just … Oh dear, I'm stuck.' She tried to slide to the other side of the bed, but her legs were entangled in the bedcovers and she only managed to rub her body clumsily against his. The hard tips of her breasts tingled as they pressed against his chest, and brought even more heat to her face.

She heard his sharp intake of breath. 'Let me help …' He put his hands on either sides of her waist, picked her up and lifted her off him before setting her on her feet by the side of the bed.

'Thanks.' What could she say now? She couldn't very well run out of the room without acknowledging the fact they had slept in the same bed, even if she didn't have any recollection of the night's events … and he didn't either, by the look of complete shock on his face. And yet, however awkward it had been to wake up in his arms, it had felt good – far too good, in fact – and somehow like the most natural thing in the world.

She bit her lip. 'Err ... How is your hand?' she asked, when what she really wanted to know was how she ended up in bed with him.

He looked down at his bandaged hand and shrugged. 'I'll live.'

He sat up and pulled the duvet right up to his chin. His dark hair was tousled, lines of tiredness bracketed either side of his mouth and his body seemed far too big for the single bed under the childish superhero duvet.

'Listen, Jenna, I'm sorry for ...' He made a wide gesture with his arms and sighed. 'Please let me explain, but first I can assure you that I didn't mean ... I don't make a habit of sleeping with women.'

He hissed an annoyed breath, and closed his eyes for a second. 'What I mean is that you were having a nightmare. I tried to wake you but you were upset so I held you to calm you down. It was only going to be for a few minutes but I must have fallen asleep and somehow we stayed ... together all night.'

'I had a nightmare?'

He nodded.

She remembered now. She'd had her usual dream about Adrian coming back from work and getting annoyed because she bought the brand of curry sauce he claims gives him hives and he says she's done it on purpose; he gets angry, grabs her arm and twists it behind her back before pushing her into the wardrobe and turning the light off. Then she gets those horrible cramps in her chest and it's so dark, there's no air and she can't breathe but there's nothing she can do except wait.

The blood left her face and she felt suddenly faint. 'Did I say anything?' Her nightmares usually felt so real she always woke up sobbing with pain, as if Adrian's anger vibrated around her and fear coated her heart with ice, and she was back at the flat, looking into his cold grey eyes ...

Daniel hesitated, and broke eye contact for a second. 'Hmm ... No ... but you were crying quite a lot.'

She narrowed her eyes and clenched her fists hard. How long would she be plagued by the all too real nightmares? She could pummel the wall with frustration. 'And you're sure I didn't speak?'

When he nodded again, her relief was so great she sagged against the wall and let out a long breath. She slowly stretched her fingers and managed a smile for Daniel, who was now looking at her with concern. It must have been awkward for him when she cried out in her sleep, and yet he hadn't hesitated to take her in his arms.

Her heart filled with gratitude and warmth as tears gathered in her eyes. 'You were very kind to comfort me. Thank you.'

'Don't mention it.' He glanced at the window and the sunshine streaming through the gap in the curtains. 'It must be late. I'd better set off for Glendale without delay. I'll come back for you as soon as I have a lift.'

'I'll come with you. I don't want to impose on Hamish any longer.'

'But your shoes are ruined.'

'They'll be fine.' She walked to the window and pulled the curtains open and gasped in delight. 'Look at this gorgeous view!'

Where there had only been grey fog and rain the day before, today the vast expanse of the sea lay in front of her, dark blue and glittering under the morning sun. Fishing boats were out in the bay, making patches of blue, white and red, and in the hazy distance were a couple of small, emerald-coloured islands.

'It's a fair morning.' He was right behind her now. She

hadn't heard him get up and she now turned and tilted her face up to look at him.

'The best morning and the best place in the world to forget horrible nightmares. After all, isn't Arrandale called the Land of Happy Dreams? I forget how you say it in Gaelic.'

He smiled. 'We say *Fearann nan Aislingean Sona*.' His deep voice brought heat and shivers to her skin. Was there anything sexier that this man smiling and speaking to her in Gaelic – anything sexier than his cobalt blue eyes and ruffled dark hair on this bright, sunny morning?

She cleared her throat, and forced herself to look away. 'I suppose we'd better get ready …'

They changed back into their own clothes, which thankfully dried overnight but were stiff with dirt and mud, and set off after Hamish insisted on making breakfast – tea so strong and bitter it stuck to her teeth, and a small mountain of toast slathered with jam and vegan butter.

Before they left, Daniel promised to get in touch and meet up at The Anchor very soon. 'I owe you a few drinks for patching me up and putting us up,' he said before giving the student a friendly clap on the shoulder.

Hamish gave Jenna a hug. 'Take care of yourself, Jen, I'll see you around.' In less than twenty-four hours it felt like the young man had become a friend.

'He's a nice lad, and clever too,' Daniel remarked as they set off in the fresh but bright morning, with the dogs running around and chasing rabbits in fields covered with wild flowers – cotton flowers and daisies, purple gentians and sunny hawkweed, and so many more.

'I only wish he gave up that pipe dream of finding the *Santa Catalina*'s treasure. He's wasting his time, not to mention endangering his life. So many people have tried and came back with nothing – if they came back at all.'

No doubt he was thinking about his brother's tragic accident. How horrible it must be to be stuck underwater, know that you are running out of oxygen and don't have a chance to make it back to the surface alive.

'If there was ever any gold,' he added, 'it has long since been secreted away, washed away by the currents or buried in silt in the seabed. There are examples of this happening – the most well known being Tobermory.'

'Is that in the Isle of Mull?'

He nodded.

'I'm not familiar with the story. What happened there?'

'In October 1588 one of the Armada ships – the *San Juan de Sicilia* – anchored there to make repairs on its way back to Spain. The galleon was rumoured to carry a huge treasure of gold and silver. It blew up, for reasons unknown and sank, and to this day lies buried in the silt somewhere at the bottom of Tobermory bay.'

Daniel plucked a long blade of grass from the side of the road, stuck one end between his lips and gave her a sideway glance. 'I've been meaning to ask you … Your trial period comes to an end in a few days, so if you want to leave … well … now would be the time to tell me.'

'Leave? I don't want to leave. Coming here was the best thing I ever did. Arrandale is a wonderful place. I've made lovely friends and I love Buttercup, and Brendon and Ruth – perhaps not in that order.' *And I love you*, she finished silently, and the realisation made her heart bump hard. Where had that come from? She'd better quash the silly thought straight away.

He let out a sigh, and looked relieved. 'Good. I am glad.'

'However, I hope the council don't ask you to get rid of me,' she added.

'Why would they? I hope you're not still thinking about Celia Kennedy or Councillor McLean.'

She bit her lip. 'Well, they have been rather critical.'

'Don't worry about them. You're doing a great job. People keep telling me how happy they are to have a proper library service again. As for McLean, I told you before not to worry.'

They didn't talk the rest of the way. The only noises around them were the occasional bark or whimper of the dogs as they ran wild in the tall grasses and meadow flowers, and the seabirds' manic calls from the cliffs ahead.

A hamlet appeared at the turn of the road, nestling in a small, green valley. 'Glendale Farm,' Daniel announced. 'Another half an hour and we'll be there.'

He turned towards her, and hesitated. 'Before we get there, I wanted to say that if you ever needed help, or wanted to talk about ... stuff – anything that is troubling you – you can talk to Ruth, or even Miona.' He took a deep breath. 'Or me, too, of course even though I'm not ... well, I'm a man and you may prefer to talk to a woman about certain ... hmm ... matters.'

It was like a punch in the stomach. She *had* talked in her sleep and he was only being tactful before when he said she hadn't. What exactly had she said? How much had he understood? Shame and misery rose inside her.

Daniel was still looking at her with concern so she forced a smile and said in an overly bright voice, 'Talk about what? There's nothing to talk about, but thanks anyway.'

But the sunshine had dimmed, the breeze felt a lot fresher, and her heart had grown cold.

Chapter Twenty-Four

'I think that's enough, love,' Daniel winced as Katrina pushed yet another pin into his hair, stabbing his skull. He'd lost count of the number of clips and pins she'd put in already. He felt like a hedgehog. He probably looked like one too – albeit a hedgehog with a penchant for purple and pink.

She tutted. 'You need another pretty bow on this side, and a bit of glitter on that side.'

He turned round. 'Glitter? You never said anything about glitter!'

The little girl slapped something wet and sticky on the patch of hair that was still free of clips and pins, and rubbed it into his scalp as if she was doing a shampoo. She had come back crying from school, although she wouldn't tell him what had upset her, so when she'd said she wanted to be a hairdresser and asked if she could practise on him he'd said yes. He hated to see her upset, and besides, it was only a bit of harmless fun. Having his hair brushed might actually be quite pleasant, and he may even catch up on some sleep. How naïve of him …

Katrina now stood in front of him with her head cocked to one side. 'All done. Let me get my mirror.'

She produced a rainbow coloured mirror with the head of a unicorn stuck on top, waved it in front of him, and almost took his eye out with the yellow plastic horn.

'Careful or I'll need an eye patch like the pirate Black Beard. I already have an injury, I don't want another one.' He showed her his hand, with the dressing that the practice nurse had redone a couple of days before after taking the stitches off. Surprisingly, she had praised Hamish's handiwork and said that the student's stitching had spared Daniel surgery.

'Don't worry, Uncle. I'll be careful. Look how pretty you are …' She held the mirror up, and he burst out laughing when he saw the mess she had made of his hair.

'I'm not sure about pretty but it's certainly very striking. I'm sure you won't have any problem getting a job at the salon.'

'You think so?' She gave him a happy smile, and her blue eyes, so similar to his own, lit up.

'Now can you take everything out? I have stuff to do on the farm and I don't want to scare the sheep and the cows off.' Or have Iain and the lads make fun of him.

Katrina nodded and started pulling the clips and pins out. 'Can you read me a story before I go to bed? Jenna says that reading is the best thing ever. She says it gives people imagination and gives them somewhere to escape to when they feel worried or sad. Oh yes, and she also said that it can give you a better vocab … vocable …' She frowned.

Daniel smiled. 'It's *vocabulary*, chick – it means, words. Well, Jenna is a librarian, so I guess reading books is part of her job, and I suppose a good story can make you pass the time if you're bored, or scared.'

Scared … Was that what Jenna had been, back in Manchester? Her cries of pain, her voice begging not to be shut in the dark still echoed in his memory. What happened to her, and who was that man – Adrian – she was pleading with in her nightmare?

'I told her that you never read books.' Katrina sounded accusing.

He sighed. 'I don't have time for reading.' But even as he spoke his excuse sounded weak and pathetic.

Katrina pulled out the last of the clips. 'I got another Zonk storybook this week.'

'Zonk, again! All you can talk about is that big purple monster!' Daniel said in a deep voice as he jumped to his feet and gathered her in his arms.

He lifted her up, turned her upside down like he used to do when she was a toddler, and tickled her tummy while she roared and squeaked and giggled in delight.

'Daniel McGregor. Put the wee lassie down immediately!' Miona's stern voice called from the doorway. 'She just had her tea and you'll make her *boke*.'

He sighed, and put Katrina down. 'Sorry, Miona.' He gave Katrina a kiss. 'You go and get ready for bed, young lady, while I tidy myself up, and I think it's going to take me a while.'

He wasn't wrong. Half an hour, a scalding hot shower and three shampoos later, he had to admit defeat. His dark hair stuck up, rigid with blue glitter glue. He would have to grin and bear it, or wear a cap.

'Can we ask Jenna to come for lunch tomorrow?' Katrina asked as he kissed her goodnight. 'She hasn't seen the baby cows yet, and Miona said she would make a chocolate cake. I could do her hair too … please, Uncle.' She batted her eyelids, and joined her hands above the sheets as if in prayer.

He drew his eyebrows in a mock cross frown and wagged his index finger. 'After what you did to me, you shouldn't get any pudding for a month, never mind Miona's chocolate cake, and I'm not sure Jenna would appreciate you putting glitter all over her hair either. But I'll see what I can do. I'll call at Mermaid's Cottage later and ask her.'

First there was something he had to do …

'Have you painted any more pebbles?'

She nodded. 'I did one after tea today. It's over there, on my chest of drawers.'

'Do you mind if I take it? It's for a … surprise …' He

couldn't tell her who it was for, of course, not yet. He would, soon – when he found out how to extricate himself from all the lies about Hugh and Shannon he'd said over the years.

'Goodnight, love.'

'Goodnight, Uncle Daniel. What can I dream of?' she asked, looking at him, her bright blue eyes already cloudy with sleep.

'Hmm … You are walking in a magical forest, with lots of flowers and animals.'

She shook her head on the pillow. 'We already had that dream. Give me another one.'

Damn, he was running out of ideas. He scratched his head, and winced at the feel of the stiff glitter glue on his hair. 'I know! You're a famous hairdresser and people come from all over the world to have their hair done by you. How's that?'

She gave him a sleepy smile. 'That's a great happy dream. Thank you. You're the best, Uncle Daniel.'

His heart tightened and tears pricked his eyes as he clutched the pebble in his hand. How long would it be before she stopped saying that?

The Weeping Stones looked exactly as Katrina had painted them – a dozen imposing standing stones forming a large semicircle facing the bay, with tombstones lining up on the opposite side.

What a striking place for a graveyard, and how poetic in a way that the McGregors should complete with their kin's tombstones the circle their Neolithic forefathers had started. Jenna walked around the graveyard, searching in vain for Lady Jane's grave. Most of the tombstones had been worn by the elements, their inscriptions illegible. Jenna however found two graves which, judging from the names and the dates must have been Daniel's parents. Next to them was Hugh McGregor's. It was plain and black, with a couple of verses chiselled under his name:

> *"Twilight and evening bell,*
> *And after that the dark!"*

Shivers ran up and down her back as she whispered the words.

A bunch of wildflowers tied with a long stem of grass was propped up against the stone. The verses were familiar but Jenna couldn't quite remember which poem they were from. She zipped her fleece against the breeze and glanced across the bay at Mermaid's Rocks, where Hugh had died.

She turned round, ready to leave, but Daniel was walking towards her, a serious, almost forbidding look on his face. Was he annoyed that she was there? Perhaps he was thinking about what she said in her sleep, that night at Hamish's cottage. She still felt nauseous with shame thinking about it. How much had she said, and how much had he understood?

He yanked his cap off. There was something odd about him, and it took her a second or two to realise that it was his hair which stuck up in stiff, blue, glittery peaks. 'Jenna? This is a surprise.'

'I hope I'm not trespassing,' she started. 'There was no sign to say it was private, and I've wanted to see this place for a long time. But I'll go now, and leave you in peace.'

She had been thinking about him all week, reliving the sensations of waking in his arms, safe and warm, but being close to him now made the feelings and the yearnings rush back.

He smiled. 'No, don't go. Actually, I'm glad to see you. I was going to call at Mermaid's Cottage to invite you for lunch tomorrow. Katrina is desperate to show you the calves.'

'Well ... thank you, but ...' She would love to spend time with Katrina and the MacKinnons ... and above all with Daniel. However, it wasn't wise, especially now that he knew she was hiding something about her past and he may want to talk to her about it.

His smile wavered. 'If the prospect of meeting the baby cows isn't tempting enough, I should tell you that Miona is baking her world-famous chocolate cake and that Katrina said she would do your hair for free.'

He ran his fingers in his hair, making a blue strand stick up. 'As you can see, her experiments with glitter gel are rather striking.' Laughter danced in his eyes and his voice had softened, like every time he spoke about his niece.

How could she resist?

'In that case, I shall be very pleased to come for lunch. Thank you for inviting me again.'

He grinned. 'Great! Katrina will be pleased.'

What about him? Was he pleased too? She wanted to ask, but instead she gestured towards the stone circle. 'I've been wondering why this place is called the Weeping Stones.'

He smiled again. 'I'll show you.'

She followed him to the tallest stone. 'Put your hand on the rock,' he said, and Jenna stroked the bumpy surface of the stone.

She opened her eyes wide. 'It's wet! How is that possible? The weather has been dry and sunny all day.'

'I'll let you into the secret. If you lick your finger you'll find that it tastes salty, that's because the stones are exposed to the wind and the sea spray, so they're always wet.'

She touched her finger to her tongue. 'You're right. It does taste salty ... Tears are salty too, that's probably why people say the stones are crying for the McGregors buried here.' She hesitated. 'I saw your brother's grave over there. May I ask which poem the verses are from? They are very striking.'

He stopped smiling. 'It's from "Crossing the Bar" by Tennyson. It felt right for him.'

'I didn't realise you knew any poetry,' she said without thinking.

A bitter line appeared at the side of his mouth. 'Why? Because I only read kids' books?'

That was what Toby Drummond had said. She felt so ashamed she wanted to cry. 'I'm sorry. I didn't mean to be rude or hurt your feelings.'

As he stood there, so tall and strong and burly, yet strangely vulnerable with the glitter in his hair and the downbeat expression on his face, she felt the pull of attraction again – the air becoming hazy and fizzing around them, the tingling on her skin, the overwhelming need to touch him, kiss him ... love him.

He shrugged. 'You'd be right anyway. Katrina told me what you said at school about the benefits of reading and she gave me a sermon about my lack of interest in books. I never had much time for literature. Every time I try sitting with a proper book I fall asleep.'

He gestured to his brother's grave. 'However, I have liked Tennyson's poem since I first read it at school and it seemed a fitting epitaph for Hugh.'

'What does crossing the bar, mean?'

'It's a sailing term that means setting out to sea. It refers to a sandbar at the entrance of a harbour. And of course, in the poem, it means ...'

His voice became a little hoarse and he didn't finish. He didn't need to. She understood that it meant dying. Her eyes welled up. She reached out and touched his unbandaged hand, and without looking at her, he held it and gripped it hard.

'Hugh was my brother,' he added in a deep, low voice. 'I should have protected him. Instead, I was only able to pull his body from the wreck. I miss him, Jenna. Don't get me wrong – we did have our disagreements ... but I miss him.'

She nodded. 'I understand. I miss my father too.'

Daniel gave her hand a slight squeeze. 'You said he'd been ill ...'

She nodded. 'He worked in construction since he was a teenager and got exposed to a lot of asbestos. In those days, people didn't know about the dangers and didn't have adequate protection against the stuff. That's what killed him in the end.'

'I am sorry.' Daniel gave her a kind, soft, all enveloping look which made her warm inside. He understood what it was to lose someone you loved, and to miss their smile and their voice, their touch and their quirky ways. Not everybody did. Adrian had often got annoyed that she still mourned her dad and felt the need to talk about him.

'What was he like, your dad?' Daniel asked.

She smiled, touched that he should ask, or care. 'He loved his gardening and spent all his spare time pottering about, trimming, cutting, seeding. It used to drive my mother crazy – not that she needed much to get annoyed at him anyway.' She let out a sad laugh.

'She never forgave him for their lack of money. He had a good job as construction manager when they got married, then he fell from a scaffolding, spent months in hospital and the company went bust. He was unemployed for a long time and in the end he got a caretaker job in the local primary school. He enjoyed it but my mother resented him ... for everything he was ... and everything he wasn't. She was – still is – a deeply unhappy woman.'

'If your father got ill because of his work, then he should have got some sort of compensation. Please tell me to mind my own business if you'd rather not talk about it.'

'His first employers' insurance paid out – quite a large sum, actually – but …' She shrugged and let out a sigh. It would never, ever, be enough to make up for the loss of her kind, loving dad.

How funny that the money may have made her mum's life more comfortable, but it hadn't made her any happier. At least she didn't seem to smile any more often – although she always had a smile for Adrian …

Adrian, who pretended he loved her and wanted her back after everything he had done. Jenna shuddered.

'It's getting cool,' Daniel said, probably mistaking her shivering for being cold. 'Shall we walk back?'

She nodded, unwilling to part with him yet.

'I need to do something first, if you don't mind.' He let go of her hand and walked to his brother's grave. Kneeling down, he took a pebble painted in bright colours out of his pocket and left it in front of the tombstone.

'Would you like to come in for a drink?' Jenna asked as they arrived at Mermaid's Cottage. 'We could go over the entries for the short story competition. I have quite a few already, and some are really funny.'

'The competition? Yes, of course.' He'd forgotten all about it. All week his mind had been too full of farm problems, and of Jenna. He liked her. He wanted to banish the sadness that so often clouded her eyes. He wanted to see her smile, hold her like he had that night at Hamish's cottage.

He wanted it again, and so much more … He wanted to kiss her until she forgot whatever it was she was afraid of – and whoever that man was she'd been having nightmares about.

It was cool in the evenings so she asked him to light the fire while she made coffee and put some biscuits on a plate.

'What have you got there?' He pointed at a piece of driftwood displayed on the mantelpiece, next to the framed photo of the calves – Buttercup's photo being already in pride of place in the mobile library – and pebbles and shells Jenna must have collected on the beach. It was an unusual, light brown colour, and as it stood propped up against the wall, he was reminded of a woman – a woman with very generous curves lifting a hand in prayer. He shook his head. He was seeing things.

'It's only a piece of wood I picked up from the beach,' she answered.

He lifted the piece and frowned. The wood was cold and smooth, and didn't feel like wood at all ... and no wonder! He frowned. 'If I'm not mistaken, this isn't wood, but ivory.'

'What?' She rushed to his side. 'But how did it get here?'

'The same way driftwood does. I think it's some kind of statuette or religious artefact.'

'Now that you mention it, I had the same idea when I first found it. It's a woman, isn't it? I think she is pregnant.'

An ivory statuette of a saint ... Ivory was used to carve religious artefacts from the twelfth century, but it was only later, in the fifteenth and sixteenth centuries when the Portuguese brought back ivory from the Ivory Coast, that its use became more widespread. Ivory. Religious artefacts. Early Renaissance. The statuette of a woman which could be the Virgin Mary – were there any other saints depicted while pregnant?

It could be a catholic artefact, transported on a Spanish Armada ship ... Excitement flared inside him. What if it belonged to the *Santa Catalina*? Next to him, Jenna touched the ivory, and their fingers met, sending searing heat through him. She didn't snatch her fingers away, but tilted her face up to look at him, like the other night in Hamish's kitchen, and the pull of her clear blue eyes, the urge to feel her soft pink lips under his mouth and her body under his hands was almost impossible to resist.

He was hard and tense, and all he could think of was kissing her ... It wasn't a good idea. Talking about the statuette wasn't a good idea either. As far as he was concerned, it would remain a piece of driftwood, so he stepped back, put it back on the mantelpiece and forced a smile. 'Where are these short stories you promised me?'

'They're there.' As she bent down to retrieve a folder from the floor, her necklace slipped out from the opening of her shirt. It was the piece of majolica she had shown him before. It didn't take long for his mind to take the leap. A piece of majolica earthenware, probably late fifteenth century, and an ivory statuette of a saint, both found on the beach at Mermaid Cove.

Was the *Santa Catalina* treasure at long last giving out clues as to its location?

Chapter Twenty-Five

'Jenna! Let's go and see the baby cows in the field.' Katrina ran across the yard, with Sam and Eddie bouncing and yapping around her, and took Jenna's hand.

The little girl's jeans were tucked into mucky wellies and her faded blue sweatshirt made her eyes stand out even more in the sunlight. Once again, Jenna was startled to see how much like Daniel's they were – same vibrant blue, same shape, same dark eyelashes ... The family resemblance was definitely striking. Hugh must have looked a lot like his elder brother.

What did Shannon look like? All she knew was that she was a "babe" – in Hamish's words, that she had a beautiful voice, swam like a siren and filled Daniel's eyes with sadness. A dark cloud of jealousy obscured the sunlight for a moment, but Jenna pushed it aside. Shannon was nothing to do with her.

She gave the dogs a quick pat, and pointed at Katrina's plaits, which today were decorated with a variety of clips and bows. 'I like what you've done with your hair.'

The little girl beamed as she tossed her plaits over her shoulders. 'I decided I wanted to be a hairdresser when I grow up, so I've been practising on Uncle Daniel. He said I was very good, even if I put too much glitter on.' Katrina giggled. 'Would you like me to do your hair later?' She gave Jenna a look so hopeful she didn't want to disappoint her.

'I'd love to, but no glitter for me, please.' She looked around the yard. Apart from the quad bike, there were no other vehicles today.

'Are you on your own? Where is everybody?'

'Scott and Jamie are in the cowshed. They help out on

the farm,' she explained. 'Miona is making lunch, and Uncle Daniel and Iain had to go to Dana this morning.'

'Oh, that's a shame.' Jenna hoped that her disappointment didn't show too much.

Katrina shrugged. 'No it's not! There'll be more chocolate cake for us.' She slipped her hand into Jenna's and pulled her forward. 'Come on. Let's go and see the cows. Maisie is a lot better now, did you know?' She led Jenna to a field of lush green grass sprinkled with daisies and buttercups. 'We have to stay near the gate,' she said. 'Uncle Daniel doesn't want me to go in the field on my own. He says cows can be *moo*-dy.'

Jenna burst out laughing. 'He's right. So, which one is Jenna?'

'It's that small one, over there! She is very cheeky.' During the next half-hour, Katrina described in detail the personality and quirky habits of every one of the twenty or so cows grazing in the field. 'They have their own language, you know. Uncle Daniel doesn't believe it, but Miona does. She knows a lot of stories, some are a bit scary.'

Katrina nodded, and gave Jenna a puzzled look. 'She was talking about you the other day. She thought I was in my bedroom but I was playing with my Lego on the stairs. She was telling Iain that she hopes you'll stay in Arrandale because Uncle Daniel likes you very much.'

'You shouldn't be listening to grown-ups' conversations, Katrina,' Jenna interrupted quickly, heat rising on her cheeks and her heart bumping hard. 'And even less repeat what you heard.' But she was smiling inside. Silly, silly woman, she should know better than to believe a seven-year-old girl. She might have misheard what Miona and Iain were saying …

'Will you stay? I really want you to stay.' Katrina's eyes were misty all of a sudden. 'I like it when you come to school with Buttercup and tell us stories. It was the best day ever when you told Archie and his friends off for being silly ... and I want to go to the beach and find lots of shells again. Uncle Daniel never has time for anything fun.'

'Miona said something else,' she carried on. 'She said you were the Cove's new mermaid, but I don't want you to be a mermaid, because then you'll go away like my mummy. I want you to be real and stay here and be my friend.'

Her throat tight, Jenna wrapped her arm around Katrina's shoulders and gave her a tight hug. 'Of course I'll stay, darling. I love it here, and I love being your friend too. And I can confirm that I am definitely no mermaid!' She gestured towards her jeans. 'I have legs, no fishtail or webbed toes, and I can't even swim that well.'

'I can swim very well. I could teach you,' Katrina said.

'Thanks, but I'd rather look after my flowers.' Jenna smiled. 'I tell you what. If Miona agrees why don't you come back to Mermaid's Cottage with me after lunch and help me in the garden? There's lots of tidying up to be done and I could do with some help. Would you like that?'

Katrina nodded enthusiastically. 'Yes, please. I can always do your hair another day ...'

They walked back to the farm, holding hands and chatting and found Miona standing in the yard, her fists curled on her hips. 'There you are. I thought you'd been taken by the water horse.'

Katrina shrugged. 'Uncle Daniel says that water horses don't exist and that they're just another of your inventions.'

'He'd better watch out next time he goes to Na Mna then, or he'll end up as a tasty supper for the water horse who lives at the bottom of the loch.' But she was laughing. 'Come on, lassies, it's time for lunch.'

They ate in the kitchen, which was a lot more welcoming than the dining room, and Miona readily agreed to Katrina spending the afternoon with Jenna. 'I'll tell Daniel to collect her if he's not too late. You never know how long a search and rescue mission is going to take.'

Her face sombre, she explained, 'They're looking for a sailing boat that didn't come back to Portree last night. There's a family on board – holidaymakers.'

'Has Iain gone out with the lifeboat too?'

Miona looked away and smiled to herself. 'No, lass. He was a crew member back in the days and looked ever so handsome in his kit. He used to make my heart go all funny.' She gave Jenna a knowing smile. 'He only helps with the maintenance now ... but he still makes my heart go a bit funny.'

Katrina put her knife and fork down and pushed her plate away from her. 'That's because you're very old and old people have bad hearts. Can we have some chocolate cake now? I ate all my pasta.'

The woman sighed. She looked tired suddenly. 'Give me a moment. I'll make some coffee for Jenna and a cup of tea for me.'

She must be in her seventies. It mustn't be easy for her to look after such a big house as Dunfiadhaich, cook and clean and care for an energetic child too. Jenna pushed her chair back and stood up. 'I'll make the drinks, and Katrina will help clear the table.'

Miona frowned. 'There's no need. I can ...'

Jenna frowned back. 'I insist. Come on, Katrina, get up and put the salt and pepper away and the dirty knives and forks in the sink. I'll deal with the plates after I've boiled the kettle.'

Katrina jumped down from her chair, and gave her a delighted smile. 'Yes, Jenna!'

Two pieces of delicious chocolate cake and a mug of coffee later, Jenna asked Katrina to get a change of clothes, some sun cream and a cap while she put the dishwasher on and gave the worktops a quick wipe down.

'Now you can have a well-deserved rest while the house is quiet,' she told Miona.

'Thank you, lass. Would you mind phoning Iain before you leave? My hearing's not so good and I struggle with phone calls.'

'Sure.' Jenna took her mobile phone and keyed in the number of the lifeboat station that Miona dictated to her.

Iain answered after a couple of rings. 'Aye, is that you, Jenna? What's up? Is there a problem at the farm?'

'No, everything's fine, don't worry. Miona wanted to know if there was any news.'

There was a silence, followed by a long sigh at the other end. 'Not yet, lass. They're still looking for the sailing boat, and there's bad weather coming our way.'

'Bad weather?' Jenna glanced at the blue sky out of the window.

'Aye, it's coming from up North – Shetland. Should hit us late afternoon.'

Jenna's fingers tightened on her phone. 'Oh ... are Daniel and the crew going to be all right?'

'Sure, lass, don't you worry about them. Tell Miona I'll stay down here until they come back.'

Jenna ended the call and told Miona what her husband had said. The woman only nodded, but she sensed she was worried. Daniel may be experienced, but accidents happened even to seasoned sailors ... and what about that family on the sailing boat?

'I'm ready!' Katrina skipped into the kitchen, waving her cap and with her rucksack bouncing on her back.

Miona sighed as she pulled the cap down on Katrina's head. 'You go and have fun, lassie. I hope Iain and your uncle aren't too late back. I'll ask Scott or Jamie to phone the lifeboat station for news later, if they're not busy.'

Jenna frowned. 'Why don't you come with us to

217

Mermaid's Cottage? That way I can phone Iain for news from time to time and you'll know straight away what's going on.'

Miona nodded. 'Now that's a good idea. I'll get my knitting, and I'll put some chocolate cake in a tin so we can have it later with a cup of tea.'

Back at Mermaid's Cottage, Jenna took a chair from the dining room and plucked the straw hat from the coat stand, and carried them both out into the garden.

Miona sat down and put the hat on. 'Thanks, lass. I'll sit here, near the rose wall. It's a lovely spot. The garden is coming on nicely.'

Jenna smiled as she surveyed the trimmed bushes and freshly dug up borders. 'I love it here. There are so many flowers, colours and scents to enjoy.' She pointed at the climbing yellow roses. 'And my sunshine wall never fails to cheer me up.'

Miona took her knitting out, and Jenna collected some garden tools from the shed together with a bag of rocks and shells to decorate the garden. This would be Katrina's job this afternoon.

Digging stones and pulling weeds out of the borders was as satisfying as ever. Jenna gave Miona a pair of secateurs and the housekeeper alternated between chatting to Katrina, doing a little bit of deadheading and knitting, and once in a while she looked at Jenna and gave her a nod and a smile. As for Katrina, she was busy singing to herself and making a complicated mosaic near the climbing yellow rose wall.

After a couple of hours the wind freshened, bringing clouds rolling in from the North ... and all of a sudden the sun was gone and the sky was black.

Miona looked up. 'That's the bad weather Iain was talking about.' She had hardly spoken the last words when fat raindrops fell on the garden, followed by a deluge.

Jenna dropped her tools to the ground. 'Quick! Katrina, run into the house. I'll get Miona's chair.'

A bolt of lightning fizzed across the sky and thunder boomed ahead. Katrina shrieked and froze on the spot, so Jenna lifted her into her arms and hurried back into the cottage, followed by Miona. The chair could wait ...

'I can't believe how quickly the weather turned,' she said once they were safely in the house. She put Katrina down and walked to the kitchen. 'Who's for a cup of tea?'

She switched the kettle on and opened the box of Toby's chocolates.

'These look fancy,' Miona remarked as she helped herself to one.

'Toby Drummond brought them, together with some flowers ... but they didn't last very long.'

Miona gave her a sharp look. 'What did he bring you flowers and chocolate for? Is he courting you?'

'Oh dear, no.' Jenna laughed at the old-fashioned word. 'He was just being kind, I suppose.' She couldn't tell her that he also needed to apologise for suggesting that she spy on Daniel and accusing him of having an affair with Shannon ...

'When will the storm go away?' Katrina asked in a frightened voice, sticking to Jenna's side as the gale shook the windows, bolts of lightning forked in the darkened sky and thunder blasted overhead.

Jenna gave her a pen and a notepad. 'Why don't you write a story about a happy dream? Many of your friends have already handed them in. Your uncle and I read them all yesterday. There are some very good ones.'

Her voice became thoughtful as she recalled how much Daniel and she had laughed the night before. It had been hard to draw a shortlist and Daniel hadn't left until late in the evening.

She stood at the window as Katrina wrote her story. Huge waves pummelled the cove as angry clouds rolled overhead. The rain battered the clifftop, the gale howled and screeched like a banshee. Were Daniel and the lifeboat crew safe, and what about the family in the missing sailing boat?

Miona put her knitting down and came to stand next to her. 'The crew will be tired and hungry when they come back to the lifeboat station. You should make a big pan of curry or bolognese then we'll phone someone to pick it up when it's ready.'

Jenna smiled. 'That's a great idea.'

Rummaging through her cupboards, she found a pack of rice, two tins of Borlotti beans, and a small jar of chilli powder. 'I could make a chilli. There's some mince beef in the fridge, a few carrots and onions. It won't be as good as the real thing, of course …'

'But it will be hot, filling and tasty, and that's all that matters.'

'I'll start cooking straight away.'

The woman gave her another small smile. 'It's good to keep busy when you're worried about your man or you'll drive yourself silly.'

Jenna gasped. Did she know? Had she guessed what she didn't want to acknowledge, even to herself? Miona was right, of course. Keeping busy was the best cure against anxiety. She cut and chopped the carrots, and fried the beef and the onions, added the beans and boiled water for the rice.

'I'll keep some for our tea,' she said, since there was no question of Miona and Katrina walking back to the farm in the raging storm. Once the chilli was ready, she asked Katrina to set the table. They ate quickly and after tea, Katrina resumed her writing, and Jenna did the washing-up, but time was dragging on, and on.

'You should phone the lifeboat station,' Miona said. 'Iain won't mind. He knows how much I used to worry when he went out with the crew.'

Jenna dried the last of the plates and put it into the cupboard. It was uncanny how the woman could read her mind ... or her heart.

It was Iain who answered again. 'They're still searching the Sound of Raasay, which is where the skipper said he was heading yesterday before he set off, but there's no sighting of the boat as yet. How are you all faring?'

'We're fine, Iain. We're at Mermaid's Cottage. We were doing some gardening but now we're stuck inside because of the storm. Miona has her knitting, and Katrina is writing a story. By the way, I made a pan of chilli for the crew. It was Miona's idea.'

'Brilliant! I'll arrange for someone to pick it up. I fear it's going to be a long evening.'

Jenna put her phone down and glanced at the window. Every gust of wind, every bolt of lightning and blast of thunder reverberated inside her, tightening her chest. Please make Daniel and his crew safe. Please make him come back soon ... The words turned incessantly in her mind like a prayer. How she wanted to be with him again, see his smile, and hear his voice.

It may be the last thing she needed, and certainly the last thing she had expected when cold, scared and seasick, she had met him on the *Riannog*, but she couldn't hide from the truth any longer. She had fallen in love with Daniel McGregor, and there was nothing she could do about it.

Another roll of thunder shook the windows of the little cottage. Iain was right. It was going to be a long evening.

Chapter Twenty-Six

As daylight faded, the thunderstorm rolled away and the rain eased off at last, even if occasional gusts of wind still rattled the cottage. Miona dozed on the sofa, her knitting discarded on her lap and Katrina curled up, fast asleep against her.

Jenna went upstairs to get a blanket to cover them both with. Next she tidied the dining room table, put the pens, colouring pencils and notepad to one side, and slipped Katrina's story into her folder. The little girl had spent ages writing and illustrating her story, before finally folding her piece of paper and giving it to Jenna. She didn't say what her happy dream was. Being reunited with her mother – the very mysterious, and very absent Siren, most probably.

And what was *her* happy dream? Being rid of Adrian for good; feeling strong and believing that she could and would make a new life here, in Arrandale. Being friends with Daniel, of course, and spending cosy evenings with him, like they had the night before ...

She snorted. Friends? Was that all she wished for? Of course not. And there had been nothing cosy about their evening at all. She had been a ball of nerves, of emotions, of desires, and not only when he held her hand and told her about his brother at the Weeping Stones, or when their fingers had met on the statuette ... She had felt the same jolt of awareness every time he looked at her, and the same crazy urge to be close to him.

Love. That's what it was. She sighed as she watched the angry grey sea roar in the cove. It was so different from the feelings she'd first had for Adrian. Adrian had dazzled

222

her, swept her away from her mundane life in a whirlwind of excitement, never leaving her time to breathe, to adjust, to think. From the moment they'd met in the trendy Manchester bar where a colleague from the library was celebrating her birthday to the day they moved into the flat, it was as if he was intent on winning her over. He sent her romantic texts ten times a day, and wrote long and poetic messages to go with the flowers he had delivered to her. She was the prettiest, the cleverest, the quirkiest and the funniest girl he'd ever met …

Except that deep down all the praise and the compliments made her feel like a fraud and she'd always wondered what he could possibly see in her.

He had never loved her, that much was true. Once they'd moved in together and after the initial honeymoon period, he had played on her insecurities, her desire to please and be loved, and her reluctance to make a fuss. He had broken her, and she had let him – that was what hurt the most.

The jingling of her phone echoed in the quiet of the room, and she rushed to answer before it could wake Miona or Katrina up.

'Jenna?' Iain's voice sounded strained. 'The lads are on their way back. They're tired, but safe.'

Thank Goodness. She closed her eyes and let out a sigh of relief. 'Did they find the sailing boat?'

'I'm afraid not. The Black Wolf had to be stood down to give the men a chance to rest. Another lifeboat from Portree and a SAR helicopter have taken over the search but they're struggling against that blasted storm and will probably have to give up soon. If they don't find anything then the Black Wolf will resume the search at first light.' He sighed. 'How are Miona and the wee lassie?'

'Fast asleep, both of them.'

'I'm afraid you're going to have to wake them up.

Brendon is on his way to collect that pan of chilli you made, but he said he'd take Miona and Katrina home first.'

She just had time to wake Miona and Katrina up before the noise of a car engine in front of the house signalled Brendon's arrival.

'Hi love … What a bad night this is,' Brendon said as Jenna opened the door. 'Has everything been all right for you? No power cut? No damage to the cottage? Good.'

A sleepy Katrina, now wearing Jenna's fleece, gave her a goodbye kiss, followed by Miona. Miona helped Katrina climb in the back of Brendon's car, and sat next to her while Brendon secured the pan of chilli in a cardboard box in the boot of his car.

As he waved Jenna goodbye, the thought of being alone was suddenly unbearable. She had to see Daniel, make sure he was all right.

'Wait!' She gestured frantically and Brendon wound down his window, a puzzled look on his face.

'What's the matter?'

'Can I come to the lifeboat station with you? Please … I could help with the food, or make tea, or whatever needs doing.' She didn't care if she sounded desperate.

Brendon nodded. 'No problem. I'll pick you up on the way back.'

She slipped a jumper on, put her trainers and her coat on and waited for Brendon by the door. It wasn't long before Brendon was back. He swung the passenger door open and she jumped in. 'Thank you. I hope you don't think I'm being a nuisance.'

'Of course not,' he said as he started on the bumpy track to the main road. The storm had blown all kinds of debris around, and he had to keep his eyes on the road. Once in Dana, he drove down along the seafront and parked near the lifeboat station.

'We're just in time.' He gestured towards the bay, where blue and white lights flickered on the horizon. Soon the lifeboat was bouncing on the dark waves as it entered the harbour.

'Why don't you run to the end of the pier to welcome Daniel home while I take the pan in? I'm sure he'll be glad to see you.' He smiled and heat flamed on her face. So he had seen through her pretext of helping with the food ...

By the time she arrived at the end of the pier, Iain and two helpers in hi-vis jackets were securing the lifeboat by tying thick ropes to bollards, while on deck half a dozen men and women kitted out in white helmets and navy and yellow waterproof gear collected equipment and got ready to disembark.

Iain frowned when he saw her. 'What are you doing here, lass?'

She gave him the same rushed explanation she had given Brendon. 'Am I allowed to stand here?'

'Sure ... Daniel will be up shortly.' He winked and walked away. So he too had seen right through her.

The men and women climbed onto the pier one by one, hardly giving her a glance. Heads were bent, shoulders sagged. No one spoke. Daniel was the last to leave. He looked tired – so tired. The harsh, glaring lights from the boat cast shadows around his eyes, and deep lines bracketed his mouth.

'Jenna? Are you all right? Has anything happened?' He frowned, took his helmet off slowly, and ran his fingers through his hair. Even in the dimming light she could see the strands of blue glitter glue he hadn't managed to wash off.

'No ... I'm fine. I made some chilli for you ... and the crew. It was Miona's idea. I'm so glad you're safe ... I've been worried.'

He glanced at the other crew members who had now

225

reached the lifeboat station at the end of the pier, then back at her again. He looked puzzled. She took a step back, now feeling awkward and embarrassed. 'Sorry ... I shouldn't have come. I'm keeping you behind when you're tired and you want to be with your friends. What must you be thinking?'

He narrowed his eyes and let out a short breath. 'If I told you what I'm thinking, you'd run away screaming,' he said in a deep, low voice. Her throat tightened. Was he angry that she had come? Yes, that must be it ...

He gestured to the lifeboat station. The lights were on. Everybody must be safe and warm inside by now. 'Did you say you brought some food?'

'Yes. Chilli con carne. I hope you'll like it.' She tried to sound upbeat when she felt that she was dying inside. What had she been hoping? That he'd be overcome with joy at seeing her and he'd take her in his arms, hold her tight and kiss her? Yes, of course, that's what she'd hoped.

'That's great. Thanks. Let's go back to the station and feed the crew. We're all in need of a good rest.'

They walked in silence side by side. No wonder he wasn't talking. He must be exhausted. The failed rescue and the fate of the family in the lost sailing boat must prey on his mind, and he was probably longing for sleep.

'We need to take our kits off and have our debrief now,' he said when they got to the station, 'but if you find your way to the kitchen someone will show you what to do. It's over there.' He pointed to a staircase, pushed a door and didn't even look back.

Brendon was already in the kitchen, stirring the chilli which was bubbling on the stove. He gestured towards a stack of plates and glasses. 'Would you mind setting the table? The cutlery is in that drawer, and there's sliced bread in that bag over there. We'll need a couple of pitchers of water too.' Thank goodness he was too busy to notice the tears in her eyes.

The lifeboat crew came in the common room a short while later. They had changed into their own clothes. Some were yawning, others rubbed their eyes, but they all greeted her and Brendon with a smile and a cheer as they sat around the table and she helped dish out the chilli.

'Thanks,' Daniel said when she handed him his plate. 'It smells good.'

She stood, her back against the wood-panelled wall as they scraped their plates clean. Nobody was talking much, even while they waited for her to make some tea and coffee. As soon as they had finished their hot drink, they stood up and bade one another goodnight. Those who were on duty making sure they had their pager in case they were called out again, the others wished them good luck for the next day.

'I'm going home now, love,' Brendon said after they loaded the dishwasher, scrubbed the chilli pan clean and tidied the kitchen. 'Do you want a lift back?'

'I'll take Jenna home,' Daniel said before she could answer. He was standing in the doorway, one shoulder leaning against the door jamb. 'If that's all right with you, of course.'

He looked at her, and she nodded. 'Sure. Thanks.'

Iain said he would lock up, so Daniel put a coat on, grabbed hold of the clean pan and they walked side by side to the Land Rover.

'It must have been very scary to be in the middle of the storm,' she remarked to fill the silence between them.

'It was pretty scary, yes, but most of all it was disappointing that we couldn't find that sailing boat. I hope the Portree crew find it tonight otherwise we'll try again tomorrow. As more time passes it becomes more and more likely that the outcome won't be good. There's a family in that sailing boat – the skipper, his wife and two kids.'

He ran his fingers in his hair, and sighed. 'I'm sorry I missed lunch, by the way. How was Katrina?'

'As chatty as ever. She showed me the calves, and after lunch we went back to Mermaid's Cottage to do some gardening. Miona came too …'

He opened the door for her and put the pan on the back seat.

It was less awkward to carry on talking as he drove back to Mermaid's Cottage. 'Katrina was a great help in the garden. She started to make a mosaic with shells and pebbles I collected, but had to stop because of the storm. She was really scared of the thunder and lightning.'

'Aye, she's been like that ever since she was a toddler. It used to take me ages to send her to sleep.'

She cast him a sideways glance. His jaw was clenched. His fingers gripped the wheel hard. His eyes stared at the road. He probably couldn't wait to be rid of her and go to bed for a good night's sleep. It had been a terrible mistake to go to the lifeboat station. She realised that now.

'She wrote a story for the competition,' she added in a quiet voice.

'Good.' He turned onto the lane leading to Mermaid's Cottage.

The Land Rover bumped along the lane, shuddering and creaking every time it hit a pothole. 'Is your car fixed now?' Immediately she bit her lip. What a silly question. Obviously it was fixed, or he wouldn't be driving it.

'As fixed as it can be,' was the short-tempered reply.

Perhaps she'd better stop chatting after all. It was obvious she was only irritating him. He pulled up in front of the cottage, and turned to look at her, his face stony and his mouth grim.

'Here we are. Listen, Jenna, it was really kind of you to bring the food over, but ...'

She panicked. She didn't want to hear what he had to say – didn't want to hear that he was grateful, but she shouldn't have come to the lifeboat station. That she'd embarrassed him in front of the crew ... and he wasn't interested in her.

She opened her door. 'There's no need for you to get out,' she said very quickly before he could get another word in. 'I'll get the pan and see myself in.' She jumped out of the car, opened the back door and grabbed hold of the pan. 'Thanks for the lift ... and good luck for the search tomorrow.' She slammed the door shut and hurried to the cottage.

She didn't wave, or look at him. Right now all she could think about was being back in the safety of her little house, and try to forget that she had made a terrible fool of herself. Why had she even believed Katrina when she told her about Miona's and Iain's conversation, when they said that Daniel liked her very much? That she was the Cove's new mermaid. She, a mermaid?

She let out a strangled laugh full of despair and derision as she fumbled to get the key in the lock, slipped inside and closed the door.

There was the rumbling of a car engine, and the screeching of tyres on the lane, and then nothing but the wind and the rain. Daniel had gone, and she was alone.

Heavy-hearted, she put the pan in the kitchen and went upstairs where she undressed, took a shower and slipped her pyjamas on. She was sitting at the dressing table, running the brush through her hair when a strong gust of wind shook the house. There was a clicking sound. The electricity went off and the cottage was plunged into darkness.

She cried out in shock. The brush fell onto the carpet with a thud, and she glanced around the velvety darkness, but couldn't see anything at all. She couldn't even breathe ...

She gripped the edge of the dressing table and drew in a few deep breaths. There was no need to panic. No need to cry. She would get the electric torch from the kitchen, light a few candles, and everything would be all right.

She was at Mermaid's cottage, not locked in the walk-in wardrobe, and this was a power cut as was to be expected with the storm. There was plenty of air to breathe …

She waited a couple of minutes until her eyes got used to the dark but as she finally stood up, her hip bumped into the side of the dressing table, catching her off balance and she banged her head on the edge of the door.

White stars flashed in front of her as tears sprang out of her eyes and a sickly feeling twisted her stomach. Still, there was still no need to panic, she repeated again and again as she padded barefoot down the stairs, holding on to the walls on either side.

She had barely reached the hallway when she heard a car engine outside. A door slammed, footsteps crunched the gravel in front of the house. She held her breath, fear constricting her chest as seconds stretched by. Who could this be at this time? A cold, slimy hand gripped her heart. What if it was Adrian? What if he had come, as promised?

The loud knock made her jump. 'Jenna … It's Daniel.'

Daniel? She started breathing again, turned the key in the lock and opened the door. He stood, tall and solid in the darkness in front of her.

'You gave me such a fright. I thought …' She heaved a breath, and wiped her cheeks with the back of her hands. What would he think if he saw she'd been crying, like a child who's afraid of the dark? Which was exactly what she was. 'Is anything the matter? Why did you come back?'

'I wanted to check you were all right. The power went off at the farm, which meant it went off here too, and I thought you may be scared. You did say that you didn't like being in the dark ...'

She frowned. When had she told him that? She couldn't remember. She nodded. 'I was scared, that's true, but I was on my way to find the torch and the candles.'

'Perhaps I can help?'

'Well, yes, if you like.' She opened the door wider and moved aside to let him in. Why had he bothered to come back to help when less than an hour before he looked as if he couldn't wait to be rid of her?

Chapter Twenty-Seven

Daniel walked into the pitch-black living room. 'I'll get the torch and the candles.' It was the least he could do when he'd hurt her feelings by behaving like an insensitive *eejit,* and was about to hurt her even more.

Being exhausted after a day at sea and anxious about the fate of the missing sailing boat didn't constitute any excuse for the way he'd greeted Jenna after she'd waited for him at the pier, and looked at him with eyes filled with kindness, and concern … and something else he didn't want to see, and had no idea how to deal with.

The truth was that he was scared stiff. Scared of what he felt for her, scared of what his heart and very fibre of his body urged him to do … and scared that it would all end in disaster if he gave in to his feelings, like the last time he had believed himself in love. When he'd seen her on the pier, he had been very close to letting his inner caveman take over, sling her over his shoulder to carry her away and make love to her until the end of the night.

Of course, Jenna was nothing like Shannon, and what he felt for her was different too. It was deeper and stronger, more luminous. It felt right too whereas there had always been doubts and shadows in his feelings for Shannon.

Jenna was full of light and sunshine, and thinking about her made him smile, whistle and hum to himself as he went about the business of running the farm. He thought about her every day, and every night. When he was out and about in Arrandale, he looked out for the yellow mobile library, hoping for a chance encounter. He wanted to hold her, protect her from harm and help her forget whatever, and whoever, she was scared of.

Jenna was kind, sincere and loving and he hated himself for hurting her tonight, but he couldn't get involved. They may have a special connection but it was altogether safer, and kinder, to block his feelings. Drummond had been right too when he'd pointed out that they had nothing in common. He was a farmer, he didn't do books and literature, and she was … Well, she was clever and educated and came from the city … Besides, he had Katrina to think about, and she would always be his number one priority.

This was more or less the speech he had rehearsed in the car as he sped back down the lane from the farm when the electricity went off and his first impulse was to rush straight back to Mermaid's Cottage to check that Jenna was all right, alone in the dark.

He knew the cottage well so it didn't take long to find the torch, locate the spare batteries he had bought before Jenna arrived, and find a couple of candles and the box of matches from under the sink.

'There. It will be all right now. I'll light the fire with a match, since there's no electricity. You'll need it. It's chilly tonight.' He looked at her and his heart lurched in his chest. She'd been crying, and there was a cut on her forehead that was bleeding. He stepped towards her, put his finger under her chin and tilted her face up. 'What happened to your head? Why didn't you say you were injured?'

She shivered but didn't move away. 'I tripped in the dark and banged against the door. It's nothing. I'll put some cold water on it.'

He moved away, ripped a piece of kitchen towel, folded it and put it under the tap for a few seconds. 'Let me do it.' He dabbed the wet paper gently on the cut. 'Does it hurt? Sorry,' he said when she winced.

'No, it's fine, don't worry.'

He put the paper on the kitchen counter. 'There ... all done.' He smiled. 'I don't think you'll need stitches.'

'That's good, because Hamish isn't here.' She smiled back. 'And I won't trust anyone else with a needle.'

He should step back, make his rubbish little speech and leave but he couldn't move. In the soft glow of the candles her hair was pale golden and her eyes the colour of aquamarines. The air thickened between them, filled with tension and longing. He knew then that he wouldn't say anything and he wouldn't walk away.

His finger traced the outline of her face, following the contours of her temple, her cheekbone, her jawline ... tiny moonstones shimmered on her earlobes, reminding him of the night she had listened to him play his fiddle on the beach. She was a little mermaid – a moonlight mermaid, he thought as his fingers moved slowly to her lips.

She let out a trembling breath and he bent down slowly until their lips were a couple of inches apart, pausing for the space of a heartbeat.

He held his breath, and the world stopped too. And then he kissed her, brushing his mouth against hers ever so lightly at first. She let out a little moan and he was lost. Wrapping his arms around her waist he pulled her to him until he felt her body against his – soft against hard, smooth against rough. He lifted her from the ground, moulded her more closely against him, and kissed her harder, deeper. How could he have ever believed he could walk away and live without her?

'Jenna ...' He hardly recognised his voice. He hardly knew what he was doing, full stop. He put her down softly, and slid one hand at the back of her head, revelling in the silkiness of her hair between his fingers and the scent of her skin, summer and wild flower meadows, made him light-headed. All he could hear was the hammering of his heart and the rustling of their clothing as they moved against each other, and all he could feel was her naked body so tantalisingly close under her flimsy pyjamas.

He was still holding her, revelling in the shape of her small waist and the flare of her hips under his hands, and the pressure of her breasts against his chest. He wanted to touch and explore. He wanted to make her his. Was it too soon? Too fast? And what about his resolution to walk away?

He steeled himself, steadied his breathing and left his hands on her hips. Kissing would have to do for now, however badly he wanted her. There were secrets between them. She had the right to know about the past. Then she could decide what to do. It was only fair.

'Jenna, I need to talk to you. There are things you must know about me and ...'

She lifted a finger to his lips. 'I have things to tell you too, but right now I want to forget about the world and everybody else in it that isn't you.'

She rose on her tiptoes and kissed him, brushing her breasts against him again, making his whole body hard and overcome with want and need. She kissed his throat, the side of his mouth. Her fingers linked behind his neck, stroked his skin, sending jolts of desire through him. His resolve melted away. His lips parted despite himself, he responded ... and took over. With a moan, he clamped one hand onto her hip, bringing her closer, and slipped the other under her pyjama top.

She threw her head back with a whimper as he trailed kisses along her throat, caressing her skin with his lips. Her chest strained against the cotton material. All it would take was a flick of his fingers to undo the buttons ...

He straightened up. 'Are you all right with ... this?'

She lay her palm against his cheek, and smiled. 'Yes. Oh yes.'

Still kissing he led her to the sofa where he lowered himself down and pulled her into his lap. The candles made moving shadows on the walls and on her body as he slowly unbuttoned her top and cupped her breasts, then bent down to kiss her.

Her breathing came out in short, shallow gasps and she responded to every caress, every touch and every kiss with little moans of pleasure that drove him more and more wild. Her lips were pink and soft, her eyes cloudy and her blonde hair spread around her face like sunshine, and he wanted her with an intensity that hurt ...

Was she dreaming? If she was, she never wanted to wake up, that way she could stay in his arms and love him forever. Would she dare tell him what she felt? Surely he must have guessed by now.

His hands felt hard and rough against her skin, but he was touching her with such exquisite tenderness that she was melting, burning, and drowning in a sea of delicious sensations all at once ... She snuggled against him and put her palm on his heart. It beat hard and fast under his tee shirt, like hers.

She circled her index finger on his chest. His body tensed, he drew in a sharp breath and his arms tightened around her. 'I want to take you upstairs and make love to you ...' he said in a deep, low voice.

And the spell was broken as an icy finger touched her spine. How could she forget, even for a few minutes, what Adrian had said about her being prim, stiff and boring in bed, about her being unimaginative and prudish? Once he had even said that he had never really enjoyed their lovemaking, and she would never find another man willing to put up with her.

What if Daniel thought the same? What if he was disappointed?

She pulled away from Daniel's grasp. 'We don't need to go upstairs yet. Perhaps we should have a drink. I have a bottle of red wine in the kitchen.' That was it! Wine would loosen her up.

He frowned and let his hands fall by his sides. 'We don't have to do anything you don't want to, Jenna. It's all right. There's no rush.'

He touched a finger to her cheek. 'The last thing I want is for you to have regrets.'

'I won't have regrets. I promise. I need to …' She jumped to her feet, hastily refastened the buttons of her top, and padded to the kitchen area where she opened a cupboard and pulled down a bottle of red wine.

He stood up too and followed her into the kitchen as she uncorked the bottle and poured some wine into a couple of glasses. She lifted her glass. 'Santé … or shall we say *Slàinte Mhath* since we're in Scotland?'

She knew she sounded slightly incoherent but she couldn't help it. If she managed to drink a glass or two of wine, she would be less boring and more able to please Daniel – the way she had failed to please Adrian.

She drank a large gulp of wine, and grimaced. 'It's not bad. But then again I was never one of those people who can tell you what country a wine is from or what grape has been used …' That was another of her many faults and Adrian had complained time and time again that she always bought the wrong wine.

Daniel took his glass, and said in a low voice, '*Slàinte Mhath* …' But he didn't drink. He looked resigned and tired again, as if all his energy and all his fire had left him. Awkward silence now filled the room as he looked at her.

'Tell me if you've changed your mind and you'd rather be alone, and I'll go,' he said at last as he put his glass on the counter. 'I knew a woman like you would never be interested in someone like me.' He let out a harsh laugh. 'I allowed myself to dream a little.'

He shrugged, looked down at his hands. A few specks of blood had come through the plaster on his wounded hand. The day at sea mustn't have done his injury any good. 'If you think you'll be all right now, I shall leave you alone.'

Her fingers shook as she put her glass down. What was she doing, acting like some silly, spoiled woman and making him think he wasn't good enough for her when it was the other way round?

'Daniel. Wait! I'm sorry for acting all stupid – it's not what you think.'

He narrowed his eyes and she got the full force of his blue glare. 'Then what is it?'

'I'm nervous, and I'm afraid you'll find me boring and inadequate – in bed, I mean. I was told many times that I was … that I wasn't …' She didn't even finish her sentence.

'What a lot of rubbish!' He closed the gap between them and wrapped one arm around her waist. Putting one finger under her chin, he tilted her face up, the way he had done before. 'Do I look like a man who is bored?'

'Well …'

He lowered his voice, and pulled her even closer. 'Do I *feel* like a man who is bored?'

She gasped. Actually he looked and felt quite angry right now.

'You are perfect … for me, at least,' he said in a growling voice. 'And I don't care what the blasted *eejit* you went out with before told you.' He glanced at her half-empty glass of wine and his own, untouched glass. 'Now, are you going to finish this or …'

She rested her face against his chest and her hands went up to his shoulders. 'I'm sorry.'

'Aye … and so you should be, for believing such stupid lies about yourself.' He bent down and kissed her softly, again, and again. And then the room tilted and she was back in his arms as he carried her to the sofa. He sat down again with her in his lap like before and proceeded to kiss her so thoroughly that she didn't think about being embarrassed or self-conscious – couldn't think anything at all except that she loved him so much her heart felt about to burst …

It was much later when they finally made it into bed, and even later still when Daniel pulled Jenna on top of him and wrapped his arms around her. 'It'll be daylight soon and I'll have to go.'

She propped herself up with one hand and touched her fingers to his face. His stubble made a scraping sound as she stroked his cheek, and she knew that various parts of her anatomy would be red and burning all day because of it … 'Won't you be too tired for another day at sea? You've hardly had any sleep.'

He smiled and kissed the palm of her hand. 'And whose fault is that? Not that I complain. It has been … quite a night.' He reclined onto the pillow and pulled her up, so that they were level and she looked into his now serious blue eyes. 'I hope you don't have any regrets.'

'Regrets? How could I have regrets? It has been the most wonderful, magical night.' And never mind that she sounded like a love-struck teenager!

He kissed the tip of her nose. 'For me too. You are very special to me, Jenna Palmer.'

Joy bubbled inside her, and it felt like her heart, her whole body, were smiling. 'You are very special to me, Daniel McGregor,' she replied before snuggling against his chest.

'That's good,' he repeated in a sleepy voice.' He closed his eyes, and after a few seconds his breathing slowed down and his hold around her loosened.

She wanted to tell him that she loved him, that he was the kindest, the most thoughtful and patient of men – of lovers – and she could never have enough of his kisses and his caresses, and that she wanted to be in his life forever? She should tell him about what she went through with Adrian. But all of that could wait. For now she was warm, safe and content in his arms, with the sound of his heartbeat and of his breathing lulling her to sleep.

Chapter Twenty-Eight

It was the popping noise of the electricity coming back on that woke her up. She was alone in bed, with the covers pulled up over her shoulders. The ceiling light was on together with the bedside table lamp, and grey daylight crept into the room through the curtains. The alarm clock on the bedside table indicated quarter past six. She had slept about three hours ... She touched the sheets on the other side of the bed. They were cold, and she couldn't hear a sound. Where was Daniel?

Shivering in the chilly bedroom, she got up, retrieved her pyjamas from the floor and put them on quickly. 'Daniel?' Her voice echoed in the cottage. There was no answer. She walked to the window and drew back the curtains. A sigh of disappointment escaped from her lips. Daniel's Land Rover wasn't at the front any longer. He had left, without waking her to say goodbye.

Was he already out with the lifeboat? The rain may have stopped but gusts of wind still swished across the clifftop with loud whistling sounds, making the grass move like waves and ruffling the surface of the sea in the bay.

Slipping a cardigan on, she went downstairs. On the table was a piece of paper folded in half with her name handwritten on the front.

I've been paged. The lifeboat has to go out again but I didn't want to wake you. I'll call round later. Daniel.

It wasn't exactly the most romantic of messages, but he must have been in a hurry to get back to Dana, and perhaps he wasn't very demonstrative when it came to writing, that was all. He had certainly been demonstrative enough during the night ...

Her face, her whole body still burned from his kisses and caresses, and the tender, loving way he had touched her, held her in his arms and made love to her. What a contrast with Adrian. After the first few months of their relationship, his lovemaking always felt perfunctory – a burden, even. And then it had stopped altogether.

She hissed an annoyed breath. She had to forget Adrian. Forget the past. What mattered now was Daniel. Never had she been so thoroughly and completely loved, so what did it matter if he didn't write her a sonnet before leaving this morning? He must be exhausted after his day at sea and a few hours of snatched sleep, and now he was out at sea again with his crew mates, ready to save lives.

What's more, she should know by now that overblown compliments, flowery words and declarations of undying love often meant nothing, and that only actions revealed somebody's true heart. And Daniel had a good heart. And she loved him. She loved him so much it made her body and soul sing and she couldn't stop smiling.

She put the paper back on the table. Now the electricity was back she could make some coffee and toast and take a hot shower before getting ready for work. It would however take a lot more than a coffee and a hot shower to wake her up from the beautiful dream she was still wrapped up in. In fact, she didn't even want to wake up at all.

She was still smiling and still half-asleep when Brendon picked her up after eight. 'Are you all right, love? You look a wee bit pale. I hope you weren't too scared here on your own during the storm last night, especially with the power cut.'

She didn't like lying to Brendon, but she didn't want to tell him about Daniel staying the night either, so she remained vague. 'I didn't sleep much, that's true, especially with the wind rattling the windows most of the night.'

'It's a good job Buttercup is scheduled to stay in Dana all day and we don't have to drive around in this weather. Let's stop at the tea shop before we take the van out of the garage. I fancy a takeaway coffee and a box of Turnock teacakes.'

The morning dragged on and on … By lunchtime, Jenna's nerves were jittery from too much coffee and too much sugar. She should know that teacakes would only make her queasy, yet she munched through the best part of the box Brendon had bought from The Buttered Scone. Waiting for news of the lifeboat crew was agonising, especially since the Radio Dana ten o'clock news bulletin had not given any update about the search.

At least Buttercup was staying on the seafront that morning, so Jenna would see the lifeboat come back. The sea was a dirty, menacing gunmetal grey, with only a few fishing boats bobbing up and down on the swell. It started raining again, and the few families who had ventured onto the beach in fleeces and raincoats packed up their buckets and spades and hurried away.

Jenna sneezed and rubbed her freezing hands together. She should have put a cardigan or a fleece on. It was cold, sitting in the draught as Buttercup's door was kept open and the wind blew in. It must be even colder at sea, and she hoped Daniel and his crew had flasks of hot drinks. Most of all she hoped they were safe and would find the missing holidaymakers at last.

'What was that? Sorry, Brendon, I wasn't listening …'

Brendon shook his head. 'I was only saying that you have stamped Mrs Nevis' book three times.'

'Oh.' Jenna looked down then gave the woman an apologetic smile. 'Sorry, Mrs Nevis.'

The woman chuckled. 'There's no harm done, lass. You must have something more important than stamping books on your mind … a young man, perhaps?'

Jenna's face grew warm, and as soon as Mrs Nevis climbed down the steps and Buttercup was empty, Brendon burst out laughing. 'So that's what it is! I should have guessed. I'm not even going to ask who the young man you're pining for is.'

What was the use of pretending? She sighed. 'I am worried, Brendon. The weather is getting worse again.'

He glanced at the windscreen and frowned. 'You're right. I don't think we'll get many customers today. We've only had three people in this morning. Shall I put the radio back on?'

'Yes, please. It's almost time for the midday news.'

The weather report started after a few adverts. A fresh storm was coming from the north, with gale-force-nine winds gusting at ten, and downpours expected later that day and through the night. The news bulletin reported some damage to the area caused by the previous night's storm and warned of further disruption.

'We have an update from the coastguards on the *Rona*, the missing sailing boat at the centre of a huge search and rescue operation,' the journalist was saying. 'The good news is that the *Rona* has been located late morning near Garbh Eilean where it appears to have run aground. However because of adverse weather conditions the rescue is proving hazardous. Dana's lifeboat is as I speak attempting a daring manoeuvre to get close to the boat, with the SAR coastguard helicopter assisting the operations. We will of course keep you updated as the situation evolves.'

Brendon put a hand on her shoulder and gave her a squeeze. 'They'll be all right, love. They know what they're doing. In the meantime, I suggest we take Buttercup back to the garage while we have some lunch. I don't want the old girl to get battered by the storm.'

Brendon was right. The seafront was now completely

deserted as gusts of wind and lashings of almost horizontal rain swept over the road and the car park, shoving and pushing poor Buttercup and rattling the books on the shelves. Even the photo of the Highland heifer which was Buttercup's namesake and which was displayed on the counter, had fallen over a couple of times. Jenna once again crossed her fingers and said a little prayer for Daniel and his crew mates, and the family's safe return.

'Where the hell are they? I can't see anyone on or around the *Rona.*' Alasdair manoeuvred the lifeboat as close to the rocks as he could.

'They're inside. They have to be,' Daniel remarked, standing next to him, his heart hammering. The alternative was too grim to contemplate. A family, two kids …

'Then why isn't someone coming out – or at least giving us a sign? They must have heard us, and the helicopter is making enough noise.' The coxswain didn't have to elaborate. He was thinking the same grim thoughts as Daniel.

'This is as close as I can get without smashing against the rocks,' he added, using all his skills and experience of the area to keep the lifeboat away from the island's rugged and dangerous coastline.

'I'm going in – there's no other way,' Daniel said. 'If there are any casualties on board, one of us will have to get them ready to be airlifted.'

A couple of minutes later, he was in the water, which boiled and swirled and raged around him. He was a strong swimmer but his clothes were bulky and heavy. It took all his energy and determination to reach the reef on which the yacht had shattered, grip hold of the wet, slippery rock and pull himself up. The Rona lay on its side, at a forty-five degree angle, the mast snapped in two. He called the name of the family members as he scrambled onboard. Ross and Melanie Grant, their two kids Becky and Ben.

Calling, and praying, he yanked open the cabin door, and jumped down the steps. He called again. His heart hammered in his chest now. Where were they?

The cabin was empty. Shit. Had they been thrown overboard? A hollow feeling spread inside him. If so, they were lost.

He scrambled back out, and updated Alasdair on his radio. 'Nobody's in the boat. I repeat, the boat is empty. Over.'

'Roger that.'

Daniel looked at the rocky shore. There were caves around there, lots of them, but most would be underwater now because of the storm and the tide. He'd explored them often enough, back in the days when he used to dive with Hugh. However, he remembered that a couple of caves further up the shore would be dry and could provide shelter.

'I'm going to see if I can find anyone. Over.'

'Take care, Daniel. Over.'

They wouldn't have gone far, he reasoned. Not in the middle of a storm. Not with young kids. He had to cling to the hope that they were still alive and had sought shelter. If they were in a cave, it would explain why they couldn't hear the lifeboat or the helicopter. He called their names again and again as he walked into the first cave, and switched on his helmet torch. And then he heard a voice – a woman's – calling back. 'Over here! We're over here!'

Taking care not to slip on the wet, slimy rocks, he hurried to the back of the cave. They were there. Pale, wet, eyes huge and looking scared. Two kids huddling together, a blanket wrapped around their shoulders. The man lay on the ground, sleeping or unconscious.

The woman stood up and burst into tears. 'Thank God

you found us. Thank God. My husband. He's injured. He broke his ankle as we stepped down from the boat. He just made it here, but then he fainted and he's been unconscious ever since. I've been so scared.'

He gave her a reassuring smile. 'It's Melanie, isn't it? My name is Daniel. Don't worry. We'll look after you. You're all right now.' Training took over. First radio the news, ask for backup. Then assess the casualty. Having swam from the lifeboat he didn't have his first aid box with him so he couldn't do much, but it seemed Ross Grant did indeed have a broken ankle and probably concussion. The kids and their mother suffered from shock and hypothermia. But they were alive ...

Chapter Twenty-Nine

'You should eat something, love.' Brendon pushed the basket filled with golden chips towards her. 'You don't want Eric to think that you don't like his food.' He gestured to the big man behind the counter.

Jenna nibbled on a couple of chips, then a couple more. They were good. 'Thanks, Brendon.' She pulled the basket closer and carried on eating.

It had been a surprise to find the pub full on this stormy Monday lunchtime, with tourists and locals alike tucking into dishes of fish or steak pies, jacket potatoes and fish and chips.

'That's an interesting necklace you have there,' Brendon said, pointing to the pendant peeping out of the neckline of her blouse. 'Very unusual. Did you get it from the ceramics shop in town?'

She unclasped the necklace and handed it to Brendon so he could take a closer look. 'I found it on the beach in Mermaid Cove. It's a piece of majolica and apparently very old – from the late sixteenth century, I believe.'

Brendon put the pendant down on the table and slipped his glasses on to examine it.

'I looked up majolica on the internet,' Jenna carried on. 'This is very similar to pieces salvaged from Spanish Armada galleons shipwrecked along the coasts of Ireland and Scotland ...' Which made Daniel's silence when he'd seen the necklace all the more puzzling as he, of all people, should have been able to identify the piece and recognise its potential significance.

Brendon arched his eyebrows. 'You think it could come from the *Santa Catalina* treasure?'

She nodded. 'I found something else on the beach. I thought it was driftwood but Daniel said it was ivory and looked like a very old religious statuette, perhaps ... So it made me think. What if the treasure was hidden in Mermaid Cove?'

Brendon handed her the pendant that she slipped into her pocket. 'I don't want to disappoint you, lass, but people have been looking for that treasure for hundreds of years, and no one as thoroughly as Angus McGregor himself.'

Professor Ferguson claimed that jealousy and trampled honour weren't the only motives for the laird's cruel treatment of his young wife. The man was greedy for power and money too; by starving Lady Jane of food and water, he tried to force her to confess where Don Pedro de Valdes and his men had hidden the treasure. Unfortunately for him, Jane died without revealing anything, and none of Valdes' men had talked either.

'Did you look for it too?'

He nodded. 'Everybody around here has had a go.'

'Including Daniel and his brother, I believe. Wasn't Hugh searching the *Santa Catalina* wreck when he died?'

Brendon stroked his beard, looking pensive. 'Aye, that's what folk think. How did you know about Hugh?'

'Someone mentioned him the other day,' she replied, recalling what Hamish had said. 'I believe it was Daniel who found him and brought him back to shore.'

Brendon drank a sip of his beer then put the pint down again. 'It was a tragedy all right. The lad loved his diving and he was brilliant at it, if a little reckless at times. Daniel loved diving too, but he had responsibilities after he became the laird. He was always the more sensible of the pair, anyway. He had to be, poor lad, because Hugh didn't help much on the estate. All he ever wanted to do was to travel, dive … and party – all the more so when he met his fiancée.'

'You mean Shannon? Katrina's mum?'

Brendon nodded. 'The Siren. That's what people used to call her.' His face grew sombre. 'She was trouble.'

'Trouble? In what way?' She couldn't help it. She was curious.

'She used to play lads against one another, cause trouble between folks – start fights for the fun of it. It was good riddance when she returned to the States after Hugh's funeral.'

'But she left Katrina here, with Daniel,' Jenna said. 'Why would she do that?'

'All I know is what Daniel told Ruth. That Shannon couldn't cope with a toddler on her own because she travelled around too much to offer the girl a stable upbringing, and felt Katrina would be happier at Dunfiadhaich Farm. Daniel had looked after the lassie more than her parents ever did, anyway, with them always jetting off somewhere on their diving expeditions.'

He shook his head. 'Beautiful, but mean and selfish – that was Shannon all right.' He reached out for his pint of bitter and drank a big gulp.

Jenna couldn't believe her ears. Brendon never had a bad word to say about anyone.

She couldn't resist a last question. 'What was Daniel's brother like?'

This time Brendon smiled. 'Almost a carbon copy of Daniel physically, but the complete opposite otherwise. He was clever but idle, and often got into bother. He loved a good time, did Hugh, and he loved adventure. He was a good lad, really, always smiling and joking, and he was a terrible flirt. Every single woman he met, young or old, fell for him, and he sure took advantage of that.'

He sighed. 'Daniel loved his brother. As they were growing up he was always making excuses for him, and covering for him when he got into scrapes, but they got on well, and as far as I know the only disagreement they ever had was over Toby Drummond.'

'Why was that?'

'Hugh and Drummond used to be best pals, back in the day. They were at boarding school together, gravitated around the same crowd in London, but Daniel never got on with him. He said he was a bad influence on Hugh. Turned out he was right.'

Jenna's eyes widened. 'Really? How?'

'Drummond was involved in buying and selling antiques and Hugh got mixed up in his business. I don't know the details, but there were rumours of a tax fiddle. Drummond left for a long holiday abroad, leaving Hugh to face the music alone. Daniel sorted everything out with the taxman, but it left a bit of a strain on their relationship.'

'There was more trouble with Drummond later, though. Ruth told you, didn't she, that they had a fight and Daniel broke his nose after Hugh's funeral?'

Jenna gasped. 'She didn't say it was after Hugh's funeral. What happened?'

Brendon put his elbows on the table and leant forward. 'I'd rather you heard it from me than from anyone else ... At the end of the ceremony, Daniel was carrying Katrina out of the churchyard, with Shannon in tears clinging to his arm, when Drummond remarked in a very loud voice that Daniel must be glad to be finally rid of his brother and would now be able to carry on with Shannon as he pleased. He even said Daniel must be relieved that Hugh would never ask for a paternity test now.'

Jenna hissed a shocked breath. Toby Drummond may have already told her that Daniel and Shannon had had an affair, but to claim that Katrina was Daniel's child at his brother's funeral and in front of the whole village was despicable.

'Drummond legged it out of the churchyard and drove back to Carloch Castle, but Daniel went after him and you know the rest.'

And Toby Drummond was still spreading rumours to this day. 'Why would he say such a vile, appalling thing, especially at his friend's funeral?'

Brendon arched his eyebrows. 'Drummond and Hugh stopped being friends after the bother with the tax people, and that's when rumours about Daniel being Katrina's dad started circulating.'

Jenna shook her head. It was a lot to digest. No wonder Daniel didn't want to talk about Shannon or his brother. 'Do you think Hugh heard the rumours?'

Brendon pulled a face. 'Who knows? But if he did, it sure would have broken his heart. He loved Shannon, and he doted on Katrina even if he wasn't often here. Every time he came back from abroad, there was always a big party and lots of fun and excitement.'

And yet the day-to-day task of bringing up Katrina had been down to Daniel, Miona and Iain even then.

'I'm only telling you this because I think you have taken a shine to Daniel ... and perhaps more than that. Am I right?' Brendon gave her a searching look, and she nodded with a shy smile.

'These nasty rumours are still flying around and I wanted to warn you beforehand. Daniel is a good man. Family is important to him. Family, and Arrandale. He's been in charge of both ever since being a lad. He would never have done anything to hurt his brother.'

Was this what Daniel wanted to tell her last night, when he said there were things he had to talk to her about? Was

252

he planning on warning her against the malicious rumours? He didn't need to – she could never believe any of them! Poor Daniel, having to put up with such accusations the day of his brother's funeral … and poor little Katrina, who may hear them when old enough to understand.

Eric walked over to clear the plates. 'Did you say that you were after news of the lifeboat?'

Brendon nodded. 'Have you heard anything?'

'I heard on my CB radio that they're on their way back. They found the family, and got them airlifted to hospital. They're all safe.'

Jenna let out a cry and pushed her chair back. 'I'm going to the pier to wait for them.' She grabbed her coat, slipped it on as she ran out of the pub and into the blustery gale and driving rain. She pulled her hood down, pulled the zip up and carried on running, not caring about stepping in puddles or the cold rain stinging her face.

Word of the successful rescue must have spread because the promenade along the seafront, deserted an hour before, was now full of people braving the weather to welcome the lifeboat back. As she hurried down to the pier, Jenna even spotted a van with the blue Scottish Television logo on its side and a satellite dish on the roof.

Iain stood at the end of the pier in his hi-vis jacket like the night before, together with another couple of men she recognised from the lifeboat station. He smiled. 'Hi, lass, so you heard they're coming back?'

Jenna nodded. 'Can I wait here again?'

'Sure … Ah. Here they are!' He pointed at the lifeboat bouncing on the waves at speed, then at the television crew who were getting out of the van and preparing their equipment. 'It looks like we're going to be on the telly.'

Jenna hardly heard him. She only had eyes for the Black Wolf. As soon as it docked, Iain and his colleagues sprung into action, and six members of the lifeboat got out on deck carrying equipment and started to climb onto the pier. Her heart was beating faster, and faster. Like last night, Daniel was the last one to come out and onto the pier.

He looked at her, smiled slowly, and this time she didn't hold back but threw herself into his arms. He wrapped his arms around her, bent down and kissed her. His lips tasted of salt and the sea. It was the sweetest, the longest; the most wonderful kiss …

Everything else blurred and disappeared – the cold, gusting wind, whipping salty raindrops onto her cheeks; the lifeboat crew waiting for Daniel on the pier; the television crew a few metres away. There was only the joy of being held by the man she loved, and the relief of touching him. He was back, and he was safe.

He encircled her waist, drew her closer. His warmth seeped into her. Her hands glided on his waterproof suit along his arms, gripped his shoulders. Breathing in scents of brine and wind, she stood on her tiptoes and linked her hands behind his neck despite the straps of his lifejacket getting in the way.

Suddenly the sounds of laughter, clapping and cheering pierced through her consciousness. 'Ooh ooh! Who would have thought McGregor got himself a lass?'

'Aye, McGregor, you lucky devil! It looks like someone is glad to see you!'

'I could do with a wee kiss too.'

'Come on, you lovebirds, we need to do the debriefing now so we can get home!' interrupted a gruff voice.

Daniel loosened his embrace but kept his arm around her waist. 'I have to go. Will you wait for me at the lifeboat station? We can go back together then …' His eyes were full of promise and made her heart beat faster.

She touched his cheek. It felt rough against the palm of her hand. 'Yes, of course,' she whispered back.

They started walking back when a man she assumed was a journalist stepped in front of them and shoved his microphone in front of Daniel. 'Can we have a word, please? STV Central – Scottish Television.' He didn't wait for Daniel to reply. 'What can you tell us about the rescue of the Grant family?'

Daniel shook his head. 'I'm afraid you'll have to wait for the press release. Now if you don't mind, I need to go.'

But the journalist still blocked their path. 'As a lifeboat crew member who regularly puts his life in danger to save others,' he insisted, 'are you angry at the family for disregarding the weather warnings and chartering a sailing boat despite having no experience of sailing and no knowledge of the local area?'

Daniel frowned. 'Angry? Of course not. I'm relieved we found them and happy they're now safe.'

The journalist nodded and turned to Jenna. 'We could all see how happy and relieved you were to greet your husband'—he looked at her hand, and must have noticed the absence of rings—'or boyfriend, back home. Do you not get scared for him when he goes on search and rescue missions, and do you always greet him on the pier when he comes back?'

Jenna's chest tightened. What had she done, making a spectacle of herself and Daniel, embarrassing him in front of everybody, and what was she supposed to say now?

'I would be more than happy if Jenna welcomed me back with a kiss every single time.' Daniel smiled and looked down at her with a twinkle in his eyes. He didn't look mad or awkward at all.

'Sorry, guys, but we really need to get back. There'll be a press release shortly if you want to hang around.' And he practically pulled her away from the journalist and his team.

As soon as they reached the lifeboat station, he closed the door behind them, took her in his arms again, and pushed her against the wall to kiss her.

'Wait for me,' he said when he released her. 'I won't be long. And then, I want to go home with you – if that's all right? Tell Brendon I'm giving him the afternoon off.'

Chapter Thirty

'What's all this about, then, son?' Iain asked as Daniel pulled off his boots and removed his waterproof kit.

'What's *what* about?' Daniel replied, pretending not to understand. He was the last to walk into the kit room, the others having already got ready and were now waiting in the common room for the debrief.

'Don't play the innocent with me, lad. You didn't rush out yesterday evening just to help the lass at the cottage when the power went off, did you? You stayed out all night too, and I guess you two weren't changing the light bulbs. We didn't have time to talk this morning, but it's fairly obvious that you and young Jenna are now ... ach ... involved. Do you know what you're doing?'

Daniel took his thermal socks and base layer off, and pulled a face as he got dressed quickly in the same clothes he'd had on that morning when he left Mermaid's Cottage – the same clothes he had the day before too. He needed to get showered and changed, but first he needed to get Iain off his back.

'Honestly? I haven't a clue what I'm doing, but it feels damned good to go with the flow for once and not plan every single thing. So I think I'll carry on and figure things out as I go along. Jenna and I are good together right now and that's what matters.' They were more than good. They were wonderful together, and he felt stupid and giddy, like he was floating on a cloud right now.

He was expecting another sermon, instead Iain's face crinkled into a broad smile and he clapped him on the shoulder.

'Good answer, lad. Hurry up now. Alasdair is waiting for you and we all know he's a grumpy old sod.'

There was a massive cheer as he entered the common room, and heat crept up on the back of his neck.

'It seems Romeo has finished serenading his Juliet at last and is gracing us with his presence. About time,' Alasdair remarked with a mock severe look on his face.

'Serenading?' another lad remarked. 'Lover boy wasn't doing much singing back there, only a lot of groping and kissing!'

Twenty minutes later, and after much banter and teasing, and Alasdair insisting that he had the bandage on his hand redone by the crew's first-aider, Daniel was out of the lifeboat station, holding Jenna's hand and striding to the side street where he'd parked the Land Rover. 'Sorry it took so long.'

'It's all right,' she said, sounding slightly out of breath. 'Don't you have to talk to the journalist from the television again?'

He realised that she was almost running to keep up with him, and he slowed down. He couldn't wait to be alone with her – couldn't wait to kiss her again and take her to bed.

'Alasdair is dealing with the press.' He looked at her and smiled. 'I have more important things in mind than talking to a journalist.' The way she blushed made his heart melt a little. They reached the car. He held open the door for her and she got in.

'I'm sorry I left without saying goodbye this morning, but my pager went off at half five and I didn't want to wake you,' he said as he climbed behind the wheel and started the engine.

'It's all right. But it felt strange to wake up without you … like it had all been a dream.' She was still slightly out of breath, and doubt crept up inside him.

Perhaps he was rushing it – rushing her. Just because she had waited for him at the pier didn't mean she wanted to be whisked away and taken to bed. What was he doing? He was behaving like an animal.

He took a deep breath, slowed down, and turned to her. 'Please tell me if I'm going too fast. It's just that … it felt like a dream to me too, and now I want to make sure it's real. I want it to be real, Jenna.'

This wasn't the place for telling her how much she meant to him. He'd never been good at expressing his feelings, but he hoped he could show her when they got back to the cottage.

She looked at him, and smiled. 'I want it to be real too. And no, you're not rushing me at all.'

He let out a sigh of relief. 'Was Brendon all right about not working this afternoon?'

This time her face turned bright red. 'He wasn't surprised since he was at the pier when the Black Wolf docked and he saw, hmm … how *pleased* we were to see each other. What's more, he said he wasn't going to argue about having time off and was going straight back to The Anchor for another pint.'

'Pleased?' Daniel laughed as he changed gears, accelerating as he left town. *Pleased* didn't even come close. His heart felt like it was going to burst.

As soon as they arrived at Mermaid's Cottage, Jenna got out of the Land Rover and unlocked the door. She had hardly stepped into the hall when Daniel shut the door, took her in his arms, and gave her a long, leisurely kiss.

'This was the kiss I wanted to give you to wake you up this morning,' he whispered against her lips.

He gave her another, more urgent kiss. 'And this one would have been to make sure you were fully awake …'

Still kissing her, he unzipped her coat, and slid it off her shoulders and let it fall to her feet. Her blazer soon followed. He bent down, untucked her shirt from her trousers and started undoing the buttons, his fingers shaking with impatience.

She now stood against the door, her blonde hair tousled, her eyes half-closed and cloudy, and her lips already pink and swollen. Her shirt was open, revealing her plain white bra underneath. Desire shot through him. He couldn't get enough of kissing her, of touching her, but he had to slow down. If he carried on like this it would all be over in five minutes.

Jenna could hardly think as he trailed a finger down the curve of her neck, along her delicate collarbones, and down towards her breasts, stroking over the soft fabric of her bra. Teasing, tormenting. He made quick work of the rest of her clothes, and when she was down to her underwear gently pushed her against the door again.

The wind gusted and the rain drummed against the door. Thunder rolled in the distance, but she hardly heard it. A cool breeze touched her skin but it didn't stop her from burning. He unclasped her bra and slipped one hand down to her stomach and further down still to caress her as she threw her head back and clung on to his shoulders. Her bra fell to the floor, and now all she was wearing was her knickers. Her heart beat so hard it hurt and her legs hardly carried her as he took his time to explore and his lips lingered on her breasts, the stubble on his cheeks rasping and grazing her skin, adding to the pleasure swelling, throbbing, peaking inside her.

He lifted her off the floor, and carried her to the living room. 'The sofa,' he said in a growl before letting her down softly on the cushions.

The stormy sky made the room dark but he didn't switch the light on as he kicked his shoes off, shrugged his coat off and undressed quickly. And then he was on top of her, their bare skin touching and shivering with jolts of desire as lightning fizzed and thunder cracked around Mermaid's Cottage.

He rolled her knickers down her hips. 'Jenna ...' His voice was dark and deep as he lifted her hips and thrust inside her, and when they moved together at last, it felt like she was riding the storm, and the thunder and the lightning echoed and reverberated around them.

'Are you cold?' he asked a while later, kissing the tip of her nose as he wrapped his arms around her.

'A little. We could go up.' She pulled the throw which she had covered Katrina with the night before on top of them and snuggled closer. It was a very tight fit, not to mention that the sofa was far too short and Daniel's feet were sticking out, but there was nowhere else she'd rather be ... except perhaps in bed with him.

'I don't know if I can move. I feel a little tired all of a sudden, my love ...' He sounded sleepy. Letting out a sigh, he ran his hand down her back slowly.

Her breath hitched in her throat. He had called her my love. It could be nothing, of course – a manner of speech. Nevertheless, hope and joy soared and bubbled inside her. Could he possibly love her? He had said earlier in the car that he wanted their relationship to be real, and he had looked eager enough to touch and kiss her ... but that didn't mean that he actually loved her.

It was too late for her, of course. She loved him already, whether he loved her back or not. She kissed his chest, his throat, his jawline, moving up to the corner of his lips. 'Then you should sleep.'

He closed his eyes, mumbled something, and his breathing slowed down. She would enjoy every single second of being in his arms. She closed her eyes and drifted to sleep too.

It was early evening when she woke up. Daniel was

snoring softly and still holding her tightly against him, but she had pins and needles from being squished against the back of the sofa and had to get up. Her heart softened and swelled as she looked at him, then at the fresh bandage on his injured hand. That strong, brave and modest man had helped save lives today …

Her conversation with Brendon and Toby Drummond's vile accusations came back to her, but she shrugged them off. She would never believe Daniel was capable of betraying his brother. Never.

She stroked his forehead gently. He twitched, mumbled a protest, and slowly opened his eyes.

'I'm sorry, I need to get up,' she said.

He glanced at the clock on the wall and hissed an annoyed breath. 'Don't tell me I've been asleep all this time,' he said, before kissing her. 'That's embarrassing. So much for my stamina – and there was me, hoping to impress you and show you how strong and manly I was by making love to you, again and again. That will have to be for later.'

Her face grew warm and she gave him a playful smile. 'Promises, promises.'

He laughed, and holding her more tightly pressed her against him. 'Trust me, I will.' He kissed the top of her head. 'For now I must go back to the farm. I haven't seen Katrina since Saturday evening, and I want to make sure she's all right. She does worry.'

It was no wonder, with her father dead and her mother absent, that the little girl would be anxious about her uncle. Daniel's concern for the little girl was another reason she loved him.

'Come with me,' Daniel said then.

'Sorry?'

'Come to Dunfiadhaich Farm with me, that way we can both spend time with Katrina. She likes you very much.' His eyes softened as he brushed her hair from her face. 'And I like you very much too.'

He grew serious. 'It may be early days, but I want you to know that I'm serious about you, Jenna. Deadly serious.'

Her heart beat hard, her chest was tight. 'I'm serious about you too,' she whispered. She wanted to say that she loved him, but she felt shy suddenly. 'I would love to come to the farm with you this evening.'

'Then we'd better get ready,' he said. He got off the sofa and held out his hand to help her up. 'I think we have time for a wee shower.' He smiled as he pulled her close and once again held her against him.

'I saw you on the telly. You were kissing Jenna.' Katrina threw herself into Daniel's arms as soon as he opened the door.

Behind him, Jenna gasped as embarrassment flooded inside her. She had forgotten all about the journalist from Scottish Television. So they had filmed everything and it had already been on the news. It wasn't only Katrina who would have watched her making a spectacle of herself, but people from Dana, from the whole of Arrandale ... or further afield. Celia Kennedy, Councillor MacLean ... And what about English television? Surely they wouldn't be interested in a local lifeboat rescue – would they? Her mother never missed the *Six O'Clock News*.

'That's right. And now I am kissing you.' Daniel lifted Katrina in his arms and gave her a big kiss. She hooked her little legs around his waist like a monkey, the way she always did.

'I've missed you, chick,' he said. 'How have you been? How was school? What about those naughty lads you're always complaining about – did they behave themselves today or did you have to boss them around again?'

'Archie was told off by Miss today for messing about with the glue sticks.' Katrina giggled, and pulled a face as she sniffed his hair. 'You smell of girly shampoo.'

'I think it's nice, don't you agree?' he replied, winking at Jenna, who smiled back as she remembered how liberally he had used her body wash in the long, hot and steamy shower they had taken together ... and how they had stumbled onto her bed afterwards, giggling and wrapped in the same bath towel.

Katrina turned round and her eyes widened as she saw Jenna standing in the doorway. 'You're here too! You were kissing my uncle and everybody was clapping and cheering. It was on the telly. You'll be famous now.'

Jenna's face burned. 'I don't know about being famous.' But she would definitely have to get used to people smirking and winking at her in the next few days ... starting with Miona and Iain who now appeared in the corridor.

What were they going to say? What if they didn't approve, or if Katrina got upset about it? She looked all right now but she may change her mind, and later tell Daniel she wasn't happy about them having a relationship. And then what would he do?

Miona scowled at Daniel. 'Are you going to stay in the hallway all evening? Take the lasses into the drawing room while I warm up something to eat for you two lovebirds. We've already had our tea but I bet you're hungry and all.'

Daniel laughed. 'I am positively ravenous.'

He gave Jenna's fingers a quick glance and frowned. 'You're doing that thing with your fingers again,' he remarked in a quiet voice.

She looked down and shoved her fists in her jeans pockets. When would she ever stop that irritating habit? It wasn't as if Adrian still had any power over her – as if he still mattered.

'You have nothing to be anxious about,' Daniel added. 'Come.' Still carrying Katrina, he led the way into the drawing room. Jenna had never been in here before. In fact, she realised that apart from the dining room and the kitchen she had no idea what the rest of Dunfiadhaich Farm looked like.

It was a cosy room dominated by a stone fireplace and with large windows overlooking a wet and windswept garden at the back of the house. Oil and watercolour paintings adorned the walls which were covered with faded flowery wallpaper. Photos were displayed on the mantelpiece and on scattered tables around the room, and children's books were piled up near the sofa next to a plastic crate filled with toys, dolls and Lego bricks. This was a room for living, playing, reading and relaxing ... a homely room, and a far cry from the stilted and sophisticated grandeur of Carloch Castle's drawing room.

'What a beautiful garden,' she said, glancing out of the window and marvelling at the white, pink and purple rhododendron bushes which were for now battered by the wind and the rain.

'Iain does much of the gardening,' Daniel said. 'I'm too busy with the farm and the estate. Do you mind if I leave you for five minutes? I need to get changed.'

'Of course not. I'll have a chat with Katrina.'

The little girl dived head first into her toy box and pulled out a brush, and a plastic bag filled with hair clips, bows and ribbons.

'I'll do your hair so you'll be pretty for your tea with Uncle Daniel. I never got to practise on you Sunday ...'

She tapped her small hand on the sofa. 'Sit here.'

'Yes, Miss Bossy Boots!' Jenna laughed and did what she was told, and for the following ten minutes suffered in silence while Katrina scraped her hair with a plastic brush, poked her skull with clips and pins, and generally created a massive bird's-nest on her head.

'Are you going to marry my uncle?' Katrina asked. 'That's what you have to do if you kiss, you know.'

'Err, well … Oh, look at that lovely ribbon,' Jenna said, holding out a pink satin ribbon, hoping to distract her.

'No. I don't want that one.' Katrina dismissed it before sticking a few more clips in her hair, 'My uncle never had a girlfriend before. You must be very kind to him and take good care of him.'

Jenna's heart immediately tightened and tears pricked her eyes, and this time it wasn't because of a hairpin digging into her skull, but because Katrina was looking out for Daniel. 'I will, don't worry. I like him very much and …'

And she should stop now, before she opened her heart to a seven-year-old girl and confessed that she was truly, deeply, madly in love with her uncle!

As Katrina carried on doing whatever she was doing to her poor head, Jenna looked at the photos scattered around the room. They were lots of Katrina – as a baby in a pram or in the arms of a man who looked like Daniel and must be her dad; as a toddler on the beach; in her school uniform, standing proudly on the front steps of Dunfiadhaich Farm, probably on her first day at primary school.

On a table near the window were a few photos of a couple in formal evening wear – the tall, attractive dark-haired man in red and green tartan, black velvet jacket, waistcoat and white shirt; the woman in a black evening dress with a sash of the same tartan, her greying blonde hair gathered in an elegant chignon. There were photos of two dark-haired boys with mischievous smiles, Daniel and Hugh; then the same boys as teenagers riding a quad bike or on the beach in swimming trunks, holding flippers, diving masks and snorkels. Jenna looked around the room, but if there were any photos of Shannon, she couldn't see them.

Daniel pushed the door open and popped his head round. 'Jenna, we're eating in the kitchen.'

'But I haven't finished her hair yet!' Katrina protested.

'It looks lovely as it is,' Daniel said. 'Come with us and you can tell us what you've been up to today.'

The meal consisted of shepherd's pie and apple crumble with custard. Katrina hovered around Jenna and insisted on finishing her hair while regaling them all of tales about her school day. Miona stood near the stove, arms crossed on her frilly apron, a beaming smile on her face, and Iain sat at the table next to Daniel and begged for second helpings of crumble.

They talked about the rescue – Daniel leaving out the details which could upset Katrina; about the weather which would thankfully be getting better in the next few days; about Buttercup and Jenna's ideas to make it a real social hub for the community; and about the farm and the tractor which still wasn't fixed.

The windows got all steamed up and the kitchen echoed with banter and laughter, even more so when Daniel let the dogs in and Sam and Eddie both rushed straight to Jenna and put their wet, muddy paws on her jeans.

Daniel kept smiling at her across the table, his blue eyes filled with warmth and something so sweet and tender it made her heart flip and spin and fly.

'I know what we should do now,' Katrina said after she'd had a cup of hot milk and the rest of them had coffee. 'Uncle Daniel, why don't you get your fiddle and play some music for Jenna? She'll need to practice the steps for the ceilidh on Saturday!'

'Now that's a good idea,' Miona said. 'It's been a while since I heard any music in this place.'

'I sing to you all the time, woman,' Iain protested.

'You don't sing. You crow!' she retorted.

'Och … That's mean,' Iain replied with a mock wounded look on his face.

Daniel pulled a face and looked at the wall clock. 'I don't know. Isn't it a bit late?'

'I can put my pyjamas on and do my teeth in five minutes.' Katrina joined her hands and gave him a cute, pleading look.

Daniel smiled. 'All right then, love. But I'll only play a few tunes. I don't want you to stay up too late.' He looked at Jenna. 'I'll show you to the library. It's the best room for dancing.'

So they pushed some furniture around to make space for the dancers on the wooden floor, and they had a party. Daniel played happy tunes which had everybody dancing and twirling, even Jenna who didn't know what to do but was shown the steps by the others. When they collapsed, dizzy and laughing, red-cheeked and out of breath, onto the library's large, battered armchairs, he played a few of the soulful melodies he played on Mermaid's Beach.

He looked at her and smiled, and her heart swelled again … God, she loved him so much.

'Right, young lassie,' he said, scooping a giggling Katrina in his arms. 'That's enough dancing for tonight. It's time for bed.'

Katrina insisted that both Daniel and Jenna come up to her room and sit on her bed to read her a bedtime story.

'Why do you call this place a farm when it's more of a manor house?' Jenna asked as she walked up the imposing staircase and trailed her fingers along the dark oak banister.

'I suppose it was one of my ancestors' canny ideas. Pretending to be farmers would deflect the greed and jealousy of other clans.'

Katrina had a room worthy of a fairytale princess. The walls were painted yellow and pale blue and a white bed with a canopy and white muslin curtains hanging down. On the white dressing table was a photo of the most beautiful woman Jenna had ever seen, surrounded by large, exotic looking sea shells. She didn't need to be told that this was Shannon.

Jenna took in the woman's sparkling green eyes and dazzling smile, and the long, curly black hair that tumbled down to her waist. No wonder people had nicknamed her the Siren.

Katrina jumped into her bed, slipped under her covers and patted the duvet. 'You can both sit on the bed and take it in turns to read the story.' She had picked up one of her favourite Zonk McPurple stories, of course.

When they had turned the last page, Daniel put the book away and bent down to give Katrina's cheek a kiss. 'Time to sleep.'

Katrina yawned, snuggled under her duvet and closed her eyes. 'Goodnight, Uncle Daniel ... Goodnight Jenna.'

Daniel frowned. 'Aren't you forgetting something, Katrina?'

The little girl shook her head. 'Nope.'

'You didn't ask me what you can dream of tonight.' Daniel sounded puzzled and slightly disappointed.

'That's because I already know,' she replied. 'But I won't tell you yet. It's a secret.'

'All right, sweet dreams then, chick.'

'Jenna?' Katrina called with a sleepy voice as Daniel was switching off the light. 'Thank you for making my uncle happy.'

Chapter Thirty-One

Daniel pulled Jenna on top of him and trailed kisses along her throat, his fingers sliding up and down her back. 'I wish we could shut the door and forget about the world for a few days.'

'What about Buttercup, Brendon ... work?' She became breathless as his hands slipped further down.

'I could give you another day off.'

'It wouldn't be fair,' she said. 'Yesterday was exceptional.'

He smiled. 'Was it? Thanks. I'm glad you enjoyed it. I did try my best.'

'I wasn't talking about *that*!' She laughed – a playful, husky laugh that made his heat bloom inside him all over again. 'I meant, the unplanned afternoon off.'

He cocked his eyebrows, and shook his head, pretending to be offended. 'I see. You know how to wound a man where it hurts, don't you?'

'*That* was exceptional too.' She drew slow patterns on his chest, and kissed him above the heart. Suddenly she heaved a sigh, propped herself up, and looked at him, deadly serious. 'Daniel. I need to talk to you.'

He looked at her, surprised by her change of tone. 'Is it anything I did, or said? Perhaps it was too much at the farm – the music and the dancing, not to mention Katrina's hairdressing. Talking of which, here is another pin ... I thought I'd taken them all out.'

He stroked her hair and dislodged yet another one of Katrina's hair accessories. He'd had great fun earlier plucking out all the clips, bows and bubbles before running his fingers through Jenna's silky blonde hair.

'It's not the music and the dancing – although it was fun

– or my hair, or Katrina's hairdressing. It's … you … and me.'

He tensed, and frowned. 'Oh.' So this was it – the moment where she told him it had all been a mistake, and she should never have got involved with him. They were too different. He was rough when she was delicate and sensitive. He didn't like reading when it was her life. He cared for a troubled little girl who took most of his time when he wasn't working. He had half-expected it but the sudden ache in his chest staggered him. It was as if someone crushed their fist into him, and pushed and rammed so hard he couldn't breathe.

He looked into her pale blue eyes. They were soft and gentle. She was about to deliver the killer blow, that's probably why she looked at him with such kindness.

His throat was tight when he asked, 'What do you mean? I thought we were getting on rather well.'

Pink bloomed on her cheeks and she heaved a shaky breath. 'Yes, we have. It's been wonderful … What I want to say is, there are things you need to know about me, about the past.'

His relief was so huge and unexpected that for a moment he lost the ability to breathe, let alone speak. He rolled over and looked down at her as he linked their fingers together and pinned her hands on the pillow on either side of her head. 'I don't *need* to know anything, Jenna. As far as I'm concerned, you're pretty much perfect.'

But *he* wasn't. As a matter of fact, he had things to tell her too, and he feared she may feel differently about him afterwards.

He would talk to her, but later, that weekend perhaps over a glass of wine or two, or during a long walk on Mermaid's Beach. For now, he enjoyed the feelings and sensations of having the woman he loved in his arms.

It was after midnight when Jenna fell asleep. He wanted to be home when Katrina woke up in the morning, give her some breakfast and take her to school. He had a pretty full-on day planned too … He disentangled himself from Jenna's embrace and got up. He gathered his clothes from the floor and got dressed quickly. Jenna looked so peaceful, her blonde hair making splashes of sunshine on the pillow. It seemed a shame to wake her up, but he'd promised to say goodbye this time, so he sat on the bed next to her when he was ready, and bent down to kiss her lips.

'I have to go, love. Don't get up. I'll close the door behind me.'

She nodded, half asleep and her eyes unfocussed. 'Hmm … All right. I'll see you after work?'

'Yes. I'll call round in the evening.'

He kissed her again and went down, retrieved his jacket from the living room where he'd thrown it on the sofa when they'd arrived back earlier in the evening. His keys were on the table, next to the blue folder in which Jenna kept the entries for the short story competition. She had said that Katrina had written her story. Curious, he opened the folder, and pulled out a folded sheet of lined paper, flipped it open and started to read.

"The Mermaid Girl" was the title … He tensed. In the margins were drawings of fish, shells and seaweed. There were mermaids too, a child one and a woman, as well as yellow flowers – roses perhaps, like in Jenna's garden – and a little house which could very well be Mermaid's Cottage.

"There was once a poor little mermaid girl called Kaya …" He started reading, his throat tight, his eyes burning, and his shoulders stiff and rigid. "… who got lost after a bad storm and woke up one day on a beach in a strange country. A peasant woman found her and adopted her."

Daniel cursed under his breath. It didn't take a child psychologist to tell him that Kaya was Katrina. "The woman was kind, but Kaya really wanted to get back into the sea, back to her mermaid mother who must be so worried about her ..."

Daniel's shoulders tensed further. Worried? Ah! Nothing could be further from the truth. Shannon didn't even reply to his emails these days. He wasn't even sure that she read his weekly updates about Katrina.

"Every night she went to the beach and she called and cried, but her mother never came."

Aye, that was more like it ...

"Time passed, and Kaya worked in the garden with the peasant woman. Kaya liked the garden, especially the yellow roses. One night she had a dream that she grew the most beautiful roses in the world and she became famous and her mummy heard about her and came to find her. So the kind peasant woman helped her grow the best roses in the country. One day, like in her dream, her mummy heard about the beautiful garden. She realised Kaya was her lost daughter, and she took her back to the mermaid kingdom ... Kaya's dream had come true. It was the best day of her life."

Daniel's hand shook as he put the paper back down.

How could he have been so presumptuous as to believe that he would succeed in giving Katrina a normal, settled and happy childhood – as normal, settled and happy as was possible under the circumstances? He had failed miserably. The little girl still suffered from her mother's absence, and all she wanted was to be reunited with her. Whatever had gone on in the past, whatever wrong Shannon had done, he couldn't ignore Katrina's feelings – Katrina's dreams. He had to do something ...

He closed his eyes, and let out the breath he'd been

holding. He put the paper back in the folder, and let himself out of the cottage. He had a lot of thinking to do.

'So I heard McGregor and you were smooching on the telly last night.' Murdo gave her a quizzical look.

'Aye, they were smooching all right! I was at the pier when the lifeboat came back and I witnessed the drama first-hand, along with half of the town,' Donald remarked.

Jenna's stomach tensed. She had become fond of the two elderly gentlemen and their good opinion mattered.

Murdo faced Donald and shook his head. 'I'm fair scunnered you didn't call me and I missed all the excitement.'

Donald only shrugged. 'You were too busy slurping whisky at the pub, you old scoundrel.' He turned to Jenna again. 'I wish you and McGregor well, lass. The lad deserves a bit of happiness after …' He frowned, and corrected himself. 'Well, he deserves a bit of happiness, that's all.'

Murdo pulled his sleeve. 'Aye, he sure does. Come on, old man, let's have a look at the books on shinty that Jenna found for us, over a cup of tea at The Buttered Scone.'

'Who are you calling an old man?' Donald knotted his bushy grey eyebrows. As usual they carried on squabbling as they climbed down Buttercup's steps.

All day and everywhere Buttercup stopped, people smiled and winked at her, including Brendon.

'You look positively glowing this morning, lass,' he had said when he picked her up that morning. To which she had replied that she was the happiest she'd ever been. And she hadn't stopped smiling.

The bad weather had passed. The sea glittered, a bright and deep blue – the colour of Daniel's eyes. There was sunshine all around, and in her heart too.

'Let's go, Jenna. This will be our last stop of the day,' Brendon said as he sat next to her and buckled his seat belt.

They were heading to the nursing home where she hoped to talk to Professor Ferguson again and show him the ceramics pendant.

Brendon glanced at her. 'You seem to be enjoying the drive today, love.'

She nodded. 'How could I not enjoy such a glorious day? Look at the loch over there with that tiny white cottage on the shore – how romantic it looks. And what about those black mountains in the distance …'

'That's Beinn Dhubh,' Brendon said.

That was where Daniel had injured his hand. So much had happened since …

Over the past few weeks, Jenna had become more skilled at negotiating the tight bends and narrow, winding lanes, and dealing with the sheep and the Highland cows that often wandered in the middle of the road or sat down on a patch of tarmac warmed by the sun. She had become a lot better at parking too, she thought as she stopped Buttercup in the lay-by in front of the nursing home.

'I hope we don't come across Drummond driving like a lunatic again today. Our last visit was traumatic enough,' Brendon said.

She nodded. She hoped she wouldn't meet him either. Her opinion of the man had taken a dive since Brendon had told her about the shocking incident in the graveyard after Hugh's funeral.

A surprise awaited Jenna when she walked into the nursing home. Professor Ferguson was engaged in an animated discussion with a couple of young men, one of whom she immediately recognised. 'Hamish! What are you doing here?'

The student rose to his feet and broke into a wide smile. 'Holy Basil … Jen! What a mega surprise. We're quizzing the Prof about the *Santa Catalina*.'

He pointed to the other young man. 'This is my friend Ben – the one who was in Glasgow when you and McGregor stayed over.'

Ben extended his hand and gave Jenna a big smile. 'Hi, Jenna. I was gutted I missed Daniel's visit – and yours, of course. McGregor has always been one of my role models. Some of the dives he made with his brother were incredible. The man's a proper legend.'

Jenna smiled, filled with pride for Daniel. What a shame that the memories of his diving days were now tainted with the tragedy of his brother's death, and that he didn't want to talk about them.

'Actually,' she said, 'perhaps you can help me. I wanted to talk to Professor Ferguson but three heads are better than one. Can you wait until I have taken care of the residents?'

'Sure. No worries,' Hamish said.

'I wanted to ask your opinion about this pendant,' she told Professor Ferguson twenty minutes later. She untied the leather thong and handed him the pendant while explaining where she found it.

'Holy Basil!' Hamish exclaimed before turning to his friend, his eyes shining with excitement. 'Are you thinking what I'm thinking?'

Chapter Thirty-Two

What a rotten day it was turning out to be ...

The car had played up again as he drove back from Mermaid's Cottage last night and he'd just made it back into the courtyard before the engine spurted out smoke and died. He hadn't even bothered going to bed, but drank coffee after coffee in the kitchen, thinking about Katrina's story and what he had to do.

When the first grey light of dawn coloured the sky he had gone out to fix the Land Rover, so he was tired and in a foul mood when Katrina refused to get dressed for school after breakfast. Instead of playing along, he'd lost his temper and declared that he wouldn't take her to the ceilidh on Saturday, which had resulted in a massive tantrum. They'd been late to school and he'd had to brave the school receptionist and stammer a vague and unconvincing excuse about car problems.

It had all been downhill after that. Celia Kennedy had called about Jenna taking unscheduled time off the previous afternoon, resulting in some grumblings from unhappy customers who had waited for the mobile library in vain and phoned to complain, even though he seriously doubted that, given the poor weather. An awkward conversation had ensued, with Daniel explaining that he was the one who had given Jenna and Brendon the afternoon off.

Then a meeting with his accountant had confirmed that the farm was barely breaking even and he wouldn't be able to buy the new equipment they needed unless he sold some land or livestock, something he'd always refused to do, except once ... And to add insult to injury, Drummond still hadn't covered the cost of the sheep he'd run over.

Katrina had come out of school looking upset again, and confessed some children had made fun of her and it wasn't the first time. 'I told some people about my story for the competition and they said it was rubbish and that I'd never win.'

He had crouched down, and got out his handkerchief to wipe her tears. 'You mean, the story you wrote at Jenna's the other day?'

She sniffed loudly and nodded. 'It's about a mermaid girl and—'

'I read it,' he interrupted. 'It's very good.'

Her eyes lit up. 'Is it? Really?'

'Really ... and I loved your illustrations too.'

Katrina let out a long sigh. 'Miss said I had to stop making things up, you know about my mummy being a mermaid. She said she'd speak to you about it at the parents' evening.'

'The parents' evening? When it that?'

'Soon.' Katrina rummaged through her coat pocket and handed him a crumpled slip of paper. His heart sank when he read it. The next parents' evening was in a couple of weeks' time. No doubt the teacher would mention Katrina's fertile imagination once again when in fact she was only repeating the stories he'd made up.

He was tired of it all. So tired.

He held her hand as they walked back to the car. Or rather he walked and she skipped.

'Don't worry about the parents' evening, Uncle Daniel. Miss won't tell you off for being naughty,' she said.

He glanced down at her. 'Naughty?'

'Well, you said a lie this morning. We weren't late because the car wouldn't start but because you were mean to me and you made me cry.'

He stopped and stared into her bright blue eyes. 'I'm sorry

if I was cross with you, love. I am sorry for everything.' His voice broke and he closed his eyes.

He felt a tug on his hand. 'Are you crying, Uncle Daniel?'

'No, of course not.' But he turned away and gave his eyes a quick wipe with his fingers.

'It was my fault you got told off at school. I should have got dressed straight away. I am sorry. Do you want me to tell Miss the truth tomorrow?' she said then in a small, quivering voice.

He grunted something which could have been a yes or a no. How he loved that child. 'Oh love. Come here. I'm sorry too.'

For everything.

And he scooped her up in his arms, held her tightly and buried his face in her dark hair, breathing in the scent of her baby shampoo. He carried her back to the car, and strapped her in her car seat at the back.

'Can we stop at Mermaid's Cottage and ask Jenna if she can have tea with us?' Katrina asked as he drove out of Dana and onto the cliff road. 'We had so much fun last night.'

Jenna … His fingers gripped the steering wheel more tightly. What should he tell her? Should he even have got involved with her at all? He knew how special she was, how she made him feel … and he had let himself hope that she could be his happy dream come true. Now he wasn't sure he hadn't made a massive mistake.

'Perhaps not tonight, love.'

He thought Katrina would protest but she said nothing. However, as he drove near the clifftop past Mermaid's Cottage he noticed a scruffy blue van parked at the front, with University of Glasgow stickers on the rear window – Hamish's and his friend Ben's perhaps?

It was about five by the time they got back to the farm, which would make it after 1 p.m. in Anna Maria Island. It wasn't the best time to call if he wanted to talk to Shannon, especially if she'd been out partying the night before or was taking clients out diving, but he had to do it before he lost his nerve. So he made some coffee, asked Miona to give Katrina her tea and keep her occupied and not disturb him and closed the door to the study behind him.

He glanced at the bookshelves lined with row upon row of dusty tomes he rarely glanced at, let alone pulled out to read. His desk was littered with invoices for fuel and cattle feed, adverts for second-hand tractors and copies of old farming magazines. Drummond was right. He was a philistine.

Would Jenna find anything to talk to him about once the initial burn of attraction had cooled and she saw him for what he was? He was hardly a catch. He may have the fancy title of Laird of Arrandale, but he was really nothing more than a near-bankrupt farmer; a man who had caused his brother's death, and a failed father substitute. Why had he been kidding himself? Getting close to Jenna had been a terrible mistake.

He dialled Shannon's number before he got cold feet and talked himself into sending an email instead, or better still, doing nothing at all. He wasn't sure whether to be glad or not that as expected she wasn't in. He left a message for her to call back, no matter what time.

Sipping his coffee, he reclined against the back of his chair, closing his eyes as he remembered …

Shannon. It was almost eight years to the day since he first laid eyes on the tall and willowy dark-haired beauty who completely and utterly bewitched him. Nine years since he thought she was the woman he wanted to spend the rest of his life with. She truly deserved her nickname – the Siren. Her voice, her beauty, her lust for love, life and diving were a drug he couldn't get enough of. When she'd responded to him he thought he'd caught his very own mermaid …

His mouth tightened in a derisive smile. What a fool he had been, and how well she had played him.

He had been so besotted he hadn't even seen it was all a game to her – a game she never had any intention of losing. When he'd finally realised what she was up to, it had been like seeing the negative of a photo. Where there had been beauty, there was only ugliness; where there had been happiness, there was only wretchedness, and where there had been life, there was only death. And the love he had believed to be an ardent fire had been nothing more than a tiny spark that had quickly fizzled out.

But out of all the mess and the tragedy, a beautiful little girl had been born – Katrina. It had been a joy and privilege to look after her all these years.

He had no idea how long he remained lost in his thoughts. The phone ringing pierced through his dark, bitter memories.

'Hi Shannon. It's good of you to ring back. We have to talk.'

'See you at the weekend!' Jenna waved Ben and Hamish goodbye and watched their battered campervan bounce away on the clifftop road.

The students had spent the last two hours on the beach, climbing onto rocks and splashing about in the water along the shore. 'There are lots of sea caves around here,' Hamish had said when they came back up the path, their wet shorts and tee shirts clinging to their lean, athletic bodies.

Jenna told them the old story about the mermaid kept captive in the derelict castle's tower, and she showed them the stone flag in the garden. 'Daniel believes that this hides the entrance to a cave.'

Hamish's eyes had almost jumped up and down with excitement. 'The old castle is only further up that hill. Imagine if ...'

He looked at Jenna. 'What if we lifted that stone flag and took a look to see what's down there? Do you think Daniel would object?'

She shrugged. 'You'd better ask him. It's his land and his cave, after all. But perhaps you should know that these'— she pointed at the marks on the stone—'are supposed to be a spell a witch scratched with her own fingernails against anyone who would remove the slab.'

She didn't add that Daniel was also very much against further investigations into the location of the *Santa Catalina*'s treasure.

Once alone, she closed the door to the cottage, got changed into a pair of jeans and her pale yellow shirt, and made some lasagne. Daniel hadn't said at what time he would come, but she wanted to have something ready in case he was hungry. She couldn't wait to feel his arms around her, kiss him, and make love to him and lose herself in his embrace. Just thinking about him made her heart beat faster and sent shivers of delight all over her skin.

She'd better do something constructive instead of daydreaming about Daniel, so she opened the folder of entries for the short story competition. She was curious about Katrina's story but her smile quickly faded as she read the little girl's story. Poor little mermaid cast to the shore after a storm, and poor Katrina. Would she ever get her wish and be reunited with her mother?

While the lasagne was in the oven, she tidied up the living room, humming to herself. An hour ticked by. When the top of the lasagne was brown and crispy she switched the oven off. Another hour passed, then another, and there was still no news of Daniel. Outside the sky had become a pale, transparent blue tinged with pink and orange as crepuscule crept in, together with the first doubts ... Would he come at all?

She looked at her phone but there was no message from him. Should she text or call him? Perhaps he'd been called to the lifeboat station or was too busy at the farm to call round as promised.

A message pinging made her jump, the sound strident in the quiet of the cottage. At last! She pressed down on the phone without thinking, and gasped as a line of emojis appeared on the screen. Yellow roses, crying faces morphing into screaming faces.

Below was written: *I'm coming for you.*

Adrian! There was no name but it could only be him. The strange thing was that she had blocked him, so how could he still send her messages? It had happened once before, when she'd been out in the tea garden with Ruth, but she had been so shocked it had skipped her attention. Now she looked at the number of the sender. It was her mother's. She must have lent her phone to him, or he'd taken it without her knowing. The message disappeared under her eyes, and the screen went dark again …

Jenna may be scared but she had to calm down, and think rationally.

It was unlikely that Adrian would come all this way. He only wanted to spoil her happiness because he couldn't bear the thought she was no longer in love with him.

Another message pinged. Her mouth dry, her heart beating fast and hard, she grabbed hold of the phone and stared at the screen. A single red rose appeared this time, a wilting rose with a petal that looked like a drop of blood with a sinister smiling face next to it and a few words underneath.

I shall bring your engagement ring with me. You shouldn't have left it behind.

Immediately the words and images disappeared again and she was once again staring at a blank screen.

Chapter Thirty-Three

'I'm sorry, lass,' Miona said when she opened the door. 'Daniel isn't here. He left for Inverness early this morning.'

'Oh … I didn't know he was going away. Will he be staying long?' Jenna couldn't hide the disappointment in her voice.

Miona sighed. 'Until Saturday. He'll definitely be back for the ceilidh in the evening. He said he had meetings with the bank and the solicitors, and of course there's that business with … Never mind, you'll find out soon enough.'

She frowned as she looked at Jenna. 'Are you all right, lass?'

'I'm fine, just tired.' Her head ached and her eyes were gritty from the lack of sleep. After Adrian's threatening message she had resolved to be brave and tell Daniel everything, but she hadn't had the chance to do so. He texted late in the evening that something had come up and he couldn't come after all – a short, impersonal text, and now she found out that he'd left.

What was going on? Why this sudden trip away? What did Miona mean by "she would find out soon enough"?

Miona opened the front door wider. 'Why don't you come in and have a cup of tea and a bite to eat? Iain is driving Katrina to school this morning. He'll give you a lift to town.'

Katrina was having breakfast in the kitchen, but she jumped down from her chair to greet her. 'Jenna! What are you doing here?'

Jenna forced a smile. 'Miona kindly invited me for breakfast.'

Katrina pushed her bowl towards her. 'You can have mine. I don't like it.'

'Eat your porridge, young lassie,' Miona scolded.

Katrina sighed in an overdramatic fashion. 'Do I have to?'

Miona nodded. 'Aye. I don't want to tell your uncle that you haven't been a good lass – not after yesterday. He's got enough on his plate at it is.'

'You're right.' Katrina climbed back on her chair and grabbed her spoon. Her blue eyes were serious now as she turned to Jenna. 'Poor Uncle Daniel. He's been working too hard. He stayed in the library all evening yesterday and he didn't kiss me goodnight or read me a story or give me an idea for a happy dream.'

That was a lot of information to process all at once. Had something upset Daniel, something that perhaps explained why he hadn't come to see her and why he'd had to leave this morning, but what?

Miona put a steaming mug of tea and a plate of buttered toasts in front of Jenna. 'That will perk you up.'

Jenna smiled. 'Thank you, Miona.'

Katrina swallowed the last spoonful of porridge then ran upstairs to get ready for school. Miona took a dishcloth and wiped blobs of milk and porridge from the table as Jenna finished her breakfast.

'You must be wondering what's going on,' Miona said quietly. 'I hope Daniel explains everything when he comes back. It's only fair you should know.'

She looked at Jenna. 'Please hear him out and don't be angry with him when he tells you about'—she pulled a face as if she had eaten a slice of lemon—'*her* and what happened in the past. He always tried to do his best by the wee lassie. It's not been easy, but he's given Katrina more love than *she*'—once again her lips turned downwards—'could ever have. He's happy with you, lass. I've not seen him that happy for a long time.'

Jenna hadn't planned to open her heart to Miona but she couldn't help it. 'I love him, Miona. I really do love him.'

Miona sighed as she put her hand on hers. 'I know, lass.'

The rest of the week passed with excruciating slowness, and even Enid's endless supply of scones and shortbread biscuits, and Donald's and Murdo's banter hadn't been able to cheer her up.

Saturday came without Jenna having heard from Daniel. She had sent him a couple of short messages, asking if he was all right but he hadn't replied. Something was definitely wrong, but what?

She was glad when Hamish and his friend Ben arrived in their old campervan for their diving expedition in Mermaid Cove.

'We've got news!' Hamish said as he kissed her cheeks. 'Why don't you tell Jenna about your discovery, Ben?'

Ben nodded. 'I went to Glasgow Uni for a meeting yesterday, and called in at the History Department archives for a spot of research. Professor Ferguson told me the other day that I may find interesting old maps of Arrandale there ... and indeed, I found a seventeenth century map of the Mermaid Cove and guess what?'

'There is a cave network that goes right into the cliff, as far as Dunfiadhaich Castle,' he carried on. 'In fact, according to the maps I found the old castle cellars joined into the cliff and would have provided a means of escape for the McGregors if the castle was under siege by enemy clans. I am sure that's where the treasure is.'

Hamish rubbed his hands together. 'So we're going to snorkel there this morning. Why don't you come with us?'

Jenna shook her head. 'I'll pass, thanks. I've never done anything like that before. I'm a rubbish swimmer too.'

Hamish shrugged. 'We'll only be a couple of hours at most. Come on, Jen. It will give you the chance to see the cove from a completely different perspective. You'll be amazed at what's down there – the corals, the star fish, and the kelp forest. We may even see a few seals.'

He cocked his head to one side and added, 'I bet Daniel would be super impressed to hear you've gone snorkelling with us.'

That made her think, as Hamish probably knew it would. She smiled. 'All right, I'll come. But I don't have a wetsuit …'

'No worries. I brought my girlfriend's wetsuit and everything you'll need for the dive – mask, fins, snorkel … even neoprene socks and a hood, and a spare waterproof head torch in case you want to go into the cave. You're about the same build, so it should work. What size shoes do you take? I'd guess a four or a five, and by chance Jess had fins both sizes.'

'I take a four.'

'Cool. You won't regret it, Jen. I promise.'

She pulled a face. Nothing was less certain, but both Ben and Hamish were experienced, and it would help pass the time until the evening.

Hamish checked his watch. 'We've plenty of time before the tide. Although they aren't that strong around here, tidal currents can still cause dangerous surges in caves so we'll have to watch out for it. Did you find anything interesting on the beach this week?'

Jenna shook her head. 'Not this week.'

'Oh well, never mind.' Hamish rummaged at the back of the van and handed her a wetsuit and a pair of fins. 'I'll show you how to fit the mask and the snorkel when we're down at the beach. We'll unload this and get geared up and will meet you down there.'

Jenna went upstairs to put her swimming costume and wetsuit on.

Ten minutes later, she stared at herself in the mirror and grimaced. 'That's not a good look.' She looked, and felt, like a big fat sausage squeezed into a skin at least five sizes too small.

She pulled the hood down and laughed. Forget the fat sausage. She now looked like a giant slug! She made her way downstairs, the suit squeaking with her every step, and walked down to the beach where the two students were already kitted out. The sun was hot and she could feel her body steaming and sweating inside the suit.

'Hello sexy!' Hamish whistled as she came closer.

She curled her fists at her hips. 'Please don't make fun of me. I can't believe I let you talk me into this.'

'You'll love it, Jen. Now, let me give you a quick tutorial about snorkelling and then we'll put the rest of the kit on. Be prepared for the most amazing experience of your life.'

A short while later, and after she got over the initial shock of the freezing cold water as she followed Hamish and Ben into the clear turquoise sea, and she got used to breathing through the snorkel, she had to acknowledge that Hamish had been right. There was a whole world out there – a silent world of beauty and colour, of coral and seaweed moving with the currents, waves of tiny fish catching beams of light and transparent jellyfish pulsing through the water.

Hamish and Ben stayed close as they swam along the cliffs, signalling once in a while when something caught their attention. When they reached a large rock near the entrance of a cave, Hamish tapped on her shoulder, took his snorkel out of his mouth and pointed at the rock. 'Why don't you wait for us here while we go in? We won't be long.'

'Good idea.' She could do with a break. She heaved herself

up onto the rock, slipped the mask, snorkel and neoprene hood off, and tilted her face up to enjoy the sunshine on her skin. Swimming had felt effortless when she was in the water, but her arms and thighs were aching now.

Hamish and Ben came back a short while later. 'That cave is huge indeed and it seems that there are lots of chambers, some barely accessible through cracks in the rock. We don't have enough time or equipment to explore it now, so we'll have to come back. In any case we'd better take you back. I don't want you to overdo it for your first time.'

The three of them swam back to the beach together, past the buoy that they said marked the entrance of the cove, and Jenna was astonished to see how big it was. They were standing knee-high in the water and taking their fins off when Hamish pointed at the cliff path. 'That's good timing ... Look who's there.'

Jenna's heart missed a beat and pleasure fizzed inside her as Daniel hurried down the cliff path. He was back, at last, but looking very unlike his usual self in a dark blue suit, blue tie and white shirt. As he came closer, she saw that he was clean-shaven and even had his hair trimmed. He looked so handsome – like some male model out of a fashion magazine, she couldn't stop herself from smiling.

'Hey, man, how are you?' Hamish called, but Daniel only gave him a sharp nod as he stood in front of her, blocking the view of the cliff path and the beach, and forcing her to tilt her chin up to look at him ... straight into his glaring blue eyes. He was angry – very angry. Her smile froze and faded and all the pleasure from her swim and from seeing him again drained away.

'Daniel ... what's the matter?'

'What the hell do you think you're playing at?' His voice was so cold and sharp she took a step back.

'I was just ... learning how to snorkel with Hamish

and ... Ben,' she stammered as tears burned her eyes. Her heart bumped so hard it hurt, and her throat was so tight she could hardly breathe. Why was he mad at her?

Anger flashed in his eyes again. He shook his head, and clenched his jaw. 'You don't know the first thing about diving. The currents can be dangerous around here, they can push you against the rocks, or you could have got caught in a whirlpool. This is beyond stupid ...'

'Hey man, cool it,' Hamish said, coming over to her and wrapping his arm around her shoulders. 'Don't get mad at Jen. We only went out for a couple of hours or so, and we took good care of her. She's been great, and she was never in any danger.'

Daniel tightened his jaw again. 'You're completely irresponsible, the three of you. Anything could have happened. Anything.'

'Chill, Dan ...' A woman spoke from behind Daniel with a slight American twang.

Jenna craned her neck to look at the woman who was talking.

Next to her, Hamish dropped his arm by his side, his mouth gaped open, and his eyes almost popped out in surprise as a tall and willowy woman with long dark hair stepped forward and slipped her arm under Daniel's.

'Holy Basil ... it's ... Shannon O'Keeffe, isn't it?' Hamish exclaimed.

The woman flashed Hamish a smile. 'Indeed – wow, this place hasn't changed at all.' She looked down at Jenna and arched her eyebrows. 'Except for the mermaids, who've become rather podgy since I was last here.'

Chapter Thirty-Four

Daniel frowned at Shannon. Why was she being so nasty? And why was she standing so close and holding onto his forearm?

'I told you to stay in the car,' he said.

She arched her eyebrows and let out a low chuckle. 'Surely you haven't forgotten that I always do exactly as I please?'

The note of challenge in her voice didn't escape him. It was a warning, of course. She may have come all the way from Florida at his request, but that didn't mean she would do everything he asked. He had to tread carefully ... for Katrina's sake.

He looked at Jenna again. Hamish had his arm around her shoulders, as if trying to shield her from his bad mood and Shannon's vicious tongue. Daniel didn't blame the student, but he sure didn't like the way he pulled Jenna against him. His chest ached again, the way it had earlier when he was driving past the cottage, spotted the three silhouettes in wetsuits and recognised Hamish, Ben and Jenna.

He hadn't even taken a second to think. Stamping on the brakes, he had swung the door open and jumped out of the car. 'Stay right here,' he barked at Shannon before running down the path.

Hamish cast him a reproachful glance, and suddenly he was boiling in that damned suit he'd had to wear for the meeting at the solicitors' that very morning while Shannon was having a lie-in at the posh country hotel she'd insisted on after he picked her up from the airport.

He took off his jacket, loosened his tie and undid his top

button. 'Where did you swim to?' he asked Hamish in a more amenable voice.

'To that rock over there so that Jenna could have a rest while Ben and I took a look at the sea cave,' the student replied. Bending towards Jenna, he added, 'Come on, Jen. Let's get changed and have a bite to eat.'

She nodded but didn't reply, and Daniel noticed that she was avoiding looking at him. He couldn't blame her. He'd behaved like a bully – a mean, angry and nasty bully. He'd overreacted, and all because of the terror that had gripped him when he'd seen her in that wetsuit.

Shannon tugged on his sleeve. 'I don't know about you, *honey*, but I'm shattered and can't wait to be home. We had so much catching up to do last night it was far too late when we fell asleep, and the bed wasn't as comfortable as it should have been, especially given that it was a five star hotel.'

What was she talking about? She had slept in her own bed, in her own hotel room last night; why was she calling Dunfiadhaich home when she used to hate the place? And she'd never called him *honey* before!

Jenna was still fiddling with her mask. It now dangled around her neck, with the snorkel entangled in the straps. He extended his hand. 'Let me help you with that. You're doing it all wrong.' Once again he managed to sound like a pompous ass.

Jenna stepped out of his reach, and yanked hard on the straps to dislodge the snorkel. 'There's no need. I've done it now. I'm going back to the cottage.'

Keeping her head down, she walked away, towards the path.

'I'll carry the stuff,' Ben said as he piled up masks, snorkels and fins into a large bag then followed her.

'I'll be right with you,' Hamish called to his friend. As

soon as Jenna was out of earshot, he added, 'You were bang out of order, man. Jenna was amazing today. And for the record, she didn't want to come, but I insisted and said you would be proud of her, so you can call me stupid, but not her. She only did it to impress you.' And with a last cold glare, he followed his friend and Jenna.

'Gee ... That went well,' Shannon remarked as she narrowed her eyes to watch Jenna and the two students walk up the cliff path. 'So the woman is Katrina's new best friend – the librarian. See? Contrary to what you think, I do read your emails.'

Her voice took on a sniggering tone. 'She'd better lay off the pies. She looks as if she's going to burst out of that diving suit. I'm surprised she didn't sink.'

He looked at her, but didn't answer. What had he ever seen in her? She may be beautiful still, but her green eyes had grown hard, her lips thin and her voice grated on his nerves. And yet they were the very same eyes, lips and voice which had mesmerised him all those years before ...

He drew in a breath and turned away but Shannon whined again. 'Are we going now? I wasn't kidding when I said I was shattered. I need a rest before ...' She sighed.

Perhaps she was anxious at the thought of meeting the daughter she hadn't seen for years – the daughter who idolised her but she'd ignored, not even bothering to reply to her letters or emails, forcing him to come up with stories about mermaids and a so-called dolphin post ...

It would be only natural for Shannon to be nervous, but somehow he wasn't sure she was, and once again, doubts ate at him. Had he done the right thing by asking her to come over – by begging her to take up her responsibilities at last, or at least get to know Katrina and try to build some kind of relationship with her?

The sun glinting on something in the sand right where

Jenna had been standing caught his attention. It looked like a pearl or a shiny pebble.

'Dan, come on,' Shannon moaned next to him.

'Just a minute.' He walked to the edge of the water and crouched down. It was one of Jenna's earrings – a tiny moonstone encased in gold. She must have lost it when she pulled on her hood and took her mask off. How lucky that he'd spotted it. Another few minutes and it would have been washed away and his midnight mermaid would have been without her piece of moonlight. He picked it up and slipped it in his breast pocket. He would find a quiet moment later to give it back to her, explain what was going on, and apologise. For everything.

'Let's go. Katrina won't be home yet. I asked Miona to take her to town and not come back before late afternoon. That will give you a few hours to rest, and prepare what you're going to tell her.'

She shrugged. 'Prepare? There's nothing to prepare.'

'We'll see you tonight at Jim's ceilidh,' Hamish said later after they'd had some lunch and he'd loaded the diving gear into the van. Ben was already behind the wheel, slipping his sunglasses on and flicking the visor down.

'I won't be going. I can't. Not after what happened at the beach …' Her voice wobbled and tears filled her eyes.

Hamish frowned. 'I see. I am sorry, Jen. It's my fault Daniel went mad at you back there. I shouldn't have insisted on you coming snorkelling with us. Actually, I think he got stressed because he was scared for you – because he cares.'

She sighed and fought to hold back the tears. 'He doesn't care, Hamish.'

She hitched a breath and forced a smile. 'It's not your fault Daniel was angry. There's no excuse for him being rude to you or to me. I know you're trying to be kind, but to tell the truth, I have a bit of a migraine – probably caused by too much sunshine.' Or rather, too much heartache …

Hamish didn't insist. As soon as the van drove off, Jenna tidied the kitchen and did the washing-up. She needed to keep busy, so she grabbed her gardening gloves and a pair of secateurs, took the straw hat from the coat stand and went outside, but even the garden didn't bring her the peace she craved. As she pulled out weeds, cut and trimmed bushes and dead-headed the climbing yellow roses, questions swirled in her mind.

Why was Shannon in Arrandale? Katrina hadn't said anything so she mustn't know that her mother was coming. Miona, however, must have known, and some of the hints she had dropped on Wednesday now made sense. She recalled the housekeeper's words – Daniel was happy with her, she should give him a chance to explain what was going on. Well, he hadn't given *her* a chance to talk, back there on the beach. All he'd done was shout and stand close to beautiful Shannon as she laughed and called her a fat mermaid.

Bitterness turned her insides to acid. Shannon said they'd done a lot of catching up. She could imagine what kind of "catching up" she meant on that supposedly uncomfortable bed. So perhaps Toby's allegations were true all along, and that Daniel and Shannon had been lovers in the past. Perhaps rumours about Katrina's biological father were true too.

She was going to be sick … Was everything she had believed about Daniel a lie?

Jenna cut off the dead roses, which looked exactly as she felt. Withered, dry and useless. All the colour, the life and the joy had been sucked out of them – and of her. Sweat stuck her top to her back, the sun burned her bare arms and her throat was parched from the heat. Her head throbbed and her heart ached so much it hurt just to breathe.

She walked back into the cottage, took her gloves and her hat off, and glanced at her reflection in the hallway mirror. Something was wrong. She touched her left ear ... she'd lost her earring!

She retraced her steps into the garden, looking down all the time, but she couldn't find it. Perhaps she lost it as she got changed out of the wetsuit in her bedroom. She rushed upstairs, examined her clothes and every inch of the carpet. Nothing.

What about the beach? It was a long shot, but she had to try. She went back outside and walked very slowly down the path and onto the beach, all the way to the edge of the water, but once again she found nothing.

Her heart heavy, she trailed back to the cottage. This felt like an omen ... Wearing the moonstone earrings was a symbol of defiance against the past, against Adrian, and her old self. A sign that from now on she wouldn't let anyone impose their opinions any longer, but be herself and make a success of her new life.

Well, she had failed. She was still a gullible fool.

A thousand shards of ice stabbed at her heart as Adrian's mocking voice calling her pathetic came to torment her again, but this time it was mixed with Daniel's angry words, calling her stupid and irresponsible, and Shannon's drawling, mocking tone when she referred to podgy mermaids ...

Chapter Thirty-Five

'Hi, sweetie pie, why don't you come closer so I can give you a kiss?' Shannon put down her drink and rose from the sofa.

Katrina stood in the doorway, clinging to Miona's hand, her blue eyes wide with shock and her face pale against the bright yellow frills of the new dress they had bought especially for the ceilidh.

Shannon on the other hand looked perfectly at ease. After a couple of hours' sleep in the guest bedroom, she had changed into a green dress and silver coloured sandals that emphasised her slim, tanned legs. With her dark hair tumbling down to her waist, she looked like a beautiful and exotic creature – a creature who was already sipping her second whisky. Perhaps she was nervous after all and the laid-back attitude was only a facade ...

'Go on, lassie, go and see your mum.' Miona gave Katrina a gentle push, but Katrina clung ever more tightly to her hand and refused to budge.

Shannon's smile froze ever so slightly. 'Are you being shy? Come here and tell me all about you, about your school and your friends. I already met one of them this afternoon on the beach. That woman you're friendly with. The one who drives the mobile library. Jennifer ...'

'Jenna,' Daniel corrected.

Shannon shrugged. 'Whatever – she'd better stick to driving vans and stamping books. She looked ridiculous in a wetsuit, and reminded me of a manatee ... Do you know what a manatee is, sweetie pie?'

Katrina didn't react, and Shannon carried on. 'They're also called sea cows. There are lots of them near my house on Anna Maria Island. They are fat and clumsy and very funny.'

Daniel cringed. Shannon was talking too much, too fast.

'You live in a house?' Katrina spoke at last and Daniel held his breath.

Shannon's smile wavered. 'That's a funny question. Of course I live in a house – a big house on an island and—'

'Did you swim to come here?' Katrina interrupted.

'Swim? Don't be silly! No one can swim across the Atlantic! What do you think I am? A fish?'

Daniel repressed a frustrated sigh. Why couldn't the woman go along with the stories he'd made up over the years, at least until she and Katrina could form some kind of bond? Then again perhaps the whisky had gone to her head and she had forgotten what he had patiently told her the evening before.

'Come here, sweetie pie, and give me a kiss.'

Katrina still didn't move, so Shannon pointed to her dress. 'Why are you wearing this horrid dress?' She glanced at Daniel and shook her head. 'I bet you're the one to blame for this. Trust you to buy something in that yucky yellow colour. We'll have a girly shopping trip to Glasgow or Edinburgh Monday or Tuesday, just you and I … Wouldn't that be fun, Katrina?'

'Yellow is Katrina's favourite colour,' he said in a cold voice. It was on the tip of his tongue to add that Shannon had lost the right to criticise his tastes in fashion when she'd abandoned her daughter and he'd become Katrina's guardian. 'And she can't go shopping during the week. She has school.'

Shannon shrugged. 'Silly me. There's school, of course. How is school, by the way? I remember you wrote about it in one of your letters.'

'You got my letters?' Katrina asked in a small voice.

Shannon nodded. 'We do have postmen in Florida, sweetie pie.'

'Human postmen?'

Shannon chuckled. 'Of course.'

'You have the internet too – for emails and things?'

'We have everything on Anna Maria Island.'

'What about fish mail and dolphin post?'

This time Shannon looked uncertain as she glanced at him. 'What is the girl talking about?'

His fingers tightened around his glass of water, so hard he felt it was going to break so he put it down on the mantelpiece. She had clearly not listened to a word he'd said.

Katrina stared at Shannon's bare legs, and Daniel knew exactly what she was thinking. Her mother lived in a house. She travelled by plane. She had normal postmen ... and she had legs. She wasn't a mermaid at all.

Then she looked at him, and the hurt in her eyes made his chest ache. 'You lied, Uncle Daniel,' she said in a small voice. 'You lied about everything.'

She yanked her hand from Miona's, turned on her heels and ran away.

Shannon frowned. 'That's not the welcome I was expecting. What horrors have you been telling her about me?'

Miona glared at her. 'Daniel only ever said nice things about you, Shannon. God knows why. I'll go and prepare the tea.'

'And a good day to you too, *hun*!' Shannon called after her. 'I see the old bat is as charming as ever. Years have not mellowed her one bit.' She took a big gulp of her whisky and flicked her hair back over her shoulders. 'She never liked me. I bet she told Katrina lots of lies and bad stuff about me.'

'I don't think Miona or I needed to make anything up after the way you behaved. The truth would have been bad enough.'

She opened her mouth to speak but he raised his hand. 'Don't play the offended party with me, Shannon. We both know there's only one victim in this mess, and that's Katrina.'

Anger flashed in her eyes. 'You've changed your tune since you called me on Wednesday. I'm starting to regret coming here. I thought I was doing you a favour. I thought—'

'You thought you would be welcomed back here with open arms as you played the loving mother in exchange for a substantial amount of cash,' he interrupted. 'Well, you're going to have to work a lot harder for your money. You have a lot to make up for. Five years of absence, silence and indifference, to be exact.'

'You never spoke to me like that before,' she hissed.

He shrugged. 'That's where I went wrong. All these years I tried to cover for you and made up the most outrageous stories so that your daughter wouldn't know that you didn't care and weren't interested in finding out what a beautiful, clever and funny child she was growing up to be. Do you have any idea how hard it's been for her? Hell, you couldn't even be bothered phoning or even sending her a card or a present for her birthday.'

'You know why. I wasn't cut out to be a mother. My job … my diving were my life, still are. And she reminded me too much of you … and of what happened. I thought it would be better if we didn't have any contact at all.'

'Better for whom? Anyway, I have to go looking for Katrina. Do you want to come?'

She pulled a face. 'Somehow I don't think she wants to talk to me.'

He left Shannon to sulk in the drawing room and ran upstairs, but Katrina wasn't in her room. He looked in the library where she liked to hide on the window seat behind the curtains, and did a quick search of the rest of the house. He went outside, checked the barn and the cowshed, and asked the lads if they'd seen her. They hadn't ... Perhaps she'd gone to the fields behind the house. She often went to the lower enclosure to talk to the cows and the sheep, or so she claimed, but she wasn't there. He went into the garden in case she'd decided to pick more flowers, getting more and more frantic by the minute.

Damn ... Anxiety made his heart beat faster. Where was she?

And then he knew ... Mermaid's Cottage, of course.

Why hadn't he guessed sooner?

Someone was banging on the door and calling her name. Jenna winced as she sat up on the sofa and glanced at the window. Katrina was outside.

Jenna cast the cushion aside. Against all odds, she had managed to fall asleep. Her head throbbed, her throat was parched and sore, even her legs ached as she made her way to the front door. One glance at her reflection in the hallway mirror confirmed that she looked as bad as she felt. Her hair was tangled, her face blotchy and her eyes red and swollen. She'd probably scare Katrina away ...

But Katrina didn't even look at her. She threw herself against her as soon as she opened the door. She encircled her waist with her arms and started sobbing. 'Uncle Daniel lied ... there's no dolphin post, no fish mail ... And *she*'s not a mermaid at all ... she has legs and she lives in a house, and she is mean and horrible and I hate her!'

'Hush, my darling. Calm down – you're going to make yourself sick.' Jenna stroked the little girl's hair. Pulling away, she kept a hand on her shoulder before bending down to look at her. Her yellow dress was wrinkled and stained and a cut at her knee was bleeding.

'Come with me. I need to put something on your knee.' Holding her hand, she led her to the kitchen where she pulled a chair out for her to sit on.

'I ran away. She said ... she said ...' Katrina hiccupped.

Jenna stopped her. 'Don't try to talk. Let's get you cleaned up first.'

She helped her sit on a chair, poured a glass of water and added some orange cordial. Katrina's little chest heaved with sobs as she sipped her drink. Jenna dabbed a cool compress against her knee and fished out a plaster from her first aid box.

'Here, all done. You were very brave.' She lifted Katrina from the chair and set her on her feet, her heart tightening again at the utter misery in the little girl's eyes that echoed her own feelings.

'I'll take you back home,' she said. If Katrina had run away like she said, Daniel would be frantic with worry.

'I want to stay with you.' Katrina snuck her hand into Jenna's and held tight.

'You can't. Your uncle will get worried, and what about your ... mother?' she finished.

'She said you looked like a sea cow, and that my dress was yucky.' That started a whole new flood of tears.

'Oh my poor darling, come here.' Jenna enfolded her into her arms and patted her back, her hair, while making soothing noises. She didn't care about Shannon calling her a sea cow or a fat mermaid, but she cared about her hurting the little girl's feelings.

The sounds of dogs barking outside cut through Katrina's sobbing. It must be Sam and Eddie, and Daniel wouldn't be far behind.

'I think your uncle is here. Let's go and talk to him.'

Katrina shook her head so Jenna left her in the living room and went to open the door.

'Have you seen Katrina?' Daniel asked as soon as Jenna stepped outside. 'She ran away and I can't find her anywhere.' He raked his fingers in his hair. 'I thought she may have come here.' There was nothing left of the hard, angry man who'd shouted at her on the beach. This was the Daniel she knew, and she loved.

She nodded. 'Yes, she's here. Don't worry.'

Closing his eyes, he let out a long sigh of relief. 'Thank heavens.'

'She's very upset.'

He frowned. 'I know. Her first contact with Shannon was rather difficult, and not at all what I had hoped. You see, I thought ...'

She stepped back and forced a tight smile to hide her bruised heart. 'I'll get Katrina. Stay here. I won't be long,' she said in a cold voice.

She didn't want him inside Mermaid's Cottage. He had pushed her away, ignored her, hadn't judged it necessary to tell her that Shannon was coming over from the States. And he had slept with her last night ... It was best to keep her relationship with the McGregor family strictly professional from now on.

Turning round, she walked back into the house.

'I don't want to go home,' the little girl whined. 'I'll get told off for running away.'

'Your uncle needs to see that you're all right, Katrina. He is very worried about you. He loves you very, very much. Everything will be fine, I promise.' She took the little girl's hand.

Daniel was waiting outside. His face lit up as soon as he saw Katrina.

'You gave me such a fright, chick,' he said in a slightly hoarse and wobbly voice that touched Jenna's heart despite her resolve to keep her distance. However badly he was hurting her, she couldn't doubt his love for the little girl.

'Never, ever, run away like that again, do you hear?' he added, crouching down to be at Katrina's level.

'I'm sorry, Uncle Daniel,' the little girl muttered as she took a few hesitant steps towards him.

He touched her tear-streaked cheek then looked at her stained dress and the plaster on her knee. 'You're hurt.'

Katrina nodded. 'I tripped on the path but Jenna made it better.'

Daniel glanced up, and gave Jenna a tight smile. 'Thank you.' He looked at Katrina again. 'What about your dress? Do you want to change before going to the ceilidh?'

'I don't want to go. Please don't make me. And I don't want to see *her*. She's nothing like you said. She's no mermaid ... and she's not nice at all.'

'She's your mum, love. Give her a chance. She has come a long way to see you. She'll be staying with us at the farm for a while.'

Jenna didn't like the bitter taste of jealousy in her mouth and the pain twisting in her chest and she felt like bursting into tears all over again.

'I'll leave you to go home, then. I hope you have a good time tonight.'

Daniel sprung to his feet. 'Are you not coming?'

How could he be so blind, so insensitive – so selfish – and think she would want to sit in a pub watching him, Shannon and Katrina play happy families?

'No. I think I'll pass.'

'But you promised!' Katrina insisted, tears filling her eyes again.

'I did but I ...'

'If Jenna doesn't come, then I'm not going either and nobody can make me!' And Katrina started crying again.

It wasn't the little girl's fault she had fallen in love with Daniel – not her fault she had mistaken a couple of nights of sex for love.

Jenna sighed, annoyed with herself for being so easily swayed. 'All right ... I'll come, but I need to get changed.' She also needed a shower, a shampoo and blow-dry to tame her hair which was stiff with salt after the snorkelling expedition despite the neoprene hood. She also needed a ton of make-up to hide the blotches caused by too much crying. Actually, it probably didn't matter what she looked like. All eyes would be on Shannon ...

Daniel smiled but his blue eyes were thoughtful. 'Iain will pick you up in an hour. I need to go early to set up and do the sound checks.' He sighed. 'Thanks, Jenna. I really appreciate it.'

'I'm doing it for Katrina, and only for Katrina,' she said, hardening her stare. And she closed the door.

Chapter Thirty-Six

By early evening the ceilidh was in full swing. Tables and chairs had been pushed against the walls to create a dance floor. The pub was full, and there were so many people up and dancing that at times the clapping and the clattering of feet on the wooden floor almost drowned the music.

Daniel's bow flew over the strings of his fiddle as the band played another rousing jig. Next to him on the tiny stage were a piper and a flute player, as well as a guitarist who called the moves. Katrina and Jenna had danced almost non-stop since they'd arrived but as the music ended Katrina now pulled on Jenna's hand.

'I'm thirsty and my feet hurt.'

'Mine hurt too. Let's sit down,' Jenna agreed, glad of a rest, even if focussing on the steps and putting a smile on her face for Katrina's sake distracted her from her heartache. It also kept her away from the table Daniel had commandeered earlier for their party and where Shannon was alone, ostensibly staring at the screen of her mobile phone.

'I'll get you a drink. Would you like an orange cordial?' she asked Katrina.

The little girl nodded enthusiastically, and climbed on the chair next to Shannon who didn't even glance at her but carried on scrolling down on the screen of her mobile. She looked stunning in an emerald green dress that matched the colour of her eyes, and with her dark hair loose on her shoulders – stunning but completely indifferent to everything and everyone around her. Her tumbler of whisky soda was almost finished. If she was aware of people staring and whispering about her, it didn't seem to bother her at all.

Ruth couldn't wait to talk to Jenna when she got to the bar. 'I couldn't believe it when I saw Shannon was here! What's going on, and how long is she staying?' she asked as Jenna shouted her order to Eric.

'I have no idea. You should ask Daniel.' She turned away so that her friend couldn't see the tears in her eyes.

Ruth looked perplexed. 'He never said she was coming over from Florida, only that he didn't need me for childminding next week.' She glanced back at Shannon and shook her head. 'Good luck to him if he hopes Shannon will look after Katrina, that's all I say. Look at her staring at her phone!'

She fiddled with the ties of her apple green blouse, and looked at Jenna. 'It may be a wee bit awkward for you, going to Dunfiadhaich Farm when she's there, but I hope you won't let her get to you. She could be a downright mean and nasty cow back in the day and I doubt very much she's changed.'

Remembering Shannon's barbed comments about sea cows and podgy mermaids, Jenna nodded. 'It's all right, Ruth, since I have no intention of going to Dunfiadhaich Farm ever again.'

'I understand you don't want to rock the boat, love, but the sooner Shannon accepts you and Daniel are together and you have every right to be at Dunfiadhaich, the better.'

Jenna heaved a sigh. 'That's the thing, Ruth – we're not together.'

Her friend stared at her in shock. 'What? But I thought ...'

'Well, you were wrong. It looks like Daniel had a change of heart – if his heart was ever involved, which I very much doubt.' Jenna's throat was so tight it was hard to talk. She took a deep breath. 'He didn't tell me he was going away or that Shannon was coming. He didn't even reply to my texts. Shannon and he … They spent last night together in a posh hotel. Shannon said they didn't get much sleep because they'd had so much catching up to do.'

Ruth looked crestfallen. 'Oh love, I'm sure you have the wrong end of the stick. I can't imagine that Daniel would cheat on you or—'

'He never made any promises,' Jenna interrupted. She really didn't want to have this conversation. Eric handed her the drinks she'd ordered, she thanked him and looked at Ruth. 'I'd better take these back. I'll see you later.'

'Thanks, Jenna,' Katrina said as she grabbed hold of her cordial and started sucking through her straw and making bubbles in her drink.

'Stop doing that. It's annoying,' Shannon admonished in a sharp voice without lifting her eyes from her phone.

Katrina stopped at once and pushed her glass away. 'I'm sorry,' she said with a sad smile.

Jenna bit her tongue. She was getting more and more annoyed at Shannon's behaviour. Why bother travelling from the States if she couldn't even be bothered to look at Katrina, let alone be nice to her? And what was going on with Daniel? He had hardly spoken a word to Shannon since they'd arrived, and every time he looked her way, it was with a glare and a frown. That wasn't the look of a man in love.

She stole another glance at him. He looked so handsome with his shorter hair. He had rolled up his sleeves, and she couldn't help shivering as she remembered those very same arms holding her tight, loving her. How could she get it so wrong?

As if he could sense her watching him, he looked at her. For a few seconds the music and the noise receded, everything around him blurred and faded, and all she could see was him; all she could hear was her heart beating too fast; and all she could feel was love and pain.

Shannon chose that very moment to look up from her phone. She glanced at her then at Daniel, and back at her, and smiled as if she knew exactly what Jenna was feeling.

'So, Jennifer ... Tell me ... Do you intend to take up snorkelling? If so, I suggest you get yourself some proper gear, starting with a wetsuit for your size. The one you were wearing today was at least two sizes too small and can't have been comfortable.'

Jenna forced a smile. She wouldn't let the woman get to her. It was her problem she was mean and rude. She didn't have to stoop to her level. 'It's Jenna, and the wetsuit wasn't mine ... but you're right, it was far too tight. I still enjoyed the snorkelling outing with Hamish and Ben. They are very experienced divers and they were very patient with me.'

'I want to go snorkelling too but Uncle Daniel says it's dangerous and I'm too young,' Katrina said.

Shannon turned to her and shrugged. 'It's only dangerous if you don't know what you're doing. Never mind what grumpy Daniel says, I'll take you snorkelling.'

Jenna's eyes widened in shock. Daniel wouldn't be happy about this.

'Here are your diving friends by the way.' Hamish and Ben were getting a pint of beer at the bar. Shannon gave them an enthusiastic wave and signalled for them to come over. They looked surprised and walked over to their table with their drinks.

'I'm glad you made it, Jen,' Hamish told Jenna.

Shannon put her phone down on the table and gave the two students a dazzling smile. 'Good evening, boys. Why don't you join us?'

Hamish blushed but he pulled out a chair and sat down, and Ben did the same.

'We were just talking about diving,' Shannon carried on. 'Some of my gear must still be at Dunfiadhaich Farm, that's if Dan hasn't chucked it away, and I was wondering if I could tag along with you two on your next dive.'

Hamish put his pint down, a shocked look on his face. 'Holy Basil! *You* want to come with *us*?'

'Why ever not? You seemed very capable young men, back there on the beach this afternoon.' Shannon gave the student another smile and put her hand on his arm. His colour shot from pink to beetroot. 'Tell me all about you, your favourite dives around Arrandale and what you're planning next.'

'We're looking for the *Santa Catalina* gold,' Ben blurted out. 'We believe we may have a lead. There's a large cave network in Mermaid Cove which goes all the way to the old castle and we want to explore it.'

'Shut up, Ben.' Hamish glared at him.

'Why?' Ben frowned, then gasped and his face paled as it dawned on him that it was the quest for the *Santa Catalina*'s gold that had killed Hugh McGregor. He looked at Shannon. 'Oh bugger. I'm sorry. I wasn't thinking. I shouldn't have mentioned the *Santa Catalina*. It was dumb of me,' he stammered, grabbed his pint and swallowed a long gulp of beer.

'Don't worry about it,' Shannon said, sipping her whisky. 'As a matter of fact, the *Santa Catalina* and I have unfinished business, so I would be happy if you included me in your plans.'

Ben gave her a beaming smile. 'Wow ... It would be great to have you onboard, wouldn't it, Hamish?'

'Sure.' Hamish nodded.

'Then we have a deal,' Shannon said. 'What about taking a look at that cave tomorrow?'

Hamish pulled a face and pointed at his pint. 'I'd rather

not. Tonight's going to be a late night, and I'd rather not dive when I'm hung-over.'

Shannon shrugged as she lifted her glass and drank a sip. 'It doesn't bother me, and you two look like men who can handle their drink. But perhaps I'm wrong ...' Her voice trailed, and her eyes sparkled with amusement. Hamish's face turned red again.

'Can I come with you?' Katrina asked. 'Can I? Please?'

'Perhaps not tomorrow, sweetie,' Shannon said. 'First you must show me you can handle yourself in the sea. Let's see ... If you can swim to the buoy in Mermaid Cove and back, then I'll take you diving, and never mind what grouchy, scaredy-cat, killjoy Uncle Daniel says,' Shannon added in a silly voice that made Katrina giggle.

'He's not that bad,' the little girl replied. 'But sometimes he is grumpy, and he never has time for fun things.'

Shannon jumped to her feet. 'Well, you and I are going to show him how to have a good time, aren't we? Starting right now. I used to be one of the best ceilidh dancers around here.' She grabbed Katrina's hand, pulled her to the dance floor, and led her into a frantic jig.

'She is extraordinary, isn't she?' Ben said with a besotted grin as he followed Shannon's moves on the dance floor.

'Stunning ...' Hamish agreed. 'But I still don't think we should dive tomorrow.' He pointed at his pint, then at Shannon's three empty whisky glasses. 'You know drinking and diving don't mix.'

'Come on, mate!' Ben sounded annoyed. 'How many opportunities will you get to dive with Shannon O'Keeffe? It would be stupid to turn her down.'

'Do you intend to go back to the cave?' Jenna asked to diffuse the tension between the two friends. She was starting to see what Brendon meant when he'd said Shannon used to stir trouble.

'Aye – I'm sure the gold is hidden there,' Ben replied. 'There were old papers in the archives about the cave being used by smugglers over the centuries, and a very interesting titbit of information about the family living at Mermaid's Cottage being involved in all kinds of illegal activities.'

'And I was talking to a geology lecturer at uni who said that recent storms and the spring tide may have caused rock falls and ground movement in the cave, creating or reopening passages to old chambers.'

'Which could explain why some artefacts were carried out by the tide and I found them on the beach,' Jenna finished.

The last notes of music died, and Shannon and Katrina came back, hot and flustered but in high spirits.

'I'm gasping for a drink,' Shannon declared as she fanned her face with a beer mat. 'Which one of you lovely young men is going to get me a Scotch and soda?'

Ben sprung to his feet. 'I will.'

'Thank you, honey. Get plenty of ice too.'

She blew him a kiss, and he strode to the bar with a beaming smile on his face. As soon as he came back, Shannon drained her glass and grabbed hold of Katrina's hand again. 'Come on, let's go for another dance,' she told Katrina, who squeaked with delight.

Hamish and Ben got up and said they had friends to talk to … and Jenna was alone. Ruth and her husband were dancing, Miona and Iain were chatting at the bar, and Katrina had well and truly forgotten her and was dancing with her mother. Which of course was exactly the way it should be.

Nobody would miss her if she left so she retrieved her handbag and slipped out of the pub with a heavy heart. It was a long and miserable trek back and she was aching all over when the cottage came into view at last, but her relief at reaching home was short-lived.

A car was parked in front of Mermaid's Cottage. A white Audi.

She didn't need to read the personalised number plate to know who it was. She knew it by heart.

So Adrian had told the truth. He had come for her.

Chapter Thirty-Seven

Her heart pounding, she stopped at the end of the lane. Perhaps Adrian hadn't seen her and she could turn round, hurry back to the pub and ask Ruth or Brendon to put her up tonight.

Or perhaps she could be brave and face him at last … That was the only way she'd truly be free of him.

Adrian couldn't hurt her any more. She wasn't the same woman who had let him trample all over her. She had seen through him and she knew how he operated. And she absolutely didn't care what he thought about her any more. She had nothing to fear. At least that's what she kept repeating as she stepped closer.

The Audi's door swung open. Adrian climbed out. And all her confidence crumbled and deserted her. Her legs turned to jelly, and she stood shaking and gasping for air in the middle of the lane as he strolled towards her.

He looked the same – tall and lean, and smartly dressed in dark chinos and a designer white shirt with the top couple of buttons undone. His face was lightly tanned and his eyes hidden by designer sunglasses.

'Jenna. At last! Where have you been? I've been waiting for ages.' His voice, so familiar with the upper-class accent, was warm and friendly – the way it used to be at the start of their relationship, or when there were people around. But it made her skin crawl.

He stopped a few feet away from her, took his glasses off. The last rays of the sun setting behind Mermaid's Rocks shone directly into his eyes, making him blink. It was lucky because it meant he probably couldn't see the effect he still had on her and gave her a few seconds to compose herself.

She squared her shoulders and tilted her chin up. 'Adrian – what are you doing here?' Incredibly, her voice didn't shake.

He took another step forward, and the scent of his aftershave wafted towards her and it almost made her retch.

'You don't seem very happy to see me, my darling,' he started, looking hurt and disappointed. He tried to put his hands on her shoulders and leant forward to kiss her cheek but she sidestepped his move.

How dare he call her darling! How dare he come here and behave as if he hadn't tried to destroy her for the past two years.

Her whole body tensed and a wave of anger washed over her. 'That's because I'm not. In fact, I'm bloody furious. So I repeat – what are you doing here?'

'I have come to rescue you from this place, and from yourself. I totally get it. You were punishing me for leaving you, for going to London, but you've made your point now. You don't have to pretend you're happy living here.'

'Ah! I don't need rescuing, and I certainly don't need you. And I'm not punishing you. In fact I should be thanking you because leaving me was the best thing you ever did for me.'

He tutted. 'My poor darling, you do sound a little unhinged and incoherent, but that's no wonder. It can't have been easy living in that *shack*'—he gestured at the cottage—'in this wilderness, surrounded no doubt by brutes and thugs. What has this place done to you? Your hair …? It used to be so soft, and now it's …' He pulled a face as his gaze swept over her.

'You've put on weight too and that dress is simply awful. And what on earth is that piece of crockery around your neck?' He frowned as he looked at her majolica pendant.

'When I think of all the clothes and jewellery we chose

together and you gave away. Such a shame. But don't worry. We'll soon get you back on track once we're in Manchester.'

He hadn't listened to a word she'd said and anger now bubbled inside her, forcing her to raise her voice. 'My hair, my waistline, my clothes are no longer anything to do with you. And since you don't seem to understand what I was saying before, I will spell it out for you once and for all. I don't want to see you. I don't want to be anywhere near you. I don't want to read your texts, hear your voice, or even think about you. So get in your car, drive back to Manchester and leave me alone. Am I making myself clear enough now?' She was almost shouting by the time she finished.

He winced and there was a moment of stunned silence. 'There is no need to yell at me like some deranged fishwife, Jenna.' He sounded so patronising she wanted to shout all over again.

'Although actually your little outburst confirms my suspicions. You're no better, are you? You moved away, managed to get this new job, God knows how, but I can see you're still deeply troubled. I blame myself, of course. I should never have left. But I'm back now and everything will get back to normal.'

'There is nothing wrong with me! There never was, and you know it. It was you all along, you who tried to make me think that I was losing my mind. My so-called memory lapses were caused by you moving my things around the flat, changing dates of meetings in the calendar, pretending to like one thing one day, then hate it or be allergic another day – basically playing sinister mind games.'

She couldn't stop now. She had so much resentment, so much anger she had to blurt it all out. 'And that's not all. You lied about my job applications too, again and again. I was stupid enough to believe you and never suspected anything.

You lied to everybody about me, even my mother ...' Her voice broke.

'Oh dear. Have you listened to yourself? You have a serious case of paranoia. Perhaps I should take you to see a psychiatrist.'

The man hadn't changed at all.

And then she realised. He would never change. She was wasting her time.

'I think you're the one who should seek medical help before you do someone serious harm.' Memories of being shut in the dark, airless walk-in wardrobe suddenly flooded her. Her throat tightened and she struggled to breathe as the black butterflies were back and fluttered around her, inside her.

She mustn't let Adrian affect her so much. She had to be strong, even if she felt suddenly drained. 'For the last time,' she said but her voice had lost its edge. 'I am not going back to Manchester, and I am certainly not getting back with you. Now get in your car, go away and don't pester me ever again.'

She should have recognised the signs. Seen the tic pulling the side of his mouth, the way his grey eyes darkened and his face turned as cold as marble, but she was desperate to be in Mermaid's Cottage. To be alone, and safe before she collapsed.

She looked down to retrieve her keys from her bag. That one second of inattention was all Adrian needed to close the gap between them and grab hold of her arm with his left hand, squeeze hard and shake her like a rag doll.

'Let go of me,' she hissed in a shocked breath.

His fingers tightened their grip like an iron clasp and he yanked her close. 'You shouldn't have talked to me like that.' His mouth contorted into a snarl. He raised his right hand ... The sky was full of black butterflies. They fluttered all around her, became bigger ... so big they choked her and she couldn't breathe.

The screeching of tyres and the frantic beeping of a car horn jerked her back to her senses. Her eyes flickered open. She was in Adrian's car, her head bumping against the passenger window as Adrian sped around a tight bend of the road and a black Ford Fiesta was coming from the opposite direction. They were going to crash into it ...

Adrian braked hard. The Audi skidded, and the driver of the Fiesta beeped his horn again. Jenna couldn't be sure, but in that split second she thought it looked like Kieran behind the wheel, with Jim and his wife as passengers.

What was she doing in Adrian's car? And how long had she been unconscious? She lifted her hand to her cheekbone. Her face throbbed with pain ... and then she remembered. He had got hold of her ... he was going to hit her, and she had fainted. Had he actually hit her or had she banged her face against the window?

'Why am I in your car, Adrian, and where are we going?'

He glanced at her. 'I'm taking you to hospital. You're hurt.'

'Oh ...' She didn't want to be cooped up with him in the Audi, especially not when he was driving like a maniac on Arrandale's narrow, winding roads, but she could cope if it was only until they reached the hospital. And then she'd tell him again to leave her alone, and phone a taxi to take her home.

Adrian however must have taken a wrong turn because they were heading towards Beinn Dhubh, not the hospital.

'You're going the wrong way,' she remarked. 'Dana's hospital is in the opposite direction. And you need to slow down. The roads are dangerous around here.'

'Be quiet and leave the driving to me.' He took one hand

off the steering wheel and rummaged through his breast pocket and threw her engagement ring into her lap. 'Here. I brought it for you. Put it on.'

Her stomach turned, and a sour taste flooded her mouth. Had he not listened to a word she'd said?

'Take it and put it on,' he repeated more forcefully.

She looked at the ring in her lap with horror. She had vowed never to wear it again, but Adrian was driving too fast and the car was veering so close to the deep, narrow ditch alongside the road. Now wasn't the time to make him angry, so she slid the ring on her finger.

'There. I've done it. Now please slow down ... these roads are dangerous, and this isn't the way to the hospital at all ...'

'Whinge, whinge, whinge – that's all you ever do.' His jaw tightened and he sped up further. The tyres squealed again as he turned another bend of the road. Fear made her blood run cold. They were going to crash.

'Say you'll resign from this stupid job and come back to me,' he snapped.

'What?'

'You heard.'

He was mad. There was no other explanation. Mad and dangerous. And she was trapped with him. She couldn't even phone 999 for help. Her mobile was in her handbag, and she had no idea what Adrian had done with it. It didn't matter anyway since there'd be no signal around here.

She had to pacify him, get him to slow down so she had a chance to get out, and that meant telling him what he wanted to hear. At least until she got the chance to get out and run ...

'Yes! Yes, all right,' she said. 'I'll do whatever you want. Stop the car.'

He slowed down a touch and cast a sidelong glance in

her direction. 'See? It wasn't that hard. It was foolish of you to run away, but at least you realised your mistake and everything will be all right now. Yes, everything will be all right,' he muttered again.

She looked at the ring's evil red glint at her finger and started shaking as if her insides had turned to ice.

Chapter Thirty-Eight

Daniel put his fiddle down and jumped off the stage. The crowd had thinned now Jim, his wife and some of their friends and family had left, but it was still hot and buzzing in the pub, and after playing almost non-stop for the best part of the evening, half a pint of bitter was exactly what he needed. First he wanted to talk to Jenna … He looked around the pub but she was nowhere to be seen.

'You don't happen to know where Jenna is?' he asked Brendon at the bar.

'Sorry, Daniel. I haven't seen her in ages. She must have left.'

Daniel's heart sank. 'I'll call at Mermaid's Cottage on my way back. I really needed to talk to her but haven't had a chance today.'

Brendon put a hand on his shoulder. 'Do you think she'll want to talk to you? I know it isn't any of my business, but Ruth was telling me that Jenna was really upset tonight with what's going on between Shannon and you.'

'Nothing's going on between Shannon and I,' Daniel insisted. 'Nothing at all – at least not in the sense you mean.' He raked his fingers in his hair. 'But I know what it must look like.'

He looked at Brendon. 'The last thing I want is to hurt her. I love her, Brendon. More than I can ever say.'

'In that case you'd better tell her. It's no good speaking to me about it.'

'I'll get my keys and drive to Mermaid's Cottage right now. The ceilidh is almost finished anyway. They'll have to carry on without me.'

Someone tapped on his shoulder. Daniel turned round

and found himself face to face with Kieran. 'Sorry ... err ... Mr McGregor,' the lad started. 'I couldn't help overhearing you're looking for Jenna. I've just seen her. She was with some bloke who was driving his fancy white Audi like a maniac. I was taking Jim and Julie home when he almost crashed into us ... Gave us such a fright I thought Jim was going to have another heart attack.'

'An Audi? Who could that be?' He raked his brain. Drummond didn't have an Audi, not unless he'd just bought one.

Brendon frowned. 'I wonder if ...'

'What is it?'

'It could be her former boyfriend – that Adrian bloke. I'm sure she mentioned that he used to drive an Audi. If it's him, it's not good news.'

Adrian ... The name gave Daniel a prick of awareness. He looked at Brendon. 'Why do you say that?'

Brendon lowered his voice. 'Well, it's a wee bit private. Jenna talked to me in confidence. I'm not sure I can say anything.'

Daniel remembered the night when Jenna had cried about being in pain and scared of the dark, and her pleas for the man not to hurt her, and later how upset she'd been in the garden of The Buttered Scone when the couple was arguing – or rather when the man was behaving like a bully towards his wife ...

His stomach twisted in a knot and his blood ran cold. 'He abused her, didn't he?'

Brendon blinked in surprise. 'You know? The man sounds like a mean bastard. Played mind games, made her believe she was mad, shouted at her, called her stupid ...'

Daniel had a sick feeling at the pit of his stomach. That was exactly what he'd done on the beach. No wonder Jenna had been so upset.

Brendon was still talking. 'He wouldn't leave her alone either. Kept texting her, wouldn't take no for an answer. He even threatened to come and get her.'

And Jenna had never breathed a word about him to Daniel ... To be fair, she had tried once but he hadn't let her speak. He'd kissed her and made love to her instead.

'It seems that's what he just did,' he said in a gloomy voice. 'Something doesn't make sense. If he was pestering her and she was that wary of him, why did she get into his car?'

'No idea,' Brendon said with a shrug.

'I'll call her now.' Daniel dialled Jenna's number. The phone rang a few times then went to voicemail. He tried again. And again. 'No answer ...'

Uneasiness spread inside him. Something wasn't right. He could sense it.

'Where were they heading when you saw them?' he asked Kieran.

'They were heading north, towards Beinn Dhubh.'

'Why would he drive there? There's nothing.' What's more the roads were dangerous, especially as night was falling and the man wouldn't know the area.

'I'll go after them,' he said. 'But first I'll ask Eric to lend me his CB radio. Mobile phones are useless over there and I may need to call for help if things turn nasty.'

'I knew you would see sense.' Adrian let out a low chuckle, lifted a hand towards her face, around her cheekbone that still throbbed with pain, and trailed a finger along her jawline.

It took all Jenna's self control not to pull away. He had a weird glint in his eyes, an even weirder smile on his face.

'We'll spend the night at that place of yours,' he carried on, sliding his finger along the curve of her neck, and gave her a smug smile when she shivered. He must think that she was enjoying his caress when it was making her sick.

'You hurt me very much, you know, when you were acting all stubborn and unreasonable ... and even more when I found out you were unfaithful. I never thought you'd be unfaithful to me.'

He glared at her and she instinctively slid closer to the door, ready to jump out, even if there was nowhere for her to go.

'Anyway,' he carried on. 'We'll have to stay at your mother's for a while until I sort myself out. I'm in a spot of bother financially but you'll help me out, won't you? You still have some money your father left you, don't you? Yes, it's going to work out very well, very well. I needn't have worried at all,' he mumbled to himself.

So he was after her savings ... Should she tell him that she had spent most of it, having to cover the rent and expenses for their Manchester city flat on her own after he left at Christmas? Perhaps that would put him off and he'd leave her alone.

At least now everything made sense. He'd only been interested in her money. Why had she never seen it before? When they'd met at that Manchester bar her colleagues from the library kept calling her Little Miss Minted and asking her to buy rounds because she'd just received some funds from her father's estate. He must have overheard them and seen straight away that she would make an easy target. She was shy and insecure, easily impressed and desperate to please, to love and be loved. And later when they were living together he often asked her to lend him some money or relied on her to pay the bills because of the irregular income from his freelance job.

'Has my mother ever lent you any money?' she asked.

He smirked. 'Your mother has been very generous,

especially over the past few weeks. Like I said, I've had a few problems in London. Some idiots didn't like my work, refused to pay me, made life impossible for me. I had to borrow money – too much money.'

'What about ... you know ... your new girlfriend?' She couldn't help but ask.

'That selfish bitch!' he snarled, making her jump and edge closer to the door again. He drew a deep breath, and shook his head. 'I don't want to talk about her, or about London. Now we're back together, everything is going to be fine. Let's go to your cottage ... and make up for lost time.'

This was a nightmare. Jenna looked at the bleak landscape and crossed her hands in her lap. The ring felt clumsy and heavy on her finger, and made her skin hot and itchy. She turned it one way, then the other, longing to rip it off and throw it away.

Adrian started the engine, did a U-turn and drove down the mountain road much too fast again. Suddenly beams of headlights appeared in the distance. A car was coming their way. This was her chance to escape.

As they came to another tight bend, she grabbed hold of the steering wheel and pulled to the right.

'What are you doing?' he yelled, his face contorted with fury.

The tyres skidded. The Audi swerved, crashed into the ditch that ran alongside the road with the deafening blast of crushed metal followed by the loud bang of the airbags inflating. Jenna's seat belt dug into her chest and shoulder as she was projected forward and her face pushed against the airbag. It took her a few seconds to get her breath back. She pushed herself up but the Audi tipped at an angle and it was difficult to sit back.

'Adrian?'

There was no answer. With a grimace of pain she twisted

her neck to look at him. His body was flopped forward, his face pressed against the airbag. He didn't move. What if she'd killed him?

A car screeched to a halt on the road. Somebody came running, and yanked the passenger door open.

'Jenna! Jenna, can you hear me? Jenna, answer me.'

Daniel? She turned to him. His shoulders filled the door frame, his face was taut and his eyes filled with worry.

'Jenna, are you hurt?' He touched her shoulders, smoothed her hair away from her face with infinite care and gentleness.

'I'm fine.' She tried to speak but her face and her mouth hurt too much, so she shook her head gingerly. 'You must see to Adrian,' she mumbled.

'I'll help you out of the car first. Move very slowly.'

She was aching all over but didn't appear to have any injury or broken bone. Once she was out of the Audi, he lifted her into his arms and carried her to the Land Rover which he'd abandoned in the middle of the road. She snuggled against his broad chest. His shirt felt soft and his heart beat loud and strong against her cheek. She could have stayed in his arms forever but he eased her down onto the passenger seat.

'I'll radio emergency services as soon as I have seen to your ...' He paused, and his voice took a more formal tone. 'To the other casualty. Try not to worry.'

As he hurried away, she looked down, and the ring glinted at her finger. With a hiss of pain and anger she pulled it off and threw it as far as she could through the Land Rover's open door.

Chapter Thirty-Nine

Daniel gave the front tyre of the Land Rover a puerile but heartfelt kick. The blasted car wouldn't start that morning and he'd wasted so much time fixing it that he'd missed Jenna being discharged from the hospital. He should have phoned and asked her to wait or booked a taxi for her. Now she must think he didn't care when she'd been on his mind all night and visions of her slumped at the front of the Audi still haunted him.

He got his keys out, ready to unlock the car when Adrian Jones walked out of the hospital's main entrance, looking bruised and crumpled. A taxi whizzed past, stopped in front of him. Jones winced as he bent down to talk to the driver through the open window. 'Do you know a place called Mermaid's Cottage outside Dana?' He nodded. 'Good. Take me there.'

After what he'd put her through the night before, the bastard still wanted to see Jenna? Daniel didn't think twice. Seething with cold white rage, his fists curled by his sides, he strode towards him and stood between Jones and the taxi.

'Hey, that's my taxi,' Jones hissed. He was shorter than Daniel, and had to crane his neck to look at him. He must have seen something in his eyes that made him think twice about complaining again because he shuffled aside and gestured to the cab. 'OK. Take it. I don't mind. I'll get another one.'

'I don't want your taxi,' Daniel growled. He had never beaten up an injured man before but it was hard to resist the urge to push Jones against the wall and add a few bruises to his impressive collection.

'I want you to listen very carefully. You won't remember

me because you were unconscious but I'm the guy who pulled you out of your car last night. More than that, I'm a friend of Jenna's.'

Jones' eyes widened as if he recognised him. 'Ah, the guy from the lifeboat … It's you, isn't it?'

'Aye, I'm that guy all right, and I have a nasty temper too, so if you know what's good for you, you will leave Arrandale never to return, and you'll never go anywhere near Jenna ever again. You won't phone or text her. You won't even *think* about her. Am I making myself clear? Now, get in that taxi and clear off before I—' He took a deep breath and clenched his fists by his side.

Jones must have recognised the murderous glint in his eyes because he mumbled an apology, rushed into the back of the taxi and shouted to the driver to take him to the train station at Kyle.

Good riddance, Daniel thought as the taxi drove out of the car park. Now he could go and see Jenna … and explain everything.

Back at Mermaid Cove, he drove past Hamish and Ben's campervan which was parked near the cliff path. He slowed down and glanced at the beach. There was a pile of towels, flip-flops and trainers, and a couple of backpacks, the kind divers used which had straps to keep fins secure. The students had gone diving again.

Then he saw Shannon's green dress and Katrina's jeans, trainers and bright yellow sweatshirt neatly folded on the sand next to the bags. Closer to the edge of the water was a pair of canvas pumps, and if he wasn't mistaken, these were Jenna's …

What was going on? Where were they all? He braked, got out of the car, and squinting against the bright sunlight surveyed the beach and the rock pools then looked at the open sea all the way towards Mermaid's Rocks.

And then he saw them ... Jenna and Katrina clinging to the buoy about sixty metres from the beach.

He took his phone out. Ran down the cliff path. Dialled 999 for the coastguards as he kicked his shoes off. Told the operator to get a boat out to Mermaid Cove. Threw his mobile, keys and wallet on the sand and dived straight into the water.

The shock of the freezing water stole his breath but he pushed his body hard, and harder still. Every second counted. If Jenna and Katrina weren't wearing wetsuits, they wouldn't have long before hypothermia set in.

'Hang on, darling.' A wave crashed over Jenna and water gushed into her mouth, her nose, choking her. Her soaked hair was plastered on her face. The tee shirt and shorts she'd changed into after coming home from hospital stuck to her body. Her fingers hurt from holding onto the metal bar that ran around the buoy. Katrina's arms tightened around her neck and her body shuddered. It was lucky she wore a shorty wetsuit, which would at least protect her from the cold for a while.

The little girl's teeth clattered. 'I'm t-tired ... and c-cold. I ... c-can't hold on to you any l-longer ...'

'Yes, you can.' Jenna tightened her grip on the little girl's waist. 'The lifeguards are coming. I called them.'

She may sound positive for Katrina's sake but her strength was fast ebbing away. She could hardly feel her arms and legs. If only she could lift Katrina onto the platform at the base of the buoy ...

'I ... am ... s-sorry ... J-jenna ...'

'Don't be silly, darling. You're doing great.'

'No ... I mean, s-sorry for last n-night ... I was mean to you at the ceilidh.'

Jenna shook her head. 'Mean? You're never mean.'

'I ignored ... you. I didn't t-talk to you.'

Another wave washed over them, the freezing salty water making them cough and gasp, and she tightened her hold on Katrina. How long would the child have managed on her own?

It had been pure chance that she'd spotted Katrina earlier on. The taxi had dropped her at the cottage and she felt achy, tearful and lonely after a mostly sleepless night in hospital. She took a shower and changed before phoning her mother to tell her what had happened with Adrian the night before. She also told her about Adrian taking advantage of her to get some money.

'I did lend him quite a lot over the past few months,' her mother said in a tearful voice, 'but that's because I believed he truly loved you. I never thought he would hurt you and put you in any danger.' She then suggested Jenna spend some time with her in Manchester, and Jenna had promised to come soon.

It would take time to mend the relationship between her mum and her but it was worth a try, and going away might give her a chance to forget about Daniel and Shannon ...

Daniel who'd hardly spoken to her at the site of the accident and hadn't been in touch since. Daniel who didn't love her, and had broken her heart.

Hamish and Ben's campervan was parked near the path, so she went down to the beach for a chat, but there was nobody there. The students' rucksacks, shoes and clothes were strewn around on the sand along with a woman's dress, a pair of flip-flops and Katrina's clothes that were folded in a neat pile with her trainers on top. Shannon must be diving with Ben and Hamish, but what about Katrina? Hamish and Ben wouldn't take her, whatever Shannon said. So where was she?

And then she'd seen her, hanging on for dear life to the buoy in the cove.

Thankfully Jenna had her mobile in the pocket of her shorts, so she called 999 before taking her pumps off and running into the freezing cold water. It felt like forever to reach Katrina, and she probably wouldn't have made it if it weren't for sheer desperation. And it was only desperation that now made her cling to the child and to the buoy.

'It's m-my uncle ... Look!' Katrina now cried out.

She was right. Daniel's was swimming towards them, his arms slashing through the waves in powerful strokes. He lifted his head up and shouted, 'Hang on. The lifeboat's coming.'

It was another couple of minutes before he reached them, but they felt like hours. At the same time the roaring of an engine filled the air as the lifeguards' dinghy bounced on the surf at full speed towards them.

Daniel reached out and lifted Katrina into his arms. She immediately wrapped her arms around his neck. 'I've got you, chick. I've got you.'

He looked at Jenna, his eyes as blue as the sea. 'Are you all right?'

She nodded. The dinghy was there now, right next to them. A woman lifeguard leant over the side, held out her hands and shouted for Daniel to hand Katrina over. Once the little girl was safely inside the boat, it was Jenna's turn to be pulled up, with Daniel helping her from behind before heaving himself onboard too.

The lifeguard immediately wrapped a thermal blanket around her shoulders while the other crew member did the same for Daniel and Katrina, and the boat whizzed round and headed towards Mermaid's Beach, with Katrina tightly enfolded in Daniel's arms. Her dark hair was soaked and her bright blue eyes – the same colour as his – seemed huge in her pale, pinched face, but she was safe. They were all safe.

Chapter Forty

Dr Kerr gave Katrina a thorough examination and declared her a fit, healthy and very lucky girl. 'Her wetsuit and the fact that she was rescued quickly stopped her from getting hypothermia,' he said before packing his medical instruments back into his bag. 'However she needs plenty of hot drinks and plenty of rest.'

Miona brought some chicken soup and a piece of apple pie with custard which the little girl ate in bed, propped up by half a dozen pillows like a little princess, and with Daniel nursing a mug of coffee by her side.

Katrina scraped the last crumb of apple pie off the bowl and licked her spoon with a contented sigh. At least the afternoon's misadventures hadn't spoiled her appetite.

'Good girl,' he said as she handed him her empty bowl. 'I know it's early but you have to sleep, love. Remember what Doctor Kerr said.'

He was expecting Katrina to protest but she only nodded.

'I am sorry for causing trouble, Uncle Daniel,' she whispered as she pulled her covers up to her chin. 'I only wanted to show Mum I was a good swimmer. She said she would take me diving if I could swim to the buoy and back, but I couldn't. It was too hard. I was very naughty, and now you're angry with me.'

He was angry all right, but not at Katrina. Never at Katrina. 'I'm not angry, chick.' He bent down to kiss her cheek and stroke her hair away from her face.

'I was so scared. It was lucky Jenna saw me. She walked straight into the sea with all her clothes on. She was very brave, wasn't she?'

Daniel's chest felt so tight it hurt. 'Yes, chick, she was

very brave.' All the more because she'd said before that she wasn't a great swimmer and she must be aching from the accident.

Katrina's eyes filled with misery. 'I was mean to her at the ceilidh. I hope she'll be my friend again.'

'Of course Jenna is still your friend.'

'Is she still your girlfriend too?'

'Hmm .... well ...' That was another matter, one he had no answer to.

Katrina started crying. 'I let Mum down too, that's why she hasn't come to say good night.'

He tightened his jaw. 'Don't worry about that, chick. She must be busy getting changed.' Shannon had paid Katrina a flying visit after Hamish and Ben dropped her off, totally unaware of what had happened while they were out diving and exploring the sea cave. She hadn't even been worried that Katrina wasn't on the beach waiting for her when they'd come back, but assumed she'd got bored and walked home.

Katrina yawned and Daniel bent down to kiss her cheek. 'It's time to sleep now. I love you.'

She gave him a sleepy smile. 'I love you too. What can I dream of?'

'Let's see ...' He scratched his chin and pretended to be deep in thought. 'Why don't you dream about the Summer Fete next Saturday? It's going to be bigger and better this year, with the regatta. And don't forget the awards for the short story competition when I get to dress up as Zonk.'

She giggled. 'I can't wait to see that. You're going to look great ... but what about your happy dream?'

He frowned. 'What's that?'

'You need to catch a happy dream in your butterfly net, like in the Zonk stories,' she insisted.

'I thought they were clouds.'

She yawned again. 'It's the same, Uncle Daniel. The fluffy clouds *are* happy dreams.'

He gathered the dirty plates, walked to the door, and turned round before going out. His heart tightened. She looked so small and fragile, and he had come very close to losing her.

'How is the lassie?' Miona asked as soon as he walked into the kitchen.

'Asleep.' He put his empty mug and Katrina's dishes in the sink.

'You need to take yourself to bed too, Daniel. You look dreadful.'

He rubbed his face. 'Aye ... but I need to see Jenna first, and thank her. Without her, things may not have turned out quite so well.' He shuddered and his voice caught in his throat.

Miona nodded. 'She's a brave lass. Iain went down to check on her earlier and took some soup and some apple pie for her tea. He said that the two students were there, making cups of tea and looking after her.'

'How was she?'

'She said she was cold and tired, but all right, considering ...'

She cleared her throat and cast Daniel a wary glance. 'I'm sorry, Daniel. I should have seen that Katrina had put her shorty wetsuit on, and that Shannon had gone into the shed for her old diving stuff. I should have guessed they were up to something. The lass almost drowned and it was my fault.'

He put his hands on her shoulders and looked down into her eyes. 'If it was anybody's fault, it was mine for leaving Katrina with Shannon. You have nothing to reproach yourself for. You have been the best, the most loving – the only grandmother Katrina has ever known.'

Miona sniffed and her eyes filled with tears she wiped

quickly with the corner of her apron. 'Thanks, Daniel. It means a lot.'

'It's nothing but the truth.' He gave her a quick hug then pulled away. 'Any idea where Shannon is?'

'In the drawing room, looking at maps.' She pursed her lips. No doubt like Daniel she was wondering why she hadn't spent more time with Katrina after coming back from Mermaid Cove, and why she wasn't holding her precious daughter's hand and watching over her as she fell asleep right now.

Shannon flashed him a smile as soon as he walked into the drawing room and patted the cushion on the sofa next to her. 'Hey. Dan ... at last! Come here, I have exciting news for you.'

She had changed into cut off jeans and a dark green sweatshirt, had pulled her hair up in a high ponytail, and was sitting on the sofa, her long legs crossed. From the doorway she looked very much like the woman who had dazzled him when they'd first met. Beautiful, carefree ... and unpredictable.

But he wasn't the same man, and she didn't dazzle him any longer. Closing the door behind him he ignored her invitation to sit next to her and walked to the French doors overlooking the garden instead.

'You're annoyed with me,' she said, her lips forming a perfect pout.

He turned round. 'Annoyed? I'm bloody furious.'

'Why? Katrina is fine, isn't she?'

'She could have drowned, Shannon, because of your stupid swimming challenge, and now she thinks she failed you, and that's why you didn't spend any time with her this evening.'

Shannon shrugged. 'I thought she needed to sleep ... That's what the doctor said, wasn't it? As for the swimming, she'll do better next time. Now, do you want to hear my big news? Hamish, Ben and I found something incredible down at the cave!'

'There won't be a next time,' he interrupted in a harsh voice. 'You shouldn't have left her alone on the beach, let alone told her to swim to the buoy and back.'

Shannon sighed. 'It wasn't that far. At her age I could already swim double that distance.'

'There are strong currents in Mermaid Cove and Katrina very nearly drowned.'

She twirled a long strand of hair around her index finger and cocked her head to one side. 'Listen to you – you've become a right mother hen. Stop wrapping the girl in cotton wool. Let her grow up. Become more independent. She'll thank you for it.'

'She's a seven-year-old lass,' he said between clenched teeth. 'She has plenty of time to grow up and become independent.'

She glared at him. 'Don't you think I know my daughter's age? I gave birth to her, remember?'

'And you swiftly left her, to travel the world with Hugh and your father, remember?' he snapped back.

'Diving is my life, you've always known that, and we made a deal. Leaving Katrina with you was the best thing I ever did. Although when you asked me to come over this week I thought ... I hoped ... you wanted me for *me*, not only for Katrina. I did have feelings for you, Daniel. I still do ...'

He said nothing. What could he say?

Pain flashed in her eyes. 'Fine. I understand. I can see you're not interested, and won't trouble you with my feelings again. But I can't believe you didn't even ask what we found in the cave. Are you not even a teeny bit interested?'

He was ... of course he was. 'No,' he lied.

She crossed her arms and tilted her chin. 'The Daniel I used to know would have quizzed me for every detail of the dive. What am I saying? He would be on the beach right now, putting his gear on to go into the cave. Well, I'll tell you anyway.'

He was tempted to listen, but he raised his hand to stop her. 'Not now, Shannon. I need to go out. You can tell me when I come back.'

'If I'm still here.'

He frowned. 'What do you mean?'

She stood up. 'I'm not going to stay where I'm not wanted. I'll find a hotel or a B&B ... But don't worry, I know we have a deal and I intend to stick around for a week or two and make arrangements to see Katrina on a regular basis after that. Believe it or not, I'd like to make things work between us. She's a great kid. I may never get a prize for being the best mum, but I would still like to be part of her life ... if you'll let me after today's fiasco.'

She smiled, and touched her fingers to her heart. 'I promise there will be no more swimming challenges, and no diving until you say she's old enough.'

She sounded sincere, and much to his surprise, he believed her. 'You don't have to go anywhere. Katrina would be disappointed if you weren't here when she wakes up tomorrow.'

'OK then, I'll stay. But I've been thinking. I don't need your money – I don't *want* your money. You don't have to sell off any land for me.'

He gasped. 'Really? Do you mean that?'

She nodded. 'Sure. I know how much Arrandale means to you.'

'Well, thanks,' he mumbled, still stunned by Shannon's decision.

She smiled. 'Now we've got that sorted out, do you want to hear the news about the sea cave? Hamish and Ben think it may be possible to access some of the chambers which were previously blocked off and ...'

Daniel shook his head. 'I don't have time to talk about that now, Shannon. I need to see Jenna.'

'Ah ... Jenna, the cove's new mermaid. So she's the one.'

He ran his fingers through his hair, and nodded. 'Aye. She's the one.'

'I don't want to talk about this afternoon. Now if you'll excuse me, it's late and I'm busy.' Jenna forced a smile and tried to close the door but Ron Donaldson stuck his foot out to stop her.

'Come on, Jenna ...'

'It's Miss Palmer to you,' she snapped. 'Now step back so I can shut the door.'

He didn't move. 'My readers need to know about what happened in Mermaid Cove. After all, the McGregor girl almost followed her father to his watery grave ... Hugh McGregor drowned in almost the exact same spot – Mermaid's Rocks and the wreck of the *Santa Catalina* being only a few hundred feet from the buoy. It's almost as if that old mermaid curse is coming true again. This story is going to make for a great headline in Monday's paper. *"The McGregor Curse Strikes Again"*,' he said in an overdramatic voice.

'Your actions were all the more commendable when you were involved in a car accident last night,' he added. 'Would you care to tell me about that?'

She stiffened. The last thing she needed was to see Adrian's name mentioned in the local paper. As far as she was concerned he had left Arrandale, and Skye, never to return.

'I have nothing to tell you.'

The man shrugged. 'Ah well, that's too bad. I believe McGregor was at the site of the car crash too. I'll have to talk to him about it.'

'Talk to me about what?'

Donaldson jumped and swirled round to face Daniel, flanked by Sam and Eddie wagging their tails. Her insides tightened and twisted. What was he doing here? He had already thanked her for calling 999 and helping Katrina as the lifeboat brought them back to the beach. Daniel gave the journalist a stern look. 'I hope you're not bothering Miss Palmer with your questions, Ron.'

'No, of course not.' Donaldson let out a nervous chuckle and took a few steps back. 'I was only doing my job ... asking about the incident involving your niece this afternoon. Actually you were there too, so perhaps you could give me your side of the story.'

'I don't think so. And I don't want to see you anywhere near Dunfiadhaich Farm, either pestering my family or my staff. Now I think you've overstayed your welcome.'

'Yes, yes of course. Good night, Jen—Miss Palmer.' He beat a hasty retreat, climbed into his car and drove off, much to Jenna's relief.

Daniel gave her a searching look, one that made her stupid heart beat a staccato. 'Jenna ... How are you?'

She gestured to the fleece that she had slipped over a sweatshirt and two tee shirts underneath and forced a smile. 'Tired and cold, no matter how many layers I put on and how many gallons of hot tea I drink ... but Miona's soup and apple pie helped perk me up.'

'Good. I am glad. I heard Hamish and Ben came to see you.'

She smiled as she remembered how the two students had fussed around her. 'They were very remorseful for leaving Katrina alone on the beach.'

They sounded like polite strangers, and it made her heart ache. Why did she have to fall in love with him? Pretending she was fine and making mundane conversation may be possible for a few minutes, but she wasn't sure how long she could keep it up.

'Now, if you don't mind, I am tired and …'

He nodded. 'I was hoping we could talk. There are so many things I need to say, to explain.' He carried on when she didn't answer. 'I should have done it before, but I was scared I'd push you away …'

A cheerless smile flickered on his lips. 'Stupid of me, I know, since I've pushed you away anyway.'

She still didn't answer.

'We could go to the beach. It's a nice evening, although you may want to take a blanket since you're feeling cold.' He took a deep breath. 'Listen, Jenna, I know you must hate me right now and I don't blame you. The way I talked to you yesterday on the beach was unforgivable. I know it's a rubbish excuse but I panicked when I saw you in that diving suit. All I could think of was my brother … things going wrong … but I shouldn't have shouted at you. I am sorry.'

He sounded sincere.

'And of course, there is Shannon.' He glanced at the dogs who were frolicking on the clifftop, then back at her. 'I have a lot of explaining to do.'

Suddenly her mind was made up. She owed him, and herself, to listen to what he had to say. She nodded. 'Yes, you do. I'll fetch that blanket.'

Chapter Forty-One

The dogs were chasing after each other and splashing in the water by the time he jumped from the path onto the sand. He held out his hand to help Jenna climb down, and much to his surprise and delight she took it with a faint smile. The feel of her skin, of her small hand in his, warmed his heart and made him hope that perhaps things could be put right between them. However he would only have one chance at this. He'd better not blow it.

It was a perfect summer evening – one of those magical evenings unique to Arrandale when the colours of the sky changed into a rainbow of blues and indigos, pale yellows and gold tinted with pinks and oranges reflecting onto the surface of the sea. Waves lapped the sand with only the faintest, silkiest murmur. Even the calls of gannets, guillemots and kittiwakes echoed soft and distant.

'Shall we sit here?' He gestured to a patch of dry white sand.

She nodded, pulled her hand from his grasp and lowered herself onto the sand. 'Here, let me …' He took the blanket off her and draped it on her shoulders, resisting the urge to touch her, run his fingers through her hair and stroke the nape of her neck. His throat tightened. How he'd missed her these past few days …

'Thank you.' Drawing her knees up, she wrapped her arms around her legs and stared right ahead, towards the buoy and Mermaid's Rocks.

He sat down next to her, suddenly unsure of how to start.

'What did Ben and Hamish say about the diving this afternoon?'

'They were very excited about a chamber which they

estimate to be underneath the stone slab in the garden. They said there were traces of a stairwell carved into the rock and what could be a collapsed tunnel to the surface. Hamish thinks it may be possible to access the chamber from the garden by removing the slab.'

'I've had my suspicions about that piece of stonework. It's well known that the family who lived in the cottage – and indeed the whole McGregor clan – used to dabble in smuggling and the occasional shipwrecking back in the days. That's what happened to the *Santa Catalina* after all. People lit fires to lure the ship into the cove in the hope it'd crash against Mermaid's Rocks …'

'Hamish believes that access to the chambers where the treasure was hidden was blocked by rock falls for hundreds of years but that recent storms and strong tidal currents may have cleared some of the passages. He said he would like you to go with him and Ben when they go back.'

His whole body tensed. 'No. I don't think so.' Diving, treasures, shipwrecks, were all part of the past.

'Don't you want to know if the treasure is down there?'

'Not really. Not any more. The *Santa Catalina* was Hugh's obsession. That's what he was after all his life – adventure and excitement. I loved it too, don't get me wrong. That's how I used to spend all my free time – diving and exploring the coast for shipwrecks, even after my parents died and I took over here.'

He stared at the rugged outline of Mermaid's Rocks sticking out of the water. 'Of course as the responsibilities of looking after Arrandale piled up, I had less and less time for fun and games.'

'What about your brother? Did he help out?'

'Not much. Hugh was never interested in the farm. He liked to travel or stay with university friends for the holidays so I didn't ask him to work on the farm with me.

Miona said I overindulged him and didn't help him grow up, and I guess she has a point.'

Jenna gave him a soft, gentle smile. 'It was very generous and selfless of you to let him enjoy himself.'

There was a bitter taste in his mouth. He might as well confess all, even the ugly tentacles of jealousy and resentment that had sometimes stifled the love he felt for his brother.

'It wasn't that noble or selfless. I was envious of Hugh's lifestyle at times and a part of me wanted to carry on having fun too, but mostly I was proud. I wanted to show people that even without academic qualifications I could manage the estate. I was the McGregor brother in charge, the one who worked hard and everybody could rely on. I contributed to casting Hugh in the part of a charming but lazy and shallow lad. He was clever and could have achieved so much more if I'd pushed him, but I always made excuses for him and gave him what he wanted instead of telling him to buckle down and work harder.'

He sighed. 'So you see I wasn't such a great a brother after all.' He fell silent for a moment, watching the dogs shaking the water off their fur, spraying water droplets everywhere.

It was time to talk about Shannon.

'Taking care of the farm was hard work but I managed ... then one summer Michael O'Keeffe arrived in Arrandale with his team of marine archaeologists. He had written asking if he could investigate the *Santa Catalina* wreck, and I'd said yes. It had been a hell of a winter and a rotten spring. I had worked non-stop from dawn to night and was shattered and in dire need of a break. O'Keeffe arrived as the weather turned warm and sunny, and for once there was no major drama on the farm and I had some free time. Hugh had graduated and was staying in London to have fun.

'O'Keeffe said that my local knowledge would be invaluable and invited me to join his team. The first few days were wonderful. I felt freer and happier than I'd been for ages, and then, Shannon arrived.'

How could he convey what he'd felt when he'd first seen her – that punch to the gut, and the bewildering belief that he had found the woman of his dreams?

'I fell head over heels in love, or at least that's what I thought at the time. I doubt that it was love at all. I was twenty-five. It was summer. I was having a great time diving again. Shannon was exciting, exotic, and a brilliant diver. Falling for her was almost unavoidable. She seemed to share my feelings too, never lost an opportunity to flatter my stupid male ego. I felt like the luckiest man alive, especially since all the men around here were falling over themselves to get noticed by her. There were even fights in The Anchor over her, would you believe?'

He shook his head. 'Anyway, it only took a few days for us to … err … get together.'

Jenna didn't say anything but she shifted ever so slightly away from him on the sand. He wanted to pull her to him and tell her it was a long time ago and what he felt for her was a thousand, a million times stronger than what he'd thought he felt for Shannon then … but he carried on. He wanted to be completely honest with her, even if it made him look like an *eejit*.

'Shannon wanted to keep our relationship a secret. Something about not upsetting her father. That was a lie, of course, but I didn't question her motives and didn't tell a soul.'

He shook his head. 'How stupid was I? Anyway shortly after Shannon's father returned to the States, Hugh came back from London. By then, farm work had picked up so he volunteered to take Shannon out on excursions and diving trips. I never thought anything of it … until I realised she was playing us both for fools. I confronted her and she admitted she'd been "having fun with Hugh", as she put it. I broke up with her there and then, but I think my pride took more of a blow than my heart and that's when I knew I didn't love her – never had.'

'Did you tell your brother what had been going on?'

'How could I? He was completely besotted with her. What's more, he wouldn't have believed me and would probably have accused me of lying out of spite – the boring older brother jealous of the more attractive and more popular younger one … a recurring joke over the years. I said nothing and they carried on *having fun* as before. After a few weeks, they travelled to Florida together to join Shannon's father and his team on a diving expedition. Hugh was over the moon at the opportunity of working with O'Keeffe.'

'When they returned, they announced they were engaged and things got … complicated.' Now came the hard part. Better get it over with …

'The evening of their engagement party at the Three Fishes, Shannon took me to one side and told me that she was pregnant and that the dates indicated the baby was mine.'

Jenna gasped and her hand flew to her mouth as she stared at him, eyes wide open in shock. 'Oh.'

He gave her a tight smile. 'She said that if I told Hugh that the baby was mine, she would deny everything, claim that I was a sad, mean and jealous man and would get Hugh to leave Arrandale and relocate to the States and I would never see them, or the baby, ever again. However, if I kept quiet they would stay at Dunfiadhaich Farm after the birth, and as they intended to carry on working with her father on dives all over the world, I could look after the child, provide care and stability when they travelled abroad.'

Jenna's face was pink with indignation, and her eyes filled with fury. 'That is the most awful blackmail I have ever heard!'

He nodded. 'Aye.' He had relived that night many times, wondering what would have happened if he'd challenged Shannon and told Hugh the truth – or said he wanted to take a paternity test.

'So I stood aside and promised to be a caring uncle. Katrina's birth was the most intense, scary, amazing and lonely experience of my life. I couldn't say anything, couldn't share my feelings with anyone when Hugh phoned from the hospital with the good news.'

'It was hard watching Hugh slip into the part of the fun dad, hard being on the sideline, although I did my fair share of nappy changing and night feeds too when Shannon and Hugh were too shattered to get up. After about six months, Shannon's father phoned and asked her to join him on a dive in the Caribbean. Hugh jumped at the chance to go with her, and Katrina stayed with me. That was the first time they left me in charge, but there would be many more over the following two years.'

'Katrina adored them. Every time they returned there were fun and games for a few weeks, then they would jet off somewhere else. In his own way Hugh loved being a dad – he loved the kisses, the cuddles and the silly games, but he got bored easily and working with Shannon and her dad was what he really wanted to do. I was never tempted to tell him the truth. None of this was his fault, and I knew it would be devastating, that it would destroy him … I was right.'

He picked up a handful of white sand, still warm from the day, and let it seep through his fingers. He didn't want to look at Jenna. He was afraid of what he'd see. Revulsion. Pity. Scorn, no doubt. What kind of man accepts living such a lie?

'It must have been hard for you. Was there nobody you could confide in? Did nobody suspect? What about Miona, or Iain …?' Her voice was gentle, and when he glanced her way, there was nothing but kindness in her eyes.

'I think Miona suspected even if she never breathed a word. She knew how much it would hurt Hugh if it all came out. Unfortunately others weren't so compassionate.'

Drummond. His fingers grabbed a pebble and clenched hard.

'Hugh foolishly invested some money in Toby Drummond's antique import-export business. Unfortunately neither paid any attention to detail or enjoyed mundane day-to-day work. To cut a long story short, they both got conned by a dodgy accountant and Hugh not only lost his investment but he also had to pay a huge fine and unpaid tax. Drummond took off on holiday and Hugh had no idea how to deal with the situation, so he begged me to sort things out. I had to sell some land to cover the fine and the taxes, and I was mad at him and Drummond. I confronted him the day he finally came back from his holidays. It was a rather stormy conversation, as you can imagine. Drummond lashed out, accused me of carrying on with Shannon behind Hugh's back, and implied that Katrina was mine. He couldn't possibly have known for sure, but he must have seen something in my face that confirmed his suspicions. The rumours about me being Katrina's real dad started in the following few days.'

He threw the pebble into the sea, and grabbed another one.

'Was Hugh aware of them?'

'Not for a while. He and Shannon were away a lot, but the night before he died, he went to The Anchor for a drink and someone said something. He came back in a terrible rage. I'd never seen him so mad. He punched me, thoroughly beat me up and I let him … what else could I do?'

347

He shrugged. 'I tried to explain, told him everything. He wouldn't listen, said he hated me, hated Shannon, that his whole life was a lie, and he stormed off. He didn't sleep at the farm that night. I was at the farm the next day when the lifeboat got a call out. A birdwatcher had seen a diver go to Mermaid's Rocks in a dinghy, but three hours later, the dinghy was still there. Call it premonition, but I knew it was Hugh, and that he was in trouble. I geared up, the lifeboat rushed to Mermaid's Rocks but we were too late.

'Did he skip the safety checks on his equipment? Was he still drunk from the night before? According to the coroner's report his alcohol level was quite high. We'll never know. People talked of the mermaid's curse claiming yet another McGregor, but there was no curse. It was my fault we argued. My fault he died.

'After Hugh died, Shannon …' He wasn't quite sure how to continue. 'I suppose she was lost, confused, scared … She said she'd always had feelings for me, and she suggested we try again.'

He rubbed his face, and let out a heavy sigh, remembering that day, not long after Hugh's funeral, when he'd found her crying in the drawing room, and had given her a hug. She had snuggled against him and kissed him on the mouth. He had tried to pull away, but she had linked her arms behind his neck, urged him to kiss her, saying that they were meant for each other, always had been …

'I said it would never happen, so she decided that if I didn't love her, she would go back to the States and leave Katrina with me. She couldn't cope with bringing her up on her own. She wasn't cut out to be a mother, and so on. Unbeknownst to me, Hugh had named me Katrina's guardian in his will so that I could support Shannon in case anything happened to him. After the will was read, Shannon was only too glad to leave Katrina with me and she flew back to Florida.'

The dogs flopped onto the sand next to him. He ruffled their coat, gave them a quick scratch behind the ears but his mind was elsewhere – back to the time when Shannon had left Katrina.

'So in the space of a few weeks, Katrina lost both her parents. She went through a terrible phase of not wanting to fall asleep, of crying and having night terrors, and the only thing that seemed to work was to sit her on my lap and tell her stories about mermaids and sea captains looking for treasures on faraway islands. Then the stories grew out of hand.'

Jenna smiled. 'Your stories are wonderful.'

'That's not what Katrina's teacher or classmates think. That's why I've tried to stop Katrina reading stories about mermaids over the past few months.'

He sighed. 'I read Katrina's story for the competition and didn't know what to do. All I could think was that I had failed her and should make her dream come true by asking Shannon to come over. I am sorry, Jenna. I should have told you, but I was afraid.'

A light breeze now blew from the sea, and Jenna wrapped the blanket more tightly around her shoulders. She said she was cold before, and they'd been out for so long it was now getting dark.

'There are things I should have told you too,' she said. 'I was so scared when I arrived in Arrandale – scared I wouldn't be good enough and you would fire me, scared people wouldn't like me – and scared of Adrian, who was texting me that he wanted me back. I was scared too that you would find me stupid and pathetic for putting up with an abusive relationship, that's why I didn't tell you anything.'

'There is nothing stupid or pathetic about you,' he said in a quiet voice. How he loved her, longed to kiss her, take her in his arms, and forever protect her from harm and sad thoughts ... What would happen now he'd told her everything?

'Shannon wants to be part of Katrina's life and for them to get to know each other,' he said. 'She's going to stay here for a while. I really want to believe that she means it, that she has changed.' Actually she had surprised him tonight by turning down his offer of money ... 'However, I was very clear about her being more responsible and safety-conscious in the future and I think she got the message. I can't expect you to walk into the sea and rescue Katrina again. I don't think my heart could take it.'

She smiled. 'Nor could mine ... today was scary enough. Unlike Shannon, I am no mermaid.'

'Tonight I decided it was time I took a paternity test,' he said. 'I can't believe I waited this long, but now I need to know, and it's the right thing to do. Besides, the rumours are still flying around and soon she'll be old enough to understand.' He'd had many nightmares about that. 'If it turns out that she is Hugh's it won't change how I feel about her.'

'And if she's yours? Will you tell her she's your daughter?'

'I'm not sure. I mean, how could I suddenly ask her to call me Daddy instead of Uncle Daniel? The poor kid would be even more confused – not to mention everybody in Arrandale would know that I deceived my brother.'

'But you didn't!' Jenna sounded quite angry all of a sudden. 'You did everything to cause the minimum fuss and make life easy for your family. You looked after Katrina like a father without ever being recognised, and in doing so you completely ignored your own feelings.

'Children are a lot wiser and a lot more flexible than we

think,' she insisted. 'After all, she seems to have adapted very quickly to her mother not being a mermaid.'

'I'll think about it if it comes to that.' And that was the best he could do for now.

She looked at him again. 'Don't you think it's time you focussed on what you want for once?'

He lifted his hand to her face, stroked the outline of her cheek with his finger and felt her shiver under his touch. 'What I want is … you.'

She didn't say anything, and the little flame of hope he'd had dimmed and went out. She wanted nothing to do with him, and he couldn't blame her. But it hurt like hell.

In the darkening light, her eyes shone like stars and her face was touched by the moonlight, and he suddenly remembered the moonstone earring in his shirt pocket. He should have given it back to her before.

He fished it out and handed it to her. 'By the way, I found your earring on the beach yesterday.'

Her eyes widened and her lips parted onto a gasp of delight as she took the tiny earring from him and closed her fingers around it. 'I thought it was lost forever. I thought it was a sign …'

He frowned. 'A sign?'

She smiled. 'I'll explain. Later …' She leant forward and kissed him, and his heart swelled with joy and relief … and love.

Chapter Forty-Two

Saturday, one week later …

'Shannon is taking Katrina to the Summer Fete so I can get back to the farm and get changed into Zonk McPurple after my meeting in town.' Daniel pulled a face and drank the last of his coffee.

'Would you think I'm a coward if I told you that I am dreading getting on that stage dressed like an ugly monster from a kids' book and making a complete fool of myself?'

Jenna laughed. 'You have nothing to worry about! I'm sure you'll look a lot more attractive in a kilt than Zonk. Your legs aren't as hairy to start with.'

'Is that the best you can come up with?'

She smiled. 'Let's see … You do have gorgeous blue eyes.'

He wriggled his eyebrows. 'And what else?' He took her in his arms and pulled her close.

She pretended to think. 'Your kisses are probably a lot better too, but as it's almost been an hour since you last kissed me, my memory is a little hazy.'

'Let me refresh it for you.' He gave her a long, leisurely kiss, which made her sigh with pleasure. 'Hmm … yes, you are definitely a very good kisser.'

'Only very good?'

'All right … an exceptional kisser.'

He kissed her again, then released her and checked his watch. 'I'd better go. I don't want to be late for my meeting with the team from the Treasure Trove Unit.'

'Isn't it exciting how it all turned out?' Jenna said as she put the mugs into the sink and they walked out of the cottage. 'Thanks to the *Santa Catalina*, Hamish and Ben have been asked to write academic papers; Shannon gets great publicity for her diving business; and hopefully you get a substantial reward for handing over what's left of the treasure.'

Daniel opened the door to the Land Rover. 'Perhaps I'll get enough to replace that old banger at last and buy some equipment for the farm.'

He sighed and looked towards the cove and the sea, blue and glittering in the sunlight, and Mermaid's Rocks in the distance. His eyes grew pensive, and Jenna knew exactly what – or rather who – he was thinking about.

'Hugh would have been so happy,' he said. 'Somehow it doesn't seem fair that I'm the one who found the treasure when he was always more passionate about it.'

'He would be really proud of you,' she said in a soft voice. She certainly was proud of him for overcoming his reluctance about getting back to diving and helping Hamish and Ben explore the Mermaid Cove cave network.

Unfortunately their first trips into the caves established that the chambers they needed to explore were still inaccessible, so after studying the old maps Ben had found in the university archives, Daniel had borrowed a small digger to shift the stone slab at the bottom of the cottage garden to get into the caves that way. Jenna couldn't help shivering with dread when she watched him and the students descend in full diving gear into the chambers. Not only was it dangerous because of the currents whooshing against the cave walls, but she couldn't help thinking about the curse the old crone had supposedly scratched into the stone with her fingernails …

It had been an anxious wait but Daniel, Hamish and Ben had finally come back up and announced with beaming smiles and excited voices that they had found a broken chest with what looked like religious artefacts, fragments of majolica crockery, as well as a few handfuls of gold and silver doubloons in one of the half-flooded caves. Much of the treasure appeared to have been washed away by the tides, or perhaps it had been stolen by the smugglers who had used the caves to hide their loot, but it was still an incredible find.

What Daniel and the others had brought back up was now at the police station in Dana, ready to be inspected and inventoried by the Scottish Treasure Trove Unit, who would send their team to survey the caves to make sure nothing had been left behind, and Daniel, Hamish, Ben and Shannon had become local and national celebrities.

'I'll bring the envelopes with the names of the short story competition winners. Do you think Katrina won't be too disappointed that she doesn't get a prize?' Jenna asked as Daniel now climbed behind the wheel.

He shook his head. 'She was fine when I explained that it wouldn't be right as we judged the entries. What's more, she said having her mother here was like winning the best prize.'

He waved and drove away, and Jenna went back inside to wash-up and tidy the cottage, singing and humming to herself. Was it possible to be so happy? Daniel had stayed over every single night that week. He came after putting Katrina to bed, and left in time to drive her to school in the morning. Shannon had surprised him by tagging along on the school run too and insisting on introducing herself to Katrina's teacher. She would stay in Arrandale for another two weeks before flying back to Florida, but there would be frequent contacts and visits. 'She has changed,' Daniel had told Jenna. 'Don't get me wrong ... she's still infuriating, but she wants to be part of Katrina's life, and that's more than I could ever have hoped for.'

At last the little girl would have a real mother instead

of a figment of her imagination, and she wouldn't have to make up stories about dolphins and mermaids any longer.

Jenna sighed and put the mugs she'd just washed by the side of the sink. What about Katrina's father? She knew that Daniel was expecting the results of the paternity test he and Katrina had done earlier that week, and that he was anxious about it even if, whatever the outcome, his feelings for the little girl would never change.

She wiped her hands on the tea towel and glanced down at her fingers. She could no longer see the white band where Adrian's ring had been, but she would never forget how scared and insecure she had been when she'd first arrived in Arrandale. Today there were no black butterflies, no fear or self-doubts – only the promise of a life filled with love and happiness.

A black BMW stopped near the cliff path. She frowned and glanced out of the window. Who could this be? She wasn't expecting anybody, having told Brendon that he didn't need to pick her up because she would walk to town this morning. Perhaps they were tourists attracted by the tales of the *Santa Catalina* treasure, or divers who wanted to take their chances in the caves of Mermaid Cove. There had been a steady flow of visitors these past few days.

She didn't think any more of it as she went upstairs to get showered and changed, turning on the radio in case there were reports about the Summer Fete. She may have laughed at Daniel's misgivings about dressing up for the short story award ceremony later on, but she felt self-conscious about standing on the stage too. She slipped her white dress on but as she retrieved her pumps from the side of the bed she found a plastic bag with Daniel's purple tee shirt inside.

She couldn't help but smile. He had forgotten his Zonk McPurple tee shirt! Perhaps he'd done it on purpose to get out of dressing up ... 'Well, that won't work, Daniel

McGregor,' she said to herself. She would take the tee shirt to him later.

She slipped her pumps on and was putting her make-up on and singing to pop tunes on Radio Dana when a loud crash downstairs shattered her happy mood and made her jump and cry out with terror.

Shaking she rushed to the window. What had happened? Had something smashed into the door? The black car was still there, but now she could see something else too ... a heap of crushed yellow roses – roses which must have been cut or ripped from the garden wall and now lay trampled in front of the house. On the ground next to the flowers was the pickaxe she had left in the garden and that someone must have used to wreck the flowers ... and break the door down.

Her heart, her whole body turned to ice. She turned the radio down and held her breath.

There were footsteps downstairs. The sound of papers and books being swept from the dining room table. The loud crashing of the mugs and cereal bowls she had just washed up and left to dry by the side of the sink.

Her heart now raced so fast and panicked thoughts flittered through her mind. Who was down there, and what did they want? Was it a burglar? But then why would a burglar waste time ripping up her flowers – and not any flowers – her yellow roses.

Perhaps it wasn't some random burglar. Perhaps it was ...

'Are you up there, bitch?' Adrian called from downstairs. 'You're not singing any more. Are you scared yet? Good. You shouldn't have made fun of me with your new man. I had to wait for the bastard to leave – had to wait to get you all to myself.' He let out a sinister, sniggering laugh that sent her whole being into panic.

He was mad. Angry. And completely insane.

What should she do? If she waited for him to come up, she would be trapped. Her only chance was to get out through the window. Footsteps echoed on the stairs. Adrian was coming up. There was no time to waste.

She pushed up the bottom half of the window, and climbed over the windowsill, crouching so that she could get out. Now what? She had to jump. She had no choice.

She landed badly, twisting her right ankle, and grazing her hands and knees on the gravel as she tried to roll on the ground to soften the shock. At the window behind her, Adrian let out a loud curse. 'You won't go far, you silly cow.'

She scrambled to her feet, crying out in pain as she hobbled away from the house and thorns from the broken roses on the ground pierced through the thin soles of her pumps. Her best chance was the garden. There were plenty of thick bushes there where she could hide, at least for a while. She didn't have her phone to call for help. All she had was her wits …

How stupid of him to forget that purple tee shirt at Mermaid's Cottage, Daniel thought as he reached the outskirts of Dana. If he went back to the cottage now, he wouldn't be too late for his meeting, so he did a U-turn and drove back along the clifftop road.

There was a black BMW parked near the cottage which was strange because Jenna hadn't mentioned having visitors that morning. Then he saw the broken front door, and the pile of yellow roses trampled all over the ground. He slammed on the brakes, jumped out of the Land Rover, all senses on alert and his heart beating a hundred miles an hour. What was going on … and where was Jenna?

A man was speaking from the far end of the garden but he couldn't see him. 'There's no point in hiding, you know.'

Adrian Jones.

Rage pulsed inside him as Daniel made for the garden gate. He touched the back pocket of his jeans to get his phone and cursed as he remembered leaving it in the Land Rover. There was no time to get it.

Jones was still talking. 'I want some of that Spanish treasure McGregor found and which has been all over the news this week. Nobody would be stupid enough to give everything to a museum. I need money, Jenna.'

Daniel heard the sound of Jones's footsteps as he walked around the gravel garden lanes. He must be near the entrance to the sea cave by now.

'You can't run away from me. I know you hurt yourself when you jumped from the window,' Jones carried on. 'I'm going to find you.'

Daniel clenched his fists. Jenna was injured and how scared must she be with this maniac coming after her? He moved as quietly as he could, crouching down so that Jones wouldn't spot him if he should turn round.

It only took him a few seconds to reach the far end of the garden where Jones was standing in front of a thick laurel bush. 'I told you I would find you.' He was talking in a weird sing-song voice. 'Here I am.'

'And here I am, you bastard!' Daniel growled, sprinting the last few yards. He reached out for the man's shoulder, yanking him back and spinning him round.

Jones' mouth gaped open, his eyes wide with shock. Daniel didn't give him time to react before smashing his fist into his face, and never mind if the man still had bruises from his car accident the week before.

Too late did he notice the pickaxe in Jones's hand. As he stumbled backwards, Jones swung the pickaxe towards Daniel. The sharp end narrowly missed his eye but grazed his cheek before slamming into his right shoulder. He grunted in pain as his arm immediately slackened, but he managed to get hold of the handle with his left hand.

'Daniel! Take care!' Jenna cried as she stepped from behind the bush where she'd been hiding.

Distracted, Daniel glanced her way and Jones managed to wrench the pickaxe from his grip. As Jones thumped the metal head hard into his stomach, white stars flashed in front of Daniel's eyes and he fell to his knees, groaning in pain. Jones yanked Jenna to him, slipped behind her and held the handle of the pickaxe against her throat, almost choking her.

'Let her go, you spineless bastard,' Daniel thundered as he rose to his feet.

Jones stepped back, pulling Jenna like a shield in front of him.

'Give me the stuff you found in the cave and I'll let her go,' he hissed. 'The news said there were gold crosses and some gold and silver coins. Where are they? Where do you keep them?'

It would do no good to tell Jones that he'd taken everything he found to Dana's police station. Daniel raised his hands in a pacifying gesture, and took a couple of steps forward. 'It's at Dunfiadhaich Farm, where I live. There's nothing here.'

'How do I know you're telling the truth?' the man shouted, his voice now edgy with panic. Only a few steps to the stone slab ... He had to steer Jones in that direction, and not towards the gaping hole in the ground leading to the sea cave. If he fell in, he would take Jenna down with him.

'How do you know I'm not? Let Jenna go and I'll take you there.' Daniel carried on walking towards Jones who took another couple of steps back. His heels hit the slab, he fell back and smacked his head on the stone, letting go of Jenna and the pickaxe.

Daniel quickly snatched Jenna off him, and pulled her to the side. 'Can you get your phone and call the police? Quick!'

'Yes. Yes.' She was pale, but she limped away as fast as she could towards the cottage, while Daniel bent down, grabbed Jones by the collar of his shirt and lifted him right off the stone slab and in front of him. He was so angry he hardly felt the pain in his shoulder any more.

'You,' he growled, 'are in big trouble. You really should have listened to me last week when I told you to keep away.'

Jones let out a pathetic whimper. It was hard to fight the urge to thump him but beating the man to a pulp would achieve nothing now, so Daniel drew in a few calming breaths, twisted Jones's arm around his back and marched him out of the garden. Jenna was safe, that was all that mattered.

Chapter Forty-Three

Dana looked even more colourful than usual that Saturday afternoon, with the blue and white bunting stretching between the lamp posts and flapping in the wind, and dozens of stalls set up along the seafront. After the events of the morning, it felt strange to be surrounded by smiling, carefree people milling around and trying their luck at the games stalls.

Food smells wafted in the air – doughnuts and candyfloss, burgers and fish and chips, and a stage had been erected on the market square for the Punch and Judy shows, the Highland dancing and bagpiping contests that ran throughout the day. Jenna's old friends Donald and Murdo had, like every year, been roped in as masters of ceremony and from the cheers and the giggles from the crowd it was fair to say they were doing a great job.

'I don't know where they get their energy from,' Ruth remarked with a smile before turning to Jenna. 'Will you be all right, love? You don't have to do this, you know. Everybody will understand if you'd rather go home.'

'Thanks, Ruth, but Daniel should be ready now and I don't want the children to be disappointed. They are so looking forward to seeing Zonk McPurple.'

'How lucky it was for you that he forgot his tee shirt this morning.'

'Indeed. I can't bear to think what would have happened if he hadn't come back to the cottage and I'd had to face Adrian alone.'

'At least the horrid man is in custody now and won't be pestering you again.'

It had only taken a few minutes for police officers to

respond to her 999 call and arrest Adrian for assault and criminal damage. By the time Jenna and Daniel had made their statement and the police had taken him away, Adrian had lost all his bravado and was a slobbering, incoherent mess.

'It was a crazy thing to do,' Ruth remarked. 'As if he could steal the *Santa Catalina* gold and get away with it! Surely he must have known you would put the police on his trail. Unless—' She stopped and bit her lip.

Jenna shuddered. Unless Adrian had planned to silence her so she couldn't give him away …

'You must have been terrified, pet,' Ruth added, wrapping her arm around Jenna's shoulders. 'Did he hurt you?'

Jenna forced a smile. 'He didn't have the chance. I jumped from the bedroom window then hid in the bushes. All I have to show for my ordeal is a broken front door, a ruined dress and a sore ankle … and lots of dead roses.'

Ruth shrugged. 'Roses grow back, and you can get a new door and a new dress … What about Daniel? Will he be all right?'

'Adrian gave him quite a blow with the pickaxe, that's why Doctor Kerr asked him to get his shoulder X-rayed. Thankfully it turns out that he's only badly bruised.'

However the doctor wanted a word with Daniel in private, which is why Jenna asked Ruth to pick her up from the surgery. Her friend decreed that what she needed now was a restorative cream tea at The Buttered Scone.

One hour later, after several cups of tea and a massive scone smothered with cream and bilberry jam, Jenna said goodbye to Ruth and limped towards the stage. It was time for the prize-giving.

A child's voice called her name, and Katrina ran towards her, followed by Shannon.

Jenna gave the little girl a hug. 'Hello, darling. Where's

your Uncle? I thought he would be here by now.' She narrowed her eyes to scan the crowd but Daniel's tall silhouette was nowhere to be seen.

Katrina giggled. 'He's hiding in Buttercup. He's dressed as Zonk and he says he feels silly.'

'I don't blame him,' Shannon said, a mock grimace on her face. 'He *looks* silly.' She looked at Jenna, this time with concern in her deep green eyes. 'I heard what happened this morning. How are you?'

'I'm all right, thanks for asking.'

'Gee … Who would have guessed there could be so much drama in this place?'

'Look! There's Buttercup!' Katrina shouted out as the mobile library drove up along the seafront, with Brendon behind the wheel, beeping as people waved and cheered.

'I'd better get on the stage,' Jenna said.

Donald, looking rather dashing in full Highland dress – kilt, black jacket and white shirt – held out his hand to help her up.

He winked at her. 'Are you ready, lass?'

Jenna nodded.

'Good.' He tapped on his microphone, making a booming sound. 'One, two,' he said a few times. 'Can you hear me, you lot? Then *haud yer wheesht* and pay attention! Our bonnie librarian would like a word.'

The small crowd went quiet. Donald handed her the microphone and she took a few uneasy steps towards the front of the stage, feeling very awkward and self-conscious. Murdo gave her a wink and a smile. 'Go on, lass.'

'Hello everybody … Good afternoon children, mums and dads, grandmas and granddads and … everybody,' she started in slightly shaky voice. 'I know that you're all impatient for the results of our short story competition.' A few people nodded.

'The first thing I'd like to say is that as far as we are concerned, each and every one of the competitors had a fantastic story to tell, and will all get a free book as a thank you at Buttercup's next school visit. However we did have to choose three stories for our top prizes. It was so hard I had to have help from a very special someone ... So without further ado, I would like to call Zonk McPurple.'

This time there was laughter, clapping and shrieks of delight as Daniel strode across the crowd, dressed in his kilt and purple tee shirt. 'It's Zonk McPurple!' some children shouted. 'No, it's not!' others protested. 'It's Mr McGregor.' 'He doesn't even have a butterfly net!' a little boy shouted.

Daniel ruffled Katrina's hair as he walked past her, then glanced up at Jenna and leapt onto the stage, showing his strong, athletic calves as the hem of his kilt swirled around his legs. The purple tee shirt looked bright and garish indeed and for a few seconds Jenna felt a bit guilty for asking him to wear it. Then all she could see was his eyes, his mouth, and his broad shoulders ... and the fact that he looked devastatingly good-looking in his kilt.

He wasn't smiling any longer as he came closer, and Jenna's heart beat so hard she felt about to faint. After what they had gone through that morning, all she wanted was to snuggle against him, and feel his arms around her. But that would have to wait.

Daniel came closer and turned to the audience and winked. 'I may not have a net but I don't need one to catch my happy dream ... Especially when she's right here.'

He must be feeling the same as her because he gave her a long, searing hot look, filled with love and promise that brought heat to Jenna's face and made her heart beat fast and hard. 'We must ... we must announce the winners,' she stammered.

He gave her a cheeky grin. 'Aye, you're right – but I'll catch you later,' he added in a low voice, making her pulse skip and dance.

She was on her own happy cloud and couldn't stop smiling as she handed him the three envelopes with the vouchers, and he called the names and handed the prizes out to the excited winners and their parents.

'Now be off, ye two,' Donald said as Jenna gave him the microphone back. Daniel took her hand, and smiling and giggling, they climbed down from the stage to meet up with Shannon and Katrina. Shannon said she was going to the pub, and would meet them back at Dunfiadhaich Farm, and Daniel took Jenna and Katrina's hands on either side of him and led them to the fair. 'Let's go for a stroll. I don't care any more if I look ridiculous in purple.'

'I think you look very nice, and very happy,' Katrina replied.

'Thanks, chick. How could I not be happy with two such bonnie lasses next to me?'

They bought ice-creams and candyfloss, looked at the craft stalls and tried their luck at some of the games, including a few rounds of tug o' war on the beach even though Daniel's shoulder wasn't quite right and Jenna's limp got more pronounced as the afternoon wore on.

When it was time to go home, Daniel scooped an exhausted Katrina into his arms. She soon fell asleep, her head in the crook of his neck, as they walked back to the Land Rover. They turned a street corner and were face to face with Drummond and a pretty and very smartly dressed young woman.

'What on earth are you wearing, McGregor?' Toby Drummond sneered. 'Don't you know that purple does nothing for your complexion?'

His companion looked uneasily between the two men, as

if she wasn't sure if Drummond was making a joke. Just then a seagull perching on top of a lamp post screamed overhead, flapped its wings and dived down, straight towards Drummond. He paled, tried to move away but he wasn't fast enough, and a massive dropping landed on his head, and ran down his cheeks.

'Damned Arrandale gulls! I swear it's all your fault, McGregor! You must tell them to attack me.' Drummond pulled a handkerchief out of his pocket and started wiping his face, leaving great smears of white.

Daniel burst out laughing, making Katrina stir in his arms. 'I wish!'

Still laughing, he looked at Jenna and added, 'Come on, love. Let's go home.'

Later that evening, once Katrina was fast asleep in bed, Daniel drove Jenna back to Mermaid's Cottage. He said he wanted to check the new door the carpenter had fitted. 'Are you all right to walk on the beach before we go in?' he asked afterwards.

Jenna nodded. 'Just don't expect me to do any running!'

She was surprised to see that he had his fiddle in the back of the Land Rover, and he took it down to the beach with them.

'I have something to tell you,' he said as they strolled hand in hand on the soft white sand in the dimming light. 'It's about the paternity test. The results arrived at the surgery this morning. That's what Doctor Kerr wanted to talk to me about.'

'Oh … And?'

He shook his head, and took a long breath. 'I'm not Katrina's father after all.'

'How do you feel about it?'

'I'm not sure. Relieved. Disappointed.' He paused. 'Mostly relieved. It won't stop me loving Katrina like my very own daughter … but I feel better knowing that she is Hugh's, and that at least I didn't take that from him.'

They stood without talking for a while. It wasn't completely dark yet but the moon was already up and painting silver on the cove and the surface of the sea. It looked magical and mysterious.

'What a shame the authorities took all the treasure you recovered from the cave and you can't keep at least some,' Jenna remarked at last.

He looked into her eyes, stroked her cheek, and said in a soft voice, 'I have everything I can possibly want, and more. Besides, I have already found my treasure.'

Her face was warm with pleasure, her heart thudding and skipping with joy. She too had found a treasure, here in Arrandale. Several in fact. Love. Family. Friends. Her self-confidence. And a place to call home.

She pointed at the fiddle and smiled. 'Why did you bring your fiddle? Are you going to serenade mermaids again?'

Holding the fiddle with one hand, he closed the gap between them, wrapped his free arm around her waist and pulled her close, until she could feel his heartbeat reverberating inside her. Until it felt that they shared the same heart, under the silvery moonlight and the darkening dusk, with the cove and the sea and the stars surrounding them.

'Aye … Just the one … The only one.'

And he kissed her.

Thank You

Dear Reader,

Thank you so much for reading *Happy Dreams at Mermaid Cove*. I hope you enjoyed travelling in Buttercup with Jenna, and spending some time with her friends and the gorgeous Daniel McGregor in Arrandale, the land of happy dreams. By the way, don't try to find Arrandale on a map of the Isle of Skye because I made it up!

If you did enjoy the story, then I would be very grateful if you could take a few minutes to leave a review. It is a wonderful feeling for an author when readers let you know that they loved your story and your characters. Reviews are invaluable, not only to raise a book's profile, but also to encourage the author to keep writing, especially when self-doubt creeps in.

Please feel free to contact me on Facebook or Twitter. You can find the details on my 'About the Author' page next.

Marie

x

About the Author

Originally from Lyon in France, Marie now lives in Lancashire and writes historical and contemporary romance. Best-selling *Little Pink Taxi* was her debut romantic comedy novel with Choc Lit. *A Paris Fairy Tale* was published in July 2019, followed by *Bluebell's Christmas Magic* in November 2019 and bestselling romantic suspense *Escape to the Little Chateau* which was shortlisted for the 2021 RNA Jackie Collins Romantic Suspense Award. Her historical novels *Angel of the Lost Treasure* and *Queen of the Desert* are also published by Choc Lit. She also writes short stories for the bestselling Miss Moonshine anthologies, and is a member of the Romantic Novelists Association and the Society of Authors.

For more information on Marie visit:
www.twitter.com/MarieLaval1
www.facebook.com/marielavalauthor

More Choc Lit

From Marie Laval

Little Pink Taxi

Take a ride with Love Taxis, the cab company with a Heart …

Rosalie Heart is a well-known face in Irlwick – well, if you drive a bright pink taxi and your signature style is a pink anorak, you're going to draw a bit of attention! But Rosalie's company Love Taxis is more than just a gimmick – for many people in the remote Scottish village, it's a lifeline.

Which is something that Marc Petersen will never understand. Marc's ruthless approach to business doesn't extend to pink taxi companies running at a loss. When he arrives in Irlwick to see to a new acquisition – Raventhorn, a rundown castle – it's apparent he poses a threat to Rosalie's entire existence; not just her business, but her childhood home too.

On the face of it Marc and Rosalie should loathe each other, but what they didn't count on was somebody playing cupid …

Visit www.choc-lit.com for details.

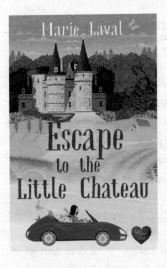

Escape to the Little Chateau

Will Amy's dreams of a Provençal escape come true?

There are many reasons Amy Carter is determined to make Bellefontaine, her farmhouse hotel in the French countryside, a success. Of course, there's the time and money she's put in to making it beautiful, but she also has something to prove – particularly to people like Fabien Coste.

Fabien is the owner of the nearby château, and he might just be the most arrogant, patronising man Amy has ever met … unfortunately, he's also the most handsome.

But as rumours circulate in the local community and secrets about the old farmhouse begin to reveal themselves, Amy quickly sees the less idyllic side of life at Bellefontaine. Could Fabien be the man to help prevent her Provençal dream from turning into a nightmare?

Visit www.choc-lit.com for details.

Bluebell's Christmas Magic

A flick of a feather duster and a sprinkle of Christmas magic …

Cassie Bell is used to mess. Her cleaning business, Bluebell Cleaning, is well known in the Cumbrian village of Red Moss. However, now it's almost Christmas and Cassie has a slightly messier situation to deal with than she's used to.

She's been hired to help Stefan Lambert, an injured army helicopter pilot who's staying at the local Belthorn Manor whilst he recovers. Stefan resents Cassie's interference and is definitely not looking for Christmas cheer. But Cassie prides herself on sparkling surfaces – so, can she bring some festive sparkle to Stefan's life too?

A Paris Fairy Tale

Is Paris the city of happily ever afters?

Workaholic art historian Aurora Black doesn't have time for fairy tales or Prince Charmings, even in the most romantic city in the world. She has recently been hired by a Parisian auction house for a job that could make or break her career. Unfortunately, daredevil journalist Cédric Castel seems intent on disrupting Aurora's routine.

As Aurora and Cédric embark on a journey across France, they get more than they bargained for as they find themselves battling rogue antiques dealers and personal demons, not to mention a growing attraction to each other.

But with the help of a fairy godmother or two, could they both find their happily ever afters?

Visit www.choc-lit.com for details.

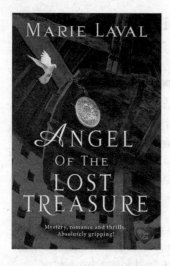

Angel of the Lost Treasure

An ancient secret hidden within a mother's song …

When young widow, Marie-Ange Norton is invited to Beauregard in France by the mysterious Monsieur Malleval to collect an inheritance, she has no choice but to accept.

But when she embarks on the voyage with her fiery-tempered travelling companion Capitaine Hugo Saintclair, little does she know what waits for her across the sea in turbulent nineteenth-century France on the eve of Napoleon's return from exile. When she arrives, she is taken aback by Malleval's fascination with her family – seemingly inspired by his belief they are connected to a sacred relic he's read about in coded manuscripts by the Knights Templar.

As it becomes clear that Malleval's obsession has driven him to madness, Marie-Ange is horrified to realise she is more the man's prisoner than his guest. Not only that, but Hugo is the only person who might be able to help her, and he could represent a different kind of danger …

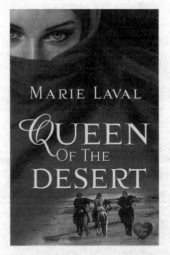

Queen of the Desert

Sometimes the most precious treasures exist in the most barren and inhospitable of places …

Harriet Montague is definitely too much of a gentlewoman to be frequenting the backstreet taverns of Algiers. But her father has been kidnapped whilst on an expedition to the tomb of an ancient desert queen, and she's on a mission to find the only person who could save him.

It's just unfortunate that Lucas Saintclair, the man Harriet hopes will rescue her father from scoundrels, is the biggest scoundrel of the lot. With a bribe in the form of a legendary pirate treasure map, securing his services is the easiest part – now Harriet must endure a treacherous journey through the desert accompanied by Saintclair's band of ruffians.

But on the long, hot Saharan nights, is it any wonder that her heart begins to thaw towards her guide – especially when she realises Lucas's roguish façade conceals something she could never have expected?

Visit www.choc-lit.com for details.

Introducing Choc Lit

We're an independent publisher creating
a delicious selection of fiction.
Where heroes are like chocolate – irresistible!
Quality stories with a romance at the heart.

See our selection here:
www.choc-lit.com

We'd love to hear how you enjoyed *Happy Dreams at Mermaid Cove*. Please visit **www.choc-lit.com** and give your feedback or leave a review where you purchased this novel.

Choc Lit novels are selected by genuine readers like yourself. We only publish stories our Choc Lit Tasting Panel want to see in print. Our reviews and awards speak for themselves.

Could you be a Star Selector and join our Tasting Panel?
Would you like to play a role in choosing which novels
we decide to publish? Do you enjoy reading women's
fiction? Then you could be perfect for our Tasting Panel.

Visit here for more details…
www.choc-lit.com/join-the-choc-lit-tasting-panel

Keep in touch:
Sign up for our monthly newsletter Spread for all the latest
news and offers: www.spread.choc-lit.com.
Follow us on Twitter: @ChocLituk,
Facebook: Choc Lit and Instagram: @ChocLituk.

Where heroes are like chocolate – irresistible!